Ghost Town

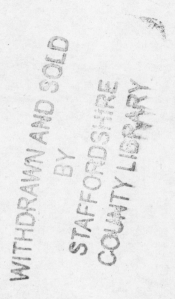

MICHAEL CLIFFORD

GHOST TOWN

HACHETTE
BOOKS
IRELAND

First published in Ireland in 2012 by
HACHETTE BOOKS IRELAND

First published in paperback in 2012 by Hachette Books Ireland

1

Cataloguing in Publication Data is available from the British Library.

ISBN 978 1 4447 2612 1

Typeset in Sabon and vtks distress by Bookends Publishing Services.

Printed and bound in Great Britain by
Clays Ltd, St Ives plc

Hachette Books Ireland policy is to use papers that are natural, renewable
and recyclable products and made from wood grown in sustainable forests.
The logging and manufacturing processes are expected to conform to the
environmental regulations of the country of origin.

Hachette Books Ireland
8 Castlecourt Centre
Castleknock
Dublin 15, Ireland
www.hachette.ie

A division of Hachette UK Ltd
338 Euston Road
London NW1 3BH
England

In memory of Niamh Long.

Acknowledgements

Many thanks are due to people who drove, cajoled or nudged me towards completion of this book. Jimmy Coughlan, Maureen Gillespie and The Coz read early sections. Ronnie Bellew was a constant source of encouragement.

My family, particularly Aideen, John and Una have always provided support in endeavours like this one.

My sister-in-law Niamh Long asked to see the earliest draft but she was taken before that could be arranged. Eoin, Laoise, Orla and Emer carry her flame. Hopefully, she would have approved and enjoyed the final cut.

Ciara Considine was, as always, an inspirational editor. Many thanks also to copy-editor Hazel Orme.

The hardy men, Luke and Tom, kept their distance. And finally, for her love, patience and making the hardy men disappear on countless weekends, the biggest thanks goes to Pauline, who made it all happen.

1

The call came through at 2.08 p.m. Joshua Molloy was told to be at the Booze To Go shop on Amiens Street at half past. It took him two minutes to polish off the mug of tea. He pulled hard on a Marlboro, checked in the box to see that he had enough for the afternoon, which might be enough for the rest of his life.

He slipped a V-neck jumper over his T-shirt, poked his feet into a pair of runners. He picked up his canvas jacket from the back of the couch and took off. He was halfway down the stairs when he copped that he had forgotten to lock the door of the bedsit. Little things like that took a bit of getting used to again.

He stepped out into a spring afternoon, looked up and saw bunched dishwater clouds lurking with intent. He slipped quickly into a rhythm, happy once he could feel his hamstrings stretch.

At 2.31 p.m., he turned on to Amiens Street. He knew the exact time because every few minutes he checked the strapless watch in his jeans pocket, as if it was a precious stone. He arrived at the Booze To Go and stood to the side of the front door.

Two minutes later, a car horn blew three sharp blasts from across the road. It took him a few seconds to recognise Harms Sullivan behind the wheel. He had aged a decade. His hair was shorter, but his face had lengthened, and the grin was plastered on, no life in it. This wasn't the pimply kid Molloy had known.

He ducked across the road, swung around the back of the motor to the passenger side. It was a velvet-black Lexus. The door opened with a plush click. The interior felt fresh. It was too clean to have been stolen for more than a day, two tops. The scene did nothing for his nerves. They wouldn't have sent hot wheels for him unless something was going down.

Sullivan thrust out a hand. 'My man,' he said. His eyes were coated with a glaze you could have skated on.

Molloy felt a damp clasp. 'All right, Harms,' he said.

The car pulled off. Sullivan tipped a volume lever to the left of the steering wheel and radio music filled the air. Toploader, 'Dancing In The Moonlight'.

'Dancer's back in town,' Sullivan said. 'Lock your daughters up in chains 'cause the man is back on the street.' He let out a whoop.

'What's the story?' Molloy said.

Sullivan was pulling out a packet of John Player Blue from beside the handbrake. He took out a cigarette and popped it into his mouth. He offered the box to Molloy, who shook his head because he couldn't be sure that his hand wouldn't tremble. Sullivan sparked his own, pulled hard and exhaled, like it was a load off his chest. 'Life is good, my man. My man. My man. Dancer Molloy is back on the streets.'

Molloy hoped that he wouldn't have to put up with too much of this bullshit. He didn't know Sullivan all that well. He had been surprised when he was told that the man would be sent to drive him.

Sullivan reached into the breast pocket of his shirt, pulled something out and passed it across. The stuff was wrapped

2

tightly in clingfilm, but Molloy could see that it was white powder. He shook his head. Offence was written on Sullivan's face, but he shrugged and returned the coke to his pocket.

'How long has it been, Dancer?'

'A few months shy of four years.'

'Four fucking years.' Sullivan glanced at him, as if to survey the damage. 'You look all right to me. Four years, man. Don't know if I could hack that. So what's the gaff like over there?'

'It's … the gaff.'

'Gear?'

'Not like the Joy.'

'So what did you do?'

'Not much. Bit of art.'

'Art?'

'Yeah. They held classes.'

'Art?'

'Yeah, art.'

'Like painting pictures.'

'Yeah, they reckon it's good for you in situations like prison. Bit like therapy. Helps you connect with yourself, your feelings.'

'Therapy?'

'Yeah.'

'Does it work?'

'Fuck knows.'

'You have to hand it to the Brits. They know how to run a gaff.' Sullivan threw back his head and let out a laugh that quickly fell into a fit of coughing. Molloy was itching for a smoke, but he still didn't trust his hands.

They were moving up on to the North Circular Road now, getting through the city, heading west. 'How's things been with you? Looks like you've moved up in the world?' Molloy tried to invest the question with some energy.

'Me? Business is flying – Junior runs a tight ship. But I'll put you right on one thing. The economy is going down the tubes, know what I mean? Fucking housing index dropping all the time. The stock market, that's fucked too. ISEQ down over thirty per cent on the year. I'm telling you, it's a killer.' He looked at Molloy as if he was about to let him in on a secret. 'I got two places on the go, yeah? A nice townhouse in a new development out in Charlestown and a two-bed in a high-rise down in the docks. Just eighteen months ago I made the punt on both of them. And now? Can't get fucking tenants. It's a killer, man. You bust your chops to make a few euro and have to watch it disappear because the muppets in charge make a balls of everything.'

Molloy listened, but he wasn't hearing much.

Harms Sullivan was little more than a runner before Molloy went away, the lowest rung of the food chain. As far as Molloy recalled, it was he who introduced Sullivan to Junior Corbett one day when both of them showed up at the flat.

Sullivan kept going: 'Cash is the only way to go these days. They can't fuck up cash. You don't have to give anybody a cut, no solicitors or stockbrokers or none of those vultures. Cash is your only man. Keep your cash and don't step on any toes. That's the way to stay alive. Me? I'm a regular Michael Flatley. Step on toes and you could—'

'End up like me?'

Sullivan looked across at him.

'You'll be OK. Junior's in good form. He's getting on with the missus, Liverpool aren't having a bad season. You're sorted. Well, hopefully.'

Molloy stole a glance to see whether Sullivan was smiling, but his face was searching for answers to his own questions.

Sullivan said, 'Maybe you could paint Junior a picture of himself and the missus. Ask him to knock that off the bill.'

Molloy felt his fists ball. At any other time in his life, he would have pulled the handbrake now, brought the motor to a stop and kicked the head off this toe-rag. He kept his eyes on the road ahead, reading the reg on the car in front. It was French.

'I'll tell you one thing,' Sullivan said. 'I admire your balls. Just back in town and facing up to your responsibilities. You have to get Brownie points for that.'

Molloy was hot, but he didn't want to wipe his brow. Don't show the fear. For all he knew, Harms Sullivan had been dispatched to do the job before he ever got to meet Junior. 'We going straight to Junior's?'

'Sure,' Sullivan said, 'unless you want to stop for an ice-cream on the way.'

Molloy closed his eyes. Accept the things I cannot change.

When Noelle Diggins replaced the receiver, everything appeared to blur. She had been told to expect this moment, but while she thought herself ready, she certainly wasn't prepared. She couldn't make out her scrawl on the yellow legal pad on the desk in front of her. The biro had two tips.

She pulled herself from the chair behind her desk. The phone rang again. She lifted the receiver.

'Noelle, it's your sister. She says it's urgent.'

Caroline. The cavalry. The line clicked.

'Noelle?'

'Hi.'

'The hounds have been at your door?'

'Just now.'

'I thought so. Where is he?'

'Not now, Caroline.'

'Oh. My. God. I knew it – I knew it months ago. You wouldn't listen. Noelle, I'm so sorry. Where is the bastard?'

'You're talking about my husband.'

'Do you know where he is?'

Noelle didn't respond. Her husband had warned her to tell nobody. And definitely not her sister.

'How much is involved?'

'How should I know?'

'Does he know?'

'Caroline, I don't need an interrogation right now.'

'You'd better get used to it. You poor pet. Who was on to you?'

'A reporter from the *Times*. I can't remember his name. He said there was a hearing scheduled for the High Court tomorrow. An application from one of the banks. He said the Law Society's investigating . . .'

'I think we should meet.'

Noelle hesitated, fishing for a second bite, a little reassurance that her sister wanted to drop everything and help her.

'Come on into town, please,' Caroline said.

Whatever the emergency, there was no chance that Caroline would come to her, Noelle thought. Her office, at Paul & Paul, was located in Phibsboro, deep in the heart of darkness: that was how her sister regarded the northside of the city. Caroline wouldn't be comfortable coming out. Once she arrived north of the river she would be agitated – the hassle, parking, not knowing how to treat the natives.

Noelle said she'd go into town. They agreed to meet at an espresso bar around the corner from Caroline's office.

Noelle replaced the receiver, reached for the bottle of water on her desk and poured a plastic cup three-quarters full. She fished in her handbag for the two Solpadeine tablets. She tore them from the packet. Apart from the stuff itself, she found refuge in the ritual: the little plop of the tablets into water, the slow fizzing of the bubbles making their way to the surface and dissolving on arrival. Then the bitter taste as she drank it down. Each time she refilled the cup and drank again, to wash the cup's walls of the residual particles. Relief. Codeine for the soul.

She buzzed Valerie in Reception. How many? Two, Valerie said, her voice lowered. Mrs Beslin was back to change her will again and that Johnny Foley person was there also.

She pulled a hand mirror from her Marc Jacobs bag. She would walk out through Reception in a flap of urgency. Something had come up, and there was nothing she could do.

The ground-floor office in which she planned her escape had been poky servants' quarters in Victorian times. These days, the large, red-brick house was entirely given over to the legal practice of Henry and Yvonne Paul. The husband and wife partners had his-and-hers offices on the first floor.

Noelle sat with her back to a small window divided into two squares by a fraying sash. The window looked out on what used to be the backyard, but now served as a parking spot for Henry Paul's BMW Series 7. On the other side of the desk, two chairs were arranged for clients. There was room for a single grey-metal filing cabinet. The walls were bare but for a Jack Yeats print and Noelle's solicitor parchment.

She walked out to Reception. The two clients were sitting on the stiff-backed leather couch. Opposite them, behind a glass partition, Valerie looked up, a pair of glasses resting on her nose. Mrs Breslin was staring ahead at a faraway spot. Noelle knew she was playing with the emotions she was hoping to evoke in the relatives to whom she would bequeath generously, and the others to whom she would not. This was her fourth visit in the last few months to divvy up the spoils. Her affection for her nephews and nieces lurched and swayed according to how often they visited her. You wouldn't mind, but the woman, despite her seventy-seven years, was as healthy as a trout and liable to be around for another decade or two.

Noelle walked towards the couch as if she were sympathising with the bereaved at a wake. Johnny Foley caught her with a crooked grin. She had to admit that she enjoyed Johnny's visits. He had a record as long as his tattooed arm, all of it fairly harmless stuff, apart from one assault causing harm. A few stints in the Joy had done little to iron out of him a compulsion to mess with the law in a manner that was beyond his control. Drink held sway over his life. As far as she knew, he was off it now, but he still had to process a few legacy issues.

Noelle stood above the pair. 'Look, I'm really sorry, but an emergency has arisen. I have a client who is housebound and has to see me immediately to change a will before the ambulance arrives.' She hated lying.

'Coronary or stroke?' Mrs Breslin said.

'I'm … not sure.'

'Stroke is on the way back, did you know that?' Mrs Breslin said. 'I've heard of three cases in the last fortnight. Shocking.'

Noelle nodded. She began reversing out of the door. Her hand reached up in a gesture towards Valerie as she mumbled something about rearranging appointments.

The air outside met her with a cool gush. She walked across the gravelled car park to her Honda Civic. Despite the clouded sky, she felt she required protection: she took from her handbag a pair of Dolce & Gabbana shades, a gift Donal had pressed on her not two months ago.

As she settled behind the wheel she felt better, wrapped up, safe from enquiring faces. She drew a long breath and turned the ignition key.

The traffic thinned out on the far side of the M50. Rain was still a threat. Harms Sullivan drove past the exit for Blanchardstown shopping centre and took the next left. A few stray drops hit the windscreen, but nothing followed. The DJ on the radio was fast getting breathless, waffling on about all the stuff that the station was giving away to listeners.

'These competitions they run,' he said, 'they give away all sorts of shite. One of these days one of them is going to come up with the ultimate prize for winning a competition. Free money and sex for the rest of your life.' He laughed at his own joke. Molloy conceded a smile. The sound of Barry White filled the air: 'My First, My Last, My Everything'.

The car swung through connecting housing estates, the road passing from one to the other, like a river between lakes. And then it flowed into the big one, Westwood, opening up broad and wide, a green on one side, a row of shops hugging the shore on the other.

Molloy noted that Callaghan's Groceries was now gone, replaced with the bright red frontage of a Spar shop. But Life Cycles was still there, around a dozen bicycles stacked outside the shop window. So, too, was Charlie's Chinese takeaway and the Wood Inn, shutters still across its door and high windows despite the afternoon hour. Out on the green, two boys were teasing a donkey on a dusty patch where the grass no longer grew.

Beyond the row of shops, they took a sharp right and drove about fifty yards along a road with steep speed bumps. The car came to a stop at the mouth of an alley on the left. Its walls were high and of white concrete blocks. Barry White died as Sullivan switched off the engine. Molloy could hear the other man's short breaths, which he hadn't noticed before.

Molloy sat forward and looked up the alley. All he could see was a row of motors parked on one side. He couldn't see the mouth of the garage but he knew it was up there. Corbett's Motors, Junior's place.

Harms Sullivan leaned forward, about to get out. 'OK, you take the wheel.'

'What?'

Sullivan exhaled a lungful of smoke. 'We're going for a drive, and you're taking the wheel.'

This wasn't good. Molloy was fairly sure that Junior wouldn't shit on his own doorstep. Once they left here, anything could happen. He got out and walked around the front of the car to the driver's side. Sullivan walked around the rear of the vehicle. An impulse prompted Molloy to run, but he didn't. When he sat in, Sullivan was already in the passenger seat, punching out a text on his phone.

'Now, my friend,' Sullivan said, raising his eyes from the screen, 'a quick toot and we're in business.' He reached into the back seat and brought forward a copy of the *Evening Herald*. He pulled out his coke and spread it on the paper, a little south of a photograph of Shakira. He chopped it up with a credit card – gold, Molloy noticed. The white line was dipping into Shakira's cleavage. Sullivan rolled up a fifty and followed the line up his nose. He threw his head back and closed his eyes. Molloy was trying to control his breathing.

The newspaper appeared before him, another line laid out, the bag sitting to the side. There was an inscription written in red on the clear plastic: 'Good luck.'

He shook his head. Sullivan pulled back the paper and hoovered up that line also. 'One for the road,' he said. He sniffed a few more times, cleaning out his hooter. Then he sparked another smoke.

He tapped digits into his mobile phone, pulling hard on his cigarette, the tip of which was growing into an orange cone. He cursed and began punching in the number again. The car was becoming stuffy. The air between them was full of smoke and a little sourness, one stray word away from a serious problem.

'We're here,' Sullivan said. He nodded, grinned, nodded again, looked over at Molloy. 'He's fine,' he said. 'Behaving himself.' He pressed the red call-end button twice, took a slow drag of his cigarette and turned to Molloy. 'Right, here's the deal. It's your lucky day. Junior's plan was to drive to a suitable location where he would clip you himself after having a little fun with you. He reckoned that was the only proper way to deal with your situation. End of story. I didn't like the idea but, hey, I don't have a say.'

Molloy felt his body tighten. Dryness was creeping up his throat.

'But it's your lucky day. It's been decided that you live. That means Junior loses out. As it happens, he has some issues that won't get resolved.' He turned towards the lane. 'He's going to come down there in about ten seconds. I will dispatch him to kingdom come and when I return you will drive like a blue-arsed fly the fuck out of here. Once that's done and the motor torched, your debt is paid and you're free to go, but we'd love to fix you up with something if you're interested.'

Molloy was trying not to puke. He got the rhythm back into his breathing. He stared at Sullivan. 'You're not fucking serious.'

Sullivan reached forward and opened the glove compartment. He brought out a semi-automatic Glock. Over Harms's shoulder, Molloy saw a figure down the lane, walking towards them. He felt a surge of anger rise within him.

Sullivan snorted, in case any coke was still hanging about his nostrils. 'Are we OK?' he said.

Molloy looked straight ahead. There were no cars on the road, no pedestrians either. He turned to face Sullivan, but beyond the man's shoulder, he could make out the figure walking towards them. He knew Junior Corbett's gait going back a long time. 'He's coming,' he said.

Harms Sullivan nodded, pushed the gun into the belt at the small of his back and opened the car door. 'Welcome home, Dancer. Here's where the fun begins.' He got out and began walking up the lane.

Molloy turned the ignition key. The sound of music crashed

to life. He banged off the radio. He noticed the gentle purr of the engine. Sullivan was now walking at pace. Junior Corbett was coming in his direction, not twenty yards from Sullivan now. Sullivan put his hand behind his back and pulled out the weapon. He crouched down. Junior Corbett froze. The sound of a shot filled the air. Corbett was falling. More shots. Corbett regained his footing, turned and tried to run, but he was hurting. Molloy touched the accelerator. What kind of a tool was this guy? The needle in the rev counter swung up. He looked out. Harms Sullivan was now walking towards him, picking up speed.

Molloy slipped the car into gear and moved off. He mounted the first ramp with a bang, and thought he'd damaged the undercarriage. The car didn't stop. He looked in the rear-view mirror to see Sullivan coming out of the alley, the gun hanging in his right hand. Molloy refocused on the road ahead. He knew the way around this estate like the back of his hand. He tried to think of somewhere he could dump the motor. His knuckles were white on the steering wheel. He felt as if he had just fallen down a deep shaft, back into a pit out of which he had climbed.

Noelle Diggins made it into town in jig time. She parked on a side-street off St Stephen's Green. At the pay-and-display, she paused to calculate: €2.70 an hour. She had just over four euro in change, but much and all as she loved her sister, there were limits to her endurance. She popped in a two-euro coin.

Caroline was seated in one of the aluminium chairs outside the coffee shop, a tall latte on the little circular table in front of her, next to her BlackBerry. As always, she was togged out for action, immaculate from head to toe. She rose to greet her sister, clasping her in a hug that lasted five seconds more than the occasion called for. Noelle couldn't help thinking that Caroline revelled in times like this, her PR training prompting her to adapt and exaggerate.

After she had ordered Noelle an espresso, she sat down again. 'So,' she said.

'How did you know?' Noelle asked.

'A friend of mine on the *Independent*? There was no way this was going to stay under wraps. When did you last hear from him?'

Noelle hesitated. Donal was in Eastern Europe – don't ask me which country – where he was sorting the thing out. Lots of people were getting into trouble over how they'd dealt in property over the last decade. He was being thrown to the wolves. The banks were ganging up on him because he wasn't from the right stock.

Caroline nodded through the version of events. Her face said she didn't believe a word of it. Did Noelle's boss know yet? What would the Pauls make of it? Noelle shook her head.

'How much?'

'I don't know.'

'Are we talking eight figures?'

Noelle had to think about that. Eight figures. Over ten million. 'Don't be ridiculous,' she said.

Caroline gave that nod again. 'Right. <u>Well</u>, the main thing is that we manage the situation as best we can?'

Noelle wished to Jesus she'd stop talking like that, the rising inflection at the end of her sentences that sounded like a question mark. 'This is my life, not a situation.'

'For the purposes of getting through it, it's a situation. We can deal with the fallout later. Noelle, I know I can be a pain in the rear end but if I'm going to add value you must listen to me.'

'Go ahead, add your value.'

'Your phone is going to start ringing. Screen every call. If you don't know the number, let it ring out. Most of them will be from the media. If you do find yourself on the phone to any of them, refer them to me. Don't get into a discussion. If you as much as say you don't know where he is, the headlines the next day will be "Fugitive Solicitor Dumps Wife".'

'There's nothing to tell. I left everything up to Donal.'

'That's what I like to hear. You devote all your time to your work with your clients. Maybe we can work with that too. I mean, your clients are hardly the city's glitterati.'

'Don't, Caroline.'

'No. They are upstanding citizens who were not in a position to make hay while the sun shone out of the Celtic Tiger's ass. That's your world. You aren't the socialite wife of a property developer. You're your own woman, representing and defending those people.'

'Stop. Now. Please.' Noelle's voice had risen beyond the pitch she intended. She looked around to see if anybody had noticed. Inside the coffee-shop window, two shabby suits were bent into each other in a conspiratorial huddle. She imagined them totting up their losses on the property market. Or could they know? Were they actually discussing the wildfire news, about her husband, Donal Diggins, the fall guy? The fugitive.

'This hearing tomorrow, you're not thinking of attending?'

'I should, shouldn't I? I am an officer of the court.'

'Could I challenge your thinking on that? So far, this has nothing to do with you. It's about your husband. Stay clear while you can. If they do come looking for you, you can claim complete ignorance?'

'But I genuinely haven't a clue what was going on.'

'There you go, you're a quick learner.'

'If this thing develops, I will be called in, you know that.'

Caroline nodded, as if the prospect had long ago occurred to her. 'Just be ready. And when the time comes, feel free to shed a few tears – it never does any harm. Why did he have to

14

run? Why couldn't he just have booked himself into a funny farm like any decent person who's fallen on hard times?'

'Caroline, would you please give it as rest? The situation, as you insist on calling it, is not out of control.'

Both women became aware of a presence at their table. The man standing above them wore a navy trench coat over a sports jacket and an open-neck grey shirt. There was grey at his temples, a whiskey paunch sprouting above his belt. 'Excuse me, I hope it's not a bad time, but I'm Alan Slate,' he said, as if that should explain everything. He reminded Noelle of somebody who might show up on her doorstep selling broadband.

'Alan Slate, formerly the darling of the tabloids,' Caroline said. She turned to Noelle. 'You must know Alan. He was a star crime reporter.' Noelle nodded out of politeness. Caroline said, 'Alan, did I read something last week about you joining that new magazine, *Upside Down*?'

'*Inside Out*,' he said.

'That's right. There was something about you getting back into the game after a few years' working,' Caroline made fresh air commas with her fingers, 'behind the scenes.'

Slate shifted on his feet. He wasn't here to talk about himself.

'Yes. Alan's speciality is gangland crime. How can I help you, Alan? My clients are all upstanding citizens. The only crimes any of them commit are against fashion.'

Slate shifted his gaze from Caroline to Noelle. 'Actually, it was your sister I was hoping to talk to.'

Noelle reached for her coffee, her eyes on the middle distance.

'You are on the ball, Alan,' Caroline said. 'You have excellent contacts. But this isn't the best time,' she said. 'Here's my card. Give me a shout at the office in about an hour and we can talk.'

Slate addressed Noelle: 'I was interested in getting a

comment from you. We could arrange something that would suit, if you like.'

'See you later, Alan,' Caroline said. 'Give me a ring.'

Slate shifted on his feet again, winding up to a response. A mobile phone sounded, to the tune of AC/DC's 'You Shook Me All Night Long'. He excused himself, fished in his jacket pocket and turned away from the table as he raised it to his ear. Noelle looked at her sister. Caroline's eyebrows were raised to transmit surprise that this pond life had shown up. Then a smile played on her lips. Keep the faith.

Slate took the phone from his ear. He rooted in a trouser pocket, his hand returning with a card. He passed it to Noelle, who pulled back into herself as Caroline intercepted it. She held the piece of cardboard between her thumb and index finger, as if it was toxic.

'Have to dash,' he said. 'But, look, I'll give you a call later.' He turned and left.

Caroline took a sip of her latte. 'Don't worry, everything is under control. He's an asshole, but he might turn out to be a useful asshole? He brings something to the table. What exactly, I haven't figured out yet, but give me time.'

Two beeps sounded from Noelle's handbag. She pulled out her mobile. Text message received. She clicked into it: 'Has de shit hit de fan?'

Alan Slate eased his five-year-old Dodge Avenger out of the bay. *Inside Out* had three spaces in the car park, which was owned by an insurance company housed in a neighbouring building. They were reserved for the MD, the editor and the organ's star reporter. It was one of the perks Slate had secured before agreeing to be poached from his old job.

He pulled out on to the south quays, directly across the river from the soaring steel and glass blocks of the Irish Financial Services Centre, the heart and soul of the Celtic Tiger, now on life support. Out on the mean streets, the traffic was rough. His impatience made itself known with a twinge on his accelerator foot. 'You Shook Me All Night Long' filled the cab. He answered. It was the magazine's snapper, Kermode. Slate had texted him to say drop whatever you're doing, a crime scene requires immediate attention. He filled him in on the directions, clipping through the roads and turns to be taken once on the far side of the M50. 'It's a jungle out there,' he told the snapper. There was no reply. In Slate's opinion, Kermode was not cut out for frontline work. He was one of the many problems at *Inside Out* that Slate viewed as preventing him fully spreading his wings.

Kermode was lost in the world of real journalism. All his experience had been with women's magazines. He was accustomed to snapping models in various states of pout and undress. Slate concluded that such work would have been lost on Kermode if he was, as Slate suspected, an arse-bandit.

Crimes scenes required a slicker hand. The angles, the detail, the blood. Kermode wasn't up to speed yet, and Slate didn't know if he ever would be. Mentally, he filed away Kermode as the next complaint he would press on his editor.

The snapper's voice came back on the line: 'Left at the church, you say?'

'No, right, right, right. Right at the church followed by another two rights. OK?'

'Right.'

'No. Left.'

'What?'

'Just kidding. It's right. All rights.'

'Fuck you, Alan. Just because you enjoy prancing around that part of the city. Wild horses wouldn't drag me out there if it wasn't for work.'

'Get used to it, brother. You're in the big league now.'

Kermode said he'd be there in twenty.

Traffic eased up once Heuston Station disappeared in the rear-view mirror. The cloud colour had lightened a little, but the threat of rain still hung in there. Slate felt the buzz welling inside him. So far this had been not a good day but a great one.

Noelle Diggins was a stroke of luck. Slate had been in the office when the call came through. A blast from the past whizzed into his orbit as he sat at his PC, gazing out on the Liffey.

'We don't need names,' the voice said. Within seconds Slate

recognised him. He was a contact from the old days, with whom Slate had had a particularly good relationship. As far as Slate knew, he had since transferred from the Bureau of Criminal Investigation to the Fraud Squad.

'You're back on the streets,' the voice said.

'Glad that word has reached you,' Slate said.

'Have a little something for you. Solicitor on the lam. Property number. Name Donal Diggins mean anything to you?'

No bells rang in Slate's memory. 'Rings a bit of a bell.'

'Poster boy for the boom,' the contact said. 'There's an application to the High Court tomorrow from two of the banks wanting their loot returned. And guess what? I'm looking at his missus right now.'

He was inside the espresso bar with another member. Slate took down the details. Noelle Diggins, also a solicitor, but nothing major. Again, the name passed him by. Slate got on his bike. In early, make the connection, and you'd never know where it might lead. The dailies would have tomorrow's court case but he could get under the skin of the story, in there where he did his best work.

The second break of the day had nothing to do with luck. He would have been more than disappointed if he hadn't got the call that Junior Corbett was down. Twenty years since he first sat at a reporters' desk and the buzz of that call still coursed through his veins. Shots fired. Man down. Blood on the streets. The scum coming up for air. Shred the front page.

He was back, no question about that. Back where he belonged, up at the top of the pile.

A queue was forming at the roundabout for the M50. It was just shy of four o'clock. He flicked on the radio, punched in his favourite pre-programmed channel, where they played 'songs to pick you up and make you feel good in the world's greatest city'.

The signature tune for the news brought on a voice, female, with an accent sprung from an ocean halfway between south County Dublin and Australia. She spewed out the headlines. Some economist from a bank was disputing that the property market was going to continue heading south. The Minister for Transport unveiled a new traffic-management plan for Dublin. And the body of a young man missing for three days had been fished from a river in the Midlands.

Nothing about today's hit. Nothing about Donal Diggins. Alan Slate allowed himself a smile. Word had not yet rippled out to the wider pools. Only he knew what was really going down in the naked city.

Fifteen minutes later he walked towards the blue and white crime-scene tape. A knot of kids with bicycles was gathered at one side, gaping up the lane where the deed had been done. Three women were in an anxious huddle, one togged out in pink polka-dot pyjamas. The snappers prowled the border of the tape. Kermode wasn't here yet, the dumbo. Slate recognised some of the reporters standing to the side, waiting for the official word.

He caught the eye of Detective Inspector Phil Wright. Wright was in conversation, but gave him a nod. A few seconds later, the cop broke away and walked over to him. Slate hadn't expected that, but it did no harm to look like he was summoning the top dog. Wright's six-foot-two-inch frame was accentuated by his erect posture. The copper carried himself like an unyielding pole. The only hair on his head was twin salt-and-pepper patches spreading out from above the ears. Slate could never imagine him without a shirt and tie, even in downtime.

'How're you, Phil?' he said.

'Haven't seen you for a while, Alan. You're still with us.'

'You know me. You can take the man out of crime, but you can't take crime out of the man.'

'I heard you were with a new outfit. *Upside Down*, is it?'
'*Inside Out*.'

'That's it. I was looking for it in my local, but they hadn't heard about it.'

'Teething problems.' He didn't want to talk about the vagaries of business, not on the stage of a crime scene. He nodded towards the lane. 'Junior was getting up somebody's nose?'

The inspector turned towards the lane as if he expected something new to emerge. 'When you've reached Mr Corbett's station in life, you can be sure that the coffin is stalking you at every turn. He's in St James's, but he won't be there too long. Took a bullet in his forearm, a graze to the temple and three wounds to his vest. He'll survive, which may not be a good result for humanity. Unless, of course, the MRSA gets him. Wouldn't it be gas, Alan, if the man they couldn't shoot was taken down by a hospital bug?'

'He had a vest on?'

'Wouldn't you, if you were him?'

'Anyone in particular?'

A few of the other reporters had drifted over. Slate caught them out of the corner of his eye. Inspector Wright looked up and waved his arm, like a farmer shooing cattle away from an electric fence. 'I'll be with ye in a few minutes, lads. Hold the fort till then.' He turned to Slate. 'An old friend of Junior's is back in town after a stretch at Her Majesty's pleasure. Dancer Molloy?'

'I've heard the name before.'

Wright looked up the alley. 'He was small fry. A waste of space. They say he could have made it in football across the water when he was younger. That's where he got the name.'

'He had form with Junior?'

'I'm not going to spoon-feed you, Alan. Look it up. I hear that he got help from this other wannabe terminator, Harms Sullivan.'

The name rang a bell, but Slate couldn't say from where. He issued a knowing nod, hoping that was enough to convince the cop he was up to speed.

'You're not really up to speed, Alan, are you?'

'Bit rusty. I'm hardly back in the game a wet week. Give me time, Phil. I haven't lost my touch.'

Wright nodded. 'Young Harms is another useless fucker at the lower rungs of Junior's ladder. If it was the pair of them, I'd take short odds on their tenure on this mortal coil. Whoever it was, they made a balls of it. They pulled off a few shots and ran. And get this, the driver panicked. Took off without the shooter, who was left wandering around, looking for a lift home. What a country.'

Wright stepped back and regarded Slate. It was obvious that the business end of things was over. When he spoke again, his voice was lower: 'No hard feelings, Alan, but you made a right eejit of yourself with that other stuff. If I was younger and greener I'd be amazed that you're still in the game.'

Slate kept his eyes on the cop's shoes, which were scuffed and could have done with a polish.

'But you're not the worst of them. Just keep your nose clean this time around and I won't stand in your way.'

Slate made to respond but the cop raised a hand. 'We'll leave it at that for now.' He turned and waved to the pack of reporters. 'OK, lads, gather round.'

Slate reversed to the fringes, his prime cut in the bag, as the pack hurried to pick at the bones. There would be nothing in this briefing that he wouldn't read about in tomorrow's dailies, but he stayed awhile just to show some interest.

Kermode arrived as the briefing broke up. He spotted

Slate and ambled over, cameras hanging by straps from his shoulders, a cigarette between the fingers of his left hand. Slate wondered whether his lazy gait could be interpreted as camp.

'All right, Alan,' the snapper said, sounding weary and resigned.

'No, it's not all right. They'll be packing up here soon.' He pointed to the lane and told him the angles required. Kermode nodded and went in search of photos, an air of resentment trailing behind him.

Two beeps sounded from his pocket of his jacket. He reached in, his index finger tapping the red button: 'C U in the Lonesome Oasis 20 mins.' The sender was notified as Seamus F. This really was turning out to be a good day.

Detective Seamus Fox was sitting at a table at the rear of the Lonesome Oasis when Slate entered. It was just after five p.m. The lighting was low, as if the place couldn't wait for the night to come. The interior was bordered by a blood red-couch. Music from what sounded like an over-forties radio station provided a background din. Slate could make out 'Stop In The Name Of Love'.

Fox was one of four patrons in the place. Another man was sitting at the bar, perusing a tabloid newspaper. A couple had commandeered a booth to spread out what looked like maps on a table. They had the cut of tourists. Slate was curious as to how tourists would end up in this place, out here in the wild west of the city, worlds away from the Book of Kells, or the Guinness Hop Store.

In the 1970s the Lonesome Oasis would have been described as a suburban lounge bar. Thirty years later, it had all the appearance of a place hanging on impatiently for a developer to walk through the door and declare it apartment fodder. The way things were looking now, though, the Lonesome Oasis had missed the boat.

Slate gestured to Fox in a drinking motion. The cop held up a near-full pint in response. Slate called for a pint of Heineken and joined the other man. They didn't bother with the formalities. Fox threw a stack of photos on the table. All were of a similar character, obviously taken in a holiday resort.

'Torremolinos,' Fox said.

Some of the photos showed men and women poolside, dressed in swim-gear, gripping cocktails, against a backdrop of powder-blue skies. A few had been taken indoors, most likely in a bar. Everybody was laughing. One man who appeared in nearly all of them had a tattoo on his left forearm.

Slate looked up. Fox was smiling. 'Junior and his homeys on tour.'

'We can use them?'

'Be my guest. I'm sure it will cheer him up in his hospital bed when he picks up this week's copy of … what do you call it?'

'*Inside Out*.'

'Yeah. The ladies in the photo there? Junior's missus and the other wives and girlfriends will be interested in them. From what the local cops told us, they didn't come cheap.'

Slate said, 'The editor will be frothing at the mouth when he sees this stuff.'

Fox took a long draw on his pint and replaced it on the beer mat. 'How's it going anyway?'

'OK. Different ballgame from newspapers, but I'm getting there. And you?'

'I'll survive. Another four years to pension. I can push their fucking pens till then.'

Slate wanted to say something else, but didn't know what would fill the void. They had both suffered, but somehow he knew that Fox's load was heavier, albeit less poisoned by the guilt that Slate felt. He moved the conversation on to football. Fox had another two pints, Slate a glass. He wasn't sure where he would stand if he was stopped to blow into the bag. In the old days, there wouldn't have been a problem. Right now, he didn't know whether the old rules applied. He suspected not.

It was pushing for seven thirty when the pair emerged from the Lonesome Oasis. The night had closed in around west Dublin. They resolved to meet again, maybe for a session, within the next few weeks.

Slate drove back to the office. *Inside Out* was based on the first and second floors of a narrow, refurbished red-brick structure on the south quays. Editorial was on the first floor, Commercial taking up the second. The ground floor had been occupied by a mortgage brokerage, but since Slate's arrival it had been replaced by a crowd buying gold. Every day, as the employees of *Inside Out* hit the stairs, they were met with a large poster telling them: 'We buy your gold for cash.'

The office was dead to the world when Slate arrived back. He switched on the lights and slipped in behind his desk. He had the choice seat in the place, next to a tall window that looked out on the Liffey and the opposite quays. Right now, it was all lit up over there against the darkness. A vessel of some sort was steaming up the river, a shaft of light boring into the water.

Apart from Slate's desk there were six on the floor, facing each other in pairs. The editor's office took up about a quarter of the floor space, located behind panels of sheetrock to waist height and glass above that. It was as cramped a working environment as Slate had experienced in his career.

He had got through a first draft of his story on Junior Corbett when his mobile rang. Seamus F came up on the screen.

'Hey, did you forget something?' Slate said.

'Junior Corbett's been busy in his hospital bed.'

'Man down?'

'Sullivan, little tosser, a nobody, really. His brother's in the frame for the job on Junior.'

'Harms Sullivan's brother?'

'Yeah, Steven. Just eighteen. He's paid the price for big brother's ambitions. They're taking him to the morgue.'

Slate put down his phone. He began reading his copy, erasing the bits that had just been overtaken by events. The city was no longer awaiting a gangland bloodbath. One had just arrived.

The streets of Dublin are about to flow with blood with an all-out gangland war, Inside Out *can exclusively reveal.*

The attempted murder of convicted drug dealer Anthony 'Junior' Corbett on Wednesday was avenged that night by the brutal slaying of Steven Sullivan, a minor figure in gangland. Sullivan is understood to have been close to one of the two assassins who attempted to gun down Corbett near his home in west Dublin. There is no evidence to suggest that Corbett was behind the revenge hit, but garda sources have told Inside Out, *'He won't be grieving for that young fella, you can be sure.'*

Sullivan died in a hail of bullets as he left a city-centre pub following an evening's drinking in the company of other gangland figures. According to impeccable garda sources, the 19-year-old was singled out by the balaclava-wearing gunmen, who brought death and degradation to the streets of the capital city.

Gardaí are predicting an all-out bloodbath following the hit and the attempted murder of Corbett.

Inside Out *has learned that Sullivan was not one of the hitmen who carried out the assassination attempt on Corbett but the would-be assassin is believed by gardaí to be a close relative of the dead teenager.*

Inside Out *has learned that Corbett has now told his gang members that he wants the would-be assassins dealt with as soon as possible.*

From his hospital bed, the multimillionaire has instructed his henchmen that there will be huge rewards for whoever avenges the attempt on his life. Sources have told this reporter that the suspected assassins were a young drug-dealer trying to make a name for himself, and a former associate of Junior Corbett's, who was recently released from prison in England.

This man had been jailed for drugs offences and is believed to have returned home with the intention of becoming a major player in the city's lucrative drugs business.

The two would-be killers went about their deadly business last Wednesday afternoon near the premises where Corbett runs his second-hand-car sales business. They tricked the drugs baron into meeting them around the corner. Then one of them opened up on him with a Czech-made Glock firearm, spraying Corbett with a rain of bullets. Shocked neighbours dived for cover as the gunman kept firing. Young mothers threw themselves in front of their children who were in danger of being caught in the crossfire.

The gunman then ran back to the stolen Lexus where his accomplice was supposed to be waiting. But the getaway driver had lost his nerve and driven off before the hit was complete. Witnesses described how the driver sped away with a look of terror on his face, when he realised the enormity of what he had been involved in. You don't mess with Junior Corbett in gangland.

Meanwhile, the gunman panicked and ran. Local people describe him tearing through their estate waving his gun like a madman. By the time the first gardaí arrived on the scene, the gunman had disappeared into thin air.

Worse was to come for this assassin. Unknown to him, Junior Corbett was wearing a bulletproof vest when the bullets rained down on him. Amazingly, he survived the assassination attempt despite shipping six bullets. Gardaí are now calling him 'The Cat' because of the number of lives he appears to have. This was at least the fifth attempt on his life. He suffered a number of superficial injuries to his body but he was saved thanks to the vest, although sources close to the investigation claim that he soiled himself in the shooting. Like a lot of other tough guys in gangland, Junior Corbett isn't as tough as he wants people to believe.

Corbett was rushed to St James's Hospital, where doctors who might otherwise have been healing law-abiding citizens were told to save his life.

But there will be no resting for this dealer in death until he tracks down the men who tried to ensure that he would deal no more. Garda sources have confirmed to this reporter that the would-be killers are intent on taking over the drug-distribution network in west Dublin.

However, Corbett won't be got rid of that easily. He has told associates that he will fight to the death to keep his business afloat.

More gardaí are to be drafted into west Dublin, but as usual there are not enough resources available to tackle the growing threat of gangland. As always, Inside Out will be first to bring you the latest grisly details.

Alan Slate, crime reporter of the year 2000, 2002, 2004

3

When it came to Molloy's turn, he said he'd just listen. The chair nodded at the man sitting to the right of Molloy. This man was wearing a dark suit with an insignia, indicating it was the property of a transport company, maybe Dublin Bus. He had a second chin folding into the first, and his cheeks looked like they were about to break out in flashing red lights. His tie was loosened for air. Once given the signal, the words flowed as if from a tap.

'Thanks, chair, it was good listening to you and the other speakers. But I'm in an awful place at the moment. I've come to the conclusion that I married the wrong woman, and I'm just glad I was drunk for fifteen years or I might have got my act together to kill her somewhere along the way.'

A guffaw rippled across the room. Molloy drifted. That was what he liked about the meetings. They provided space to do some thinking, in a room where the air was thick with long thoughts seeping out and being chewed over by a bunch of fuck-ups.

The room was in the basement of a day centre in the north inner city. The building was located between a mechanic's workshop and a small, family-run grocery, which was holding out against the march of the multiples. Upstairs in the day centre, Molloy noted, a whole lot of effort was going into helping people avoid pitfalls. Down in the basement, a clean-up operation was under way.

The room was lit by three bulbs, hanging from the ceiling and shaded by basic plate lampshades. There were seven rows of plastic chairs, four deep, and a long wooden bench at the back. About half of the chairs were occupied. Molloy counted five women in the room. To the side at the back there was an alcove, which housed a sink, kettle and work counter. A man stood sentry there. He was built like a brick shithouse, although the pudginess around his eyes evoked the image of a child. The fella guarded the tea like it was high-grade whiskey. A cup could be obtained before the meeting kicked off, and again at its conclusion. None would be dispensed while a meeting was in progress. If you had a problem with that, take it to the big man and await his considered response.

At the front of the room, facing the gathering, two people were seated behind a table on which burned a nightlight candle. Molloy knew this evening's chair, Johnny Foley, a harmless sort with whom he'd been in school many moons ago.

Beside Foley sat the group secretary, a woman who wore hard years on her face, which meant she could pass for anything between thirty and fifty. Behind them, on the wall, two long scrolls were hanging: 'The Twelve Steps' and 'The Twelve Traditions'. On the table there were a number of slogans: 'Let Go Let God'; 'One Day At A Time'; 'Easy Does It'; 'Think Think Think'. Whenever Molloy looked at the slogans he always visualised one that was not there: 'Don't Fuck Up'.

On the first night Molloy had walked into the meeting,

he'd spotted Foley. Their paths hadn't crossed in years, but an ember of kinship still burned from schooldays. Foley told him he'd been in and out of the rooms. It had taken a bit of getting used to, but the gargle had been dragging him into all sorts of fixes. 'It's a shelter from the storm for me,' Foley said. 'Just keep the head down, do the programme and don't pick up a drink. Have you got a sponsor?'

Molloy muttered something about taking it handy for the moment.

'Trust in your higher power. Me, my higher power is my probation officer. She has Jennifer Aniston's body and the face of Angelina Jolie. I go to sleep at night thinking of her and I know I won't pick up a drink for another twenty-four hours.'

Now, more than a week later, Foley was at the top table, kicking off the meeting with his life and times. Molloy wasn't listening, but he was shaken from his own musings every now and again by laughter rolling across the room as Foley gave it welly.

Three more speakers had their say before Foley called the meeting to an end. The secretary thanked him and asked for a sign of appreciation. A round of applause rang out as everybody stood for the serenity prayer: 'God, grant me the serenity to accept the things I cannot change, courage to change the things I can and wisdom to know the difference.'

At that, most drifted towards the alcove, now that Brick Shithouse had given the OK to break open the tea. Molloy bolted for the door. He needed to change some of the things he thought he could still change.

At the top of the stone steps outside, two men were leaning against a railing. An hour earlier they had been sitting on the pavement, but the ground was now wet with a fallen shower. The pair had the streets written all over their clothes and faces.

One of the men held a green bottle in a low grip. The other

extended a Burger King paper cup towards Molloy. He looked at it and moved on. He was gone only a few yards when he heard the shout in his wake: 'Fucking alcoholic.'

The clock was pushing for nine thirty p.m. Yvonne Paul stuck her head into the office. 'Noelle, a word?'

Noelle Diggins was seated behind her desk. She looked up at Yvonne with what she hoped was a face of pure innocence. 'Of course,' she said. 'Didn't expect to see you in here at this hour.' Less than a month previously, Yvonne Paul had given birth to her first child.

'Henry suggested I come in. He thought it best that the three of us have a chat.'

Noelle had been waiting for this since she got back to the office in the late afternoon. She had put down a routine day in the district court, but the day had been like no other in her career. Every time she rose to address the court, she felt the eyes of the place on her. Whenever she saw a copy of a newspaper, she turned away. Her head, for the most part, stayed buried in the files in front of her. The only eyes she consciously met were those of the judge. Behind every stare, she felt, there lurked the possibility of a finger of accusation. Through the day, only half of her mind had been in the courtroom. The other half was down the road in the Four Courts, where an application was being heard in the High Court to freeze her husband's assets.

Afterwards, she came straight back and all but locked herself into the office. A stack of eight phone messages was on her in-tray. Four were from reporters. Valerie popped in as she was leaving, some time around six. After that, silence seemed to descend on the world outside her door until Yvonne appeared, wrapped in a maternal glow.

Noelle followed Yvonne upstairs to Henry Paul's office. A brass fireplace and elaborate cornices testified that this had once been the master bedroom. Henry Paul was seated behind his desk. He looked up when the two women entered. Darkness had claimed much of the room, apart from the desk area, which was lit by a green-shaded lamp. Henry Paul pushed himself back from the desk on the wheels of his leather-upholstered chair.

Yvonne sat into one of two chairs opposite the desk, an extended hand guiding Noelle into the other.

'How're you bearing up?' Yvonne said.

Noelle considered her reply. 'I'm OK, I suppose. Nobody's died. Worse things happen to people.'

'Today can't have been easy for you.' Yvonne's face had softened in sympathy. It made Noelle think of those chat-show hosts who ask the kind of questions they hope will elicit tears.

'I've had better days.'

Yvonne nodded slowly. 'And how is Donal?'

'OK.'

'Have you spoken to him?'

'Should I consult my solicitor before answering that?'

Yvonne allowed herself a smile, but Henry Paul's face gave nothing away.

Noelle had always got on better with Yvonne. For the last few months, as business had begun to slow down, Yvonne's presence in the office had been more sporadic, in deference to her condition and then the birth. It might have been a coincidence but Noelle had noticed a harder edge about the place.

'I always liked Donal,' Henry Paul said.

'He hasn't died,' Noelle said.

'No, of course. I just mean ... I liked him before all this ... hullabaloo. He struck me as somebody who got the most out of life.'

The feeling wasn't mutual, to the best of Noelle's knowledge. Donal had played a few games of golf with Henry and bumped into him at the odd bash in town. His verdict had been that Noelle's boss was a dry shite, who could do with a course in not taking himself so seriously. Their few encounters had left Noelle uneasy. She wanted to fireproof her job from the world beyond. She didn't tell Donal, but at the time she was relieved that her husband and her employer would never become buddies.

Yvonne said, 'Everybody's been under such pressure for the last few years.'

Noelle nodded.

Henry Paul stood up, and buried his hands in the pockets of his suit trousers. The pinstripe was wide enough to walk along. His shirt was pink with a white collar, the loosened tie a burgundy silk. He looked down on Noelle. 'You heard about today's application?'

'To be honest,' Noelle said, 'I was in court today and I've been snowed under. I didn't want to get into it until I'd finished work.'

'I can understand that.'

'It's been all over the radio,' Yvonne said.

'I've been up the walls, Yvonne. I wanted to get the day's work done first.' Yvonne issued her counsellor's nod again.

Henry Paul lifted a thin envelope from the desk and handed it to Yvonne. 'You needn't open it here. It arrived about an hour ago when I was outside for a smoke. According to the radio, it's a summons for you to appear before Mr Justice Cornelius Neilon tomorrow. He wants to know where Donal is. Judge Connie isn't a happy camper.'

'Nice judge,' Yvonne said. 'Very courteous, I met him at a dinner party last year and he—'

'Yvonne …'

'Well, we have to look on the bright side.'

34

'We?' her husband said.

'I don't know where Donal is,' Noelle said. 'I'll go in there tomorrow and tell him. There's no problem. Is there?' She looked at Yvonne, whose face in the half-light betrayed just tiredness, her eyes lassoed in puffy bags, exhibits to nights robbed of sleep.

'Of course I'll represent you. It's only right,' Yvonne said. 'I know a young counsel who would be ideal for something like this.'

Henry Paul moved around to the back of his chair. He stepped towards the window. He fingered the horizontal wooden blinds, prising two of them apart, and peering out into the darkness. 'Perception is the only problem for the moment,' he said. 'Yvonne and I are willing to do whatever we can to help.' At this, Yvonne nodded and moved forward, in what appeared an effort to extend her hand to Noelle. But there was too much distance between their chairs so she confined herself to widening the smile.

Henry Paul turned to face her. 'But if this gets worse, we will have to revisit the situation. You do realise there could be collateral damage to the practice and that's something I would have to examine. Times are not what they used to be and we must retain our existing business. There are livelihoods to consider.'

'And Henry Junior,' his wife said.

Noelle was gripped by a stray thought. Tell him to shove it where the sun don't shine. Tell him that this was never more than a stopgap, somewhere to hide until she figured out what she wanted to do with her life. 'Thank you, Henry. I do appreciate that you and Yvonne can be so understanding about what has happened,' she said. She got up, but Yvonne was already out of the chair. Before she could lurch to the door, Yvonne moved in for the kill, wrapping two arms around her and pressing their bodies together. Noelle's own arms hung limply by her sides. She and Yvonne had never hugged before. Yvonne smelt of baby puke.

Five minutes after leaving the meeting, Molloy was rooting around in a skip. He was careful where he put his hand in the pools of half-light from streetlamps. After a few dips he found what he was looking for and slipped it into his jacket pocket. He was just leaving when he spotted something else that might come in handy: a small, sealed plastic bag stuffed with wood shavings. He opened the bag, emptied the contents into the skip. Then he folded it and put it in his jacket pocket.

Parnell Street was quiet when he stepped on to it. He entered a public house trading under the name Yellow Peril. The place had been taken over by Chinese owners as the traditional pub trade had contracted in recent years. These days, it was a karaoke bar.

Inside, there was a Chinese man behind the bar. There were two Chinese men sitting at it, both talking at the speed of light. There was a Chinese couple in a booth at the back. Glittering globes hung from the ceiling. On the stage a petite Chinese woman was rending the air with her interpretation of 'Money Money Money' in front of three other females. She was very happy in a rich man's world. There was no sign of Sullivan. The barman was looking at him, waiting for an order, or maybe an attempt at armed robbery. He left.

Molloy had taken a trip here an hour before the meeting. Across the street there was an African hairdresser, a Polish foodstore and next to that another pub, fronted by a porch. On his recce, there had been no doorman at the entrance to this pub. That was still the case now. He stepped inside the porch.

At 10.04 p.m., Harms Sullivan walked up to the Yellow Peril.

He was wearing a blue beanie and had the collar of a navy fleece pulled up around his neck. Molloy stepped further back into the porch. He was surprised that Sullivan had shown up. When they had spoken on the phone that afternoon, Sullivan had sounded jumpy, as if he'd half thought Molloy was setting him up. He had just visited the morgue with his mother to identify his brother's body. Molloy had assured him that they were in the same boat and that two heads were better than one in finding a way out of it.

Now Sullivan had kept the appointment. He was inside the karaoke bar for all of thirty seconds. When he emerged he looked up and down the street and raised his right arm to view a wristwatch. He threw a glance over his shoulder at the singing pub. He pulled out a mobile and punched in a number. Molloy looked down as his own phone flashed on silent.

He could see Sullivan talking into the phone, leaving a message. Sullivan began walking towards O'Connell Street. At Marlborough Street he turned left. Molloy followed on the far side of the road. There was little pedestrian traffic. A couple passed Molloy, the woman apparently holding up her man by the arm.

Harms Sullivan kept moving at pace. Molloy knew these streets. Up ahead a lane led to the offices of a courier company, or it had four years ago. Molloy ran across the road, came up behind his prey. He pulled from his pocket the four-inch-long piece of lead piping he had retrieved from the skip. In one movement he grabbed Sullivan on the left shoulder and stuck the pipe into the small of his back. 'Act the bollocks and you die.'

'Dancer?'

Molloy pushed him towards the lane.

Sullivan attempted to turn, but Molloy put some pressure on the piping. 'Keep walking.'

'Jesus Christ, Dancer, you're not going to do me.'

They walked into the darkness. Molloy grabbed the collar of Sullivan's fleece and began patting him down. The Glock was in the inside breast pocket of the jacket. He took the gun in his left hand and stuck it into the small of Sullivan's back. He tossed aside the lead piping. Sullivan's head turned slightly to the sound of the piping clanking on to the ground. 'Fuckin' eejit,' Molloy said.

'Dancer, please …'

Molloy stepped back and swung with his right into Sullivan's ear, connecting, and sending his target staggering. Sullivan let out a yelp, like a stricken animal, crouched down and raised his hands to his head. Molloy pocketed the Glock in his jacket, and pulled up the pocket's zip. He grabbed Sullivan by the hair, raised him up and landed a blow to his nose. Sullivan's face twisted in pain. Molloy hit him in the eye, his left fist still in Sullivan's hair. His right hand hurt after that, but giving the dig felt cathartic, as if the anger was physically leaving his body. Sullivan went limp. Molloy dropped him to the street.

'Please, Dancer, please,' he said. 'They've killed my brother.'

'My name is not Dancer. Don't call me that, do you hear?'

Sullivan was hiding behind a raised arm. He dropped it and looked up at Molloy. 'I don't know your real name, Dancer.'

Molloy paused. He raised his right leg as if to kick the fool. Sullivan curled into a ball. 'Junior has put a contract out on us,' he said, from behind his arms.

'Us? What us?' Now Molloy swung a boot and connected with Sullivan's ribs. There was another yelp. Molloy lowered himself to his haunches. Sullivan began to weep. Molloy looked at him, a pathetic heap, just a day and a fucked-up hit away from the chest-thumping coked-up gangster living in the fast lane. 'Who?'

Sullivan was heaving with sobs. 'They're going to kill me. I don't know what—'

'Who put you up to it? Who knows I was in that car?'

'Dancer – sorry. Jesus, listen. Those two properties I told you about? They still have a great yield. One of them is yours if you can get me out of—'

Molloy stood up and kicked him again, this time in the stomach. 'Who knows?'

'My share portfolio, take it. All I want is my life. If you can help me … I'm sorry, man, for landing you in this … We have to find a way back.'

Molloy looked down at him, fists balled. 'Who?'

'Johnny Cash.'

'Johnny Cash?'

'It was Johnny's plan.'

'Aw, fuck.' Molloy swung his boot into Sullivan's midriff again, the time with even greater force. 'The man in black?' he said, as if hoping that he had misheard. Sullivan attempted to nod, fear bulging out of his eyes.

'Fuck,' Molloy said. He swung a boot at fresh air. 'Fuck, fuck, fuck.' This was bad. Johnny Cash was Junior's enforcer. He had acquired his name because of his dislike of credit cards and a penchant for black threads. His real name was Johnny Herbert, but even the cops knew him as Cash.

A dark cloud settled over Molloy's thoughts. He had sought refuge in the notion that Sullivan had been acting alone, that it might be possible to salvage something. Now exit doors were slamming in his face. 'If you're lying …'

'Why would I lie? Johnny wants Junior out of the way. He promised to bump me up to his number two. He was keeping it tight. Nobody else knew. He didn't trust any of the rest of the crew. Once he heard you were out and wanted to meet Junior, he set the thing up. It would look like you were moving against Junior before he got you.'

Sullivan looked up at him. A large bruise was mushrooming below his left eye. The other was wide with pleading. The rest of his face was a mask of blood.

'Were you going to kill me when we got rid of the motor or was it to be later?'

'It wasn't me ...'

Molloy kicked him in the chest and he rolled once more. 'And you thought he'd let you live. What kind of a fucking muppet are you? You don't come near me again. You don't speak to anybody about me. We never met. I hardly know you. Do you hear me?'

Sullivan didn't move. Molloy knew the choices now before him: kill this man and he himself might live. He lowered himself again, and this time spoke without a threat in his voice. 'Did you hear what I said?'

Sullivan was curled into the foetal position. His head moved. When he spoke, his voice was a whisper: 'What am I going to do?'

'I don't give a shit,' Molloy said. He got up and walked towards the street. At the mouth of the lane, he turned to look back. Sullivan was still on the ground, a hand fumbling in a pocket, like a man fishing for relief.

Molloy walked down Marlborough Street and across the Luas line. A couple was coming towards him, but suddenly veered off the path, as people do when faced with a regal procession or a threat. Down by the Liffey, he stepped on to the boardwalk. Streetlights bobbed on the dank waters below.

There was little traffic on the walkway. He kept a constant pace. Half a mile further upriver, two junkies lost inside tatty overcoats were leaning against the railing. They eyed Molloy, measuring him up. He willed them to come on. Just give me an excuse. Plenty of anger here, looking for a home.

The smell of low tide rose from the Liffey. When the boardwalk ended at Capel Street Bridge, he crossed the road and kept motoring along the footpath next to the river. He tried talking to himself but it was no good. He felt the anger on his face and in his thighs as he stormed through the night.

At the end of the quays, he crossed the road and the Luas line on to Parkgate Street, and made for Phoenix Park. Along its main drag, there was only a scattering of people, a jogger emerging from the darkness, a few cyclists using the lanes. Traffic on the road was light. A squad car came up behind him and passed on.

At the first roundabout, he left the road and took to the fields. It was soft underfoot. He could hear the rustle of tall grass against the lower legs of his jeans. His eyes grew accustomed to the dark. The traffic in the distance sounded like the sea.

He found the path he was looking for, a beaten passage through the longer grass. It skirted the park's cricket club, where lights still burned.

He hadn't been up this way in years, but that week when the park had been home, soon after his mother's death, had left him with a sense of direction that time hadn't taken. He found the grove of trees within fifteen minutes. He moved between a few, his hand feeling around the bark until he recognised the one he was looking for. The carved-out figure was still there, no longer smooth, but intact. His seagull. At the base, he began digging through the soft topsoil with his hands. .Once down a foot or so, he took the gun from one pocket, the plastic bag from the other. He wrapped the gun, placed it in the shallow hole and refilled it.

He retraced his steps all the way back into town along the boardwalk. By the time he got to the bedsit, his legs were heavy, but he had left the anger somewhere out there, floating down the Liffey. The stairs, which he routinely took two at a time, went on for an age.

Inside, he fell straight into bed, barely managing to pull off his jeans. He dreamed that he was back in the gaff, sharing a cell with Harms Sullivan, who was doing his head in, talking about the opportunities for property in China.

Teresa Sullivan noticed that her glass was empty. She looked at the TV: the signature tune for the late news on RTÉ was sounding. It was eleven twenty. The room in which she sat was bathed in a faded light from the hat-stand lamp that stood in the corner. She reached for the remote control and killed the screen. No more news. All it could bring was further pain. She had to identify her younger son today. The baby she had brought into the world, the boy she had tried to rear. Today he was a piece of meat on a slab, a neat bullet hole in the back of his head where death had entered.

She raised her eyes from the TV to the colour photograph sitting atop the set. A woman and two boys smiled out. Teresa had been younger then, still clinging to the looks that had set the odd pulse racing. The boys had matching patterned jumpers, big collars and compliant smiles. Their haircuts were tight to ensure barren terrain for lice.

Teresa Sullivan wouldn't have been surprised if it emerged that the gardaí had been responsible for shooting her son to death. Hadn't they been hassling the lad since he was boy, calling at all hours of the day and night looking for him and his brother? Wasn't it really the guards' fault that both boys had ended up doing what they'd done? Weren't they forced into it?

Teresa rose wearily from her chair. She was just entering the kitchen when she heard the commotion. Somebody was banging on her front door. 'Who is it?' she called.

'Ma, I haven't got me key.'

Peter. She opened the door. Her surviving son looked at her, his eyes seeking pity through the blood and bruises. The zip on his fleece was open, more dark stains marking his shirt. 'Mother of Jesus,' she said. 'What happened?'

As she spoke, she saw somebody advancing along the path of her garden. 'Peter, is he with you?'

Her son turned and saw what was coming. He lurched forward, pushing his mother before him. Teresa Sullivan fell over. Her son grabbed her arm, tried to lift her from the ground. She looked up and saw a man dressed in a black suit, black shirt and tie, his head wrapped in a balaclava. She thought it unusual that the man was wearing a suit, as if he was en route to a night out and had stopped to pick up something.

He pointed the gun at her son and pulled the trigger. The sound was deafening to Teresa Sullivan's ears. She screamed. Her son fell into her arms. Two more shots rang out. She held her son. The boy she had given birth to was dying in her arms, his blood pouring over her.

'Oh, Jesus, Peter. Oh, Jesus. What have they done to you?'

4

When Noelle awoke, Michael O'Leary was in the bedroom. Her eyelids were slow to open, pitching for more sleep. There was a little pressure at the base of her skull. Then, as she came to life, O'Leary was before her, wearing a checked shirt and a demented look, his arms spread wide like one of his Ryanair planes.

She opened her left eye. He was still there. It took her a few moments to get her bearings. She was in the spare room of Caroline's apartment. Last night they had drained a bottle of sauvignon blanc. The after-effects were renting space in her body. She raised the duvet above her head, willing herself back to sleep.

There was a knock on the door. Caroline's head came round. Her face was rearing to go for this hour of the morning, eyes as bright and shiny as her lipstick. Her hair looked like a great wave on the point of breaking. The bottle-green trouser suit was straight off the rack. Worst of all was the smile, as if she had recently awoken from a long sleep of the just.

'Can't be late for your appointment,' she said.

Noelle pointed at the poster on the wall, her nose wrinkling, as if at a bad smell.

'Isn't he gorgeous?' Caroline said. She came around to the side of the bed to get a better view.

'I remember when your wall was all Duran Duran.' Caroline bent her head to view the poster from another angle. 'I was thinking of getting it framed,' she said.

'You are an adult.'

'Look at him, the easy way he wears his power.'

'Michael O'Leary is your fantasy shag?'

'What other multi-millionaire goes to work dressed like a lumberjack? You can't bottle that kind of confidence.'

Noelle ducked beneath the duvet again. Her sister clapped her hands. 'OK, I have to fly. Come on, you have to be there by half eleven – you can't leave the judge waiting. Now, a few pointers before I go?'

Noelle got out of bed, reached for her dressing-gown and pulled it around her shoulders.

'You know that the media horde will be all over you before you even arrive at the place. Just be ready. They'll come at you like a pack? Don't be frightened. They won't touch you. They'll look intimidating, terrible dress sense, one or two could do with a course in personal hygiene, but they're not violent.

'They'll stop six inches from you and begin clicking and filming and farting and whatever else it is they do with those ... weapons of theirs. Then they'll move with you, like a rugby scrum. Ignore them. Don't smile. Don't respond to your name being called. Look ahead. Your countenance should be serious but not sad.'

'I'm going to court, not an audition.'

'Just remember, you, too, are a victim, but not a self-pitying one. Blue-sky thinking all the way.' Caroline blew a kiss and then she was gone.

After a few minutes enjoying the silence, Noelle advanced out of the bedroom. The apartment was on the third floor of a block on the south quays, built when the Celtic Tiger was at a gallop. Caroline had captured her unit off the plans.

This was going to be Noelle's home for a while. Caroline was adamant: she had even done the run out to Skellig to pick up a few bits and bobs for Noelle. When she returned, she said it was as she had imagined. The media had the place under siege. Caroline had been brilliant, no question about that.

The large living room was flooded with light, pouring through a glass wall that looked out on the Liffey. One end was dominated by a beige couch facing a plasma TV screen. At the far end, next to the glass wall, a circular table looked lonely. It was a minimalist affair, reflecting Caroline's neat and tidy mind.

Beyond a bowl of fruit and a box of Special K, there was little sign of food in the kitchenette. A compact fridge held a carton of milk, another of cream, three miniatures of white wine and a Marks & Spencer TV dinner that looked like an abandoned idea.

A radio was playing through speakers mounted high in the corners of the room. She became aware of voices. It was the news, something about a man dying in his mother's arms. She looked around to find the source. The remote control was on the couch. She pressed the red button to restore calm.

Breakfast was a bowl of the cereal and a pear that looked to be hovering on its eat-by date. She found solace in her headache. Popping two Solps now would be perfectly justified. She switched on the kettle, reached into her handbag and extracted the tablets.

Outside, the wind was blowing a shiver across the Liffey's skin. Traffic on the far quays appeared to be at a standstill.

She was surprised by how calm she felt. She was adapting to her new circumstances quite well. If she had read about somebody like herself, a life cast out from a sheltered harbour, she would have felt sympathy. Yet she was moving with the swell. There was no panic.

Of course she was angry. Donal's secret life was opening up, like a dark ocean, with God knew what lurking beneath the surface. Why hadn't he told her? Did he not trust her? Was he afraid of how she might react? Angry, yes, but she wasn't surprised. Donal loved the idea of adventure. She could have killed him now, though, landing her with a summons to the High Court.

The silence in the apartment was broken by the faint ring of her mobile phone from the bedroom. She found it on the floor at the end of the bed, in the shadow of Michael O'Leary's grin.

'Noelle, it is I.'

Natalie, her cleaner. Of course, this was Thursday.

'Natalie, I'm so sorry, I meant to ring you.'

'Yes. I am standing now outside. You don't answer. Are you hot out of the shower? Is it possible to let me in?'

Natalie was from Latvia or Lithuania, Noelle could never remember which. She came twice a week, but was just back from a holiday in the old country. 'Natalie, something came up earlier in the week. I'm not at home at the moment.'

'You are not here? But the place is chock-a-block. There are lots of people, with cameras and vans. Come on, did you win the lotto?'

'Something's come up, Natalie. I won't be home for a while. I'll ring you when I'm back.'

'But what shall I do? This is Thursday. It is not good. You are third person this week who says no more work. What is happening?'

Noelle said she'd be in touch and rang off. The luminous digits on the alarm clock next to her bed said it was 9:50 a.m. She walked into the bathroom and turned on the shower.

Alan Slate liked to be at work early. Arriving into an empty office reassured him that he was ahead of the game. It had always been thus, even when he was in Purgatory.

There was a stack of photographs on his desk, the prints delivered by Detective Seamus Fox. The top print showed Junior Corbett with the late Sullivan brothers. Slate noted that Corbett was sprouting a gut while the siblings were still in six-pack territory.

Corbett was closer to his own vintage. He must be at least thirty-five, at the foothills of middle age, five short of Alan's span. The Sullivan brothers had the advantage of youth to gift them perfect physiques. They were also dead, which provided Slate with some consolation. No point in having a six-pack to die for if you were pushing up daisies.

Alan Slate sucked in his potter. He couldn't rightly place when it had first appeared. It must be five years now, around the time he'd packed in the Astro-turf soccer. Back then, the Wednesday-night game was one of the first elements of his hectic lifestyle that had had to be shelved. Now, back at base camp, all he carried from the good times was this potter, growing by the day, which weighed on his sunny nature whenever he thought about it.

Underneath the photos, there was a cardboard folder, in which he had begun compiling the life and times of Joshua 'the Dancer' Molloy, the genius whom the cops had fingered for the amateur hit on Junior Corbett. The folder contained a sheaf of A4 pages, printed-out copies of newspaper articles retrieved from the net. There were articles from the *Ipswich Evening Star*, the *Daily Telegraph* and the *Sun* in England. Cuttings from the *Irish Daily Star* and the *Evening Herald* gave a local angle on the story.

Slate read through them again and began typing out his own narrative on Dancer Molloy. This way, he would need only to top and tail it whenever the fella's number was up. In Slate's opinion, he was a dead man walking, just another thug joining the lengthening queue earmarked for target practice after a walk-on role in gangland. There was nothing in the cuttings prior to Molloy being arrested in England, behind the wheel of a Range Rover.

It began on an early-morning patrol by two members of the Suffolk Constabulary. They spotted a car in a lay-by on the A12, a few miles south of Ipswich at five thirty a.m. on 3 April 2005. Slate was surprised when he saw the date. He knew it well: the day his own world had crumbled. According to the press reports, the morning was cold but clear with a full moon. The vehicle was parked in an 'erratic manner which naturally gave rise to a general suspicion' (PC Kevin Willoughby, *Ipswich Evening Star*).

With considerable difficulty, the man was awoken. He was quite obviously drunk in charge of his vehicle. On the floor of the passenger side, PC Willoughby immediately noticed a near-empty bottle of Stolichnaya vodka. There was also a six-pack of Heineken, from which two bottles had been torn away. There was no sign of the empty bottles in the vehicle's interior.

Things took off when PC Willoughby's colleague, PC Sonia McWilliams, spotted that the door panel on the driver's side was not fully fixed. When she tugged at it with her finger, she saw that there were packages of matter behind it. She pulled out one, about the size of a small brick, vacuum-packed and containing what she immediately concluded was hashish.

When she presented it to the driver, he 'looked as if he was about to be physically sick' (PC McWilliams the *Daily*

Telegraph), which is exactly what he did five seconds later, throwing up all over the policewoman's tunic.

He was arrested and offered no resistance, which was a relief to the two cops because any struggle might have resulted in the suspect throwing up further regurgitated matter on their uniforms and general persons.

After handcuffing him, the constables had a quick root around in the Range Rover's interior, while the suspect was put standing beside the open driver's door. From there, with his hands cuffed behind his back, he attempted to escape. He ran across the road but, before reaching the far side, he stumbled and fell, resulting in a large cut to his left temple, which required treatment.

He was taken to Ipswich police station, where he was placed in a cell and later woken when two detectives came on duty. He was questioned for seven hours, but said little beyond providing what turned out to be a false name and address.

PC Willoughby later told the local rag that they could not believe their luck. 'Either the panel was not replaced properly, which would be quite amazing, or the suspect himself had attempted to access the drugs after they were packed in place,' he was quoted as saying.

Meanwhile, the vehicle was searched, resulting in the discovery of false door panels and floors, behind and under which were found thirty-eight more blocks. The total haul was estimated to have a 'street value of £1.3 million and was destined for the Dublin market' (the *Daily Telegraph*).

The belief, articulated in the subsequent trial, was that the drugs had been transported to London, via the Channel Tunnel, where the accused had picked them up with the intention of bringing them back to Ireland for sale on the streets. Further enquiries had revealed that the suspect was a twenty-three-year-old native of west Dublin by the name of

Joshua Molloy and the Garda Síochána believed him to be a mid-level operative in a major drugs gang.

The abiding mystery about the case was how he ended up in Ipswich. One theory was that he lost his way, which was understandable considering the state he was found in.

Back in Ireland, the *Daily Star* speculated that 'The gang leader whose drugs were seized believes that Molloy was doing a runner with the merchandise, making towards the north of England where he hoped to get a ferry from Hull to Rotterdam.' This theme was further explored in the *Evening Herald*, which credited unnamed sources as saying that Molloy had fallen out with the gang leader and had been 'fleeing to mainland Europe with the intention of starting out in business, most likely in the greater Amsterdam area'. Slate knew, from his days on the tabloids, that much of that stuff was attributable to the imagination of the reporters, but what harm was there in some innocent speculation?

Molloy pleaded guilty to possession with intent to supply at Ipswich Crown Court and received a sentence of six years. The court was told that he had a list of priors in Ireland, about half of which had been processed in the Children's Court. These included one for assault on a garda officer, in which the officer sustained a fractured jaw. Molloy had done 240 hours of community service in lieu of six months in custody. His most recent offences were two for drink-driving, the second of which occurred when his licence was under suspension for the first. He served three months in Mountjoy Prison as a result.

His solicitor pleaded mitigation. Molloy had no previous convictions for drugs, and had had a tough upbringing. He was a minor player. He had never known his father, and his mother had died when he was still in his early teens. He had shown great potential as a footballer, and had come to England as a teenager for a trial with a Premiership team.

'Little did he think then that one day he would arrive back in our country under the current circumstances, but such is Fate's arrow that it can drag us down dark alleys all the way to ultimate degradation,' the solicitor told the court. (*Ipswich Evening Star*).

The judge's reply formed the lead headline for the *Herald* that afternoon: 'THUG DESERVES AN ARROW UP HIS REAR END'. The judge told him he was 'a dealer in death who had brought his foul cargo to this peaceful corner of England'. (*Ipswich Evening Star*).

And that was the last that was heard of Joshua 'Dancer' Molloy until recent days when he had exploded on to gangland again.

Slate liked the look of this one: it had great prospects. Molloy would do nicely as the basis for a serious study into the modern gangster. Ideally, the way to go would be to sketch out the details of his life, particularly the personal stuff, and have it ready to go into a major feature when he snuffed it. The details would have to be sexed up. A crazy moll would come in handy, or any victims on whom he might have inflicted violence, but these were elements that could be embellished along the road. If he was still alive in a few weeks' time, a feature could be run without the name attached. The subject would be provided instead with a tabloid moniker. 'The Footballer' was already in use. 'The Dancer' would do the job. Slate pulled down an instant headline – 'DEAD DANCER WALKING'. No doubt about it, he had the touch.

He looked up and saw it was ten thirty. Shit, he was supposed to be covering the appearance of that solicitor in the High Court, his other project, which was also pregnant with possibilities.

Four other reporters were at their desks when he got up and slipped into his jacket. He whispered hellos as he walked past. At the bottom of the stairs, the magazine's entertainment editor, Karen Small, was rooting around in her handbag in front of the poster offering cash for gold.

'Things aren't that bad,' he said. She looked up and, as he had for the last week or so, he detected in her smile something more than just platonic warmth.

'Oh, hi,' she said. She tossed a strand of hair from her face.

'You're not thinking of flogging your worldly possessions,' he said, nodding at the poster.

She laughed all the way to her eyes. 'No, I thought I had some change on me,' she said. 'I'm not important enough to get a space in the car park.'

He smiled and pulled a couple of two-euro coins from his pocket. 'Throw that in and fix me up later,' he said.

She accepted the money without argument. 'I owe you one.'

'You can buy me a drink tonight after work.'

She looked at the coins in her palm. 'Do I come that cheap?'

'It will cost you a lot more than that to get to know me. But tonight I'm buying. Deal?'

She began mounting the stairs. 'Deal,' she said, without looking back at him.

Slate turned and walked through the door. Outside the sun shone down on him. Who cared about carrying a potter when everything in the garden was rosier than it had been for a long time?

It was pushing eleven when Molloy got out of bed. He had woken as the dawn announced itself beyond the curtains. After that, there was tossing and turning but little rest. He felt groggy and narky.

He threw on his jeans and T-shirt and padded down to the bathroom. The water was cold on his face and hands. He looked closely at himself in the mirror above the basin, which was cracked in one corner and stained with specks of dried toothpaste and soap. He didn't look too bad. There was nothing he could do about the premature receding hairline, but it would be years before baldness really took hold. His face was lean, his eyes, despite the lack of sleep, alert. He was in good shape. These last two years, he had no problem looking in the mirror.

He held up his right hand and flexed the fingers, still sore from punching Harms Sullivan. The knuckles of his three middle fingers were scraped, but otherwise there were no marks.

After a cup of coffee and a smoke, he went to work. He broke the two eggs on the side of an aluminium saucepan. A fork was all he had to beat them. He cut a slab of butter and dropped it in, added a sprinkling of salt and pepper. He peeled two slices of bacon from a packet and placed them under the grill. Within minutes, they were spitting fat. He stood by the cooker, a fresh mug of coffee in his hand.

If his ma could see him now, she'd have some laugh. Her Josh cooking. She would have cackled away to herself before the coughing took hold. Her pride would have been expressed in her eyes.

He had never cooked as much as a sausage before he'd gone into the gaff. Cooking was something he had always regarded as an exotic activity, like playing golf or ballroom dancing. There hadn't been much of it at home. More often than not his mother had got their evening meal in the chipper. To this day, the sharp scent of vinegar brought him back to the table in the kitchen at home. Himself, Ma and Ivan digging into chips and battered fish, a tin of Batchelor's peas the only concession his mother made to the cooker. Now there was just him and Ivan, and they were hardly bosom buddies. Ivan had visited him once in prison and had sorted out this bedsit.

The food was gone and his third smoke heading rapidly for the butt when the phone rang. No caller ID. He hesitated before pressing the answer button.

'Joshua?'

Not even his brother called him that. 'Who wants to know?'

'It's your favourite alcoholic.'

Wally. He was phoning from the gaff.

'You're some fuckin' wanker,' Molloy said.

There was no response. Molloy thought he heard familiar sounds in the background: the clank of metal on metal, doors closing. In his mind's eye he could see Wally there, lying on the top bunk, his face to the wall, hands up around his head as if asleep. The mobile pinned to his left ear. 'Are you still there?' Molloy said.

'I'm here, mate. What's the issue?'

'The issue is your advice on how best to solve my problem. Go to the man, you said. Go to the man and apologise and offer to make good. Go to the man and that will be the end of it, the past washed away. I went to the man. Now I'm up shit creek in a boat that's leaking fast.'

'Joshua, have you had a slip?'

'What the fuck difference does it make now?'

'Have you?'

'I might as well have.'

'Hang in there, brother.'

'Don't give me that shit. I got pulled into a set-up. There was a hit planned on Junior and guess who found himself chauffeuring the shooter. It didn't happen and now there's a contract out on my head. What do you want me to do? Ring him up, tell him I'm on the fucking programme and I want to make amends?'

'Step Nine, Joshua. We won't get anywhere without at least an effort to make amends. You made that effort. You can do no more. Whatever happened, the main thing is you didn't pick up a drink. But I hear you, brother. Let that anger flow. Get those toxins out of your body—'

Molloy knew the drill. A screw was at Wally's door. He had to slip the phone under the pillow and hope for the best. Wally was one of the few fellas he had made a connection with in there. Wally had introduced him to the meetings.

It had been a long road to that point. He had tried the pills inside, but they hadn't done much for him. He had got his hands on a few grams of speed in the early days, but that had done even less. His drug of choice wasn't to hand, and nothing else would satisfy the longing.

There had been one encounter with hooch, a bottle of which he had bought about a year into his stretch. It had left him puking all over the cell and a loss of privileges for a week. He could have handled all that but the stuff was pure piss. It just didn't reach the parts where proper booze had brought him for as long as he could remember.

After that he tried to stay dry and clean, just as an experiment. It worked for the best part of a year, much to his amazement. He read a lot, even played the odd game of football, become a fixture in the prison gym. But things still weren't right. He begun to dread facing it on the outside. He kept seeing himself on the day of his release, walking fast to the nearest offy, demanding a pint of painkiller at the counter.

He had known about the meetings, but had long resolved never to go near that bunch of Jesus freaks. Then one day he ran into Wally, whom he knew from a distance. Wally asked him along, and this time he didn't bother with the resistance.

From the very first one, something made him keep coming back.

Wally was full of shit but he could set out a situation clearly, especially when it came to the sauce and all that flowed from it. You would never have put him down as somebody who was doing a ten-year stretch for armed robbery. He told Molloy that he was a driver, and, on the day in question, his driving had been a little erratic on account of the half-dozen pints he had skulled that morning.

They became friends. Wally had even convinced him to straighten things out with Junior, for the sake of his sobriety. He kept banging on about the monkey who would take up residence on his back, telling him it was all right to have a little drink. 'Except, Joshua, your monkey will be carrying a semi-automatic, playing Russian roulette with your sobriety.'

Wally came back on the line, his voice dropped to a whisper. 'Joshua, Fate intervened, my brother. Fate's a bitch at times but it's one of the things we can't change. You must accept it and try to move on.'

'Accept that somebody is going to put a bullet in my head?'

'There is triumph in this adversity, Joshua.'

'Wally, would you ever—'

'Listen to me. Listen to me. You didn't pick up a drink. You're still going to the rooms, aren't you? You're still alive. The only thing that can kill you is the next drink. There is no certainty that this Junior dude will put a gun to your head. You lift a drink and you pull the trigger yourself. Pop. Pop. Pop. End of story. Remember, Joshua, you're one drink away from a drunk. You don't want to go back.'

The line went dead.

He could see Wally now, packing away his phone, lunch ahead, then the afternoon work schedule, dinner, maybe a game of pool, an hour of TV and another lock-down for the night.

When he was in there, he couldn't wait to get out. The long chain of days stretching towards infinity. The grinding monotony. The threat of violence lurking around the next corner. Right now, it shimmered in the distance like a mirage.

He looked at his watch. He could catch a lunchtime meeting in the city centre before tackling the other matter.

He lit another smoke and grabbed his jacket. This time he remembered to lock the door on the way out.

The signature tune for the eleven o'clock news came on the car radio. Noelle was about to reach to kill it, but curiosity got the better of her. It led with that story she had caught a snatch of earlier, some gangster shot in his mother's arms. The details didn't register with her. She waited. It was the fourth item.

'The High Court is expected to hear this morning from the wife of missing solicitor Donal Diggins.' Missing solicitor. It made him sound as if he was a drowning victim, or one of those suicides whose clothes were found neatly folded on a rocky outcrop of Howth Head. Donal wasn't missing. He was just absent.

The car park was on the far side of the river from the Four Courts. Her mobile phone pinged for attention as she was turning off the ignition. A text message from Caroline: 'Good luck.'

A foul smell drifted up from the low-tide Liffey. She walked at a clip, the briefcase swinging from her left hand. Caroline had said to expect them at the far side of the river, just down from the entrance.

She hadn't arrived at the bridge when the first one approached. He was tall with a thatch of grey hair, but his head quickly ducked behind a television camera. He back-pedalled in front of her as she walked. Her face was a stone of seriousness. For a few seconds, it looked as if the cameraman might fall over as he reversed. She had to stop herself reaching out to push him, sending him and his equipment over the wall and down into the smelly riverbed.

As she turned on to the Church Street Bridge, they began rushing like bees to honey. Two men sprinting and another weaving between the traffic stopped on the bridge. Out of the corner of her eye, she saw another cameraman, this one trailed by a helper with one of those furry things they carried around. She kept eyes front.

Initially, they all moved as one. Through the cracks of the scrum, she could see motorists gaping at the spectacle. At the far end of the bridge, she had to wait for the pedestrian lights. This gave the less athletic among them the chance to grab a few shots. She kept her chin up, focused on the middle distance. They didn't say anything, just kept clicking, filming, recording her arrival, as if she was one of those men on trial for murdering their wives.

She turned in at the entrance. A guard was standing outside the security cabin through which she had to pass. He looked at her with the same curiosity as the others.

Inside, she flashed her Court Service-issued ID and was ushered past the queue at the metal detector. She could feel tension seeping from her body. Now all she had to deal with was the law.

5

Their heels echoed on stone as they moved along the corridor on the first floor of the Four Courts building. Yvonne Paul walked beside Noelle. The ten-minute consultation in the room downstairs had gone well. Yvonne had introduced her to the lawyer and they ran through what to expect.

Now they were approaching Court 12. The lawyer, his name Paul Hutchinson, walked a few paces ahead of them, his gown billowing against his stride. He held a wig in his right hand, his left wrapped around a clutch of folders and papers. Noelle had been expecting somebody older. This man was younger than her, still on the right side of thirty. He was tall and thin, with a face that betrayed the last vestiges of acne, and he wore rimless glasses with thick bifocals.

As they walked, Yvonne bent over and whispered, 'Paul is hungry.' Noelle nodded.

The lawyer pushed at the door into Court 12 but met resistance. He stuck his head around it to announce his arrival. Something gave. The room was packed with bodies. They eased their way in and beat a path through to the far end. The lawyer turned and pointed towards a wooden bench that already accommodated gowned lawyers. Noelle sat into the bench. Her lawyer entered the one in front of her, and Yvonne slipped into another, facing the lawyer, Noelle and the rest of the court. The room was smaller than she expected. Four bulbous lamps hung from the ceiling. Tall windows with square sashes looked out on to the quays and the Liffey.

In her four years of practice, she had never darkened the door of this superior court. Usually the work brought her to the district court up the road in the Old Richmond Hospital, although she occasionally appeared at the chaotic Bridewell, sitting across the Luas line from the Four Courts. Her only forays into the main complex were to the Circuit Criminal Court, which sat in the annex to the main building. The High Court was where the moneyed came to sort out their differences.

She felt the eyes of the room on her. Hutchinson turned and whispered something inaudible, which, she assumed, was designed to reassure. She nodded and smiled. She took a quick look around and recognised one face immediately. In the absence of a jury, the designated box was occupied by a platoon of what could only be reporters. Seated in the front row was the man who had interrupted her and Caroline on Tuesday last, the day the whole thing blew up. He met her stare with a grin. She looked away. She knew none of the other faces. Within Donal's social orbit, there had been many solicitors and not a few barristers, but they were scarce today, as far as she could make out.

'All rise,' somebody said, and they did. The judge came through a door and leaped the steps up to his elevated position. He nodded, and most of the gowns bowed in response, one or two from the waist.

Judge Cornelius Neilon had a quick glance around the

room as he took a pair of glasses from a case. 'Right so, off we go,' he said.

Then they started. One by one, a series of lawyers addressed the judge and applied for relief.

'My lord, I represent AIB and we would like to join the proceedings ...'

'Your lordship, I am seeking relief ...'

'My lord, I am here for Permanent TSB, and it has come to our notice ...'

'Judge, it is with great regret that I must impose myself on the court in such circumstances, but my client Anglo Irish Bank ...'

'My lord, my lord.' A cry came up from the rear of the room. 'Might I be permitted to apply on my client's behalf for much-needed relief?'

At least another four barristers competed for the attention of the judge. Noelle willed them to stop. With each application, further dark prairies began opening up. As they spoke and applied, bowed and scraped, she looked across at Yvonne, whose mouth remained firm, although her eyes appeared to soften.

While the applications rained in, the judge diverted his attention from the barristers now and then to look down on Noelle. She met his eyes, but couldn't detect anything in his gaze.

'My lord, the issue of Cape Isis is one that ...'

The judge raised his right hand. 'Sorry, Mr Sempleton. Your client?'

A wigless, reedy guy, who looked like he could do with a good feed, had raised a long-fingered hand into the air at the rear of the room. 'A group of investors in one of Mr Diggins's ventures, my lord. The Thaidye consortium. They provided Mr Diggins with over two million euro towards a leisure and apartment complex in Cape Isis.'

'Where?'

'Cape Isis, my lord. Apparently it's an island off the west coast of Africa.'

'This man's activities spread to Africa?'

'Yes, my lord,' he said. 'I have a brochure for the venture, which bills it as the discovery of Cape Isis.'

'He discovered the island?'

'In a manner of speaking, my lord. He located it as the new frontier in property. Unfortunately, my clients were given the impression he was some class of a pioneer.'

'In the footprints of St Brendan, no doubt,' the judge said.

Another barrister was on his feet, launching through the gap he had spotted. He was large, red-faced, and wearing a wig that could have done with a little straightening on his head. 'My lord, as you can observe from the applications of my friends, this matter is perhaps a lot more serious than first envisaged.'

'Nice understatement, Mr Bennett,' the judge said.

'It would appear that Mr Diggins was engaged in what I might neutrally refer to as grossly unorthodox practices. His ability to acquire money from various financial institutions appears to have been staggering.'

Noelle detected a rumbling of sorts in her stomach. Of course she knew all about Cape Isis, or at least she thought she did. Donal arrived home one evening, it must have been about two years ago. She had her feet curled underneath her on the couch, watching *Coronation Street*. He threw a colour brochure down beside her. 'Keys to the kingdom,' he said. She began leafing through the brochure, lots of sand, sea the colour of sapphire, and what appeared to be a shanty town.

'This is where we move into the super-league. Ireland on tour. Welcome to a little patch of Paradise that is going to be just a Ryanair flight away from your front door.' He slipped out of his suit jacket and stood directly in her line of sight of the TV, his hands resting on an imaginary lectern in front of him. 'Roll up, roll up, a three-bed unit with six per cent yield, going forward. Capital growth of twenty points annually. You can be in when they're shifting the muck, for that is where you'll grow your buck.

'What we have here is a little slice of Paradise that will forever be Ireland. Leave the weather behind, hop on your €1 flight and take a break in heaven. Terms and conditions apply, but none of them mean your money is at risk.' His arms were spread wide now, the better to welcome investors into his plan.

She smiled, uncurled herself from the couch and walked over to kiss him. He had that something, no doubt about it.

The booming voice of the barrister brought her back. 'At the kernel of the matter is a simple question,' Mr Bennett continued. 'And that is the location of the man whose activities have served to bring us all here together, like, if I may, my lord, a posse of righteous officers appealing to the majesty of the law. I speak, my lord, of Mr Donal Diggins. He is our Banquo, the ghost at the feast that is this hearing in front of your lordship.'

'Let's keep it moving, Mr Bennett,' the judge said.

'If Mr Diggins could be located, we could at least begin to unravel what exactly has happened. Only he can answer the myriad questions that keep mounting, like rotten tyres on a ritual bonfire.' Bennett paused, and swivelled his head slightly. Silent applause wafted into his ears.

The judge leaned forward. 'Mr Bennett, your point?'

'My point, my lord, can only really be framed as a question. And that is, where is he? Where is Mr Donal Diggins?

At that very moment, he was lying on a bed. It was in a room on the fourth floor of a hotel located on a side-street off the Marqués de Larios in the centre of Málaga.

The room was small, as befitted a three-star hotel in a tourist city. The only natural light pouring into the room came from the single window, which was barred and opened on to a narrow yard, hollowed out from the centre of the building.

Donal Diggins was buck naked. Directly above him, suspended from the ceiling, a fan chopped and hummed its way through the air of an unseasonably warm day. Just beyond the foot of the bed, directly in his line of view, were the two pale cheeks of a woman's ass. She was bent forward on to a dresser. Diggins heard a loud sniffle, and the woman straightened, as if in reaction, throwing her head back. She closed her eyes for a second, then turned to him. 'It's good, no?'

'No,' he said. Donal Diggins felt agitated. The coke was not delivering for him. In particular, it was not delivering for his member, which, despite the woman's best efforts, was as limp as a week-old lettuce leaf. He was agitated also by the suspicion that he was getting done.

Through the party years, whenever he had succumbed to temptation, the coke had never left him high and dry. Yet now, at a time of great stress when he was surely entitled to some relief, it was simply not doing the business. Quality was the problem. This whore was pushing low-grade shite on him because she presumed he was a tourist. No repeat business. What did she care?

He lifted a watch from the bedside locker. With the time difference, Noelle would be in court by now. A shooting gallery of barristers would be lining up to blow away his reputation. At least he could rely on Noelle. No bother to her. Like him, she was strong. They wouldn't let the bastards grind them down. He closed his eyes.

The woman walked around to the side of the bed. 'And what about me?' she asked him. She was slim, although her breasts could have done with a bit of firming up. Her most attractive feature was a pair of large blue innocent eyes. The accent was Eastern European. She claimed to be Albanian. Now she looked down at him with those big eyes, and said, 'I am good, no?'

'How does it break down, the grand?'

'Say again?'

'How much for you, how much for the coke.'

'I am eight hundred, the drugs two.'

'So you should be four times as good as the coke?'

She looked at him with a question mark on her face. 'Who say I am the problem?'

He would have told her to clear out with her bag of rat poison, except he couldn't be alone right now. He had called the agency soon after six a.m. when he'd got back to the hotel. He knew the significance of this day back home, and a trough of despair was beckoning. He needed distraction. He needed to get high. He needed some relief. He needed, above all, to stay away from his own company.

'It's OK if I go for a shower? When I come back we can try you again. You still have at least half-hour.' She walked into the bathroom. The shower jets squealed from behind the door.

He swung his legs off the bed and walked over to the dresser. She had left a department-store card beside the small bag. He picked up the bag and shook out enough for another line. There was an inscription on the bag: 'Good luck'.

'Mrs Diggins, please.' Noelle felt the eyes in the room on her. The lawyer turned to her and motioned to the far side of the room. She moved through the bodies, only raising her eyes when she stepped up into the box. A man approached her with a Bible. She shook her head. She wasn't a believer and she had no intention of swearing on it now. The man asked her to raise her right hand. He began:

'I affirm to this court that I will tell the truth, the whole truth and nothing but the truth.'

The Bennett man with the red face got to his feet. 'Mrs Diggins, you are aware why we are all gathered here?'

When she looked up, she noticed her elevated perch, raised above the rabble. She gazed at the Bennett man and could see now that his face was a picture of innocence, as if he was a little boy asking questions about a big bad world beyond his comprehension. 'It would be extremely difficult for me not to be aware of what is going on at the moment,' she said.

'Quite,' he said. 'Mrs Diggins, I have some documents here you might cast your eye over.' He passed the pages across.

Noelle looked down. There was a stack of different sheets, which appeared to be application forms.

'Mrs Diggins, what you have before you are mortgage applications to my client in five separate incidences. In each case you will see that the application was on behalf of you and your husband. Is that correct?'

She scanned the documents. Her name was in the space reserved for the second named applicant. The addresses were alien to her. What looked like a house in south County Dublin. An estate of sixteen luxury units in County Kerry. An application related to three apartments in Nerja, southern Spain. An address that meant nothing to her except that the country in question was Bulgaria. There was another, the address of which was indecipherable, apart from the last line, Cape Isis, West Africa.

'Now, Mrs Diggins, are you familiar with any of these properties?

'No.'

'Would any, for instance, represent a holiday home for you and your husband?'

'Not that I know of.'

'I see. And we can take it that if you and your husband had a holiday home you would know about it?'

Smart bastard. 'Yes, you could say that.'

'Now, if you look at the bottom of the second document, relating to the property in Cape Isis, the island the judge was enquiring into earlier, do you see the two signatures? One, I think we can take it, is your husband's. And the second is signed Noelle Diggins, your name. Is that your signature?'

Noelle felt herself getting hot. 'Judge, I'm not sure what the status of this hearing is.'

The barrister cranked his voice up a few notches. 'Can you tell the court whether that is your signature, Mrs Diggins? It's a fairly simple question.' He turned his head away from her again, offering his audience the benefit of his superlative skills.

Her own guy was on his feet. 'My lord, we are not here to investigate Mrs Diggins, or any knowledge she may have had of her husband's activities. She appeared here at your request to see if she could assist in locating her husband.'

The judge brought his hands together and placed them before him, as if in prayer, to consider his response, or at least give the impression that he was considering it.

When the whore came out of the bathroom, she went to her handbag and extracted a small instrument. For a second Diggins thought she was reaching for a gun. She turned towards him, a mobile credit-card machine in her hand, like a naked waitress presenting a restaurant bill.

'We fix now, before going more,' she said. He shrugged. He

pulled his wallet from his trousers and fished his credit card from one of the pockets. He slipped it into the machine.

'OK, is good. We can try while we wait for it to work out.'

Diggins lay back on the bed. She sat beside him and pushed the machine towards him. He punched in the four-digit code. She got down to work. He closed his eyes and tried to think of better days.

He had to stop this. OK, it wasn't a regular thing, certainly not the way it had been a few years ago when everybody was doing it. But he had to stop it. If Noelle ever rumbled him … Besides, he owed it to her to stop. He owed it to himself. He didn't even enjoy it any more. It was now just a habit: he tried to chase sensations that had disappeared down a dark corridor of his memory. Even when the stuff was good, it was no good.

He remembered how a friend had once described the coke hit. 'It's a bit like being at the races, and having lost on the first six, everything is riding on the last. At home, the electricity is about to be cut off because you're so far behind on your bills. There is no prospect of work and the wife doesn't even know how bad things are. Everything is riding on the seventh. That is your buzz.'

That was the buzz he got from the game as well, and look where that was now. Still, he wasn't out of it yet. The contingency plan was in place, and all he needed was a little help in executing it. That was where Noelle came in. They were a team. Maybe, afterwards, they could seek out their own Cape Isis. He tried to picture the pair of them flying in low over the island's shore, a settlement of sorts there, men and women going about simple lives, children splashing among the breakers, waving to the great god coming from the sky, bearing manna for the village of mud huts. Welcome to Paradise.

And the waves, gathering power out in the blue yonder, rolling endlessly towards the shore, turning, churning, marching, more and more and … A great wave of release began to wash over him.

He heard a voice. His eyelids parted. She was looking down at him, big blue pools in her face sparkling at a job well done. He didn't want to hear anything right now. She raised the credit-card machine above her head, like a mallet poised to deliver a violent blow to his climactic moment. 'I think we have a problem,' she said.

The judge looked down at her from his higher perch, paternal concern etched on his face. 'Mrs Diggins, you don't have to answer but in the name of bringing some clarity to these proceedings, might I ask whether that actually is your signature?'

Noelle paused. 'As you know, Judge, I'm an officer of the court myself and I'd like to keep things on the right procedural track. I was under the impression I was asked here to assist in locating my husband.'

The judge's face hardened. 'Correct,' he said.

'Judge, the last time I spoke to my husband was three days ago. He was in Bulgaria at the time. He has been under considerable strain, as you can imagine, and he said he wouldn't be home for a while as he had work to complete in Eastern Europe.'

The judge's head moved up and down in the makings of a nod. 'Any indications when?'

'No. He said that what he was doing might in turn assist any issues that are still outstanding here.'

The red-faced barrister said, 'My lord, if I may—'

'No, you may not. Mrs Diggins, do you have a contact address for your husband?'

'No, Judge, he's moving around a lot.'

'And does he sleep at night?'

'Not very well at the moment.'

'Mrs Diggins, I'm asking whether he has specific addresses at which he stays when he's ... moving around.'

'None that I'm aware of, Judge. He said he would contact me.'

Judge Cornelius Neilon leaned back in his chair. 'I see,' he said.

Scarlet Face was on his feet again, waving a sheet of paper in his right hand. 'Mrs Diggins, are we to take it that you are not in a position to assist the court at all in locating your husband?'

'I think I've answered that question.'

'You are aware of the gravity of the situation, I take it.'

'Mr Bennett, for you this is a job. For me it's my life. I know exactly what is at stake, but thanks for the benefit of your wisdom.'

Bennett recoiled as if he had been exposed to a foul smell. He looked up to the judge, his eyebrows inching on to his forehead, but the judge just nodded at him. 'Yes, but can you see how I, how we, his lordship, me, my fellow counsel who are applying for relief, how we have great difficulty in understanding how you cannot give absolutely any assistance in locating your husband? Can you see where we're coming from, Mrs Diggins?'

'You're not the only one flying blind, Mr Bennett. I've been left in the dark too, you know. None of this is easy ...' She felt herself going weak. She tried to speak, but nothing came except a loud sniffle. Her body began trembling. She reached into her handbag, but there were no hankies there. She looked up at the judge. 'Sorry,' she said.

'Take your time.' He poured a glass of water from a carafe on his bench and handed it to his gowned assistant, who brought it over to Noelle. She sipped from it. Somebody passed her a tissue. The room was so silent that when she blew her nose it sounded like a volcano erupting. She wondered what had brought her to this. Either way, Caroline would be proud of her. Tears on the button.

'You can understand our position, Mr Diggins?'

'Actually, I can't. What's the problem?' He was pacing around the room, which didn't have much space for pacing, leaving him with the appearance of a caged beast. The whore was sitting up on the bed. She had put her clothes on. He was still in the nip. 'My account is in credit. Why would you stop a payment?'

There was a pause on the line before the clipped English tone resumed. He had dealt with so many of these bankers in the City of London. They all talked the same, as if there was a banker school they went to where accents were filed down to a single specification. 'Mr Diggins, in these turbulent times, you will understand that we have some obligations. The payment being requested on your card, to an organisation La Mejor Chica, is the fourth such payment in the last fortnight. Such large transactions can give rise to suspicion and we have an automated warning system in place.'

Diggins stopped pacing. 'The only thing you need to concern yourself with is that my account with you is in credit.'

'Of course, but under the circumstances I required more information. You have now supplied it. I am happy that the transaction is genuine. The payment will now be authorised.'

The woman was sawing at her nails. When she looked up, there was confusion on her face.

He nodded at her that he had it under control. 'Well, that's good, but I can tell you – what's your name again? . . . Yeah, yeah, it doesn't matter. I can tell you that you're lucky to still be in a job. I've been a customer of your bank for the last ten years, a valued customer, and this is the first time I've had to put up with shit like this.'

'Mr Diggins, please, I understand that you are under some pressure—'

'Whoa. Whoa. Who said anything about pressure? Don't get off the topic. You and your people have let me down, OK? What are you talking about – pressure?'

'Well, sir, the credit crunch has all manner of people under pressure. We have heard about your travails in southern Ireland.'

'Yo. Back it up there,' he said, his voice now clicking up the notches. 'Just make the payment, OK? We'll leave it at that for now, but you'd better know who you're dealing with. This is not the last you'll hear from me.'

'Certainly, sir. Consider it done. By the way, how's the weather over there?'

Diggins pulled the phone from his ear, held it out and looked at it. When he spoke again, he was shouting: 'Fuck you.' He terminated the call.

The woman was off the bed now, alert to the changed atmosphere. 'All OK,' she said.

He looked at her. All she gave a shit about was her money. She didn't care that he was under pressure, that his reputation was being flaked around the courts, that all his hopes were vested in his wife, who was a real woman. All this whore cared about was getting her wad and moving on to the next john. 'It's coming, it's coming,' he said. She nodded, and moved towards the dresser, stood beside the credit-card machine. She picked up her handbag. Right now, she just wanted out. Warning lights were flashing amber in her head.

He grabbed his trousers from the back of the chair and poked his legs into them. 'Before you go,' he said.

'I not going anywhere until the thing pays,' she said.

He stepped up on to the bed and paced back and forth, from top to bottom. The chopping fan was less than a foot from his head. 'I want to talk to you,' he said.

'Don't lose your head.'

He looked up and saw the blades. He stepped down from the bed, and kept pacing. 'Will you forget about the money for one moment, just for a single second? What about the coke? I mean, that was the greatest load of shite I've ever shovelled up my nose and I've snorted some awful stuff in my day. Did you see me coming?'

'I don't understand. You say the coke no good, then you saw you coming, but I think that means the coke is good, no?

He turned from her, faced the bedroom door and began doing karate moves, his arms and legs shooting out against imaginary opponents. He grunted with each kick and chop, like a tennis player serving for the match. Her hands went to her face. The amber light in her head was flashing wildly now.

The credit-card machine began clicking out paper. She tore the receipt from it and shoved it into her bag. He turned and looked at her.

'I go now,' she said. 'They expect me at the agency.' His face was flushed. Beads of sweat trailed rivulets down from his temples. She smiled and walked to the door. He stood aside. She shouldn't be getting away with this. He thought about it. He deserved a refund, something, anything, to show him he wasn't getting done. They were all trying to do him now. He was the fall-guy for bankers and whores and everybody in between. All he had was his integrity and his wife.

He heard the door shut. He was alone again. The bag on the dresser still had something in it. He began putting a line together. Then he would go for a walk, get some breakfast, try to get a bit of shut-eye. This had to stop. It just wasn't the same these days.

The office was dozing through lunch hour when Alan Slate arrived back. He could see Frank Fastneck hunched over a terminal behind the glass partition. Otherwise the silence was broken only by the static echo of an abandoned radio buried beneath newspapers on one of the desks.

That had been a wasted few hours. The Diggins woman was giving little away, and no chance of a chat with her. At least there was some tears to brighten up dull copy. Afterwards, when the platoon of reporters had gathered on the corridor to watch Diggins and the wig have a quick confab, that was the question being passed around: were they real? The general consensus was they were too convenient when she was under pressure.

Slate sat into his desk.

'Alan, a minute.' He looked up to see Frank Fastneck's head sticking out from his office door. If the door had been a blade, and it was slammed shut abruptly, it could have decapitated Fastneck.

Slate got up and entered the inner sanctum. The editor was standing behind his desk, holding up a copy of that day's Evening Herald. Frank Fastneck was an imposing figure in any confined space. Standing at six three, he was just a few years out of a professional football career that had brought him to England and back.

He had been a journeyman player, plying his trade in the lower English divisions, with a single season in the Premiership, when his club at the time was promoted. What he lacked in skill, he made up for with heart, as a bustling centre forward of the old school.

His chiselled good looks – some social columnists made comparisons with JFK – ensured that he became something of a celebrity during his playing days.

Through most of his career he had written, through a ghost writer, a weekly column on football for a Sunday paper. On retiring, he did a bit of TV punditry. He had also invested his money wisely over the years. Then, at the height of the boom, he gathered together a consortium to start up a magazine: *Inside Out*.

A few eyebrows in the media were raised when it was announced that he would edit the venture himself. He had no experience at management level but, as he pointed out in a TV interview, he had no experience as a professional footballer before he had gone to England, and look what that had led to.

The current gibe around town was that one of Frank's weaknesses as a player was his sense of timing in making runs into the box. That lack of awareness was now haunting *Inside Out*: it launched a few months before the economy began to turn.

'Alan, this Diggins woman, what have we got on her?'

Slate raised his spiral-bound notebook and began flicking back through the pages. 'We got the waterworks in court today, but otherwise she wasn't giving much away. I have her number, but she won't pick up. I was maybe going to do something on it this week if we could bring the story on. She has a sister, PR honcho who's wrapped her in cotton wool.'

Fastneck was looking at a photograph in the paper, showing Noelle Diggins surrounded by cameramen outside the court.

'Would you?'

'Would I?'

'Would you?'

'Jesus, I don't know. She's OK, I suppose. Yeah, why not?' Slate didn't like where this was headed.

'She's going to do a job for us. She's just what we need right now.' Fastneck threw down the paper, leaned on the desk, the fingers of both his hands splayed. He looked Alan Slate in the eye. 'Women hold the key to this business, Alan. If you haven't got women, going forward, you're dead. Advertising is dropping through the floor right now. If I'm to be honest, we're just about holding on with our fingertips. We need something special. She is that something.'

Slate nodded slowly. Just two months ago he had been in this same office. The venture was about to be relaunched, just a year into its existence. He was there to be wooed by Fastneck. The magazine was going to be a new departure, going where journalism had never gone before, adapting print to the Internet age, taking on the big boys in guerrilla warfare. Now it was holding on by its fingertips.

Fastneck sat into his seat, threw another glance at the newspaper photograph.

'She's a victim and not bad-looking either, which is a big help. Men would give her one while women empathise with her victimhood. She could be a role model.'

'She could?'

'Who gives a shit as long as they buy our magazine? This is going to be big, Alan, and I want our best reporter on it. I've been talking to people. There's a lot more to come out about her husband. He was up to his bollocks in it, playing loans off against each other.'

'He sounds like a fly boy all right,' Slate said.

Fastneck looked at him as if he had run off on some irrelevant tangent. 'Alan, mind if I ask you? Did you take a punt while all this madness was going on?'

Slate felt a stab of pride. 'I'm one of the lucky ones, Frank. My situation, you know, that other business, my divorce, between it all I didn't have the cash. Anyway, I knew it couldn't last. It didn't make sense.'

'You knew?'

Slate got a kick out of this any time it came up in the last few months. He went through the same routine with friends who had got burned in the property game. He knew all along it couldn't last, which was why he'd stayed clear of it. They looked at him as if he was the oracle. He told them he had studied the form. The evidence said it couldn't last. He had the capacity to stand aside from the mob, and look at it from a rational point of view. There was no way it could last. That was his story and he was sticking to it. The fact that he'd had no money to throw around at the time was neither here nor there.

'It couldn't last, Frank. Pure madness.'

'But what did you see that the rest of us missed?'

'Intuition, I suppose,' he said. 'Look, it was like nothing as much as a gold rush. You ever read about the gold rush in the American west, nineteenth century?'

'Not recently.'

Slate was on a roll. This was his latest line. He had read it one day in a magazine at the barber's. He was surprised he hadn't heard anybody else peddling it on the airwaves. 'Back then, rational thinking went out the window, Frank. People sold up everything and headed west chasing a dream that for most of them was just pie in the sky. They were never going to make it. All the odds said they wouldn't. Sure, a few people walked away with all the serious bucks, but most of them got rightly fucked over. And it was obvious that they would. It would be a bit like getting on a plane with all your worldly possessions and heading off to buy a lotto ticket in, I don't know, Outer Mongolia.

'Anyway, that's what happened here with property. People lost all sense of reason. They kept thinking that the pyramid had proper foundations. But you keep building a pyramid and you end up running into fresh air. Do you know what I mean?'

Fastneck was giving him that look, as if he was the oracle. 'Yes, I do. Pity I didn't know you when all this shit was going on. You shouldn't be in crime. Economics is where your talents lie.'

'We're all economists now, Frank. Open your paper, listen to the talking heads of radio. Everybody knows everything now. How badly burned did you get?'

'You don't want to know. Too many pies, not enough fingers. They're very messy now. I pray daily.' Fastneck raised his hands to his head, ran the tips of his fingers from his hairline to his mouth, his eyes wide, as if he was looking out on the ills of the world. He took a deep breath and shook his head fast. 'Anyway, that's why this Diggins woman could be gold for us. There are thousands out there whose fingers are burned to a crisp. They want to read about the people who're to blame. That's where you come in, Alan. This is your baby. Not just your investigative skills, but your writing. You know I think you're the dog's bollocks. That's why I brought you to our operation. That's why you're on the big money. Bring this home and we're all going to be moving to a different plane.

'You must get on this Diggins woman's case. Stick with her until we get the exclusive. We are going to take ownership of her. Check out her background. We need something to present her as a victim. Look for cancer, or even alcoholism.

A former relationship that turned sour. Anything to paint her victimhood.'

'What if she turns out to be in cahoots with him?'

'By then we'll have flailed the arse out of the victim stuff and she can turn into a femme fatale. Readers' memories don't outlast the life of an ice cube in the sun.'

Slate had been warned about Fastneck. He had been told to sit tight, that doors would begin opening for him again in the mainstream. He had been told that Fastneck was as loose a cannon as there was in the business, and that was saying something. Impatience and ambition had got the better of him. Now he had blasted off in this Starship Enterprise of a magazine. 'Whatever you think, Frank. Do you want me to hold back on that gangsters spread and concentrate on the Diggins woman?'

Fastneck sat down in his seat. He picked up a biro, twirled it around in his fingers and leaned forward, looking Slate in the eye once more. 'Alan, your gangland stuff is tops. I mean, you're the king of crime.'

Slate felt a little pressure on his bladder, which he recognised as a pump being applied to his ego.

'But we have to move the situation forward, bring it on to the next level. Those photos of the crims on their holliers got me thinking. What about a series on lifestyles of the filthy scum? We do it over the course of a month, throw open a spread. We can do the normal stuff – the restaurants they eat at, the clubs they go to, even the hookers they use. We do everything right down to the fittings they put on their bathrooms. We could market it as Hello! for gangsters.'

There was something in Slate's throat. He coughed to clear it, and said,

'I don't know if I'd be able to get that level of detail.'

'So what? Make it up. I mean, they're hardly going to sue.'

'No, they won't sue, but they might come after me. If there's one thing these fuckers hate more than having the truth told about them, it's having lies told about them.'

'Hey, look who's talking. You're not suggesting you're afraid of these lowlifes? Where is the man I hired, the fearless crime reporter who is keeping an eye on the scum?'

It was Slate's turn to lean forward. 'Frank, I'm a crime reporter, not an entertainment correspondent. A gang war is about to explode and I think that's where I should be. Out there at the frontline.'

A mobile vibrated on the table. Fastneck looked down at it. 'Got to take this,' he said. 'Just try and get an interview with the Diggins woman. We'll park the gangsters till then, but keep the lifestyle thing in mind. We're going to make this happen, Alan. You and me, we're going to take it to the top.'

Slate returned to his desk. Two of the younger reporters walked into the room in a cocoon of giggles. The door to the editor's office opened, and they fell silent. Fastneck raised his chin in Slate's direction. 'That was CityWide. They want you to give them a heads-up on the gangland killings for the three o'clock news. Great exposure. What did I tell you, Alan? We're motoring and you're behind the wheel.'

Life had been different for Alan Slate four years earlier when the incident had occurred. He had been at the top of his game. His third book, Scum Central, was two months at number one in the bestseller list. Hardly a week went by when he wasn't invited on to radio programmes to warn the nation of the dangers of gangland. His TV appearances, while less frequent, had an even greater impact on the public consciousness. He had been told on more than one occasion that the ratings went through the roof when he appeared on *The Late Late Show*.

Rumour had it he was the best-paid journalist in the country, and whenever he was asked on air to comment on the rumour, he indulged in the false-modesty routine but pointedly never denied it. Privately, he reckoned two others were making more than him, but their main source of income was broadcasting.

When it came to the printed page, he was the top dog. Nearly two hundred grand per annum. He wouldn't be human if he wasn't quite proud of himself.

The money was just a marker, which was just as well. The divorce from Paula was taking an age and burning serious holes in his pocket. She was determined to extract her pound of flesh for a decade of marriage in which she had grown into a gangland widow. The main problem with their relationship, as he had seen it, was her failure to appreciate his role in society. She was more interested in reproducing, but when nothing was happening in that department, things began to fall apart. She wanted to investigate the situation further, take a look at IVF. He hadn't the time to invest in that sort of thing. The relationship lingered in the departure lounge for at least two years before finally heading west. Alan could see Paula's point of view, but whenever he brooded on things, and all it was costing him, he couldn't stop the resentment welling up. Outside his home, the whole world appreciated him, yet his wife just didn't get it.

One of the rare jokes he and Paula shared during the final months was that there was actually three of them in the marriage. That was where Detective Seamus Fox came in. He was the lead detective in the assignment to provide full garda protection for Alan Slate. There had been death threats. The relentless exposés Slate ran into the world of gangsters had lit fires of anger in the worst of them, including Junior Corbett, who ruled the west of the city, and the kingpin of the northside, Landy Towers. Both were known to be hopping mad at the bad publicity Slate was showering on them.

He had been subjected to bog-standard intimidation, threats

on the phone and through the post. Little reminders about his mortality. Some of it had entered an uglier realm. The worst incident involved a car driving up and down outside his home, a gun being waved out of the passenger window.

Slate had written extensively about the death threats. Whole radio phone-in shows had been taken up with the subject. In one show, hosted by Slate's friend-since-college Jumpin' JJ Fitzgerald, listeners were asked to poll by text whether or not Slate should be given full garda protection. Just over 93 per cent of respondents answered in the affirmative. Once the result was known, Jumpin' JJ told his listeners that if there wasn't movement within a week he would lead a protest to the gates of Leinster House.

Three days after that poll was conducted, the garda moved. A press release announced that, following talks with Slate, his editor and the Minister for Justice, full garda protection was to be given to him as there was a real and present danger of an attempt on his life.

The move made front-page news, and Jumpin' JJ was photographed with a protective arm around Slate. The two friends were taking on gangland together, standing up on behalf of the man and woman in the street.

3 April 2005 began brightly. Slate was treating JJ to lunch as a thank-you for all he had done. They were dining in L'Ecrivain. Around the corner on Baggot Street, Detective Seamus Fox sat behind the wheel of a Ford Focus. Fox didn't mind his current assignment, considered it something of a holiday. He had one hand wrapped around a cardboard cup of tea, the other holding a Roddy Doyle paperback. He knew and liked Slate. He didn't know, but was already growing to dislike, JJ.

The two boys emerged from the restaurant, foddered and

watered, just before three p.m. After a brief chat, it was agreed that JJ leave his car and everybody would travel in the garda vehicle. The subsequent investigation pointed to this as the first error of judgement on Fox's part.

They proceeded out of the city, en route to Dundrum shopping centre. Slate was due to appear at a book-signing event at four. Scum Central was flying out the door, and his publisher was pulling out all the stops to keep sales at fever pitch.

Red wine flowed through the bookshop. Slate read a chapter before an audience of about thirty, predominantly middle-aged women, then sat down to sign copies. He made a point of thanking the gardaí, and invited the audience to give a round of applause to his own protector, 'all that stands between me and a bullet from the likes of Junior Corbett'. Fox was surprised that he enjoyed the attention when everyone in the shop turned to his position by the door and clapped with great vigour. He was about to give a bow but caught himself just in time. JJ was at the far end, skulling his third glass of wine.

From the shop, they moved back towards town, but already the evening had momentum. Both Slate and JJ were on a few days off, and determined to make the most of it.

'Seamus, do you think the city can manage without myself and Alan for forty-eight hours?' Jumpin' JJ asked from the back seat, as they waited in line for the barriers to rise at the Dart crossing at Merrion Gate.

'It might well manage without Alan,' Fox said, as he slipped the car into gear, 'but I'd say the place will fall apart if you're not behind the microphone.'

Jumpin' JJ threw his head back and laughed, either missing or ignoring the barb. Slate looked over at Fox, a smile on his face. He reckoned all tension would seep away if he could get Seamus to knock back a few pints.

Fox relented at the next stop, Ryan's of Sandymount. By

then there was no question of him waiting in the car. As Slate had correctly forecast, the lubricant did wonders for relations within the gathering.

By the time they got back to town, Detective Seamus Fox was bulling for more. He offered to take the men to one of the most notorious hostelries in the south inner city, Time's Up, the scene of two gangland shootings in the last eighteen months.

It was a dingy affair, a narrow bar, with a mounted TV at one end, a slot machine at the other. The barman recognised Fox and nodded towards the back, where stairs led to another room. There were only three drinkers in the bar, none of whom paid much heed to the procession. JJ was in his element, lapping up the surroundings, out of his mind on the narcotic whiff of cordite. *Reelin' In The Years* was on the box. Slate recognised an early shot of U2 performing when they were teenagers.

Upstairs could have passed for a small function room. It included six small tables with stools, a barely elevated stage and a half-moon-shaped bar. The barman ferried the pints from downstairs, explaining that the taps up here weren't hooked up.

Everybody was cool. The tension that had permeated the car earlier was now ancient history. Fox had reassessed his opinion of JJ. He wasn't such a bad asshole after all.

'How do you do it, man, coming in here knowing there are scumbags who would love to take you out?' JJ asked Fox.

The detective pulled back his jacket to reveal a holster and the smooth handle of a weapon. 'Meet my baby, Mrs .38 Smith & Wesson. She don't take no shit from nobody.'

They all laughed, and JJ raised his glass to the cop.

At some point the conversation turned to The Sopranos. All three agreed that the show hit all the right spots. Jumpin' JJ moved into his Tony Soprano impersonation. 'Whaddaya do, ya goomba?' he said, his hand swiping into the imaginary head of an imaginary family soldier who had done wrong. Everybody had put away enough drink to find it funny. Seamus Fox said that the show highlighted how difficult it was for police to bring down gangland figures.

'Tell me about it,' Slate said, and all three laughed again.

Jumpin' JJ got up and said he had to take a leak. Slate and Fox exchanged glances. Slate knew that his friend was powdering his nose, and he knew that Fox knew it, but neither of them wanted to make an issue of it.

'What if there was a hit here tonight?' Fox said, as he stood an empty pint glass on a beer mat.

Slate pushed a full pint towards him. 'Say again.' Slate was barely keeping it together. Pints on top of wine rarely worked for him. He was toying with the idea of asking JJ about the coke. He had never bothered with it, but he knew that the stuff was supposed pick you up when the booze was kicking in.

'What if JJ came jumpin' out of the jacks and was facing down the barrel of Smith & Wesson's finest, held by one of those gangsters who make him go weak at the knees?'

The pair looked at each other and laughed. Fox sat forward in his chair, pulled up the flap of his jacket to expose the holstered gun. 'Now, if you were to grab my weapon, sure I'd be way too slow to stop you,' he said.

Slate looked at him. A grin, lopsided with drink, hung on his face. Slate licked his lips. He got up and felt the cold handle of the gun, gently raised it from the holster with his thumb and forefinger. He sat down again. Fox took a draw from his pint. Slate joined him, then got to his feet. He reached over for his anorak and dipped into the side pocket, his hand re-emerging with a black woolly hat. When he pulled it down over his face, he could still see through the threads of wool, if not too well.

The door to the toilet opened. Jumpin' JJ's eyes were on the floor as he walked through.

'Freeze, motherfucker,' Slate said. His feet were planted

apart, the weapon in his hands, held out front. JJ looked up and paled. He turned to Fox, who was observing the proceedings as if attending a movie.

'Don't move a fucking muscle,' the gunman said. His words came out muffled from behind the woolly hat. JJ looked again and shook his head, like a man trying to get rid of lingering sleep. Then he grinned, his world coming back together again.

'Jesus Christ, if it isn't the abominable gangster. Hey, fucko, you need a few eye slits in that arseways balaclava of yours.'

'I said don't move,' the gunman said. Slate couldn't believe the power he felt surging through his body. He could make this guy do whatever he wanted. He felt himself swaying. He raised his right foot and replanted it on the floor, locating his balance again. He could make this fucker dance.

'Jump, JJ,' he said. 'Jump up and down like a clown. Jump, I said.' He began to wave the gun around loosely, like he remembered Joe Pesci doing in *Goodfellas*, just before he shot the young kid who was waiting on the poker table. The gun was now pointing at JJ's feet.

'Get cracking, Jumpin' JJ. Jump. One, two, three. Jump now or you'll jump no more.'

JJ raised his hands and waved. His face twisted into what he believed would look scary. 'Whoo-aa,' he shouted at the gunman, as if he was a ghost.

Fox was laughing. He got to his feet. 'OK, lads, the fun's over. Alan, the weapon?'

'Jump, I said, jump, motherfucker.'

'Yeah, yeah, what are you going to do about it, man?'

Fox raised his voice. 'OK, lads, come on, that's it.'

Slate glanced at him, and pulled the hat off his head. The gun remained trained on the target. 'Ah, Seamus,' he said. 'Sure it's only a bit of—' The sound of the shot and the recoil in his hand hit Slate at the same time. Fox reared back, like a horse. Slate's ears were ringing. He looked at JJ, who was on the floor, his mouth wide open, his left hand reaching down to his left ankle, which was fast disappearing under a fountain of blood. Slate felt the gun snatched from his hand. Detective Seamus Fox ran to JJ and got down on his hunkers as he reholstered the weapon. Now a wail filled the air. A voice bellowed from the stairwell, 'What's going on up there?' The barman knew from experience it was best not to run into a room where shots were being fired.

'Get an ambulance,' Fox shouted. Blood was pooling around the injured man's foot.

Slate put his hands to his head and walked over. 'Jesus, JJ,' he said.

'You shot me,' Jumpin' JJ said. 'You fucking shot me because I wouldn't jump.'

The local uniforms were on the scene within minutes. Fox calmed everybody down, then handed his weapon to the investigators. Slate wanted to accompany his friend in the ambulance, but it was explained to him that he would instead have to accompany the officers to Pearse Street station.

An investigation into the shooting concluded that Fox had made significant errors of judgement in allowing his garda vehicle to be used for the 'entertainment of the man whom he was protecting and the victim'. While there was no conclusive evidence that he was above the legal limit for drink-driving, the investigating officers reported that quite obviously he had drink taken.

Slate told the investigators that he had grabbed Fox's weapon from the holster and pointed it at the door of the toilet just as JJ was opening it. He absolved the detective of any blame, and expressed huge remorse for the hassle his actions were now visiting on his protector. No conclusions were reached on how Slate had gained possession of the standard-issue firearm. Slate's statement that he had caught the garda unawares most likely saved Fox his job.

No official action was recommended, but the result was obvious to anybody who knew the routine in these matters. Fox was to be relegated to desk duty until such time as his full pension entitlements kicked in.

Against all the odds, considering who was involved, the story was kept out of the press. Poor Jumpin' JJ was on crutches for three months, and his five-a-side football on Tuesday evenings came to an end. He issued proceedings against the gardaí. The case was settled before it even got into its stride, with JJ pulling in a quarter of a million euro plus costs.

Slate didn't emerge unscathed. Sources in the upper echelons of the force made it plain to his editor in the best-selling City Gazette tabloid that he was no longer welcome on the crime beat. He was relegated to the sub-editors' bench, which saw his salary nose-dive by two-thirds. The divorce gobbled up all his spare cash. He had to shelve plans to take a punt on property.

He spent nearly four years in Purgatory, as he referred to the subs' desk, before a new career at the frontline beckoned through Frank Fastneck and *Inside Out*.

After his recuperation, Jumpin' JJ never really got back into the loud-mouth groove on the airwaves. He left for a new life in Australia, where he was last heard from reading the farming news at a radio station near Ayers Rock.

7

There was one other person in the waiting room. An elderly woman sat at the end of the leather couch, gripping a handbag as if it held the Third Secret of Fatima.

The receptionist was behind a glass partition, a pair of glasses hanging from her neck. Radio music purred through the room.

Molloy gave the woman behind the glass his name. She told him to sit down. He was surprised by how relaxed he felt. Any other time he had been in a solicitor's office, he was trying to beat the law. This time he was seeking a leg up.

A door at the far end opened. A woman showed her head and beckoned to the pensioner. Just as the door closed, the booming signature tune for the news killed the music.

'Man gunned down in his mother's arms in latest gangland killing.'

Molloy threw a glance at the woman behind the glass partition, but her head was still bent into something.

The voice came on again: 'A twenty-two-year-old man was shot dead in his mother's arms last night as he fled from his killers in a housing estate in the west of the city. The killing is believed to be the latest execution in a brutal gangland war that erupted earlier this week with the attempted murder of a leading criminal figure in the same area. The dead man is understood to have been a member of one of the gangs that are now locked in a struggle for control of the city's lucrative drugs business. And on the line we have the reporter who has the inside story on this outbreak of gangland warfare, Alan Slate of *Inside Out*.'

Molloy knew the name. When he had worked for Junior, some of the lads in the crew were obsessed with everything Alan Slate wrote. Molloy could never figure it out. They would fume and rage about him, never letting up with talk of blowing his arse halfway into next week or putting his head into a bench vice. Then, if one of them recognised that Slate was writing about them, or a job they had been involved in, they were over the moon, famous for a morning.

'Alan, welcome back to the airwaves. Glad to have you with us.'

'Glad to be here, Karen.'

'What can you tell us about this latest brutal killing?'

'The situation is really getting out of control. This man was well known to gardaí as a thug and a violent criminal. He arrived home last night to his mother's house where his killer was waiting for him. As he entered the house, the gunman came up behind him and shot him four times. He died in his mother's arms.

'My sources in the gardaí are saying that the dead man had been beaten up and possibly tortured before he was shot dead. They are working on the theory that he escaped from his killers and they followed him home to finish off their dirty work.'

'Alan, has this dead criminal been identified?'

'Yes, Karen. I can reveal exclusively to your listeners that the dead man was Peter Sullivan, better known on the street as Harms Sullivan. He was the older brother of nineteen-year-old Steven Sullivan, who was shot last Tuesday a few hours after ...'

Molloy felt a chill course through his body.

'My magazine *Inside Out* will be reporting the detail of this war on Friday, Karen, and it is available from all good newsagents, although we're experiencing some difficulty with distribution at the moment.'

'Should we be worried that the gangland situation is getting out of control?'

'Karen, I'm always worried that it's getting out of control but I have faith in the gardaí. They're putting their lives on the line every day of the week. But on Friday when *Inside Out* hits the streets, I'll be revealing all about this outbreak of gang warfare and I can promise you it will make fascinating reading.'

'Alan Slate, thank you as always for your insight. Keep up the good work.

Now, elsewhere, there was further bad news for the housing market today with a survey ...'

The woman behind the glass partition called his name. 'Mrs Diggins can see you now.' He got up and paused for a moment to kill the dizziness.

Molloy didn't take in much about her office. He still wasn't steady on his feet. The solicitor got up and extended her hand. It felt soft, reminded him he hadn't touched a woman's flesh since he'd gone in. She had her eyes on him the way women often did, as if surprised by his appearance, pleasantly so. She didn't look too bad herself. 'Are you all right?' she said, sitting down.

'Me?' he said.

'You look a bit … shook.'

'I'm fine.' He took the seat on his side of the desk.

'So, what can I do for you, Mr Molloy?'

She was straight down to business, no fannying about, no nice-to-meet-you. Her head was already bent, as if she was trying to regain formality after staring at him when he'd entered. A pen was poised in the fingers of her right hand.

'I want to get custody of my son.'

She began writing on a yellow pad on her desk. He spotted gold on the ring finger of her left hand.

'Are you married?'

'No.'

'How old is your son?'

'Three and a half.'

'And you and his mother have fallen out.'

'I was away when he was born. I'm just back.'

She looked up at him.

'I got into a spot of bother in England. Her Majesty thought it best to detain me. I got out last week.'

'And the nature of your conviction?' Her head was lowered again. He didn't respond immediately. She filled the void. 'Drugs?'

'That's what they charged me with.'

She kept writing. Molloy had been expecting something a bit more, some enthusiasm, an effort on her part to empathise with his predicament. He tried not to think of Sullivan being shot in his mother's arms. They must have nabbed him on his way home. He'd be next. Tortured. Unless there had been no torture. Maybe somebody had beaten him up before he'd gone home. Maybe somebody had seen them last night.

'Mr Molloy?'

'Sorry?'

'Your son's name?'

'Alexander. Not my choice, but that's the way it goes. His mother had notions.'

'Have you had any contact with your son or his mother since you got out of prison?'

'I haven't had any contact since I went into prison. My brother tried to keep in touch with her for me. He found out about the birth and the name six months after Alexander was born. It was bad enough she called him that, but then she told my brother she'd make sure I had nothing to do with the child. I don't even know where she is right now.'

'Were there problems in the relationship before your departure?'

'What kind of problems?'

'I think you know what I'm talking about.'

'She got out a barring order two months before I was arrested. It was all trumped-up stuff.'

The solicitor took off her glasses and rubbed her eyes. When she looked up, her face was all business. 'Mr Molloy, if I'm going to represent you, I need to know all the facts. It will be of no help to you or me if you hold something back until we're in court and I'm flying in the dark.'

He didn't say anything. He had hoped they wouldn't have to rake over this terrain.

'I presume there was some evidence of an assault that enabled the issuing of a barring order?'

'Assault is a big word.'

'Was Miss ...'

'Rogers, Stephanie. And she was well able to use her fists herself.'

'Was she assaulted?'

'I've a problem with that word, "assault". If I go out and box some fella, that's assault. What happened between me and Stephanie was just a bit of jostling.'

'Did she attend a doctor?'

He felt his muscles tightening. When he came in that night, she was in a state. She was frustrated. Since getting pregnant, she'd tried to lay off the coke, her drug of choice, and the booze, which she wasn't shy of either. He didn't see any reason why he should sit at home and hold her hand while she craved a lift.

She came at him with a saucepan, swinging wildly, her hair flying after each lurch. She connected at least once, but he just reared back. He laughed at first, but then she got him a right wallop over his left ear. She kept calling him a cunt, saying over and over that she didn't want his child, she didn't want anything more to do with him. Through the barrage he had maintained his grip on the six cans of Bud in his right hand. When the saucepan crashed against his skull the second time, he lost it, swung his left, connected with her cheek, sent her flying across the room, back on to the couch. It was only then that he realised he might have done damage to the life inside her. She lost consciousness for a few minutes.

Of course she attended a doctor. Molloy was the one who rang for the ambulance. 'Look, there was an incident. I was defending myself. She was out of control.'

'Was substance abuse involved?'

'Loads of it. Steph wasn't one for clean living. And, from what I hear, becoming a mother hasn't changed her.'

She was looking at him again, as if she was having difficulty keeping her eyes off him. 'And what about you?'

'Booze was my poison, but that's all behind me.' He moved forward on the chair. 'I'm an alcoholic. It's taken a while but I am getting help. No more gargle. I'm finished with the life and everything it dragged me into … with what I was involved in. All I'm saying is things are different now. I'm a different person today. I've done a lot of things I'm not proud of. I'm not dodging my responsibilities. I have paid my debt to society. All I want is access to my son. All I want is a break.'

She took off her glasses again and laid the pen on the page. Her face softened into a smile in which he detected a smidgen of what he had been looking for when he walked in. 'I hear you, Mr Molloy. You sound to me like you're entitled to a break. First of all we have to find out where exactly your son is.'

Two men occupied the front seat of the powder blue Toyota Avensis parked on the street opposite the offices of Paul & Paul. Rocco Sansom sat in the passenger seat. He wore a replica jersey of the Dublin Gaelic football team, sky blue with navy trimmings. The fingers of his left hand were wrapped around a can of Red Bull.

His brother Kyle sat behind the steering wheel. He was two minutes older than Rocco. He was dressed in a Liverpool Football Club strip, red with white trimmings. The number 23 was on the back of the jersey, above which was the legend 'Carragher'. Kyle had a John Player Blue clasped between the fingers of his right hand. The window on his side was rolled down two inches, which was just as well because the car was full of smoke and the smell of Colonel Sanders's finest deep-fried chicken breasts. Both men wore black tracksuit bottoms. Rocco was shod in Nike Air runners; Kyle preferred Adidas.

On first impressions, most people found it difficult to distinguish between the twenty-year-old Sansom twins. But it soon became apparent that Kyle was the one with the scar, which described a curve from an inch beneath his right eye around to the tip of his right nostril. He had acquired the injury some two years previously following a misunderstanding over the merits of Liverpool Football Club in its current incarnation. The man who had attempted to settle the affair with a broken bottle was now a long-term resident in Beaumont Hospital, where he lay in a vegetative state.

Rocco took a swig of his Red Bull. 'It's him all right.'

Kyle pulled hard on his cigarette, the tip stretching into a horn. 'Why don't we just do him now?'

'Out on the street?'

'Why not?'

'Kyle, listen to me. Doing a fucker is the last option, not the first, OK? This isn't PlayStation.'

Kyle shrugged. His brother tapped on his mobile. He raised it to his right ear.

'Johnny, yeah. You're not going to believe this. Guess who just walked into our woman's office? The all-singing all-dancing Georgie Best himself.'

There was silence on the line for five seconds before Johnny Cash filled the void. 'You're joking?'

'Nope.'

'You're sure?'

'It's him.'

There was another silence, the sound of Johnny Cash doing some thinking. 'Is he going in to see her?'

'The other two ain't there. He must be.'

'Fuck it,' Johnny Cash spat out. 'Fuck it, fuck it, fuck it.'

Rocco pulled the phone back from his ear to give the venom a little room to foment. 'Maybe he's decided to turn rat,' Rocco said.

'To rat about what? He's been away for the last four years. What's there to rat about?'

'I dunno. The hit on Junior maybe?'

'So he's going to do what? Rat on himself? He organised the hit, remember? You have to think, Rocco. I can't be doing all the thinking for everybody.'

'Jesus, sorry, Johnny.' Rocco bit his lip. Johnny Cash had not been himself since that attempt on Junior. Everybody was up in a heap since then. And all that bad shit was being flushed down the line, from Junior to Johnny and on to Rocco and Kyle. It wasn't fair, but that was life.

Rocco knew one thing. Now was not the time to express his individuality or to make a move or to do anything that might raise nerves or hackles. Now was the time to keep the head down. So far, he and his brother had been managing fine doing just that. Their number was to keep an eye on the solicitor. Neither Junior nor Johnny told them why, and they knew better than to ask. It had something to do with her husband, the guy who'd gone missing with a lot of loot unspoken for. Now there were complications. Johnny was up in a heap again. It could only mean headaches and hassle.

'Are you tooled up?' Johnny said.

Rocco looked across at his brother. Kyle carried a knife with a four-inch blade. It wouldn't take much in the way of encouragement to get him to use it. 'We can do a job if need be.'

There was another silence. Rocco found himself hoping that they wouldn't have to kill again. He worried about Kyle in that department. Kyle had the kind of enthusiasm that would do nobody any good in the long run because it was inevitable that one day the wrong man would end up dead.

That was how it seemed when they shot Harms Sullivan's brother on the night of the hit on Junior. It was a clean job. He drove and Kyle got out and walked up to Sullivan and did the business from behind. Two other punters turned and ran. Kyle stood over Sullivan and put two more slugs in the back of his head. When they were driving away, Kyle was like a man riding an eight-ball of coke.

Anyway, Rocco heard later that young Sullivan hadn't been involved in the hit on Junior. It was just a message for his brother. Rocco felt a bit iffy about it. The news didn't bother Kyle one bit.

'OK,' Johnny said. 'Leave the solicitor for the moment. There's no sign of her husband showing up and we know where to get her. Follow Molloy. Find out where he's staying, but don't do anything. Yet.'

Rocco emitted a silent sigh of relief. He looked across at his brother, whose face showed he was impatient to find out whether there was any action to be had.

'Will do,' Rocco said, and pressed the call-end button. He turned to his brother. 'Sorry about that. Nothing doing for you today.'

8

They were still at the top of the stone steps. Molloy was first out again, and when he got to the street, the two boys were seated on the pavement, under the streetlamp's pool of light, just as they had been when he had gone in an hour earlier. A smile creased his face, but he walked straight past them. The paper cup, he noted, had been replaced by a flat cloth cap.

He walked on and had to wait only six seconds. 'Youse alcoholics are all the same, mean as shite.'

He turned right at the end of the street and picked up pace. From an open window, he heard the tolling bells of the Angelus on TV. The meeting had been good. He hadn't spoken, but he had heard plenty.

Ten minutes later he pushed open the heavy door of the Georgian building. The air was musty and silent. He had seen little of his housemates since moving in.

The wide staircase, with its worn green carpet, had seen better days. Five steps shy of the top he stopped in his tracks.

The door to his flat was ajar. He felt something run through his body. He'd be better off taking his chances on the street.

He turned to descend the stairs, but there was a figure on the landing below. The man was wearing a dark football shirt, tracksuit bottoms and runners. His hair was short, as if it had been cut using a bowl. His face was long but smooth. He held a gun in his hand. He moved towards the stairs and waved it, indicating to Molloy that he should enter the flat.

Molloy pushed open the door. There was a man sitting on the couch, swept-back gelled hair, leather jacket, two and a half chins, and a handlebar moustache, borrowed from Central Casting for Mexican bandits. Johnny Cash had put on a bit of weight since Molloy had last seen him.

Another man was standing in the kitchenette. He wore a Liverpool jersey and a serious scar, but otherwise bore a striking resemblance to the one with the gun. The one with the gun shut the door. Molloy could see that he was wearing a Dublin GAA jersey.

Cash nodded at Liverpool, who pulled a plastic tie from his pocket, and moved towards Molloy.

'You know the drill,' Cash said. Liverpool began to pat Molloy down. He pulled two ten-euro notes from Molloy's jeans pocket. He took a set of keys from the other.

'Is this girl enjoying herself?' Molloy said. The blow to his kidneys sent him doubling over. The one with the gun now came towards him and tried to kick him in the balls, but Molloy managed to protect himself with his thigh, which took the brunt of the blow. His leg went numb with pain. His kidneys felt as if they had been used as a squash ball. Liverpool pulled on the tie, the plastic digging into Molloy's wrists. He was hauled to his feet and pushed on to the couch. Johnny Cash got up and moved towards the door, as if he required distance from Molloy to do whatever had to be done.

Molloy looked up at the pair, the Dub and Liverpool. They had to be brothers.

'You've really fucked up this time,' Cash said. Molloy didn't reply. The situation was beyond his control, but he wasn't going to put up with more than was necessary.

Cash turned to the two sportsmen. 'Boys, meet the tough guy who tried to plug Junior.'

Liverpool's face twisted into a smirk. The Dub held his stare, the gun dangling by his side.

'OK, let's get moving. Junior wants to have some fun with this asshole.'

The ride through rush-hour traffic had been slow and now this. The driver checked twice with her when she asked to be dropped at Arrivals. Noelle just confirmed the instruction without any explanation. Donal had told her to pass through Arrivals as a precaution. He was getting good at this subterfuge stuff.

Inside, the terminal was black with people. She moved between the knots forming to greet relatives or friends. She was negotiating her way through the masses, trailing her wheelie-bag when she detected a flurry behind her. She turned to see a woman in a canary yellow suit running towards her on heels as long as steak knives, wielding a microphone like a gun. Taking up the rear, a barrel of a man was labouring under the weight of a television camera.

Noelle froze. Not now, please, not when I've nearly made it. She kept her eyes lowered as the woman reached her and only raised them when the puffing cameraman was passing by in her wake, focused on other prey. Noelle paused to compose herself.

She felt her head throbbing again. The plan had been to stave off the next Solps until she arrived, but the headache was now demanding swift remedy.

Upstairs in Departures, she walked the length of the hall, just as Donal had told her. At the far end, she joined the queue for an ATM machine. She did a quick recce. The faces she scanned gave little away, but none was likely to belong to a reporter or a cop. God, listen to her. A cop.

She pulled a hand mirror from her bag, and it was only when she opened it that she saw the pair of shades shielding her eyes. She had been wearing them since leaving Caroline's place. She pulled them off.

It was then that a current of electricity coursed through her body. Fear? Thrill? Guilt? The expectation of meeting Donal after nearly three weeks apart? Whatever it was, it was keeping her on her toes. She was looking forward to seeing him, to giving him a piece of her mind.

She requested two hundred pounds in sterling, deposited it in her purse. Next she went to check-in where a machine spewed out her boarding pass. The queue for security was not as bad as she had expected.

Inside Departures, she sought out a café. The cappuccino cost nearly four euro and they said they had no tap water so she had to buy a bottle. The Solps went down well. Already, she was feeling better.

The flight was practically full. The other seats in her row were occupied by a young couple who had student written all over them. An uneventful journey was punctuated by a mild pocket of turbulence as the Welsh coast hove into view.

At Heathrow, she found her way down into the bowels of the terminal, following the sign for the Underground. She paid at the automatic ticket machine and made straight for the platform. It was now pushing for seven thirty p.m. and the rush-hour had thinned out. As the train rocked towards the city, she pulled the written instructions from her handbag for a final consultation.

At Hammersmith, she alighted. It took her a few seconds

to get her bearings. Up the stairs, across the bridge and down onto the platform for local District Line train heading back west. It arrived within minutes.

Two stops later, she got out at Stamford Brook. The doors swished closed behind her and the train pulled away at a lazy beat.

Descending the stairs, she wondered if it was possible that he mightn't show up. At the bottom she lifted her wheelie-bag on to the concrete floor. She looked up.

He'd seen her through the barrier. When she spotted him, he had a smile on his face as broad as the Shannon. He was wearing a jumper, which wasn't like him, and a waxed jacket. He looked thinner. The smile was too nervous to reach as far as his eyes.

From where Molloy lay, both the view and his prospects were constrained. His wrists and ankles burned with the pain from tightly bound plastic ties. His throat was parched. The gag itched at the corners of his mouth. The only sound in the room was the ebb and flow of the breath delivered through his nose, steady and constant as the tide on a lonely beach.

He was lying on a sheet of transparent industrial plastic. A rope manacled his wrists to a bed, across which lay a duvet, in a cover depicting Spiderman in reds and blues.

Beyond the walls, he could hear an occasional grunt or whoop from one of the twins. They had to be playing a computer game against each other.

The blood on the plastic had dried. He could smell its sweetness, only inches from his nostrils. He could see it in little jagged stains on the clear plastic, like a cluster of islands that harboured dark secrets.

After they had arrived, tied his ankles and manacled him to

the bed, Johnny Cash swung a kick at his head, not full force, but enough to daze him. It connected with his left ear. Blood flowed, and for a while he thought the buzzing would stay for good.

In the intervening hour or so – maybe it was two hours, he wasn't keeping track – he had straightened out a few things. He wouldn't beg for his life. He would do his damnedest not to show pain if they got stuck into torture. He wouldn't plead for the mercy of death if the pain got too bad.

The main thing was that he was still alive. He had been around long enough to know that killing was usually undertaken quickly, when surprise provided advantage, when there would be little fuss on the precipice of death, when the potential for anything messy was eliminated. Were they forgoing convention to ensure he died in the fullness of pain? Or were they really going to look for answers? Johnny Cash didn't want to hear the answers he had to give.

He had been on the other side of that door, another house, another time, about a year before he went away. He had arrived for a pick-up. Being escorted into the sitting room, he heard a muffled cry from the bedroom, then the bang of a struggle, another shout and then silence. The fella who was with him searched his face for a reaction, but Molloy carried on as if he hadn't heard.

The following day, it was all over the news. The body of a twenty-two-year-old had been found under a bush in a park, not half a mile from the house, by two Poles en route to a building site. When the photograph appeared in the newspapers, Molloy saw that he had known the dead man, but not well. They had been in the same company on different nights out, but had never exchanged more than a few words.

It was the usual job, bullet to the back of the head, but the body also gave up signs of the terror inflicted prior to death.

The muffled cry from the bedroom stayed with him for a

long time after that. He didn't harbour guilt or regret. It had nothing to do with him. But the sound of a man grappling for his life, like a drowning swimmer who knows too late that he's trusted too much in the sea, kept bugging him, a constant reminder of the fragility of his existence.

There would be no muffled cry today. If the chance arose, he'd make a fist of getting out, but he wasn't going to beg. He would hold on tight to his dignity until they wrestled it from him. He would accept the things he could not change.

From where he lay, Molloy could see the outline of a little boy's world. A pair of Bob the Builder slippers was neatly pushed under the bed. A hurley leaned against one wall, standing over a sliotar and a football. The two shades of blue worn by the Dublin county team hung from a pennant. He felt like an intruder in this cave of innocence. The child who slept in the room couldn't be much older than his own son. This was no place to die.

Donal reached for her hand and she didn't resist, but she let her arm hang limply from her body. Small-talk filled the void as they walked through the evening. He was grand, he said, bearing up well. She was looking great. Noelle said little, letting him stew. She hadn't been in this part of London since before she'd left for a year in Australia, soon after college, more than a decade ago now.

He led her into a pub, the Thirsty Quill. There were only a handful of other patrons, most of them focused on a football match on the TV. She opted for a glass of white wine. He had a pint of bitter. After depositing the drinks on the table at which she sat, he said he had to go to the little boys' room. She looked vacantly at the football, wondering how well she knew the man to whom she was married.

When he returned, he sat down and said, 'You've every right to be angry.'

Her eyes were on the glass of wine. 'That's very big of you, letting me know my rights.'

'You have no idea how sorry I am.'

She described a pattern with her index finger on the frosted wine glass. 'You've never given evidence in the High Court before a room baying for your blood. You really haven't a clue what it's like. Sitting there, looking out on all these strangers while a fat barrister exposes your marriage as a web of lies. You've never really been exposed to that kind of humiliation, have you?'

He leaned in towards her. 'I will never forget what you've done for me.'

'Don't worry, I won't let you. How could you, Donal? How could you have lied to me for so long?'

'Noelle, come on, you're making it sound as if I was having an affair.'

'You were. With property. The new sex – isn't that what they were calling it a few years ago?'

'Listen to me. Hey, I got in over my head, I made a few mistakes. Does that turn me into a mass murderer? Are you seriously trying to tell me I deserve what's happening back home?'

'I didn't say that.'

He pushed the pint aside and leaned over the table. His hand crept across and wrapped itself around hers. When she looked up, his eyes were all over her, pushing everything else in the pub back into the shadows. 'Whatever I did, it was for us. For the future. For…our family. The family you and me want to have.'

She felt his hand applying pressure. 'How long?'

'How long what?'

'How long was it going on for?'

He straightened in the chair again, his hand drifting back

across the table, tactically retreating in order to regroup. 'I don't know. I didn't set out to do anything wrong. When things don't work out like you have them planned you just have to keep moving stuff around or else the whole house comes tumbling down around your ears.'

'You gave undertakings to the banks that you knew were lies, just plain, barefaced lies.'

He shook his head. 'Look at it from my point of view. The banks were throwing out money at everybody. It was nearly your national duty to take out a loan. I was the go-between, the solicitor who handled sales.'

'And you were trusted. The undertakings, Donal, the whole system put huge trust in you. So did the clients.'

His eyes went towards the ceiling, as if he was seeking patience to convey what had to be perfectly obvious. 'Let's be straight, babe. The system of undertakings was brought in to cut down on legal fees. It meant the banks didn't have to have their own solicitor. I tell the bank there is no other mortgage on the property, the bank take that as read. They're supposed to ask me for the deeds. They don't bother. I see money for old rope and take a punt that nothing will be rumbled if I get a few mortgages on a single property. And it would all have been fine if the whole market hadn't got ripped apart by the sub-prime thing in America.'

'Donal, it was fraud.'

'Says who?'

'Jesus, Donal, says the law. We are officers of the court.'

'Look at what was going on out there. It was the law of the jungle, and I was supposed to stand back as if I was batting for Mother Teresa? You have to get real, Noelle. Besides, I didn't see you complaining about the spoils.'

'What?'

'Skellig, the holidays, the lifestyle, you didn't question any of it.'

It was her turn to straighten her back. 'Well, maybe I should have.'

'Why didn't you?'

'Donal, I wasn't a gangster's moll who turned a blind eye to some extravagant lifestyle, asking no awkward questions. I assumed you were legit. You were – you are – a solicitor, for Christ's sake, not a drugs-dealer or something.'

'All I'm saying, babe, is that everybody was on the make. Some more than others. Everybody was turning a buck and nobody questioned how all this wealth was being created. The whole country lost the run of itself, and now that the house has come down, I'm the only one getting it in the neck.'

She took another sip of wine. 'You've never mentioned family before,' she said.

His hand strayed across again. 'This whole thing has given me a chance to think about the things that really matter. Look, babe, what's done is done. It was done with the best of intentions, for us, for the future. We can't go back there now. I can't even go home. But we still have a future. And what better time to start than now?'

A warm feeling came over her. She knew it of an old day, since soon after they had met. She had always been aware that he would keep her on her toes, that things would never be dull. She wanted to believe him. She did believe him.

'Let's get out of here,' she said.

Molloy didn't know how long had passed when he detected that there was a fourth person in the house. He heard Cash walking into the adjoining bedroom and telling the twins to get moving. He felt his body stiffen.

The door opened. From where he lay, he could see under the bed towards the door. A pair of scuffed shoes came in first, worn, he was sure, by Johnny Cash. There followed two sets of runners, different brands but both blue. The three pairs of feet came around to his side of the bed. He kept his head down, lying on his left ear. He wasn't going to look up at the bastards. Then the fourth pair entered. These were brogues, advancing slowly, deliberately, and looking so shiny they might have just walked out of the sea.

He shut his eyes and every fibre in him tightened. The brogues walked around to his side of the bed, where the other three pairs of shoes surrounded him, as if he was some exotic capture. The brogues stepped on to the plastic, scrunching the dried blood underfoot. Molloy felt hot breath on his ear as the owner of the brogues bent down to him. He heard chewing and caught a current of gum. Something touched his skull. It felt like leather, a glove. The fingers drummed on his head for a moment. Then the breath receded. The brogues stepped back, and the other three pairs retreated as if following an unspoken instruction. He opened his eyes and saw a brogue swinging towards his midriff. It caught him square in the stomach. At first he thought he had gone into shock, but worse was the knowledge that he was about to vomit. He felt it rise, travelling up through his throat, into his mouth, trying to squeeze out past the gag. He began choking. Jesus Christ, this was how it was going to end. He struggled against his bindings until somebody tore the gag from his mouth. The puke flowed on to the plastic, right across his blood and on to the carpet.

'Oh, for fuck's sakes,' one of the twins said. 'The state of this. Little Vinny is going to have a canary.'

'Fuck Vinny,' the other said. 'Ma will go through the fucking roof.'

Molloy was having difficulty breathing through his nose. He took big gulps of air through his mouth, and tried to ignore the rancid taste.

'Molloy,' Junior said. Molloy looked up at him. The last

time he had seen Junior was from afar, behind the wheel of the Lexus. Junior had been running for his life, and now the brogue was on the other foot. 'How do you want to die?'

Molloy concentrated on his breathing.

'It's not a trick question. Johnny here thinks we need to send out a message. He wants to put your balls in a clamp and begin the process from there. Me? I think you might go too fast that way. A useless fucker like yourself would probably die of shock before we could really get down to business.'

Molloy stayed silent. He had a rhythm going now. He suppressed an impulse to share with Junior what he knew about his great friend Mr Johnny fucking Cash. This was not the time. Maybe when there was nothing left to lose.

Junior Corbett lowered himself to his haunches again. Molloy could hear him chewing gum.

'Whose idea was it?'

Molloy took a deep breath. 'I thought I was going to you to fix up about the debt.'

'Do I have to hurt you to get an answer?'

He looked up. Johnny Cash was at Junior's shoulder, staring down at him through cold eyes. He couldn't see Cash's hands, but would have wagered that the fucker had his fingers on the butt of a weapon in case events took a sour turn.

'Sullivan,' Molloy said. 'He didn't say who was behind it or whether it was his own gig.'

Junior Corbett raised himself up to a standing position. 'A gig,' he said. 'Hear that, lads? This tough guy reduced killing me to a gig.' The lads responded with grunts, which passed for nervous laughs.

'As it turns out, it's your lucky day. First and foremost I am a businessman. Your sentence is being suspended because I hear that you may be in a position to make some reparation for your crime.'

Molloy looked up again. Four pairs of eyes were staring down at him, as if into a black hole.

'Now, what do you know about this Diggins woman and her thieving husband?'

They retraced their steps to the tube station. The apartment was just across the road. A friend of Donal's from home had bought it as an investment and it was now between tenants. They took the lift to the fourth floor. He brought her down the wrong corridor first, before doubling back and finding the apartment's door. She laughed, asked him whether he was doing his spy thing, but it was a genuine mistake on his part. He had only been in the place for the first time earlier that day.

She followed him as he moved through the rooms, like a pair of amateur burglars checking out a job.

When they entered what must have been the main bedroom, he looked out on the London sky. She threw herself on to the bed and he turned and came to her. Neither pulled the curtains.

Afterwards she dozed for some minutes. When she opened her eyes, he was staring at the ceiling. 'You have a plan,' she said. It wasn't a question.

He released a long sigh, and drew himself out of the bed. He padded out of the room. She heard a noise from the corridor outside the apartment. A toilet flushed. She could see out through the window. The lights of London reaching up into the night sky reminded her of wartime movies about the Blitz.

Donal came back in, sat on the bed. 'Are you up for it?'

'If it involves a bit of excitement.'

He searched her face for a sign that she was codding. She couldn't hold back the smile. 'It's just ... Well, apart from the fact that you've been a, well, a complete bastard, escaping over here was a bit of fun. Never thought I'd see it like that but …'

He reached over and kissed her. 'I have cash,' he said.

'Does that mean I'm going to get fed tonight?'

'No, seriously. I have a lot of cash. I'm talking about enough to sort out our problems.'

'How much?'

'Three million.'

'What?' She sat up in the bed.

'The big three.'

'In cash?'

'Yes, cash, cash, the only currency that matters. Property and shares can disappear when some half-wit broker in Tokyo is having a bad-hair day. Cash is king.'

'Jesus,' she said. She stared at the ceiling, which had a white stucco finish, just like the master bedroom in Skellig. 'Where did you get it?'

'I robbed a bank.'

She looked at him.

'Clients, where else? Lots of people dealt in cash. Everybody from shopkeepers up to barristers, and including every business in between. They came to me with cash and asked me to translate it into property. I did.'

'Where is it?'

'Believe it or not, hidden in a wall.' He stood up and slipped into his trousers. He took a grey shirt from the suitcase at the foot of the bed. He put it on and began buttoning it from the bottom up. 'Let's get something to eat,' he said.

The restaurant was a fifteen-minute walk along Chiswick High Road. They were greeted by a round man with a clipped moustache and a tight waistcoat. The lights were low, glowing from behind red shades hugging the walls. They took a table near the back, Noelle facing out into the restaurant, Donal with nothing in his vision but his wife. On the table before them an old green wine bottle served as a candle-holder, dried wax spilling down the neck. The waiter lit it and murmured something about the limits of the menu tonight.

Donal ordered a bottle of Chablis after a cursory perusal of the wine list. Noelle smiled. As long as she'd known him, she had noticed him attempting to affect an air of knowledge about wine whenever they dined, particularly in company. She didn't buy it. He still couldn't tell one bottle of plonk from another. At least that was one affectation he seemed to have surrendered in his new incarnation.

'What about those people?' she said.

Donal unfolded a napkin and laid it on his lap. 'They knew the risks.'

'But everyone thought there was no risk. Property was a sure thing.'

'There are always risks.'

'But they didn't know you were the risk.'

He looked at her full of surprise that she would wound him like that.

'Sorry, but all that money, and all those people out of pocket. I mean, shouldn't you be giving it back?'

'To whom? The banks? You were in court. The banks have first call on anything I, we, have. Surely you don't want me to give it to them. There were all sorts of rackets going on over the last few years. And I'm supposed to give up what I have, what we have, just because I had the foresight to know that the whole shebang would come crumbling down? I'm not a charity, Noelle. This is our future we're talking about here.'

The waiter appeared with the bottle of wine. He poured a little into two glasses and waited for a verdict. Donal nodded at Noelle. She took a sip, waited for what she guessed would be the appropriate time for her palate to form an opinion, then smiled at the waiter. He filled the glasses and left.

'What are we going to do?' she said.

'Look, we have to be ahead of the curve. That's what it's all about now. We have the seed capital for a new life. Right now, nothing else matters.'

'What about my family – Caroline?'

'We're not going into a witness-protection programme. Caroline can visit, if she promises to behave herself. There's nothing to stop you popping home for a break, and once the heat dies down, I'll be able to zip back now and again. We can have the best of both worlds. A proper life and easy access to home.'

Noelle picked up her napkin, began fidgeting with it. 'Do we have any choice?'

'Yes, and the reason we have choice is that I took care of things. I put away the rainy-day money. The future is ours. All we have to do is get the money out of the country. And that's where you come in. What do you think?'

She looked at him, her husband. He reminded her of somebody who had just completed a presentation for a corporate audience. 'We were drifting along, Donal, weren't we? I mean, I was anyway. When the Pauls called me in, I was half hoping they would give me my P45. How did I end up working for them?'

'You didn't want to go down the corporate route, remember? You said you'd give general practice a shot. You know how I felt about that.'

'Come on, Donal, I was never cut out for that corporate stuff.'

'You do get a better class of client.'

'A better class of gangster.'

'Ouch.'

'The clients are the only good part about the job I do have. At least they bring a bit of humanity to the work.'

'You can't eat humanity.'

'This guy came to me the other day, good-looking guy, just out of prison.'

'How good-looking?'

'He wants to get access to his son. He's never seen the child. Can you imagine that?'

'Did you tell him he should be seeing a social worker? You're a solicitor.'

'Well, that's the job. Sometimes the lines are blurred. He had problems with drink, but he's stopped now. You know, it lifted my day. He doesn't look like somebody who's ever had any breaks.'

'Some of us made our own breaks.'

'He was arrested in England on the third of April 2005.'

'That's a coincidence.'

'As I was walking down the aisle, heading for a new life, he was off for a new life in prison.'

'Are we getting off the point here?'

'To be fair, he seems to be trying to forge a new life for himself.'

'Run that good-looking bit by me again?'

'That's the difference between what we do.'

Donal stayed silent, which she interpreted as him holding his tongue, thinking better than to say what he really thought. He took a sip of wine and said, 'If things work out for us, it will open up a whole new life. You could retrain, go back to college even.'

'Where?'

'I was thinking of Portugal.'

The waiter appeared with pen and notebook, his moustache twitching at the corners. Neither of them was up on Greek food, so they ordered what looked the blandest. Moussaka.

When the waiter was gone, she raised the wine glass to her lips and passed her hand across the table. He gave it a squeeze, but she didn't hear what he was saying because her attention was caught by a commotion at the door. A man was pointing in their direction, the maître d' looking over in confusion. The man appeared vaguely familiar in the low light. He began walking towards their table, a companion in tow. When he was halfway across the room, horror began to manifest itself on her face. Donal stopped mid-flow.

'What is it?' She pointed towards the advancing pair, as if she had been struck dumb. Donal turned as the men arrived.

'Noelle, sorry to bother you in the middle of a meal, but this seemed to be the only chance we would get,' the man said. He turned to Donal. 'Hello, Alan Slate, *Inside Out*.'

The second man was smiling over Slate's shoulder, a vulture with a photographer's eye, scouring the carcass of a romantic meal.

'You know this man?' Donal asked, turning back to Noelle as if the pair weren't there. She nodded.

'Mr Diggins, have you anything to say to the people of Ireland about your activities in the property market?'

Donal got up from his chair. He towered over the reporter. 'You're representing the people of Ireland?'

'Why are you on the run, Mr Diggins?'

Noelle pushed back her chair. 'Come on, we're out of here,' she said.

As she got up, the second man reversed, before turning to jog lightly towards the door. Slate held his ground. 'Mr Diggins, what about the people you left high and dry, taking multiple mortgages out on properties?'

'I've nothing to say to you.'

'Mr Diggins, what about the children?'

Noelle glared at him. 'What kind of a man are you?'

'Noelle, we can do this in a way that suits you. I have a few questions for your husband and one or two for yourself.'

Donal looked down at the reporter, conveying what he

considered to be menace. Slate looked back, no sign of fear on his face. Donal pushed in his chair. He moved towards Slate, who began reversing. 'You come in here and hassle my wife, after all she's been through. Haven't you done enough to her?' He advanced towards the reporter, who turned and walked quickly towards the door. He pulled it open in a deft gesture and disappeared outside.

The waiter intercepted Donal. 'Excuse me, sir, there is a problem?'

'No problem,' he said.

'We're leaving,' Noelle said. She tossed her hair outside the collar of her coat.

Donal handed the waiter a twenty-pound note for the wine. He grabbed Noelle's hand and exited through the door.

The snapper was outside, standing directly across from them, backing on to the road. His positioning left him room for manoeuvre, able to run ahead whether they turned left or right. He reeled them off. She had a face to kill for, all confusion and hurt.

Inside Out has tracked down the solicitor who ran off with millions of euro given to him by hard-pressed investors. The fugitive, 41-year-old Donal Diggins, was tracked by this reporter to an expensive restaurant in west London. He was dining with his wife, who had made a furtive journey to the British capital for a rendezvous with him.

As our exclusive pictures of the couple reveal, they left in a hurry when confronted by this reporter and photographer Julian Kermode. Both Mr and Mrs Diggins refused to answer questions relating to the missing money, which is estimated to be more than €10 million.

Diggins is currently the subject of an inquiry by the High Court. The file on the case has also been passed to the Fraud Squad.

Inside Out *received information that Noelle Diggins was travelling to meet her husband in London and the magazine's investigative unit immediately swung into action. Noelle Diggins is herself a solicitor, working out of a small practice in north Dublin run by a husband-and-wife team.*

The couple were tracked first to a local bar and then an apartment in Chiswick, west London, and from there they travelled to enjoy a meal in the restaurant. When asked to explain himself, Donal Diggins approached this reporter in an aggressive manner and refused to answer any questions. Despite the intimidation, the Inside Out *team persisted with enquiries and ensured that the meeting with the couple would be recorded for publication.*

Today we publish three pages of pictures of the couple on a London street where they were fleeing not just their responsibilities in this country but also a legitimate media inquiry.

Commenting on the scoop, Inside Out *editor Frank Fastneck said that it showed journalism at its best in this time of national crisis. 'We are at the frontline in bringing the real stories to the public,' Mr Fastneck said. 'We will track down these fugitives and ensure that they are brought to justice.'*

Meanwhile, Inside Out *is also publishing exclusive pictures of the criminal Junior Corbett on holidays in Spain with members of his gang. The photos were taken by Spanish police, who were keeping an eye on Corbett for the gardaí. But now you can feast your eye on what Corbett and his gang get up to when they go on holiday.*

For more, see pages 3–10 on the extraordinary life and times of a fugitive and pages 11–14 for Junior Corbett's summer holiday.

Alan Slate, Crime Reporter of the Year 2000, 2002, 2004

9

Noelle waited in her room until the mystery man had gone. She lay on her back on the bed and looked up at Michael O'Leary on the wall. She didn't last long. That crazy grin of his – it was as if he was laughing at the wild gales blowing through her life.

She turned on her side, facing the door and, beside it, her suitcase, which remained unopened. Sitting atop the case was the trashy magazine. She was now officially a cover girl, her photo plastered across the glossy front page.

Nobody should ever be photographed looking as angry as that, all lines and sharp angles hardening a face, skin stretching as if it was the work of a drunken plastic surgeon. 'FUGITIVE SOLICITOR'S RENDEVOUS WITH WIFE', the headline read. They were so stupid they couldn't even spell 'rendezvous' correctly. All they were interested in was prurience. Well, they were messing with the wrong woman.

She had caught the early flight back from London, after two nights with her husband. At Dublin Airport, she popped into the Spar shop for a bottle of water, only to see the photograph on the rack next to the till. She didn't believe it at first. After leaving the shop, she returned and bought a copy. In the back of the taxi, all the way to Caroline's place, she read and reread the story, as if the words or meaning might change the next time. As if she was dreaming. The story was bad, inaccurate and downright cheap. The photos were just awful.

By the time she arrived at the apartment, she was gagging to let loose her fury. The first thing she noticed in the living room was the Crombie thrown across the sofa. It was pushing ten o'clock, yet there wasn't a sound in the place. Caroline had company. Noelle slipped into the spare room, to wait and see.

She heard something in the living room. She resisted the urge to go out and have a gander. Caroline was unattached, so this could be the start of something.

More likely, he was a ship in the night. Noelle could never understand her sister's finicky taste in men. Each first date was followed by a mental ticking of the boxes. The number of ticks never amounted to the pass mark.

The apartment's front door closed. She gave it a minute before she left the bedroom. Caroline was coming out of hers at that moment, wrapped in a pink towelling robe. 'How was the trip?'

'Have you seen this?' Noelle handed the magazine to her sister, her nose tilted to warn there was a smell off it.

Caroline glanced at the cover. 'It hit the streets last night. I was going to break the news gently once you got in.'

'Have you read it?'

Caroline's face said she had. She took her sister's shoulders and pulled her into a hug.

'It's a terrible picture,' Noelle said.

'I know. Well, it's not that bad.'

'It's awful. How could they be so low?'

'They love catching people at their worst. Especially celebrities. They want to reassure their readers that these people can look like shit too.'

'I'm not a celebrity.'

'You are now.'

'I'm going to sue.'

'Over the picture?'

'No, the story, the whole thing. It's a serious invasion of privacy. It's inaccurate. It makes us out to be Bonnie and Clyde.'

'Honey, you know the law better than me, but I've read it and I can't see where they've left themselves open to an action? Let's just relax for a minute.'

Caroline gently prised the magazine from her sister's fingers. She padded across to the kitchenette in her rabbit-head slippers, and raised the magazine high above the pedal bin. 'Let's give this trash a home?' she said. She dropped it into the bin. She took the kettle and filled it at the sink. Noelle walked over to the window and looked out on the Liffey. It was low tide and the river looked sad and lonely.

'What about the Pauls?' Caroline said. She sat down across the table from where Noelle looked out on the river.

'I'd say that's it. There's no way Henry will put up with this.'

'You think he'll fire you?'

'He's likely to do anything. I wouldn't mind letting him know he's a prize shit.'

'Could I challenge your thinking on that?'

Jesus, she was barely out of bed and into the groove already. 'No, you couldn't. Not right now. I need to feel angry at somebody, and he's the only person I can think of, apart from that toe-rag of a journalist.'

'I could think of somebody else.'

Noelle turned to her. The kettle began to whistle. Caroline smiled and slipped out of the chair. 'So how was it?' she said. She took two mugs from the cupboard and dropped in teabags.

'Strange.'

'How is he?'

'A lot more upbeat than me.'

'He always was, I'll give him that. Nobody could ever say that Donal didn't have oodles of confidence. Did you let him know how you felt?' Caroline slipped into the chair. 'Did you?'

Her sister was wearing the look that meant she was trying to hide her scepticism. 'Of course I did.'

'And?'

'He's had to put up with a lot, Caroline. What he's been through would knock the wind out of anybody's sails, but he's hanging in there. It would suit a lot of people to have him as a scapegoat. He wasn't the only one cutting corners.'

Caroline tapped her fingers on the table. 'So the marriage vows are still intact?'

'Yes, dear sister. The marriage vows are still intact.'

'What's the plan?'

'Who said there was a plan?'

Caroline smiled but there was no warmth in it. She wrapped her hands around her mug. Noelle got up and turned towards the window again. The river didn't look any better.

'Come on,' Caroline said. 'Switzerland or Liechtenstein? It has to be one of the two.'

Noelle turned back to her, hoping her face could lie. 'As a matter of fact he doesn't have a plan.'

'He has no money?'

'I didn't say that. Caroline, please, I could do with a little support.'

'You know I'm just worried about you.' Caroline got up and went to her sister. She brought Noelle into her arms. Noelle didn't resist. 'I'm sorry, hon, but I knew he was trouble from day one.'

'And how come I didn't see it?'

'Maybe you did. Maybe that's what you were looking for.'

'Trouble?'

'Danger. You were never going to marry a quiet accountant and live happily ever after. Donal fitted the bill. Nice guy, or so you thought, with that whiff of danger. Just like . . . well, just like Dad.'

Noelle pulled away. 'Oh, for Christ's sakes. Thanks for that, Dr Freud.'

'Listen, you're the one I'm worried about. Let it go. If he doesn't want to come back here, that doesn't mean you have to go running to him. And don't get involved in any of his schemes.'

Noelle's eyes were back on the Liffey. There was what looked like a car accident on the quay at the far side. She spoke to the window. 'If I'm so in love with danger, how did I end up doing what I do?'

'Ahem, I think you know very well why. One of us had to follow Dad into the practice, and it was obvious who he wanted. You weren't going to break his heart.

'And then just to show that you had your own mind, when you did settle down to work, you went to an incy-wincy practice in the northside where, let's face it, you were never going to set the world alight.'

Noelle threw her left arm into the air, turned and walked towards the bedroom. 'I know you only want to help, but let's just leave it for the moment.'

Her sister waved. 'OK, whatever you want.'

Molloy alighted from the 39A bus at the Blanchardstown shopping centre. He set off on foot. The day was fresh, but last night's showers were still on the ground. He wore a beanie and his canvas jacket was zipped up to the neck, the collar pulled in around his throat. It wasn't the cold he wanted to protect himself from so much as the past. The contours of his childhood lay across here. He didn't call it home. He felt like a stranger returning, keeping an eye out for ghosts.

His ear was still buzzing. Apart from a meeting yesterday, he spent most of the day in the bedsit. After darkness fell, he walked the length of the boardwalk, the smell of low tide rising to meet him. On the way back, he called into Hickey's pharmacy on O'Connell Bridge and bought a packet of Panadol for his head. The night was good to him. When he awoke, he felt fresh and ready to get cracking. He caught the bus at Eden Quay and sat on the upper deck.

Now he walked west, out past the shopping centre. Within fifteen minutes he was nearing the shops in Westwood. There was nobody on the green, no donkey, no kids. He saw two middle-aged women leaving the Spar shop. He kept his head down.

Beyond Westwood, the road narrowed and he was in the country. Half a mile on, a beast of a building rose from behind a line of poplars. It looked like something that had died on the side of the road. It was finished in brown stucco, with columns of long windows. A car park, which looked like a hurried job, lay in front of the building. This ground had once been hallowed to him. It was here he had become the Dancer, setting the place alight. Now they had buried his field of dreams under a block of apartments.

He moved across the car park. From the distance came the jagged rhythm of shouts at a match. He walked around the side of the building. Green fields opened up. There were two soccer pitches side by side. Only one had posts and nets. A match was in progress, kids, under sixteen, he reckoned. One of the teams wore a strip of pink bodies with white arms and piping. Molloy didn't recognise them. Their opponents were playing in a strip of black with an amber sash running diagonally across the body. Dynamo Westwood.

At the height of the property bubble, the club agreed a land swap deal with a developer to allow for the new block. A clubhouse was to be built as a sweetener. Beyond the far pitch, Molloy could see a concrete platform on the grass, which he took to be the abandoned foundations of the clubhouse. He walked towards the pitch. A long ball came out from the Westwood defence. A lanky guy hugging the left wing brought it down with one touch. He set off towards goal. He rode one tackle, pulled inside when a second loomed. Molloy felt his pulse quicken. Go, fella, go. He played it inside to a team mate, who took the ball, didn't move but played it back to Lanky. He was through now, coming in from the left-hand side of the large box. There was nothing between him and the net but the goalkeeper. 'Do it,' Molloy said. 'Let it rip.'

The shot whizzed towards the goal and the keeper went down, but it was beyond the reach of his left hand. It skidded across, kicking up the lime that marked out the small box in front of goal. Just wide of the post. A groan went up from the sideline. Molloy heard a voice from his past echo across the pitch.

'Good effort, pick it up.' He looked over and saw the familiar gait. Mick Santry was patrolling the far touchline in the long strides that Molloy had always felt made him look like a farmer, marking out territory.

The game continued. Lanky on the left wing saw a lot of the ball. He took on opponents at will, jinking inside and out. Twice he came close to scoring, the second effort thundering off the crossbar. Molloy didn't know the kid but felt a kinship with him. He was the main man, carrying the rest of the team. His name, according to the shouts that followed his every touch, was Tommy.

Afterwards the two teams retreated into their own huddles, surrounded by gear bags and empty plastic bottles. Santry broke away, headed towards the goal nearest Molloy. He was carrying a plastic chair. Molloy walked up as he was unhooking the net at the left-hand post. Santry looked up, returned to the net, then did a double-take.

'You've got a prospect there,' Molloy said.

Santry looked at him again, stood on the chair and began unhooking the net at the upper end. 'Tommy Wills? A few Premiership clubs are sniffing around. Some of the older heads at the club, the kind of fellas who claim to know about these things, they reckon he's the best prospect we've had in over ten years since another kid had something big in his grasp.'

Molloy said nothing. Santry stepped down from the chair, picked it up and moved to the other post. 'All you can do is hope he doesn't turn out the same kind of fuck-up that fella was.'

Molloy shifted on his feet. 'Has he had any trials?'

'Why? Do you want to have a word in his shell-like? Tell him how exactly you can make a complete bollocks of the greatest chance life can offer you? Do you want to tell him how to puke your guts out in Man City's training ground?'

Molloy looked over at the huddle of Dynamo players on the far touchline. Two of them, stripped to the waist, were messing about with a plastic bottle, trying to spray water on each other.

'What are you doing here, anyway?'

'I'm looking for Stephanie.'

'You're the last thing my niece needs right now.'

'I want to see my son.'

The older man stepped down from the chair. Molloy looked him in the eye.

'You broke my heart, Dancer, you know that? You were a

jewel on a slag heap. You took that talent and pissed it down the drain.'

Molloy kept his feet on the brown patch of ground in front of the goal. He could have been back there, listening to Santry after a game, telling him he had to put in more effort. 'That's all behind me.'

'What am I reading about in the papers? You come home to start shooting people. Not that I'd mind Junior Corbett getting a bullet to his head after all he's done for this place. But you? I don't know you. The kid I knew ... Just go.'

Molloy bent to pick up the net. Santry pulled it from him. 'Give me that. I don't want you around here. These kids have enough to fight without looking at the likes of you.'

Molloy let the net fall from his fingers.

'Things are not what you read. I'm going straight. That other stuff is finished with. Look, I need to find Stephanie. I need to see my son.'

Santry was looking back towards the huddle on the far touchline. Most of the players were now dressed, some of them scooping up gear-bags. He turned back to Molloy. When he spoke, his voice had fallen a notch. 'She's lost to the family. After you went away, she— She's hardcore now. The social services were in there last year, but they couldn't do anything about the kid. It wasn't an emergency, they said. There was no abuse, so they walked away. I'm told they don't have the resources to cope with plain old neglect. The boy is still with her.'

'Where?'

'She doesn't have a home. She moves around. I've been trying to do something about that child but ... Your friends probably know more about where she is than I do.' Santry gathered the net up into himself, like a child hugging a comfy blanket.

'What friends?'

'Your friends on the dark side. They take care of her habit. They own her. Don't come around here again.' Santry walked back towards the huddle of players who were now breaking away. Molloy noted that the tall guy was the only one still togged out. He was playing keepy-uppy with the match ball, like a kid who just wanted to keep playing long after the final whistle had sounded.

It was at times like these that Alan Slate wondered about his call. OK, life had been bleak in Purgatory. Every day he sat on the sub-editors' bench, correcting spelling. And then he went home in the dark. His byline didn't grace any covers. Radio stations never rang, asking for his opinion on the latest murders. But at least he could take pride in his work.

Here, at *Inside Out*, he was surrounded by amateurs. The headline on his front-page scoop. They'd spelled 'rendezvous' wrong. How could a national magazine, fronted by a highly rated reporter like himself, make such a basic error? He could barely look at the thing and that hurt him. This business about the missing solicitor wasn't top of his agenda. He would have preferred to give the story a wide berth and concentrate on chasing down the scum. But once he had been put on it, he brought all his talents to the story. And now this. All his good work sacrificed on the altar of idiocy.

As usual in life, luck had informed his scoop. The amazing thing was that Kermode the snapper was the man of the moment.

Fastneck had detailed him to stay with the Diggins woman. Once they hit the airport, Kermode worked out her flight and rang a cousin of his in London who was in the same game. The cousin picked her up at Heathrow and followed her all the way to the address in Chiswick. Kermode and Slate were on the next flight across the Irish Sea. Kermode said he'd take care of the cousin. Slate was reassessing his opinion of the snapper. He did have a brain.

Right now, though, there was a matter that demanded resolution. It was time to lay down a marker. He had to go into the editor's office and explain that it was not acceptable for the magazine to publish a headline on the front page with a spelling error. If he didn't act now, standards would continue to slip. Like it or not, and he was beginning to like it less every day, his immediate future was tied to the magazine.

Since his arrival there, he and Fastneck had never had a cross word. They were still circling each other, unsure of where the boundaries lay. But there would come a time when the way forward had to be mapped out. If good men were willing to stand idly by, appalling standards would prevail. He ran this through his head three times before knocking on the editor's door.

Fastneck was behind his desk. He was togged out in his usual starched white shirt, a canary yellow lie loosened at the collar. He beckoned Slate to enter. He didn't bother getting up. He wore a pained expression, as if he had piles or something.

'Good scoop,' he said, raising his eyes for just a second.

Slate sat down on the other side of the desk. Fastneck was peering at what appeared to be a stack of typed sheets full of tables in front of him. 'Frank, the headline,'

Fastneck looked up. There was impatience on his face, suggesting he was in no mood for hassle. 'I thought it worked,' he said.

'Worked fine if it was spelled properly.'

Fastneck looked up again. He riffled through the sheets until he located a copy of the magazine. He held it out in front of him, as if he had difficulty reading it.

'"Rendezvous",' Slate said. 'There's no z.'

'I can see that. So what?'

'It's spelt with a z.'

'I know that.'

'It's a bad mistake. It makes me look bad.'

Fastneck dropped the magazine back on to his desk. He stretched his arms high in the air, then brought his hands to his face, slowly dragging them down over his high cheekbones. It dawned on Slate that this was the first he knew that there had been a cock-up.

'No z,' Fastneck said. 'No fucking z.'

'Frank, I'm not making a big deal of this but—'

'You're not making a big deal of it? Well, what are you doing?' He got up, turned and looked out on to the Liffey.

Slate thought it best to stay silent.

'We've lost Tesco,' Fastneck said to the window. 'Gone. Four colour pages.'

'Jesus.'

'Yeah. We could do with a few loaves and fishes right now.' He was still talking to the window.

'Maybe we could beef up the advertising department,' Slate said.

'The advertising department, as you call it, is gone too.'

'What?'

'We had to let Kavanagh go last week. Useless fucker that he was. Petra – you know Petra?' He turned from the window. 'Maybe you haven't noticed her. She's not much to look at but she could sell snow to the Eskimos. She rang me last night. She's off to the *Independent*.'

'Not good.'

'My wife is joining the team. Julie worked in advertising for years before she stayed at home to raise the kids. She'll be in this afternoon after she drops our youngest to her mother's. My wife, Alan. She's leaving our children to come in here and rescue us.'

'I'm sure it's only short term, Frank.'

Fastneck dropped his hands on to the desk in fists. He leaned down and looked across at Slate. 'My family is facing serious

132

upheaval. All our money is tied up in this magazine. I love my wife, but I dread the thought of working with her. Can you see where I'm coming from?'

'Sure, Frank, but we'll manage.'

Fastneck picked up a few of the sheets on the desk, waved them in his right hand, as if he had just got a full house at bingo. 'Circulation is flat.'

'It's a jungle out there, Frank.'

Fastneck straightened. He stood ramrod straight, his hands now resting on his hips. Slate noticed that the hairs hanging from his nostrils were twitching. He could see why Fastneck had been described in his playing days as a centre forward who terrorised defences.

'You can understand why right now I don't give a shit about your z.'

Slate recoiled as if he had been slapped across the face. 'Forget it, Frank. I was just thinking about standards. Readers care about them.'

'So do I, Alan, so do I.' He eased himself into the chair again, the expression on his face lapsing into pain. 'Look, never mind me. It's just a tough time. I'm all wound up. I was driving in this morning, just thinking,' he began to hammer his fists on the desk rhythmically with each word, 'Forward. Forward. Forward.'

Slate coughed. 'Are we in trouble?'

'Nothing that we can't handle. This is when I'm at my best, Alan. Backs to the wall. Two down at the start of the second half.'

'Everything to play for?'

'Now you're talking. Our courage is our best asset. And you, Alan. You're a major asset. You and me together, we can make this thing work.'

Slate felt the tension in his body ease.

Fastneck pulled open a drawer, took out a sheet of notepaper. 'What we need is serious material, something that will wipe the floor with all of our competitors, the dailies, the Sundays, the lot.'

Slate nodded. Fastneck handed him the piece of paper. 'She's got a yarn about this solicitor. She got badly burned and she's in the mood for singing.'

Slate looked at the mobile number and rose to leave. 'No problem, Frank.'

'By the way, I know her. You won't mind if I tag along for the interview.'

Slate reeled in the first thought to enter his head. He wants to tag along. The fucking editor wants to sit in on an interview because he knows the subject. Forget about the z. Standards were way down in the hole.

'Wally?'

'Hey, my brother. Life on the outside looking good?'

'Is it fuck.'

'No picnic in here either. You're still getting in the meetings?'

'None of this is easy.'

'Don't fade on me, brother. Pain and suffering are necessary, misery optional.'

'I met a fella today, football coach. He knows me since I was in short trousers.'

'You was making amends. Made a list of all the persons we had harmed.'

'Will you shut up for a minute? I was looking for my son.'

'OK.'

'This guy knows the places I been. He was there when I messed up that time I went to Manchester. I hadn't seen him in years. He was talking to me as if I was a different person from the kid he knew.'

'You are.'

'It was as if all the best bits of me had died, and all that was left was the fuck-up.'

'Joshua, this takes time. Some people look at you and they say, "Yeah, he's just putting on an act or looking to score something." You have to give it time. You have to show that you're serious about this.'

'I don't have time.'

'Sure you do, brother, all the time in the world.'

'Just going back to the pitch today, it made me think.'

'Regrets, you have a lot.'

'Things could have been different.'

'The past. Accept the things you can't change.'

'I'm a dead man walking.'

'Well, walk yourself out of town.'

'I can't. You know that TV show, things to do before you die?'

'Tell me about it.'

'I have to see my kid.'

'You are one morbid fucker. Get yourself a higher power.'

'Wally?'

'Yeah.'

'Go fuck yourself.'

'Until the next time, brother.'

'Hi.'

'How are you?'

'OK. What's that noise? Have you got a cold?'

'Naw, just a runny nose. You got back all right?'

'Yeah, well. Until I came across that magazine. Have you seen it yet?'

'I can get by without it.'

'Easy for you to say.'

'Sorry.'

'They made me look awful.'

'Can't imagine I came out of it smelling like Mother Teresa.'

'You're Clyde to my Bonnie.'

'I wish I'd given that reporter one good haymaker in the restaurant that time. Have you thought about things?'

'Nothing else.'

'And?'

'Do we have to do it your way?'

'Babe, there is no other way. How can we begin again unless we have something to survive with? We're talking about seed capital for our new life together and, right now, you're the only person who can get your hands on that. You know I'd be picked up within an hour of touching down. You're all I've got ...'

'What's that noise?'

'Room service.'

'Very nice.'

'Noelle, if we're going to do it, we need to move soon. The longer we leave things the greater the chance that it won't come off.'

'I know. It's a long drive, the far side of the country.'

'It will be worth it. It's the foundation of our future.'

'And then we emigrate.'

'Yeah. It's no longer the place where we want to raise our family.'

'Our family?'

'Well, maybe it's time we got our skates on. Listen, one thing. The laptop in Skellig. Could you get it? Just to be on the safe side. If the guards ever put a bit of effort into this, they could get a warrant. I don't want anybody opening up the laptop.'

'The keys to your secret life.'

'There could be burglars sniffing around the place as well.'

'OK.'

'We'll talk tomorrow?'

'Are you in a hurry off somewhere?'

'No, no, I just have a stack of work here that I have to get through. It never ends. Listen, you sound tired yourself. Get a night's sleep and we'll talk in the morning. And I do love you.'

'Glad to hear it.' She hit the red button.

10

Rocco couldn't get his head around the size of the place. The front porch wasn't a porch at all but a greenhouse, thick with plants and shrubs like something in *I'm A Celebrity . . . Get Me Out Of Here*. He half expected an exotic creature with a long neck to leap out.

So far so handy. The front door behind them had shipped a bit of damage when they'd worked the lock, but it wasn't as if they were on a main street. From the road, you'd have to leap above the steel gate and get a good eye at the front door before noticing that it was hanging ajar.

He tried the handle on the glass door from the porch into the house proper. No go. Kyle's breath, hot with stale beer, came over his shoulder. He had a screwdriver in his hand. He reversed the grip and thrust the handle through the glass, shattering the silence. No alarm. Even after cutting the power at the line outside, there always remained a fear that the alarm would begin hopping. Not this time. Rocco put his hand through the hole in the glass, and slowly turned the Yale lock.

Inside, there was a corridor as wide as Ma's front room. Rocco's runners squeaked on the polished floor. He could hear his breathing and a current of noise coming from Kyle's headphones.

He pushed at the first door to his right. The torch fingered tiles inside, white and brilliant. And then he saw the jacks. The handle on the cistern was gold. A gold fucking handle. He sat down on the lid. There was a whiff of lemons in the black air. He turned off the torch, closed his eyes, waiting a moment. Then he got up and wrapped his fingers around the gold handle, smooth and cold, pushing down against the gentle pressure. The sound of flushing filled the air. Hallelujah, these people really knew how to take a dump.

When he came out of the bathroom, Kyle was down the far end of the corridor, his torch jerking about.

'Yo,' Rocco said. There was no response from Kyle. As if it wasn't bad enough that he was half tanked, Kyle was also getting a load of the Black Eyed Peas. Sometimes Rocco found it hard to believe they were brothers, not to mind twins. He loved Kyle but, man, that boy gave a whole new meaning to the word 'stupid'.

He walked up and tapped his brother on the back. Kyle jumped, turned and pulled the bud from his left ear. 'Easy on,' he said.

Rocco took away the one on his brother's right ear. 'We're not here to party.'

Kyle gave him that look, half bored, half stupid, fully in need of something to set him back on the road.

Just then Rocco thought he saw movement. He turned, reaching for the Beretta in the pocket of his tracksuit bottoms. He held out his left hand to protect Kyle. That was when he saw the mirror, as big as a 48-inch TV screen. The reflection showed two men in black woolly hats, black Adidas tops, both wearing faces like startled earwigs.

Kyle began to giggle. 'Why don't I head up there?' he said, pointing towards the stairs to the side of the hall. 'You stick to the ground level.'

Rocco pushed him towards them. 'Don't be afraid of wrecking the joint. No harm in making it look like a professional job.'

Kyle nodded, and Rocco added, 'Just stay away from her underwear.'

Rocco turned back to exploring. Junior had wanted this job done more than a week ago, when the whole thing had blown up. But until now any attempt to get into the house would have been recorded by the media hordes waiting outside. Smile, you're on *Candid Camera* for the *Six O'Clock News*, mugs gracing the front pages of every paper. Now that the fizz had drained from the story, the cameras had left and there was space to do a little work.

Rocco moved through another door into what he thought must be the sitting room. Faint light poured in through two windows at the far end. Between them sat a flat-screen TV mounted on a fitted table, 24-inch. It looked like the Sky Plus recording box was there too, with various bits and bobs he couldn't make out but would, at any other time, have coveted.

He walked over to one of the windows. The moon was high in a clear sky, stars sparkling on the dark sea below. These people knew how to live.

His torch fingered around the place. There was a large cream-coloured couch that looked like it might swallow you up. At one end there was a fireplace, about three times the size of any other Rocco had ever come across. It looked to be cast iron, topped with a mantelpiece swaying in curves of treated wood.

There was a photograph on the mantelpiece, fitted inside a silver frame, shaped like a fish. He shone his light on a smiling couple. They were looking out from a background of sand meeting a cobalt blue sea. Of course he recognised the woman, although the lens was kinder to her than she had appeared over the last week or so.

The man, well, he looked the business, as fine a specimen to shine out of the Celtic Tiger's ass as you were likely to find this side of the Atlantic. He had the cut of a TV star, all chiselled features and a smile that spread out like a warm embrace.

Rocco took the frame down, opened it at the back and folded the photograph. He just knew his ma would love the frame.

He heard Kyle call his name through the house. He went out into the hall. Kyle shone his torch down on his face. 'Follow me, brother. I is the burglar in chief tonight. Think I found what we're looking for.'

Somebody was banging on Molloy's front door. He jumped from the bed, hauled straight out of a dream in which he had been sitting at a bar on his own, waiting. The first thing to enter his head was the window. It was a long way down from the first floor, but with a shake of luck he might survive. He couldn't say the same for what faced him on the far side of the door.

'Open up! Gardaí!' someone shouted. Well, the accent was right. Pure culchie. They kept pounding.

He pulled on his jeans, slipped into a T-shirt. His bedside clock said it was just gone six a.m. Pulling back the edge of a curtain, he saw a white Ford Mondeo double-parked on the street. Nothing else was moving down there in the half-light, the city squeezing the last out of the night behind closed doors.

When he opened the door he was met with two faces. No question about it, these boys were the real deal. An older guy stood to the front, tall, bald, apart from salt-and-pepper wings, with a face that said he had come out of the womb as a fully formed pig. The other guy was younger, but carrying enough pounds for the pair of them. His hair was cut tight and two nicks on the left side of his jaw betrayed a bad-shaving day.

'Detective Inspector Phil Wright,' the older guy said. 'And this is Sergeant Mattie Kerins.'

'What's the problem?'

'How does this fine morning find you, Joshua?' His face was lapsing into the bored look Molloy recognised as standard fare on older cops.

'Why are you harassing me?'

'You must be very glad to see us, Joshua.'

'If you haven't got a warrant, just fuck off.'

Wright stepped back, turned himself halfway to let the gorilla Sergeant move past him. The gorilla pushed Molloy in the chest, sending him reeling back into the room. He had to steady himself from falling backwards. He checked an impulse to swing for the fucker.

Wright shut the door. 'You're a lucky boy that it's us who've come calling, Joshua, because from what I'm hearing, you're due some visitors who wouldn't be half as accommodating.'

Molloy found a spot on the wall, just below the ceiling, where the wallpaper had peeled off in a jagged line.

Wright moved across to the window. He pulled the curtains, letting in the dawn. 'Now, we have some good news and some bad news. Which first?'

Molloy kept his eyes on his chosen spot.

'Well, in the great tradition of these things, Joshua, I'm going to give you the bad news first.' He pulled a sky blue sheet of paper from his jacket pocket. 'I am hereby notifying you that An Garda Síochána has information that suggests there is an imminent threat to your life. We would advise caution on your part. There, that was easy.'

Molloy kept his eyes on the peeling wallpaper. Was it peeling or tearing? That was the question. Wright looked around, seeking somewhere to deposit his tidings. He let the sheet float from his hand on to the two-seater. 'Unofficially, Joshua, we couldn't give a fiddler's if Junior Corbett's boys blow your head halfway into next week. The problem is, if they splatter your brains all over this place or, worse, out on the street, that constitutes a violent breach of the peace. People get upset with that sort of thing. I presume you do know that you're in line for an OBE?'

'A what?'

'Hear that, Mattie? It speaks. You've heard of an OBE, Joshua. Footballers and pop stars and all these big shots get it from the Queen. In England.'

'What the fuck are you talking about?'

The other one came in here, smirking: 'The inspector is talking about an OBE Dublin style, One Behind the Ear.' He made a gun out of his right hand and laughed. Inspector Wright smiled, but it was a mean smile.

Molloy didn't move. If only you knew, bogman. Been there, dealt with that. Sentence suspended. Now clear the fuck out.

'The good news is that we are here to provide you with an opportunity. We are your confessors, Joshua. We are going to allow you to confide in us all you know about the murder of that fine young man Peter Sullivan.'

'Who?'

'Peter Sullivan, your buddy Harms, who was going to help you get rid of Junior so you could move to the top of the tree. Tell me, Joshua, how in the name of sweet Jesus were you stupid enough to organise a hit on Junior with a young fella whose brain went on safari around the time he got out of short trousers?'

Molloy's eyes were closed, as if in prayer.

'Anyway, what we really want to talk about is the night you met him after that disaster, and how you followed him back to his sainted mother's house where you shot him to death.'

Molloy was looking at him now. This had to be a shakedown.

They couldn't have anything on him. 'I don't know who you're talking about. Now, if you wouldn't mind, I have some sleeping to do, so if you could clear off, I'd be really grateful.'

He tensed himself to take a blow, but it didn't come.

Wright let out a long sigh, heavy with exaggerated resignation. 'Joshua Molloy, you are under arrest in connection with the murder of Peter Sullivan. You are not obliged to say anything unless you wish to do so…'

By seven a.m., there were four of them at it. The three males were stripped to the waist, the woman still wore a tank top, but nobody was betting it would remain in place. They were at the back end of the establishment, giving it loads to Beyoncé. Now and then, the girl leaned into one of the men, singing into her fist. Rocco reckoned she was so far gone she believed she was Beyoncé reincarnated in a Dublin pub.

The early house was rocking. Hugging the Luas line, a stone's throw from the Four Courts, there was no problem with the volume of music here. Rocco and Kyle were sitting at a small circular table. Apart from the party crowd, there was a knot of four middle-aged guys at the bar, nursing pints, night-shifters who had wandered in for a quart and found themselves in the middle of a party. It didn't seem to bother them.

As far as Rocco was concerned, he and his brother were in the same boat. They had just finished work, and were now entitled to a few scoops before heading off home. He was on his third. The job on the house had left Kyle particularly thirsty and he was racing ahead, skulling his fifth. Behind the bar, a goateed pile of beef had his eyes fixed on the TV mounted in a corner. A recorded boxing match was in progress.

The only element of the morning that kept Rocco from fully relaxing was the presence of two other men at another table.

They had exchanged nods when they entered. Rocco recognised both of them, Landy Towers's brother and his mate, a junkie toe-rag whom Landy used whenever help was hard to find. There hadn't been any trouble between Landy and Junior for at least a year, as far as Rocco knew, and he didn't want any hassle with anybody this morning.

He had done a satisfactory job. Junior and Johnny would be pleased. He was entitled to a few pints and a bit of blow now that work was over.

Apart from the thing, they had helped themselves to two cameras, one video recorder and a drawer full of jewellery. They had had a barney as they were going out of the door – Kyle was insisting on dragging out three of Diggins's suits. OK, they were top-notch stuff, a couple of Italian jobs and a pin-striped German number but . . . In the end, when Rocco wouldn't give an inch, Kyle had stormed out. They had left the suits hanging on one of those bushes that filled the porch. That was the only minor worry from the job. Why would anybody abandon a few choice tins of fruit at the front door on the way out?

Now it was time to relax, even if that pair of toe-rags looked as if they were fit to throw shapes.

Kyle came out of the toilet, swayed back towards the table. Rocco noticed the looks that passed between his brother and the other two. 'Fuckin' pricks,' Kyle said, as he sat down.

Rocco was more interested in his brother's attempt to snort life back into the day – Kyle was fading fast. He had to shout to be heard above Kanye West, who had taken over from Beyoncé. 'How was it?'

'Yeah, great. What are we going to do about those two?'

Rocco took a long draw from his pint. 'There's nothing *to* do. We're going to enjoy a few pints and, right now, I'm going to join you on the upper level.' He extended his hand. Kyle fished in his trouser pocket and passed the small package to his brother.

The toilet floor was wet, but that was nothing compared to the smell of piss. Still, nobody came to the early house for a hot date. The only sound in the cubicle was the hissing of the pipes above the cistern. He wiped the top with his sleeve and laid out the stuff, chopping it up with his credit card. Two quick toots and he was in business. He dipped his index finger into the package and rubbed the particles into his upper gums. Now he was ready for whatever else the day wanted to throw at him.

The first thing he noticed when he came out of the toilet was that the two boys were gone. Then he saw that Kyle was no longer at their table. Two half-finished pints were sitting there, looking lost. The night-shifters were at the front window, peering out on to the street. The party people were now doing their thing to Fergie, 'Big Girls Don't Cry'. The girl was at the centre, fingering her tank top, fenced in by her three shirtless friends.

Rocco moved towards the window. One of the night-shifters turned, saying, to nobody in particular, 'Somebody call the law. There's a psychopath going crazy with a knife out there.' He turned and found himself looking at Rocco and something clicked, a connection between this man and the psychopath.

The light of the day hit Rocco the second he came through the door. He saw the junkie lying on the pavement. Blood was flowing from his stomach, like a slow purple spring, spilling out on to the ground. His whole body was twitching, eyes barely open. A few yards away Kyle was thrusting down into the prostrate body of Landy Towers's brother. He kept repeating what sounded like 'Cunt,' as he brought his knife down into the man, who was grunting in pain.

A bell sounded. Rocco looked behind him to see the Luas approaching. The train passed in a blur, carriages full, some of the passengers turning to look out at murder rending the rush-hour.

He grabbed Kyle by the back of the collar, hauled him to his feet. Kyle kept swinging at Landy Towers's brother, whose eyes were now on the sky above. Rocco grabbed his brother's stabbing arm and held it aloft. 'Out of here, now,' he said.

Kyle looked down at his victim. 'Who's a fucking pansy now, big man?' He swung a kick into the man's ribs, and Landy Towers's brother's eyes closed for a moment. The blood on his shirt was dark and spreading.

Rocco had his brother by the arm, breaking into a jog. He could see the Luas train disappearing into the distance up ahead. They rounded a corner, ran the fifty yards or so to the Toyota Avensis. Just as they were getting into the car, two schoolgirls in green pinafore uniforms approached. The one on the outside had long pigtails. She looked in at the two men. Rocco turned the ignition and slipped into gear. He told Kyle to get down, sit on the floor in the front passenger side. His hands were shaking on the steering wheel. It had nearly been a great night.

Slate was in the shower when his phone began hopping. He turned off the knob, opened the shower door and grabbed the phone from the lip of the sink. It showed 'private number' on the screen. He was due at the interview that Fastneck had set up. With any luck, this was a call to cancel.

'Beauty-sleep interruption.'

'Who this?'

'Your old confederate.'

Now he recognised the voice: Seamus Fox. 'You've pulled the early shift.'

'Manning the desk of my woes here, buddy. And guess who is occupying interview room number two down the hall from me right now in the company of Inspector Phil Wright?'

Slate thought about it. Maybe it was the solicitor: his type always eventually came home. Maybe he'd get out of this interview today. Then he could move back to chasing big game. 'Tell me you have Donal Diggins down there. Please tell me I'm right.'

'Who?'

'Diggins, the solicitor on the lam.'

The line gave way to a brief pause, before Fox said, 'That lowlife ... I got a pad in Bulgaria. Have you ever been to Bulgaria? No, me neither. But I was told that it was the new thing, Marbella on the Dead Sea or the Black Sea or whatever fucking sea it's on. Anyways, the missus says she'll go along with it ...'

Slate clasped the phone between shoulder and jaw. He reached out and pulled a towel around himself in a wrap. This was the high maintenance part of the job. You let people rabbit on with whatever it was they wanted to get off their chest. You waited. You tried to sift through the chaff to find the few grains of wheat. And when you were dealing with a friend in the force, you knew that the wheat was in there somewhere. Let it out, Seamus.

'... a sure thing. We all went out there to a hotel by the airport. They had this Bulgarian footballer there, played for Barcelona, or maybe it was Real. I can't remember his name but he didn't say much. He just stood there as if to say to us, "This is what Bulgarian people look like."

'Yeah, and he had a hurler from Cork as well, tall lad. He said even less. I remember thinking, What is he doing here? What do footballers and hurlers know about whether an apartment in Bulgaria is a good bet or not? Do you get me?'

'Celebrity appeal, Seamus. Celebrities know everything about everything.'

'Yeah. Anyways, the thing is a dud. We got word last month. All this shite about guaranteed tenants and ten per cent yield, it's all bollocks. They've stopped building the place. My apartment in the sun doesn't even have walls.'

'And Diggins was behind it?'

'Who?'

'Diggins, the solicitor on the lam.'

'No, no, it was this outfit from down the country. We're suing the bastards but they haven't a bean at this stage anyway.'

Slate walked into his bedroom, pulled open the curtains. The sky held some bright promise.

'You didn't get caught, Alan, did you?'

'Nope.'

'Did you really see this coming? Were you smarter than the rest of us?'

'Seamus, I was so far up my own hole in those years that the Celtic Tiger passed me by. Now, please, who is in the interview room?'

'What?'

'Who have you got down there?'

'Oh. It's your man, Molloy, the Dancer, you know, the footballer. The fella who's back in town to kick up a gang war. Wright is down there going through him for a short cut.'

Slate exhaled silently. 'Thanks, Seamus,' he said.

'Yeah. Listen, one other thing. He's asked for a solicitor.'

'So what?'

'A Noelle Diggins. Mean anything to you?'

Molloy thought about the colour of the walls. Lemon yellow. The chair he was sitting on was nailed to the floor, a metal contraption with armrests. On the other side of the table there were two plastic seats, waiting to be occupied by good cop and bad cop. High on the wall opposite his chair the eye of a camera looked down on him.

He had been dragged in a couple of times before, but nothing ever came of it. The second time, they'd lifted him from the street as he was coming off a three-day bender. It was the usual stuff. Photographs of Junior, sightings of him in the company of Junior, bullshit about information from others that put him as a major link in the chain. He kept his trap shut. It was all over in an afternoon.

All he remembered from that episode was needing a drink. He could still feel the shivers that ran through him, the sweats, his head ready to explode. Two days after he got out, Junior sent him back to get the tape. They watched it over vodka and orange juice the following night.

Right now, his main craving was for a meeting. Between one thing and another, he hadn't gone yesterday. He was feeling it now.

The door opened and the two boys who had made the early-morning call lumbered in. They sat down and each placed a cardboard folder on the desk. Wright, the inspector, began talking. 'OK, Joshua.. You know why we're here. We're investigating the death of Peter Sullivan on the twelfth of March.'

'I don't know anything about that.'

'How long did you know Peter Sullivan?'

'What was the name again?'

Wright acted as if he hadn't even heard him. 'Where were you on the evening of the twelfth of March?'

'I was in my bedsit, listening to music.'

Now it was the other guy's turn. 'You're sure about that? That you were listening to music? What about TV, Josh? Remember any programmes you might have seen that evening?'

'Josh' it was now. 'No, I was listening to music. No law against that.'

'Did you stay in all evening?'

Molloy paused. 'I have a problem here.'

'What's your problem, Josh?'

'I don't know if I can trust you people.'

The two cops looked at one another.

'Do you want to get something off your chest?'

'Nothing about me, but there's other stuff.'

'If you co-operate with us, we will do everything possible to protect you.'

He shifted in his seat, looked up at the camera. 'What can you offer me?'

That look passed between the pair of them again.

'I think perhaps we'd better terminate the interview at this point. It is now eleven oh four a.m.' Wright said.

Kerins raised his Africa-sized posterior from the seat and went out through the door. He returned seconds later. 'OK, it's off,' he said.

Wright spoke, his tone now softened into one of friendship. 'Now, Josh, what have you got for us?'

'About what?'

The pair of them looked at each other again. Wright said, 'About Junior and what happened to Harms Sullivan. If you can hand us Junior's arse on a plate, it will make a big difference to you.'

'How so?'

Wright shrugged, threw his arms out, as if to embrace all possibilities. 'Well, immunity might be on the cards. Witness protection, there's a lot can be done these days.'

'But I thought you had me in the frame for Sullivan?'

'We do,' Kerins said. 'For starters we have CCTV from a Spar shop off Parnell Street. Sullivan passes down, you follow a few seconds later. That was an hour or so before he was shot dead.'

'That's all you have?'

'That's for openers. We also have Sullivan calling your mobile a few minutes before you were caught following him.'

Molloy leaned forward. 'Do you really think I would have been stupid enough to get a mobile in my own name if I was going around killing people?'

Wright said, 'I have learned from long experience never to underestimate the stupidity of some of you people.'

Kerins interrupted, before Molloy could reply, 'What do you want, Josh? Things can be done ...' Trailing off to more possibilities.

'But we haven't got all day.'

'So I rat out Junior ...'

'You got it in one. Now, what have you?'

Molloy straightened. 'Nah. I think we've got crossed purposes here, fellas. I was just wondering whether I'd be able to get a piss break in the middle of this. Better turn the tape back on.'

Kerins grabbed Molloy by the front of his T-shirt. He moved around the table, shoving Molloy back across the armrest. Wright came from the other side and stepped between them. 'Go out and cool down,' he told his colleague.

There was thunder on Kerins's face. He pulled the door after him on the way out.

'Now I know which of you is the bad cop,' Molloy said. He didn't see the back of Wright's fist describe a curve as it swept in from behind and smacked him hard on the left ear.

The walls in the room were bare. There was no recording equipment, or anything else to distract attention, apart from the peeling brown paint on the door. Noelle had a quick sconce around to make sure there was nothing under the scarred table or the metal chair on the far side of it.

She looked at her watch. Seven minutes had crawled by since she was deposited here. She'd give them another five, before making a song and dance. The suspect was entitled to counsel as soon as she arrived in the station. There should be no fannying about. She took a yellow legal pad from her briefcase, and opened it on the table.

Her head hurt. She was agitated, not so much by being called down to the station but the circumstances around it. She was surprised to hear that it was Joshua Molloy. He had genuinely seemed like somebody who was turning things around. But surprises had been coming at her thick and fast of late.

The next surprise hit her when she left the apartment. Her car, her seven-year-old beloved Honda Civic, had been singled out and neutralised by a clamp. It was just gone eight thirty a.m., and the bastards had been out already, hunting down innocent prey. By the time the taxi left her at Mountjoy station, her head was politely requesting its daily bread. The call had thrown her from her Solp ration with breakfast.

It was just after the ten-minute mark when the door opened. Molloy walked in. He looked to be in good shape, apart from the guilt she detected on his face. He was still kinda cute. She got up and extended her hand, although the formality felt awkward. The door closed behind him. His hand was warm.

'No camera here. Does that mean you're free to beat up on me?' he said.

'I can't say I don't feel like doing just that.'

He looked around the room, bent down and stuck his head under the table.

'I've already checked it,' she said. He eased himself into the nailed-down chair. 'I presume you've been treated all right.'

'Yeah, apart from a slap.'

'One of them assaulted you?' She reached for her pad on the table.

'Forget it. I was asking for it.'

'I need the details now. I want a doctor in here to examine you. Was it here or when they arrested you?'

'No assault. I was asking for it. I got a slap. I don't need the hassle of chasing cops on a brutality rap. End of story. They don't have anything on me.'

She looked at him as if he had two heads. 'You were asking for it?'

He threw his head back and laughed. 'You should see your face. Look, I yanked his chain and he reacted. Forget about it. Sorry for dragging you in here.'

He looked like he meant it. 'What happened to the new leaf you had turned over?'

'They're on a fishing expedition.'

'You don't go fishing on dry land. I'm your solicitor, or at least that's the way it appears now. If you tell me you're innocent, that's fine. But don't yank my chain by launching into some spiel as if you're about to join the Legion of Mary. Frankly, I'm not in the mood.'

Molloy nodded, giving nothing away. 'About my son …'

'We will deal with your son later. Right now, you're the focus. My advice is to say nothing. It's their job to get you to make admissions, and the best thing you can do is stay schtum. If they have a case against you, let them build it.'

'There is no case.'

'If you have an alibi we'll deal with that later, but don't get into it with them. Just keep your mouth closed.'

The door behind opened. Noelle got to her feet, turning to face whoever had the temerity to enter at this point. The inspector was standing there, filling the door frame. 'Excuse me, but I am not finished with my client.'

'Sorry about this, Mrs Diggins, but something else has come up. I just thought it best that I tell you. There has been a robbery at your home.'

The fight went out of Noelle. 'Which home?' she said. As

154

soon as the words came out, she realised how stupid they sounded, as if she was a jet-setter, living between countries or continents. Truth was, she didn't know where she considered home any more.

'Ah, your ... home in Killiney,' he said.

'Sorry, I'm staying with my sister at the moment. I wasn't sure where you were referring to.'

'There are two officers at the house now. I know this is a bad time, but the sooner you could meet them, the better.'

She looked down at Molloy, still sitting in his chair. He shrugged. 'Go on ahead. I'll be all right. These lads will treat me with kid gloves. Ain't that the case, Inspector?'

Wright ignored him. Noelle scooped up her writing pad, opened the briefcase.

'Are you driving?' Wright said.

'No,' she said. 'No. The clampers came for it at the crack of dawn. Could I organise a taxi?'

Wright thrust his hands into his trouser pockets. 'I'll give you a lift. Your client can cool his heels for a few hours. It's only fair.'

Noelle was taken aback. The usual tack in a situation like this would be for them to press home an advantage. 'That sounds reasonable, thank you,' she said. She turned to Molloy, who was now on his feet. 'They aren't going to tell me how long they're detaining you, but if you're not out by this afternoon, I'll drop by.'

Molloy nodded. 'And my young fella.'

'We need to move on that once you get out of here.' Her head was really hurting now.

The sun was climbing high above the North Circular Road when Noelle Diggins and Inspector Phil Wright emerged from the station. The morning rush-hour had rushed on by. An ambulance siren wailed up the road from Drumcondra, arriving with a skid at the entrance to the Mater Hospital, opposite the station.

From the far side of the road, Alan Slate watched the pair descend the stone steps at the entrance. He didn't really want to encounter the woman at this stage. You'd never know how she might react to her starring role in *Inside Out*. He suspected that the missing z would be the last thing on her mind, and that she was unlikely to embrace her new status as a cover girl.

Still, he needed to be here for the colour. If he was going to do a major piece on the missing solicitor, this kind of stuff was necessary for the padding: the stricken wife going about her business representing the scum while her husband, the fraudster, is holed up abroad.

Wright was pointing down the road to where, Slate surmised, his motor was parked. They began walking. Slate tracked them from his side of the street. A truck rumbled between them, carrying livestock. A stretch limo followed. There was a man on a black bicycle fronted by a blue canvas contraption for carrying children.

The pair came to a set of pedestrian lights. They crossed to Slate's side of the street. He was now ten feet from them, caught unawares. He thought he might be better served to put a bit of distance between them. But too late: Wright had caught his eye. The policeman's widened in surprise. Whether the woman sensed it or not, her attention was now drawn to Slate. The look on her face went from curiosity to anger in four seconds flat. She stalked over to him. The inspector trailed in her wake. Slate braced himself. 'Hi,' he said, all sheepish.

'What kind of a man are you?' That was the same line he remembered her firing out in London. She looked good in the morning light, a lot better than her image on the cover of the magazine.

'How are you this morning?' he said.

'Do you have absolutely no respect for other people? How could you do what you did to me?'

Her hands had moved to her hips now. Inspector Wright was standing just behind her, concern on his face that he might have to intervene in the event of a breach of the peace. Slate couldn't make out whether he was putting it on. 'I'm just reporting the news,' he said.

'News? What you wrote about me was lies. And you printed that awful photograph – you didn't even ask for my permission. Do you have any idea the upset you caused?'

Slate looked to the inspector. He was a cop: he could see where this was going. It was his duty to protect all citizens. The woman's head was tilted to the side, better to vent her anger. 'I'm sorry you feel that way.'

'You're not sorry for anything. All you want is to print whatever you think will sell. You'll crawl around in the gutter just to appeal to the basest instinct.'

'I'm sorry, but your husband has left a lot of people out of pocket. It's a legitimate story to follow.'

She was boring a hole into his face with her eyes, but Wright got in before her. 'OK, Mrs Diggins, I think it's best that we leave things now. Nothing is going to get solved here on a public street. Might I suggest that you can pursue this elsewhere?'

She gave him a look that would have burned coals before turning on her heels and taking off. When she was out of earshot, Wright winked and said, 'You're some fucker all right. Great story by the way.'

11

The traffic was settling into a mid-morning flow as Inspector Phil Wright's unmarked Ford Mondeo made its way towards the East-Link toll bridge. For the first mile or so, they didn't speak. The only sound echoing through the car was the sporadic crackling of the police radio. Noelle found herself squinting against a low sun, which looked all set to make the most of the day. Her shades were in the glove compartment of her clamped car. The journey took them down through Clonliffe Road, with the great hulk of Croke Park on the right, like a prehistoric beast.

She pulled her mobile from her handbag and began a text to Valerie. At this rate, she'd hardly be back in the office before lunchtime. Between the break, and her general distraction over the last week, work was mounting up. She revised it a few times before settling on: 'Val, Called to Mountjoy for client this morn. Now gone to Killiney for robbery. In later. Noelle.'

'I apologise for that back there, it wasn't very professional of me,' she said.

'You can't be blamed for it. There were times when I felt like doing that fella some damage myself,' he said.

'You know him?'

'Of an old day. He has his own skeletons.'

'That's what I can't understand. The way he wrote that story, you'd swear he was whiter than white himself or something.'

'I'd go with the something. Do you think it's connected?'

'What?'

'The robbery and the story, your husband's problems.'

The thought had occurred to her. Would it be pushing things to ask him to stop at a chemist on the way out there? Maybe he would think he was enabling her habit. 'I don't know, Inspector. Do you think they're connected?'

He heaved out a sigh that sounded like a deflating balloon. 'Could be. Depends on what might be there of interest to anybody. Your husband left a lot of curiosity behind when he took off. By the way, you can call me Phil.'

She didn't say anything. The car came to a halt in the queue for the toll bridge. The tide on the Liffey was high. If she turned towards the city, she could almost see Caroline's apartment block. Her car was back there. It began to dawn on her that she would have preferred to return to Skellig alone.

He turned on the car radio to the sound of the signature tune for the news. Since all this had blown up, Noelle regarded the sound as a toll of further doom, but she couldn't very well ask him to turn it off.

'One man has died and another is in intensive care in Mater Hospital following an early-morning stabbing in Dublin city centre. The incident, which occurred outside a public house, was witnessed by passengers in a passing Luas train.'

Inspector Wright snorted. 'That's what the city is coming to. They don't even bother killing each other in private any more. It's a public spectacle.'

'Plenty of witnesses,' she said.

'I'll wager you that not one person in that train will come forward. I wouldn't like to be the poor sod assigned to tracking down each of them for useless statements.'

Within twenty minutes, they were swinging on to Killiney Hill. Around a corner, the bay hove into view, sparkling in the sun like tiny shards of glass.

'Just about halfway down this road,' she said. He nodded, although his gaze was now moving between the sea on the left and the properties on the right. 'No two-up-two-down out this way,' he said.

She smiled. 'Only the trouble-free rich live out here.'

'Trouble follows everybody at some point or another. The rich tend to be better equipped to meet it.'

'It's just here,' she said. She felt a stab of something in her gut as the car came to a halt on the road. The entrance gate of steel was closed. It was flanked by twin piers of pointed red brick. There was a cast-iron lantern on each pier and the intercom pad on the one to the right. Noelle passed her remote control to Wright. He rolled down his window and flashed it. The gates opened inwards. She heard the familiar sound of wheels grinding across the crushed shells that carpeted the driveway. Wright was leaning forward in his seat, like a man gearing up to go through the window.

She could see that the front door was ajar. As she got out of the car, two men were walking through the gate. One wore a uniform, the other was in civvies.

Wright went over to them, threw out a hand. She wandered towards the front door, turned, folded her arms and waited for them to approach. The open door made her feel cold, as if she expected that somebody might still be in there, rooting through her life.

Wright saw her and said something, and the three of them walked over. She didn't wait for introductions. As they came up behind, she pushed the door open. Inside the porch, three of Donal's suits were lying on a potted geraniums.

'They must have left in a hurry,' Wright said, behind her.

She felt something under the heel of her left shoe, and only then noticed the broken window on the porch door.

'Could I ask you not to touch anything for the moment?' one of them said.

She walked on down the hall to the foot of the stairs. Her first concern was their bedroom, on the upper split. 'If you could give me a minute,' she said, to nobody in particular. She climbed the stairs, moving with caution.

Pushing open the bedroom door, she sensed that something was amiss. Clothes were strewn across the room and on the bed. An olive green suit of Donal's and one of her summer dresses were lying in a heap in front of her dressing-table.

She checked the walk-in wardrobe. The drawer just inside the door was open, exposing the empty space where her jewellery had been.

There was a knock on the door. Wright stuck his head around it as she left the wardrobe. 'Just checking you're OK,' he said. She nodded. She had asked for a minute but she hadn't meant it literally. He must have known that.

'Sloppy job,' he said, surveying the room.

'You sound disappointed.'

'Only by their standards. I think there's a digital box missing downstairs. Whenever you're ready.'

She took another look around the room. Deep down, she knew she wouldn't be coming back here. There was a sense of closure in the manner in which the burglars had left the room. It was no longer hers in anything but name, part of a life that had been whipped from her.

Downstairs, the kitchen was still more or less as she had left it. The inspector was over at the window, looking out on the bay. She couldn't see the other pair. She sat down on one of the long stools standing at the four sides of the island, which had been something of a clincher for her.

When she had first seen it, with its ceramic hobs, the extractor hood and fan overhead, domestic dreams had begun to foment in her mind. She saw kids lapping around her apron, as she welcomed Donal home. Now all she saw was half-baked notions to fill a hole where real plans should have been.

She took a tall glass from the overhead cabinet, ran the tap and filled it. When it was done she realised she didn't have any Solps. Panic gripped her for a moment. Calm down. This would be over in half an hour and she could nip down to the chemist.

The french windows leading to the patio were locked. The key was in the drawer, next to the sink, where she had kept pages of recipes cut out from the magazines in Sunday newspapers.

The key turned in the lock with reassuring ease. Once outside, the smell of the sea came over her, like a balm. She sat down on one of the oak chairs that formed part of the garden furniture set. Out in the bay, a passenger liner was heading towards the city.

Like much else with Donal, the buying of Skellig had occurred in jig time. They first viewed it on a Saturday. He was sold on it straight away. There was no argument about the interior. The history reeled him in. It had been built in the early 1890s by an absentee landlord, who resided in the English home counties. Since then it had been redeveloped a few times, the latest transformation having been effected less than a decade previously.

The house was bigger than anything Noelle had ever seen before. All of 3,700 square feet, according to the brochure. It was set behind large cut-stone walls, centred on a half-acre that rolled down towards the sea. A system of floodlights lit up the grounds. The ground floor held reception rooms and a kitchen the size of a house itself. Upstairs, there were four bedrooms, the master bedroom at the rear of the house having a sun terrace. Most of all, though, it had the feel of a home. The estate agent said the previous owners were a family who were relocating with work to Silicon Valley. Noelle could feel the warmth they left in their wake.

One of the nice features in the garden rolling down towards the sea, was an old Second World War bunker. According to the estate agent, the owner at the time was a wealthy English businessman who was known to be something of a recluse. He had the bunker built during the Emergency, as it was known, and had often been seen by neighbours retreating to spend nights there in case of attack. The bunker had survived the couple of redesigns and was now used as a wine cellar.

The agent filled them in on their neighbours. 'You know all about Bono and The Edge, I'm sure,' she said. Donal nodded. She went on to talk about Neil (Jordan), Eddie (Irvine) and Van, all of whom had made their home here. Lisa Stansfield was another celebrity they might get to call on for a spare teabag or whatever, but they'd want to hurry because she was moving back to England. The agent reminded them of Lisa's chart-topping hit, 'All Around The World'.

After that there was no talking to Donal. They repaired to the Killiney Bay Hotel to discuss things. Noelle said she thought gold handles in the loos were a bit over the top.

'Listen, babe, when in Killiney you have to wash like the Killinians do,' Donal said. The clincher for Donal happened as they were getting ready to leave. Bono and The Edge walked into the place and took a table across the room from theirs. Donal ordered more coffee. The two men sat down and moved into a conspiratorial huddle. A waiter brought them a pot of tea and a plate of triangular brown-bread sandwiches.

Noelle couldn't get over the sandwiches. 'Rock 'n' roll, how are you?' she said, but Donal was already blinded by the reflected glow.

Of course, they ended up offering what she considered to be well above the odds: €2.7 million. Donal wouldn't listen to her protests. Wasn't he the expert? Wasn't their wealth and good fortune built on his genius in the property market?

'What's a few hundred thousand here and there when measured against a home?' he said. Trust me, he said. So she did.

They had a party the week after they moved in. She was lukewarm to the idea, but Donal insisted on it. He wanted to announce to all and sundry that they had arrived on the Hill.

When it was too late, Donal discovered that the date for the shindig was the same as another birthday party in the neighbourhood. The latter was for a horse that was a favourite of the racecourse. Its owner was giving it the full birthday treatment, throwing a bash for the great and good of the horse world. So, as it turned out, only a few of the neighbours showed up at the Digginses' house-warming affair. There was no sign of Bono or even The Edge. Lisa was most likely gone home, Neil away filming. Donal didn't let the disappointment get to him. He had invited enough property developers to fill a small to middling convention centre and remarked that the absence of glitter from the bash would be compensated for by the gold, in the form of new business.

Later on, when only stragglers stood on the floodlit lawn, and the hired help scoured, in their monkey suits, for stray glasses and plates, she had sat on the decking to look at her new life. The pear trees on the patio fluttered in a night breeze. The lawn rolled down to the border, the shrubs and flowers looking, at this time of night, like blobs advancing towards the house. A shaft of light from the moon was boring into Dublin Bay below. She liked what she saw, the security of comfort, the signposts.

And now, what?, four years down the line, she could recall the nagging feeling she had at the time that something wasn't right.

'Great view,' a voice said behind her. She turned to see Inspector Wright's eyes on the bay. She wished to Christ he would stop complimenting the place.

Slate arrived early. It was a practised routine. Check out the place; find a quiet corner where piped music or the clatter of plates won't interfere with a recording; get comfortable.

The hotel was on the quays, one of those deals that were all the rage during the boom. Inside, the design was about squares and rectangles, done in shades of black and white. The chairs in the lobby were square on the seat and the backrest, big things that hadn't been designed for comfort.

He found a corner in the bar where the light was soft and low. Pan pipes sailed through the speakers on the wall, next to a large Knuttel. A waitress in black and white approached. She wore a welcoming face and a strong apron that looked as if it had been borrowed from a butcher's shop.

Slate ordered coffee and asked for the pan pipes to be turned down. He placed his mini recorder on the glass table, ran through the notes one more time. All that Fastneck had given him was that the woman was 'a classy bird', as he had recorded on the page. Her name was Ciara Savage and she had a tale to tell, which would bring the Diggins story on.

He saw them at the far end of the bar before they spotted

him. Fastneck had his left hand on her elbow, a man in charge, guiding his subject to the printed page.

He came over without bothering to offer any gesture. He whispered in the woman's ear. Slate rose to greet them.

'Alan, Ciara Savage.' Slate extended his right hand. A gold chain closed around the wrist. Her hand was soft to the touch, limp with caution. He could see why she would register as a classy bird with his editor. She reeked of easy money. Her copper hair was cut in a bob, framing a face that glowed with translucent skin. Her eyes were blue and ringed with just enough liner. She slipped out of a cotton coat to reveal a cream V-neck jumper that clung to her full figure. That and the indigo jeans made up the expensive casual look that was the preserve of serious money. Slate reckoned she was on the far side of forty but would have little trouble in shaving a decade off her age for the record.

The waitress hovered. Fastneck ordered a coffee without raising his head. Ciara Savage looked up and asked for an Earl Grey tea.

Fastneck took the reins. 'Now, Ciara, I just want you to know that I will be giving Alan's copy the once-over before publication so you needn't worry about any slips of the tongue.'

Ciara nodded and flashed a quick smile. Slate looked at his boss with what he hoped was injured innocence. Giving the copy the once-over?

'I've put Alan here on the story because he is our best reporter. Crime is his speciality and, Ciara, you have been the victim of a horrific crime. Alan is so good that I see him more as a crime fighter than just a crime reporter.'

Slate straightened in his chair, satisfied that the slight had been rectified. He reached over to the tape-recorder. 'Do you mind?' he said.

Ciara Savage looked to Fastneck for reassurance. He nodded, as if to a child unsure whether to proceed across the road.

Slate slipped into bedside-manner mode. 'Why don't we start at the start?' he said.

She did.

Ciara Savage told her story and, Slate had to admit, she had everything his boss was looking for in a victim. She was a mother of three. She was negotiating middle age with good grace and fortitude.

Ciara was married to Don. He worked in financial services, although times were tougher in that game now. Don had done well. The family lived in salubrious Foxrock. 'I suppose if somebody was looking at my life, they would have thought that I had everything,' she said.

Slate nodded. 'But you didn't.'

She raised her head and met his eyes. 'There was something missing, some big empty space at the centre of my life.'

'A God-shaped hole,' Slate said.

'A what?'

'A God-shaped hole. It's . . . just a cliche' He could see that Fastneck was not impressed.

'I'm not religious.' Her face had melted into confusion.

'Oh, no, I'm not saying you are. It's just something I heard to describe people who feel that something is missing in their lives but can't put their finger on it.'

'I knew what was missing. I wasn't looking for God.'

Slate said, 'I'm sorry, I shouldn't have introduced God. What does He know about property? Why don't we get to the point where you met Donal Diggins?'

She took a sip from her coffee. 'Well, it was my friend Shauna. She knew how I felt. She had been through the same trauma. Her remedy had been to have an affair, but that turned out to be a disaster. Then she came across Diggins with his dreams for sale. Shauna had bought a pad in Portugal through him a few months after the disastrous affair ended.

'She said I should never underestimate the value of retail therapy. I mean, hello, it's not as if I was a stranger to a binge in Brown Thomas, but she said this was different, that I needed something that would deliver more than just instant gratification.'

'That's interesting.'

'Yes.'

Slate and Fastneck swapped glances.

She turned to Fastneck. 'I don't want this written in a way that makes me look like a bored housewife who thought buying property would bring some excitement into her life.'

'Of course not.'

'Because that's not what happened.'

'What did happen?' Slate said.

'I wish you'd stop interrupting me,' she said. Slate inched back in his seat, conceding ground. Keep talking, baby. You're doing just fine.

'Anyway, Donal Diggins was conducting one of his seminars in a hotel up by the airport. We went along. It was very impressive. You were greeted at the door with a glass of Dom Pérignon and canapés. There were a lot of attractive young women hovering around and a number of, I suppose, what you would call stands.'

'Stands?'

'Like at a fair or a festival, except these stands were selling money. All the banks were there, as far as I could see. And there were a few I didn't know. At the top of the room there was a large overhead projector, and all along the walls they had put these huge photos of the most wonderful beaches you could imagine. I mean, the sand was practically golden, set against palm trees and stuff, like the start of a jungle. And the sea looked divine. In a few of the photos there were these shantytown places, with little huts at the side of a road. It was kind of cute. Except there were no people in these shots. That was the first time I saw the Cape.'

Fastneck had been nodding his way through her story. Now he looked at Slate.

'The Cape?'

'Yes, that's what we called it, the Cape. Cape Isis.'

'Paradise found,' Slate said.

'And in the background they were playing this African music – you know, a low drum thingy and a high-pitched voice, that kind of stuff. It was easy on the ear, not like the pan pipes we have to put up with in places like this. But the most impressive part, and in a way it kills me now to say this, was the man himself. You know when somebody sort of emits a glow, a kind of combination of sex and charisma and just sheer magnetism?'

Fastneck straightened, as if he expected her to put him forward as an example. 'Yeah, I suppose so.'

'That was Donal Diggins. Catch his eye for the briefest moment and he made you feel like you were the only person in the room. He just exuded it, especially with all that music and the images of the Cape. He was like a tribal chief in a Louis Copeland suit.

'Anyway, after greeting everybody and doing his mingling thing, he took the controls at the top of the room. By then I was on my third glass of Dommy, as I'd say most in the room were, so the atmosphere was very good. He started off by welcoming us, *yada, yada, yada*, and then he got into why we simply had to buy property. I got a bit lost at this stage, but the way he played around with the figures and the country and what-have-you, the gist of it was that you would be, like, really stupid if you didn't get into the market. The one phrase I remember from it all was "releasing the equity".'

'Releasing the equity?'

'Yes. He was saying you were completely brain dead if you

didn't release the equity from your home. He made it sound as if the equity was something you were hiding under the bed. He said it was dead money, and you had to release it to make it work for you.'

Slate was about to launch into his own experience, how he had avoided the rush, how he had left his equity at home, alone and undisturbed, but he stopped himself, and then congratulated himself. 'It sounds persuasive,' he said.

'It was. By then, he was coming across like a champion Zen Buddhist, spreading wealth and peace.' She threw her eyes to the ceiling, brought back to a day when she had been seduced by booze and charm. She took a sip of her tea, and looked up again. 'Then he introduced the Cape. The music was put back on and a whole series of slides came up on the projector. The place looked even better on the slides. He said it was the new frontier. Let me get this right. It was a place where the dreams of the property buyer met and married the dreams of the Paradise seeker. Well, I can tell you, after all that champers, I thought Shauna was going to have an orgasm there on the seat beside me.

'The thing he kept pushing was we were discovering the place for the first time. That was his great line. He said we would be like that guy, the saint who took off in his little boat across the world. St Jude, is it?'

'He's the saint for hopeless causes.'

Fastneck spoke up through a dry throat: 'St Brendan is the one, I think. He was the explorer.'

'That's him, except Donal Diggins made him sound a lot more exciting than just a saint. Of course, I signed up on the spot.'

'Who wouldn't?' Slate said.

'For four apartments.'

'Four?'

'That was the other thing. He made the point that it wasn't worth your while buying just one. He said that would be like winning a bit of a lotto instead of the whole thing.'

'Who was there, Ciara?' Fastneck said, his voice dropping to the level of a concerned doctor.

'Pardon me?'

'The people in the room? Who did you see?'

'Oh, yes, I forgot that bit. When I went in there first, there was this man, a scary creature. He was dressed in a grey suit, navy silk shirt and a striped burgundy tie, very noticeable. He was with a younger man, could have been his son. I overheard him a few times calling the younger guy Rocco. You remember a name like that. There were also a few policemen there.'

'Security?'

'No, no. They were there to buy the dream themselves. It was just last week or so when I read in the paper about one of those shootings. There were photographs. It showed the man who was shot, although he wasn't killed. And there was a picture of the garda who was in charge of the investigation. I thought, Now that is some coincidence. Both of those men were in the room that day.'

She picked up her handbag from the floor and fished out a folded piece of newspaper. She gave it to Slate. It was a clipping from one of the dailies, the attempted murder of Junior Corbett. A large photograph showed the crime scene with the blue and white tape and everything. And there were two headshots on each side of the main picture. One was of the intended target, Junior Corbett. The other was of the garda leading the investigation, Inspector Phil Wright.

'It's amazing, isn't it?' Ciara said. 'The two of them on opposite sides of the law but brought together by Donal Diggins to buy the dream.'

Inspector Phil Wright and the two local boys were standing beside Wright's Mondeo. The uniform was scribbling in his notebook. The detective was futhering at the crushed shells with the Hush Puppy on his right foot.

'Any ideas, lads?' Wright said. The detective buried his hands in his trouser pockets. 'No self-respecting pro would have walked out without the suits,' he said.

The uniform said, 'I couldn't see junkies making it in here past the alarm.'

'You know who she is,' Wright said.

The uniform spoke first: 'Do I what? I've been outside at least three times last week with the media. The place only calmed down in the last few days. Neighbours were getting antsy about their privacy.'

'They know how to live out here, don't they?' Wright said.

'It's their world, we just exist in it.'

'Keep them safe in their beds at night.'

'You said it.'

'So they can get up in the morning and figure out new ways to make shedloads of money.'

Wright said, 'You think this is about her old man?'

'Are you on the husband's case, Inspector?'

Wright met his eyes. 'I've been asked to check out a few angles on it. Give me a few minutes with her. The technical boys will be here soon.'

He walked back into the house, along the corridor. He couldn't help giving himself the once-over in the television-sized mirror..

Noelle Diggins was locking the french windows as he entered the kitchen. She walked over to the island and dropped the key into a drawer.

'We'll have to prepare a full inventory of what's missing,' he said. She nodded. Wright looked at her. She could easily know more than she was letting on.

'It's a strange case,' he said.

'Strange how?'

'Having had a look around, I can't see junkies finding a way in here. Whoever it was knew what they were doing.'

'And?' She walked towards the fireplace, her back to him.

'And why leave stuff behind? Like the suits. Anyway, the fingerprints boys will be here soon.'

She ran her hand along the top of the mantelpiece.. "There was a photograph..."

"Why would burglars take a photo, Mrs Diggins? If you know anything that might be of assistance, now is the time to tell me.'

She turned to face him. He noticed the colour rising in her cheeks. 'Now I really am confused, Inspector.'

'If there's anything missing that might point to a link to your husband.'

'Excuse me, but what exactly are you saying? My husband has some issues about his business that need to be processed. And you appear to be trying to connect him to a robbery. Maybe, Inspector, you're getting confused with *The Bill*.'

'No confusion, Mrs Diggins. This may not be the best time to fill you in, but your husband wasn't too bothered on who he did business with.'

'That's a serious allegation.'

'I know. And some unsavoury people have been left out of pocket. They are very anxious to find him.'

12

They released Molloy at 3.12 p.m. He saw the exact time on the clock in Reception as he walked through the door, out into the day. At the bottom of the stone steps, he paused. The traffic on the North Circular Road was light. Any passing car could be carrying a bullet for him. If it was, there was precious little he could do about it now.

He turned right and began walking towards Phibsboro. A man pushing a buggy and holding a little girl's hand walked past. He and Molloy exchanged glances. He looked like he knew his way around the inside of a cop shop.

They could have held him for the rest of the day, but what would have been the point? Both he and they knew it was going nowhere. Once the inspector took off with Molloy's solicitor, the steam went out of it. It was one for the books. His solicitor takes the cop out of the picture to sort out a burglary in her home. They had nothing more than phone calls and putting him on the same street a few hours before Sullivan was shot. The DPP would laugh them out of his office.

The sun was on his back now, reminding him that he hadn't showered since yesterday. He felt dirty, jumpy, all over the shop. What he needed most right now was a meeting.

He walked past the entrance to the prison. How different would things be now if he'd done his stint in there? His only experience of the Joy was the three months he put down over that thick motor-insurance rap, when he was nineteen. It wasn't too bad. He knew a lot of heads in there, but the time crawled. There was little in the way of work or even distraction for somebody on a short sentence. His only memory was of lying on a top bunk, staring at the ceiling, willing away the chain of minutes.

If he'd done his four years there, he might have been a big shot now, climbing up the ladder like that poor useless fucker Harms Sullivan. He might even have his own crew. He wouldn't be sober and clean. The fear would be with him bigger than ever. He would be all but dead inside, waiting for somebody to call time on his life. Which, when he thought about it, was where he was at right now. But at least he could still feel.

At Phibsboro Cross, he passed in front of Doyle's Pub just as a stooped man was coming through the door. Currents of beer blew out into his path like incense. There was an answer in there. He could, for a few hours, put it all to bed. He stopped and tried to breathe in the beer, but it was gone now. First of all, he'd deal with the hunger. See where things go.

Outside Abrakebabra, he pulled the smokes from his jacket pocket. He put fire to a Marlboro, watching the traffic queuing at the lights, engines idling, fumes thick in the air. It bugged the shit out of him that he had to smoke on the street like some class of a hobo. The smoking ban had only just come in when went away. He didn't think for a minute it would last. The notion that you couldn't smoke in pubs, restaurants, even taxis was bananas. When he came back and found that the whole country was going along with it, he knew the place was fucked.

A woman passed him, trailing three kids, two girls and a boy. The boy was kitted out in the red of Manchester United. He couldn't have been more than five. Molloy had never much noticed kids before. He stopped himself tapping the woman's shoulder to ask the price of the jerseys. Dynamo Westwood might have gear for kids that young.

Abrakebabra was empty, save the two heads behind the counter. One was Asian, most likely from a place where kebabs were a staple. The other was a pimply kid, his face as pale as a sheet. He wore a paper hat of green and red.

Molloy walked to the counter opposite the kid. He ordered a doner meal, with 7-Up and slid into the booth at the very end, his back to the wall, where he had a good view of the door. The Kings of Leon came out of the speakers. The kid began sawing meat from the spit, taking his time, careful to get his slices right. Molloy wondered how he felt about the hat. He knew he would wear no hat if he ever had to work in a place like this. It was going too far.

Ivan wore a hat once. His brother was just fourteen when he pulled a gig in Charlie's Chinese back home. Molloy knew his brother's exact age because word came through about the job on the same day that he arrived home with the under-13 cup for the west Dublin leagues. Ma was already sick by then, but she got out of bed to celebrate all the good news.

Ivan brought home the dinner from Charlie's and they sat around the table, the three of them, like they did before the cancer began to eat away at Ma. The air was thick with chow mein and sweet and sour. The fluorescent tube in the ceiling was fading, and the TV required a belt now and again to light up the picture. But for an hour at least that evening they were a family again, insulated from all the shit outside their door.

It was only when they finished the meal, and Ma moved

to sit before the TV, that it dawned on Molloy she had hardly asked about the game. It was Ivan, Ivan, Ivan, the boy with a job, the boy who was going to make something of himself, get out of the war zone. You'd swear he'd just landed a number running Guinness, instead of taking food orders for three fifty an hour.

Sure, Ma patted him on the back, said, 'Well done in the game.' But she didn't ask about any details, or how he'd played, or what the day meant to his dreams. Football was only a game, whereas Ivan was opening up new prairies of hope.

He went out that night to meet up with a few of the lads on the team. They slugged from plastic flagons of Strongbow under the stars. But celebration was beyond his reach. He knew things weren't right, but he didn't know what was wrong. Only when he began raking over the past in recent months had it dawned on him that he'd been running even then, the fear tapping at his ankles.

A couple of days later he and a few mates, Bandy Maguire and Adam Lynam, were hanging out at the shops. One of the lads noticed Ivan behind the counter inside the window of Charlie's Chinese, taking orders in the paper hat. They began making faces through the glass at him. Molloy slipped out of his brother's line of sight, but the two boys kept at it, switching between calling Molloy over, and pulling silly faces at his brother.

When he returned to drag them away, he could see that Ivan was trying hard to ignore them, but there was thunder on his face. It was all he could do to stop himself coming out and kicking the heads off them.

'That brother of yours, Dancer, he looks the business in his hat,' Bandy said.

'Yeah, if he keeps going at this rate he'll make it all the way to the circus,' Lynam said.

Molloy didn't say anything. He knew that when he got home, Ivan would give him a few digs, maybe, get in his ear about hanging out with those wasters. He knew he should tell the lads to quit, but he couldn't defend his brother's submitting to the system. Come what may, he was never going to wear a hat for the fuckers.

Bandy Maguire died in a car crash when he was nineteen. Molloy had lost touch with him by then, but he'd gone to the funeral. Lynam never worked a day in his life. He did a few short stretches for thieving, and somewhere along the way, the gear got ahold of him and eventually shook the life from him. Molloy didn't know where he was now and had no wish to look him up.

Ivan got out. He was living in Kerry, about as far as he could get from Westwood. He served his time as a wood-turner. He married a girl he met while still in Dublin. They had two kids now, both boys, and Ivan said there was no way he was raising boys in the city.

They kept in touch, but there was no bonding. Any time they met before Molloy went away, awkwardness hung between them like a curtain. Ivan never asked him what he was doing for a crust. He didn't have to.

And when Ivan was eking out a living as an apprentice, Molloy offered to give him a dig-out a few times. Ivan just shook his head, said he would beat his own path.

Ivan was the only person who visited him inside. He flew over to Portsmouth and came across to the prison. He often sent newspapers. Molloy didn't tell him about it, and Ivan never asked. There was a vague invitation to visit in Kerry but, without saying it, both of them thought it best to leave it for a while.

He was making short work of the kebab. The sauce was on his fingers, sticky and warm. He reached over and lifted a napkin from the tray. When he looked up, Johnny Cash was walking towards him, his gait unhurried, a blank expression on his face. He wore a black leather jacket that fell in a long style over his legs, a black polo neck and black slacks. His hands were by his sides.

Molloy began to slide from the seat. Cash raised his hands, out wide, where they could be seen. Then he tamped them down into the air, telling Molloy to stay sitting. 'You don't think I'd walk in here in broad daylight to kiss you goodbye?' he said. Molloy could barely hear him above the music. The Killers: 'Human?'

Cash slid into the seat opposite. Molloy saw him up close for the first time. His receding hair was the colour of iron filings, swept back and kept in place with a tub of gel. He had a drinking head, flushed pallor, watery eyes and a nose he might have borrowed from a clown. Deep crevices ran across his forehead. For a second, he looked vulnerable, a man with his own struggles. Then he set his mouth, focused his eyes on Molloy and struck the pose that was his bread and butter.

'What did they want with you?' Cash said.

Molloy dipped a chip into a little mound of salt he had spilled on to a napkin. 'Usual shite,' he said.

The kid in the hat came upon their table. Cash looked up at him and shook his head. The kid stopped for a minute, a question forming on his face. He looked at Cash but whatever he saw told him to go back behind the counter.

'I'm gonna ask you nicely, just on account of the relationship you have with us. Understand? What specifically did they want with you?'

Molloy chewed his chip, reached for another. Cash grabbed his wrist. 'Are you deaf?'

'No, I'm hungry,' Molloy said. He thought he noticed the colour in Cash's face deepen. He pulled his wrist free, took a chip, salted it and slowly placed it in his mouth. He met Cash's gaze head on.

'I think, perhaps, you may not be aware of the situation we have here,' Cash said. He bent low in towards Molloy. There was a whiff of stale booze on his breath.

'Your sentence has only been suspended, Molloy. Junior was in a generous mood when he let you live, way too generous by my reckoning. But now if I have to report back that you ain't keeping to the conditions, well, that will be too bad. Do you understand me, fuck-head?'

All of the chips were gone. Molloy felt like he still had a hole in his stomach. He took a sip from his 7-Up. There was a palm tree drawn in green on the white paper cup, as if they were in some exotic location, a different world from Phibsboro. If the chance ever arose to kick the head off this prick, he would take it with both hands.

'The way I remember it, Junior didn't do me because I may be of some help to him,' Molloy said.

Cash swung his head around, as if to reassure himself that nobody was within earshot. Molloy watched him. He was no Johnny Cash, but he could have passed for John fucking Wayne with ham acting like that. 'I'll ask once more. What did they want?'

'They wanted to know who was behind the botched job on Junior,' Molloy said, now looking closer at the other man. He thought he detected something, a twitch, maybe of fear, but perhaps that was just wishful thinking.

'What did you tell them?'

'What I told Junior. I was dragged into it. I know nothing about who was behind it. But I'll tell you one thing. I'd like to know, because whoever it was has landed me in a whole heap of shit.'

'What about Sullivan, your partner in crime? Did they ask about him?'

'They wanted to know who killed him. They had somehow got the notion that I had something to do with it.'

'What did you tell them?'

'I put them right on me not being the shooter. And I told them that whoever organised the job on Junior, he must have been the one that did Harms Sullivan. But they knew that already. Their only problem is figuring out who that could be.'

He thought he saw a bead of sweat on Cash's forehead. But then it was gone. Sweat, you fucker, sweat, just like you've made me sweat.

Cash said, 'And who do you reckon that could be?'

'Oh, I haven't an clue, man. I'm just back in town. What do I know? People are playing games, shooting and getting shot, and I'm trying to make a fresh start. What do I know?'

'OK, you live for now.'

'Go fuck yourself.'

'That situation can be revised very easily. Now, about your part of the bargain. We need to speed things up.'

'I'm doing what I can.'

'It's time you did a little more.'

'Like what? Tie her to the chair in her office and beat it out of her?'

'I bet you'd like that.'

'All I can do is keep my eyes and ears open. She's cagey. She's been through a lot.'

'Whoa. She's been through a lot? Well, looky here, the man is coming over all sympathetic. Listen, fella, she and her husband stole Junior's money. When people do that, my job is to get it back, put down a marker, and just make sure the thief's stealing days are done. Now, you are going to help me, or else ...'

Molloy raised his hand to get the attention of the kid in the hat. The kid began walking over.

'What's this?' Cash said.

'I'm getting a coffee.'

'Are you fuck. We have somewhere to go and I'm not waiting all day.'

The kid arrived at the table. He didn't look too comfortable.

'Coffee,' Molloy said.

Cash kept his eyes on Molloy. 'Forget it,' Cash said. The corners of Molloy's mouth curled in defiance. He was about to say something, when Cash said, 'This man has some family to see.'

Molloy put fisted hands on the table. The kid in the hat just stood there, as if waiting for a riposte. Molloy nodded at him and he shuffled off.

'Now, you behave yourself, because I've asked Stephanie to meet you and see what might be done about you getting acquainted with your son. But if you act the bollocks in any way, I can't be responsible for how she might react, either towards you or the brat. Do you understand what I'm saying?'

Something cold was travelling through Molloy's body, moving fast. 'Where is she?'

Cash leaned across the table. 'Be a good boy and everything will work out fine.'

The motor was parked on Leinster Street, around the corner from the Phibsboro shopping centre. It was a BMW X3 with the windows blacked out. Cash pulled out and eased into the traffic heading out of town on the N2. The radio was tuned into RTÉ 1, somebody blabbering on about gardening.

Molloy reached into his jacket for smokes. Cash looked across at him and shook his head. 'No smoking in the vehicle,' he said.

'Jesus Christ, this smoking ban has gone to everybody's head. You smoke, what's the problem?'

'I'm not having this baby stinking,' he said, his left hand

reaching out to caress the dashboard. Molloy saw something protruding from the ashtray. He pulled it open. Inside there was a three butts on a bed of ash. He looked across at Cash.

'That's emergency stuff. I smoke in the car in times of extreme stress. Otherwise you can forget about it.'

Molloy pressed a button to lower the window. A gush of air hit the left side of his face. 'So, how did you end up with Junior?' he said.

Cash looked startled, as if the question had come from somewhere beyond the bounds of their business. He remained silent for a few seconds. 'You remember Tommy Summers? Had an operation over on the southside.'

'Never came across him, but I heard of him. He copped it a good few years back.'

'I worked with Tommy. He got careless. Started stepping on the wrong toes, pushing people.'

'Who killed him?'

'Who do you think?'

'So you went to work for the conqueror.'

'That's what they did in the Roman times. The fellas who lost out, they killed the top man and those further down the chain went to work for the conqueror.'

'Did you get a free toga from Junior?'

Cash didn't react, kept his eyes on the road, as if he was happy thinking about the time in question.

Molloy fiddled with his hands. He really could have done with a smoke. 'And what about when Junior cops it? Will you go to work for the new man again?'

Cash looked over at him. Molloy kept his eyes on the road. A camper van was ahead of them, two bicycles tied to it. Cash threw back his head and laughed, but the sound was hollow. 'You mean if you'd got to plug Junior would I come working for you?'

'It wasn't me organised the hit. Whoever it was, they wanted

Junior out of the picture. Just wondering would you have gone working for the new guy.'

The signature tune for the news filled the car. A woman introduced herself and set off in a solemn tone. A man had died in the Mater Hospital following an early-morning stabbing incident outside a pub on the Luas red line. Another man had died earlier. The station's crime correspondent reported, 'The scene has been sealed off for forensic examination,' he said. 'Gardaí are appealing to witnesses to come forward. It is understood that a Luas train full of passengers was passing as the stabbings occurred. So far, there have been three anonymous calls from witnesses who said they were on the train. Two witnesses have described the killer as a young man wearing a Liverpool football jersey.'

Cash was looking at the radio, the lines on his face stretched, his eyes wide.

'What the fuck?'

'I know a guy wears a Liverpool jersey,' Molloy said.

'Lots of people wear Liverpool jerseys.'

'Yeah, but the fella I know struck me as a psychopath. Must be him.'

'Shut it.'

In fifteen minutes, they were pulling into a housing estate on the western fringes of the city. Cash drove deeper into the estate. Kids playing football stopped to stare at the BMW.

Eventually, the car eased down a road that looked to be going nowhere. Nearly every other house was boarded up with plywood or rusting corrugated iron. Cash pulled in at the second but last, before the road ran into a large green steel fence. Beyond it lay fields with little mounds of concrete rubble rising like landmines.

Cash tooted on the horn, and stepped from the car. The smokes were out of Molloy's pocket by the time his feet touched the road. He put fire to a stick as he closed the door.

He followed Cash, who was walking down a path of cracked concrete slabs towards the front door. They went into what might once have been a front room. A sheet of plywood over the window kept out the light. The only furniture was a couple of upturned milk crates. The floor was bare concrete, with loose patches of dark linoleum, most of it under a film of dust. There was a vague smell of shit, either human or animal. Molloy's eyes adjusted to the darkness.

A figure moved out from a door at the far end and a woman walked towards them. A rain jacket and sweat pants fell loose against her body, her hair hung below her shoulders in stringy mats. Molloy felt a stab as he recognised her.

'OK, take a few minutes to get reacquainted,' Johnny Cash said. 'I'll be outside, Steph. If lover boy here gets out of order, just shout.'

They waited until Cash's footsteps faded from hearing. She looked to be in bad shape, but her mouth was set at a defiant angle, as if she was determined to hold on to her dignity. She had lost weight, scaled down from a size twelve to size junkie.

'You were looking for me,' she said. 'Here I am.' She pulled a box of John Player Blue from the pocket of her jacket. When she flicked on the lighter, he could see that her eyes were hooded in dark sockets.

'How have you been?'

A cackle trying to sound like a laugh escaped her mouth. She shrugged and looked somewhere into the distance where there would be no fear of eye contact.

'Managing. It's not easy with a son and a habit. I get by.'

'How long?'

'Don't get all high and mighty with me. How long? How long have you been a lush? How long were you inside?'

She had never been into the gear. Coke was always her twist. Coke and Bacardi and Coke. The combination kept her up and kept the party going. And, man, she could party.

He could still recall the rush he got the first time he laid eyes on her. One evening he entered the Silver Topper on Junior Corbett's coat tails. There had been about six of them, all going for a pint after taking charge of half a ton of weed that had come in through Dublin port.

They were his family, all in the game together, making a better life for themselves, walking on air. Whenever they entered a pub or club, he could feel the frisson run through the place, like a current of electricity. Here were the local boys made good. Come and get a piece of the action.

Stephanie did all the running that night. She walked up to him as if it was a dare, but she knew what she wanted. She'd always known what she wanted.

She brought him back to her place that first night. They shared each other with six cans of Carlsberg and a bag of weed. The night ended in a blur, but they fucked their way through the far side of a hangover the following morning.

Some of the boys took the piss afterwards. Women on top. Was he as much into domination in the sack as he was out of it? None of it bothered him. She was doing something for him, making inroads into the big hole inside, keeping the fear at bay.

She was working as a receptionist at a gym in the city centre but packed that in soon after they moved in together. He rented a place, semi-d on a new estate in Blanch. Among her stuff, he always remembered the seven pairs of boots she brought with her. That, and an old padded chair that her grandmother had handed down as an heirloom. Molloy wondered where the hell it might be now.

For a while, he felt as if he was on the lower rungs to stability, but the sauce kept getting in the way. And she was no angel either. The baby wasn't planned. Nothing was planned beyond the next party.

'I want to see my son,' he said.

'Alexander is getting on fine without you.'

'I'm entitled to see him. I've gone to a solicitor.'

She exhaled, her mouth tilted towards the cracked ceiling, a perfect column of smoke rising before dissipating into the air. It was a gesture plucked straight from his memory, one that had always stirred him, that eat-shit-and-die pose of hers. Right now, he didn't feel anything.

'That's up to me. I'm the one rearing him. Where were you when I needed a hand?'

'You know where I was,' he said.

'Yeah. Coming back here, starting trouble, trying to shoot Junior. When did you become such a big noise?'

'Where's the boy?'

She exhaled slowly. 'He's safe. Safe from you, anyways.'

Molloy nodded towards the door. 'And safe from that cunt?'

'Johnny takes care of me. I just do what he says and there's no problem.'

'Yeah, he tells you when you have to suffer and when he'll take the pain away.'

Her arm shot out, the cigarette burning between her fingers. She began shouting. 'Just who the fuck do you think you are, looking down on me? On me? The likes of you? How's the view from up there, you bastard? You think you're better than me? Me?'

Johnny Cash appeared at the doorway. His right hand was by his side, holding a gun. 'OK, that's enough,' he said. 'Leave it, Steph. I'll deal with this.' She half turned, pulled furiously on her cigarette and spat out the smoke.

Cash said, 'We need results, Molloy. We are dealing with serious issues here, and we need to know what's going on. You get the see the kid when you deliver. Not before.'

Molloy felt his fists balling. He didn't trust himself. He turned and walked through the door. He was on to the road when she called from behind him. She walked up, dropped the remains of the cigarette on the path and put her foot on it. She looked pale in the light of the day, even thinner than when she had been set against shadows. She pressed a piece of paper into his hand and spoke in a low, soft voice:

'Ring me. I'll see what I can do,' she said. 'He asks about his daddy. He knows there's something missing.'

Johnny Cash appeared at the door. 'OK, let's go, Molloy.'

Molloy turned away from him. 'I'm walking,' he said.

13

Junior was pumping iron when the twins arrived at Corbett's Motors. They walked out of the morning rain through the mouth of the garage, from the light of the day into a windowless cave.

Junior was at the back, in a corner lit by a naked bulb on a lamp-stand. There was a radio playing somewhere. Wallpaper pop music sailed through the air, mingling with the waft of engine oil. There was a leg-press machine back there and a simple bench, where Junior was now panned out, the weighted bar rising and falling above his chest to the sound of steady grunts. You didn't disturb Junior when he was working out.

Rocco and Kyle moved towards the office. Rocco had on his Dublin jersey. After that business outside the early house, Rocco made Kyle burn the Liverpool strip, much as it killed Kyle to do so. Now Kyle was wearing the yellow away strip. He didn't yet have the one with Jamie Carragher's name on the back, but he was working on it.

The office consisted of nothing more than a few square

metres of floor space, cordoned off with dirty yellow sheetrock sitting on aluminium frames and a plywood door, the top half paned glass.

In the office, Johnny Cash was sitting on the desk, holding a tabloid newspaper. His eyes narrowed when the twins walked through the door. Rocco met his stare. Kyle kept his eyes on the girlie calendar behind the desk. The only outstanding feature in the office was a reindeer dressed as Santa Claus. He was standing on his hind legs in the corner at the rear, where Junior had put him one Christmas after an impulsive purchase in a Henry Street market. The reindeer had since lost an eye and his Santa tunic had seen better days.

Johnny had on his long leather coat and black Levi's, but he was wearing a grey silk shirt. Rocco wondered about the grey. It wasn't like Johnny to mess around with his colours. Maybe somebody had died.

Kyle closed the door behind them. Johnny Cash held up the tabloid, exhibit A. 'You've made the front page,' he said. 'Two easy lessons on how to be a grade-one muppet.' The headline was in black lettering: 'MURDER IN MORNING RUSH HOUR'. A line underneath read, 'Gangland motive suspected for stabbings outside pub'. Johnny Cash said, 'I like the gangland-motive bit. What was the motive, Kyle? Did one of them look at you sideways?'

Kyle was focusing on Miss March. She was bent all the way over, nearly touching the ground with the fingers of her left hand, a fuel pump in her right, all set for some action. 'They were dissing me big time, Johnny, trying to draw me out. You wouldn't have put up with it.'

Cash's face melted into mock sympathy. 'Tell your uncle Johnny how you went all Crocodile Dundee with that Falcon of yours. Oh, and please, please tell me it's been disposed of.'

Rocco came in here, swinging a life-raft for his brother. 'The knife is gone, and there won't be any witnesses.'

Johnny Cash raised the newspaper again. 'Apart from a trainload of passengers.'

'Nobody's going to be a hero.'

'You're beginning to sound like you approve of little brother acting the fucking eejit.'

Rocco shifted on his feet. He was looking at Johnny's crocodile-skin loafers. The fella always had great footwear, but he'd better go easy. There was only so far Kyle could be pushed. Cash must know by now he hated being called the little brother. Kyle had been out first, a good two minutes before Rocco entered the world. He said, 'You'd be hard pressed to find a bigger prick than Landy Towers' brother.'

The door opened and Junior walked in. His bald pate glistened with sweat. He was wearing a T-shirt and sweat pants and was shod in Nike Airs. A towel covered his left shoulder, falling down on a tattoo of a coiled mermaid on his forearm. He was carrying a large plastic bottle of water. He didn't offer any greeting. Johnny Cash got off the desk, and Junior sat in behind it. He uncapped the bottle and drew long from it. 'You have the laptop,' he said.

'It's in the car,' Rocco said. 'Kyle, get the computer, will you?' He pulled keys from his pocket and handed them to his brother. He waited for Kyle to leave and shut the door behind him before speaking again. 'Junior, it shouldn't have happened, but they were really asking for it.'

Junior raised his right hand, signalling that either he didn't want to hear any explanation or none was necessary. He picked up a magazine from the desk. Rocco knew what it was. By now the whole city knew what it was. Junior and the crew, including the twins, on holiday in Spain. Pages of photographs of the partying. Rocco wondered whether Junior's wife had said anything about the hookers. The last thing anybody needed right now was Junior losing the rag.

Junior looked up at Rocco. 'You've a starring role in here,' he said. Johnny Cash was trying to keep a smirk from his face. He hadn't come on that trip.

'Want us to do something about it?' Rocco said.

'Like what?'

'The reporter. He shouldn't be let get away with that shit.'

Junior Corbett threw the magazine on to the table. 'My first priority is getting my money back. Now, apart from those games you play, I presume what you know about computers would fit on the back of an envelope.'

'I never done it in school, Junior.'

'And Johnny here is no Bill Gates.'

'Who?'

'Forget it. That college kid who does business with you?'

'Fionn? Yeah, he knows about computers, told me he did a course on it.'

'Well, let's find out. If there's answers to what I'm looking for in that laptop, I need to know about it. Go and fetch him.'

Kyle walked through the door with a canvas bag. He put it on the table. 'Junior, that thing with Landy Towers' brother …'

Junior gave Kyle a look that could have been a box in the ear. His hand went north again. 'Leave it for the moment. I need to think about what to do.'

The twins left. Johnny Cash walked to the door of the office, watched the pair exit the garage. 'The shit is flying already, from all directions,' he said. 'Towers is hopping mad and the law is under serious pressure. They all want a body.'

Junior lifted the bottle of water from the desk, swivelled in his chair, looked up at the one-eyed reindeer. 'I can't afford to lose Rocco,' he said. He drew from the bottle. 'He's got a brain, which is a rare enough commodity.'

'Separating him from Kyle won't be easy.' Johnny was looking out at the garage, where there was plenty of nothing going on.

'It will need a bit of sensitive handling.' Junior was focused on the reindeer. He couldn't remember how the fucker had lost his eye.

Cash said, 'You're looking at Mr Sensitive.'

'If Rocco ever gets wind of this ...'

'He won't.'

'OK. We need to nip it in the bud before everybody starts shooting.'

Cash turned back towards his boss. 'Just let them sort out the laptop guy. I need a few days. I've promised Esther a break in Torremolinos.'

Junior looked up at him. 'You and the missus?'

'Yeah, it's a pain in the hole, but she's been on my case since Christmas. Nothing's going to happen for a few days. When I get back, I'll handle the stuff with Kyle. Sensitively.'

Junior nodded. 'Might be time to bring an end to the Dancer's last waltz too. He's not producing, and it bugs me that he's still walking around after what he tried to pull.'

Cash walked over to the desk. 'Glad you've finally copped that. I would have done him on day one.'

Junior took a key from his pocket, slotted it into a hole in the right of his desk. He fingered around inside the drawer for a few seconds and his hand came out with eight fifties. He laid them on the table. 'Enjoy yourself. We've a lot on our plate once you get back.'

Johnny Cash scooped up the money. He thanked Junior and left. Junior finished the bottle of water, swivelled once more to regard the reindeer. He sat there for a while, figuring things out. He reached over to the desk, picked up his mobile and began tapping out a number.

Alan Slate pulled into the car park of the Yacht public house in Clontarf. It was a bitch of a day. Rain was beating down steadily at an angle, wind whipping in from the bay. There were only two other vehicles parked. The lunchtime surge was still the guts of two hours away. He killed the engine, but before long, the chill had permeated the interior of the Avenger AX.

He kicked the ignition into life again, turned up the heating. On the radio, they were having a discussion on who exactly was to blame for the collapse of the economy.

Presently the figure of Inspector Phil Wright appeared in the doorway of the pub. He looked out and spotted Slate through the driving rain. He moved across the car park, bent low against the elements. 'That's a cat and a dog of a day,' he said, as he sat in. Slate could smell whiskey. 'A day to be warming the cockles.'

'Much happening,' Slate said, like a man who had just unpacked his fishing rod. He was surprised that Wright was drinking at this hour.

'Divil a bit,' Wright said. 'Just talking inside there to a fella whose business went down the Swanee. Had to lay off ten men and now he's thinking of heading for Australia. There's plenty like him. We had a grand little country here, Alan, and they fucked the whole thing up. That magazine of yours got it right. The whole place is upside down right now.'

Slate didn't bother correcting him this time. A couple were framed in the pub's doorway, looking out on the rain with trepidation. Slate imagined them to be engaged on an illicit tryst. They were leaving the pub now for some rock 'n' roll in a friend's apartment.

He was feeling frisky. Things hadn't yet taken off with Karen Small at the magazine. He had had to cancel their first date when the blood was flowing on the street. They were due to meet again tonight.

'So, what's all this about Cape Isis?' Wright said. The name of the island slipped off his tongue with easy familiarity.

When Slate had rung the previous evening, Wright hadn't

been very communicative, deploying the caution that Slate noticed was routine for most cops he contacted these days. Then he mentioned the Cape, and a telltale pause had followed. The inspector was suddenly very eager not just to talk but to meet up.

'This woman came to us, Foxrock, well to do,' Slate said. 'She got into the property game, bought into a few apartments there.'

'Do I know her?'

'Ciara Savage.'

'Name means nothing. Keep going.'

'She got into it at this seminar, in the North City Hotel. She says you were there that same day.'

'And?'

'She recognised you from your pic in the papers after the Junior Corbett hit. She saw Junior's mug in the same piece. She made the connection. Junior was there that day as well.'

'She should have been a copper,' Inspector Phil Wright said.

The couple made a dash for it. He had hitched his jacket up over his head to give running cover to both of them. Slate followed their progress. They arrived at their car, a Lexus, both hunched under the jacket as the man flashed his key. He accompanied her to the passenger door, then went around to the driver's side. Slate couldn't get any kind of a take on her.

'As you can guess, Inspector, I was a bit surprised by the news.' He knew he was using Wright's title pointedly, and he knew Wright knew it too. 'Didn't know what to do so I thought it best to come to you first.'

Wright didn't miss a beat. 'Anybody else in the frame?'

'My editor.'

'The footballer? I've seen him on TV. He wouldn't strike you as being over-endowed with brain matter.'

'Chalk it down.'

'When they're stupid, they're dangerous. How did you end up working for a muppet like that, Alan?'

'Needs must. After my little incident, I wasn't exactly flavour of the month. Frank Fastneck offered me a way back and here I am.'

Inspector Phil Wright said nothing. Slate could hear his breathing. The rain was now driving in sheets across the car park. The Lexus pulled out. Slate wondered where they were headed. He saw an empty apartment with a chilled bottle of bubbly.

Karen Small lived in an apartment in the city centre, this he knew. He tried to imagine the interior, most likely soft lighting and candles and all that shit. He had overheard her one day mention negative equity. Jesus, that was all they talked about. Negative equity. In terms of small-talk, it was the new property.

'Pub business is fucked, you know that,' Wright said.

'The way things are looking, everything is fucked.'

'I've seen members when they retired and they don't know what to do with themselves. Some of them used to buy pubs, maybe down the country. Time was it was a grand number. Steady few bob coming in, get yourself a good manager and you can have a fine life. Bit restrictive, having to be there at night time and that, but there are worse ways to invest your lump sum. I thought about it at one time a few years back. It had its attractions.'

'Pubs are going the way of farming,' Slate said. He was rehashing a line he had heard a business reporter at the magazine use a few days before. 'Good only as part-time gigs. They ripped the arse out of it and now they're walking around balls naked.'

Wright looked at him, surprised that Slate could come up with something so profound. 'I could get out in a couple of years, if I don't make super. Thought about a pub for a while but, like you say, the good days are gone there. Property is your only man, they said. Getting the money was no problem, as you know. So I queued up to hop on the ladder. And who was waiting with his hand out to give me a leg up?'

'Our friend.'

'I'm not a bad judge of character, but I never saw him coming. By Jesus, he could sell.'

'So I heard. He was a great man for releasing equity on your home.'

'Release the fucking equity. I've woken up in cold sweats for the last few months with that line screaming through my head.'

'How much did you ...?'

'Four hundred thousand. The bank wanted to give me even more. My retirement has been flushed down the toilet.' He stopped to accommodate whatever was rising in his throat. Slate was taken aback. A detective inspector of An Garda Síochána, a man who had faced down the worst elements of humanity thrown up by the city, was about to start blubbing in his car. He heard a sniffle. He reached across and opened the glove compartment. Inside, next to a torch and the vehicle manual, there was a packet of tissues.

Wright pulled out the packet and blew his nose.

'I began looking into it after he took off. Some job. He kept making arrangements to take a group of us out there, but it never came off. I began to get uneasy, but I kept shoving a lid on those thoughts. I couldn't afford to believe there was anything wrong with it.'

'Maybe the stuff still has value. There hasn't been a crash on Cape Isis.'

'It was all Irish. Everybody who owned was Irish. And the idea was to flog it to other people here as a slice of Paradise, away from the rain. Bad enough that we were just flogging houses to each other here. The next move was to do it in the arse end of nowhere off the coast of Africa.'

The car was filled with the sound of Inspector Phil Wright blowing his nose. He held the tissue when he finished, unsure what to do with it. He stuffed it into his coat pocket.

'Has he anything stashed away?' Slate said.

'Dead right he does. If he was sitting here now, I'd tear him limb from limb until he handed over what's mine. Alan, I want my money back. I need you to keep this under wraps for the time being.'

'I'd say you're not the only one looking for him.'

'What about your editor? Will he want to drag me into it?'

'One thing I've learned is to treat him like mushrooms – keep him in the dark and feed him shite. What about your end? Is there any investigation into Diggins yet?'

'Are you joking? With all the other banking shit going on? No resources, no will there to nail a fella like this. It'll be next year before they even get around to him.' The policeman reached for the door handle with his left hand, threw his right across at Slate. 'Anything you need, Alan, you let me know. There's a thousand stories out there in the naked city. We can help each other.'

The rain had eased off now. Slate watched him walk across the car park to his Mondeo, hunched down against the disappointment of his life. He tried to feel sorry for him, but right now, he just had to suppress a feeling of elation that was prompting him to unleash a roar. Back in the game. Lining out for the A team, and set up to start banging in goals like there's no tomorrow.

She had just downed her afternoon Solps when Valerie rang through. 'He wants to see you,' she said.

Noelle ran her right index finger along the inside of the glass. 'Thanks, Val.' She replaced the receiver and put the finger into her mouth, licking the sour particles from it. She was glad that she had downed them before going up to see him. The last thing you needed during an audience with Henry Paul was a headache.

Immediately she walked through the door she knew what was on the agenda. Yvonne was sitting in the same seat she had occupied at their last confab. She got to her feet as Noelle entered, and smiled. No hugs this time. Yvonne looked better than she had in months. She wore the face of somebody who had had a good night's sleep, and the trouser suit was kind on her readapting figure.

Henry was seated behind the desk, togged out in a sky blue shirt with white collar, and a sunny yellow tie, loosened at the neck. His cuffs were turned over, as if the weight on his mind had led to instinctive fidgeting. He got slowly to his feet, more in response to his wife's lead than any effort at politeness. He waved a hand at the chair beside Yvonne. Everybody sat down.

'Thanks for coming,' Yvonne said.

Noelle was about to ask whether she had had any choice, but let it pass.

'We need to talk,' Henry said.

'Sure. What's up?' Noelle was trying hard to sound surprised. There was no way she was going to make this easy for him.

'It's the continuing fallout,' Henry said.

'None of it can be easy on you,' Yvonne said.

'I'm coping. It hasn't affected my work, not as far as I'm concerned anyway.'

Henry Paul said, 'With all due respect, Noelle, we have to consider more than the effect it's having on you personally.' She looked him in the eye to see what he was trying to convey. Rule number one: whenever anybody offers all due respect, assume they're about to do something that shows no respect for you at all.

'What Henry means is that of course we're worried about your personal welfare, but there are other things to consider.'

'I'm listening.'

'Perception is everything in this business,' he said. His eyes drifted down to his desk. He was looking at a page of a magazine. 'The coverage of the whole affair, it's just ... It does nothing for the business.' He picked up the magazine and she recognised it. 'Paul & Paul is mentioned in this – I don't know what you'd call it – diatribe. You've been an excellent employee, Noelle. I can't think of any complaint I could have made of your work once you'd settled into the routine here.'

Noelle felt herself getting hot. She had known this was coming and, for the most part, she welcomed it. But there was a certain humiliation in being fired. She had never been fired before. Well, there had been that time when she was picking fruit in South Australia, but she had long lost interest by the time she was told her services were no longer required.

'They're down in the gutter,' Yvonne said. 'Crawling around down there. I mean, it must have been awful for you when you read it.'

'I've had better days,' Noelle said. 'What did you think of the photograph?'

Henry looked at her as if she was a client for whom he was trying to suppress his distaste.

Yvonne reached over and took the magazine from his fingers. She closed it and regarded the cover. 'It's not the worst,' she said.

'Really?'

Henry got to his feet, pulling against the drift in conversation. He walked over to the window, hands thrust deep into the pockets of his trousers. He spoke with his back to the two women. 'If that was all, I'd be willing to go out on a limb for you,' he said.

Noelle looked at his back. The creases on the shirt were like deep crevices on a cliff face. He must have ironed it himself, now that Yvonne was up the walls with the baby and the state of business meant he couldn't send the shirts out to be ironed any more. She couldn't handle the idea of Henry going out on a limb for her. She said, 'There's more?'

He turned to her. Out of the corner of her eye, she could see the back of Yvonne's head, as if she felt compelled to look away from what was to be delivered.

'You must have heard the rumours.'

'Which rumours are they, Henry?'

'Yvonne?'

Yvonne looked to be on the point of tears. When she spoke her voice was just above a whisper, as if the walls had ears. 'Some are saying that Donal was involved with unseemly individuals. I'm sure it's nothing more than people thinking the worst. The way things are now, everybody is losing the run of themselves. I appreciate that you're not going to say anything here that might cast Donal in a bad light, but you must have heard what they're saying.'

Noelle switched her gaze to Henry. He was focusing on his desk, as if he was trying to read a document from his spot by the window. 'No, Yvonne, I haven't, but I would be very grateful if you could tell me what exactly it is that they're saying.'

'Well. Henry?'

He raised his eyes and met hers. 'There's probably no truth to it,' he said, 'but they're saying that some serious criminals were laundering their money through Donal. That he was buying property for them, and that now they're looking for their money. One name in particular is being bandied about.'

Noelle felt something hollow in her stomach.

'Junior Corbett,' he said.

Yvonne emitted what sounded like a yelp. She bowed her head, brought a hand up to her forehead and began massaging it. 'The pits,' she said. 'That man . . .'

'OK, we've established that malicious rumours about Donal are flying around. Where exactly does that leave me?'

Henry sat down again, picked up a pen and began twirling it in the fingers of his right hand. 'I'm just giving you the big picture. The reality is that business is contracting at a serious rate, and I don't think there's enough here to justify three solicitors.'

'Bullshit.'

'Oh, Noelle.' Yvonne spoke from behind her hands.

'Pardon me?'

'You're afraid of the smell, there's nothing more to it.'

'Well, I did say—'

'You want to hang Donal without trial and me by extension.'

Yvonne looked up. 'Oh, Noelle, please. It's not like that.'

Noelle beat back her first impulse. Don't give him the satisfaction of losing it. Keep calm. In the unlikely event that she would be taking action, what she did now would come into play. 'I'm sorry you feel that way, Henry. But I believe I'm being treated very unfairly, if not illegally.'

The last word acted like a lightning bolt on the couple. Yvonne straightened herself as if answering a call to arms. Henry appeared to turn a shade of grey, all humanity draining from his face. 'It's probably best that you clear your desk today,' he said. 'Obviously you'll get the statutory.'

Noelle took a breath. OK, she could let rip, tell him where exactly he could stick it. But there was no percentage in that. She took another breath. The room was quiet now. Yvonne plucked some imaginary fluff from her blouse. The pen twirled in the fingers of Henry's right hand. She heard the leather squeal under his ass as he stretched himself. They were all waiting to arrive at the point where she would transmogrify into the hysteric.

Various emotions were welling up inside her for a riot. She wanted to ring Donal, tell him what they were saying. But she didn't want to ring him in case he confirmed it. A wicked impulse was urging her to shout in Henry's face, and throw things around the room.

She also wanted to gather her stuff, never darken the door of this place again. Revenge would be sweet but it could also be expensive.

She got up. Yvonne was on her feet nearly as fast, lining up, Noelle imagined, for one last hug. Henry stayed put. 'Goodbye, Yvonne,' she said, from a safe distance. Yvonne just nodded. Noelle turned on her heels and made for the door.

He was reading about José Mourinho on the back page of a tabloid when she appeared at the foot of the stairs. She looked as if the world was weighing her down.

'Hi,' she said, approaching him, her hand extended. 'You have an appointment, don't you?'

He got to his feet. 'You told me to ring in. Here I am.' He waited for the excuse. She didn't look to be in the shape for any kind of discussion. 'Your face says something has come up.'

'Is it that obvious?'

'Sorry.'

She looked across at Valerie, who was busy not looking at them.

She lowered her voice. 'Something big has come up. I've just been asked to leave the building.'

'Is it on fire?'

Her laugh was coated with bitterness. 'No, but I am. I've just been fired. Anyway, I'm still a solicitor, I'm still in a position to take on your case, but if you would prefer, I'm sure Valerie can organise an appointment with one of the Pauls for you.'

'They don't know my dark secrets. If I was to start sharing them with somebody else in here, the place might turn into an AA meeting. I'm sticking with you.'

'In that case, you might help me to clear out my office, and we'll arrange for a more formal meeting later.'

'Lead the way,' he said.

She approached Valerie and began speaking in tones a notch above a whisper. Valerie looked up as if she hadn't been aware of anybody's presence in the room. She listened for a few seconds. Sympathy replaced fake surprise on her face. She opened a door at the side of her glass partition and came out. The two women hugged.

Then Noelle led Molloy into her office. He noticed that her desk was in disarray compared to the first time he'd been in there. She looked around, deciding on a plan of action. She took the framed parchment off the wall and laid it on the desk, on top of the scattering of papers and files. She took a print down from the wall and carefully placed it on top of the parchment.

'Is this going to be a quick getaway?' he said.

'If we're intercepted by Henry there may be a scene. He may get it into his head that some of the stuff I'm taking is his.'

The metal filing cabinet creaked as she pulled it open. She began flicking through the files, taking out selected ones and handing them to Molloy. A stack began to grow in his outstretched arms. She did the same with the lower drawer of the cabinet. As she went along, she picked up pace. 'According to the letter of the law, these client files belong to the firm,' she said, 'but I suspect the particular clients I'm taking would have something to say about that.' She shut the cabinet with a bang of finality. 'OK,' she said. 'Let's make a break for it.'

They walked into the reception area, Noelle leading the way. Henry Paul was standing at the foot of the stairs, Yvonne on the second step behind him, looking over his shoulder. Valerie was busy being busy again. Henry took a step forward, his left hand extended. 'What's this?' he said.

'This is me leaving, Henry. And these,' she said, turning and waving towards the stack in Molloy's arms, 'are my effects.'

Henry looked beyond the files to Molloy's face,. 'Noelle, this is the firm's property,' he said.

'Oh, Noelle,' Yvonne said.

Noelle stopped in her tracks. 'Henry,' she said. 'You remind me of my favourite phrase, one I read in a book a long time ago.'

'Noelle, please. We can deal with this in a civilised manner. I don't want to bring in any outside agency.'

His wife piped up behind him, 'What phrase?'

'Why don't you take a flying fuck at a rolled doughnut?'

A rippling giggle escaped Yvonne, like something alien that had appeared from nowhere. Her husband turned and glared at her. When he turned again, towards his departing employee, he saw only the back of the thug, walking through the door.

14

Rocco was just about to press the buzzer when he heard a wail coming through an open window on the first floor. He looked at Kyle, whose eyes went up towards the window. 'Our man is scaring the shit out of the neighbours again,' Rocco said. Kyle allowed himself a smile. The twins were standing outside an apartment block of six units, built on a patch of ground in the salubrious suburb of Rathgar, which a developer had colonised five years previously.

They were visiting one Fionn Higgins, college graduate, budding musician and coke fiend, who did a little business to make a crust because the music wasn't going anywhere.

The steady stream of fiends visiting Fionn's place didn't seem to bother the neighbours, but Rocco could never understand why none of them had kicked up over the music. Most of the time it was nothing short of brutal. Fionn's weapon of choice was an Ibanez electric guitar. To Rocco's ear, it sounded something like a neutered wildcat on speed. Not that Rocco wished the fella ill. If Fionn made it into the big-time, which he was always saying was around the corner, then new prairies of fertile markets might open up.

Fionn took twenty seconds to arrive down at the door. When he opened it, his face fell, as if the boys were cops or the harbingers of some family tragedy. He hesitated a moment too long. 'Hey, guys,' he said, trying manfully to sound casual.

'We were just in the neighbourhood,' Rocco said. 'Thought we'd make a social call.'

'A social call?' Fionn didn't look any worse than normal. He was a big lad, carrying a few stone more than he should have. His ash-blond hair fell in sweaty wisps over his eyes, which in turn were all but falling off his chin. Irrespective of what time the twins called, he looked like he had been dragged backwards through a hedge.

Rocco said, 'Yeah, a social call, Fionn. Which part of that do you not understand?'

'Sure, sure. It's just, like, I didn't expect you guys till next week.'

'Well, it's your lucky day, then.'

'Sure, sure. The only problem is I'm rehearsing for a gig I got coming up next week. I'm really up to my tits, man.'

Rocco slapped him on the back. 'It's *our* lucky day so. We can get a sneak preview. Hey, how do you like that, Kyle?'

Kyle spoke for the first time: 'Do you have any chocolate biscuits?' He moved towards the door as if accepting an invitation, and Fionn stepped aside. Kyle walked on down a windowless corridor towards the stairs. Fionn called after him, 'Kyle, listen, man, I got company.'

Kyle turned and smiled before continuing on his way.

Rocco held his arm out for Fionn to go next. 'Is your bird here?'

'Yeah, man, she's giving me a hand.'

'I'm sure she is, and all the rest of it too.'

Poor Fionn looked like his day was coming apart. Rocco

just loved this guy. Of all the people who were distributing for him, Fionn was the one who gave Rocco the most pleasure in exercising power over him. Rocco liked holding the reins over his life, a turning of the tables on the natural order of things. If Rocco had been forced to scrape for a living in some shit-kicking job, it would have been the likes of Fionn to whom he would have had to answer. Not Fionn himself, obviously. He was good for nothing. But a Fionn type.

Upstairs, Fionn's bird was sprawled on the couch. Rocco had met her twice before and it crossed his mind that if Fionn ever fucked up in a major way he would take it upon himself to give her one. She could have done more with what she had, no question about that. She had perfect skin and if she'd given her body a chance it might have shown her in an even better light, but she was dressed in a knitted jumper, jeans and tan Ugg boots. She wore the lazy face known best to the very rich or the very stoned. Rocco reckoned she qualified under both categories.

'You guys know Emma,' Fionn said.

She raised her right hand, which had a pencil-thin joint balanced between thumb and index finger. She didn't straighten herself or sit up to make room for the new arrivals. Rocco had noticed the same arrogance on their previous encounters.

Fionn picked up his guitar and plectrum. He swung the guitar strap over his shoulder and adopted the pose. He touched a few strings delicately, before looking up at the twins. There had been no invitation to sit down so Kyle took the initiative and eased himself into a soft chair beside Emma's couch. Rocco went to the dining-table and pulled out a chair for himself.

There followed five minutes of torture. After tuning up, or whatever the fuck it was he did, Fionn switched on a drum machine. Then he took off, making noise, searching desperately for rhythm, moving his body to a beat that Rocco couldn't locate. 'The man been down on my life,' Fionn sang, his eyes closed.

On the couch, Emma's head was bobbing was if she were lost in the music.

'Kept my sweet girl in the groove, but she gone and said she gonna move. Out.'

At that line, Emma cranked up the head bobbing. The twins looked at each other. Kyle's face was all serious. There hadn't been any offer of a line or beer or even a chocolate biscuit.

When Fionn's guitar fell silent, he looked up, ready to drink in some lovin'. Emma clapped madly, even if she still didn't raise herself into a seated position.

'OK, that's enough,' Rocco said.

'Whaddaya mean?'

'We got somewhere to go, Fionn, and we don't have all day.'

'Rocco, man, you don't understand. I can't go anywhere right now. Is there some kind of a problem?'

'Don't worry, we just need to borrow your skills for a few hours.'

Kyle got to his feet in a quick movement. He gave Fionn a look that was an instruction. Fionn flinched, reared back like a startled horse.

'Hey, give the guy a break.' Emma was at last straightening herself, Rocco noted, with a little satisfaction. 'He's got to, like, rehearse? This gig is a very big deal for Fionn.'

Kyle said, 'You shut the fuck up.'

'Hey, man.'

'What did you say?' Kyle's feet stayed planted on the same spot but he thrust out his chest.

'Take it easy, man, She was just saying that—'

Rocco raised his hand. 'Let's go, Fionn. Kyle is a little upset that you don't appear to be showing him any respect.'

'Jesus, man, I wasn't dissing anybody.'

Rocco walked over to him. 'What are you going to do? Call the law? You have three seconds to walk through that door. Kyle is a patient man, but right now you're testing him to the limit. Maid Marion here will have to manage without you for a while.'

'How long will I be gone?'

At the rate you're going, for ever, thought Rocco. 'Not long, let's go.'

'Can I bring my axe?'

'What do you think this is? You want to bring a fucking axe?'

'He means his guitar,' Emma said. She was sitting upright, ramrod straight.

'No, no, no. Come on, out of here.'

Fionn went over to Emma, who got up off the couch, all action now. He kissed her and they hugged.

Kyle walked through the door, followed by Fionn. Rocco turned to give the bird the once-over one last time before leaving. One day maybe.

There were a few practical pointers that kept coming up at the meetings. Don't go looking for trouble. Stay away from your old mates. Remember, the common bond you shared with them was the need to get out of your head. Occupy your time with something, anything, to take your mind off the sauce.

The number-one pointer was, stay out of pubs. Why torture yourself? Why put yourself in harm's way? Why go looking for trouble?

It was now going on for two hours since he had entered this particular pub, and things could have been a lot worse. First of all, it wasn't like any pub he had known before. It was on the south quays, in the basement of a building that was offices above ground level. The place was dark with soft lighting and all nooks and crannies, each one with its own curving roof of stone, a feature retained since the place had been, he reckoned, a warehouse of some sort, where men had done an honest day's work.

He still hadn't figured out where the bar was. Noelle seemed to know her way around the place. He had slipped into calling her Noelle, no bother. She said her sister's place was around the corner, but she couldn't face going back yet.

After they entered their own nook, a waiter in a waistcoat materialised like a genie.

She asked for a wine spritzer and turned to him. Molloy didn't know what you drank in a place like this if you weren't drinking. He asked for a Coke. It all felt very strange, but the genie didn't bat an eyelid.

After he had gone, she said, 'Of course. I forgot. How stupid of me. Do you mind?'

He shrugged. 'No problem,' he said. 'It's not as if this place is a real pub.' That drew a laugh from her that was more nerves than mirth.

Since they left the office, she had given off the vibe of a coiled spring, talking mad, saying nothing, yabbering on about everything that came into her head. He asked her about the burglary, and she waved away his concern, as if it was no big deal.

He mentioned his son and how things were going, but he didn't get into telling her the details. He needed her full attention for that.

On the way there, as the traffic lights at the foot of Gardiner Street turned green, and she was grappling with the gearstick, she had asked him had he ever been fired. He had to think about that one. 'I suppose the day I got nabbed in England was a firing of sorts,' he said. 'But apart from that, I've never been in a job where you get fired. You might get shot, but you wouldn't get fired.'

She glanced at him when he said that, but he was smiling until he shouted at her to brake. They were nearly upon a stationary double-decker. She two feet from the rear where, Molloy noted, somebody had traced the word 'Revenge' in the street grime.

So, by the time the genie brought her spritzer, and a napkin for a beermat – a fuckin' napkin for a beermat – he was hoping the booze would work its way to relaxing her. The second did the trick. After that, she switched to Bailey's and ice. He was on his third Coke and his stomach was beginning to rebel.

They had been down every avenue of small-talk. Even when she relaxed, she remained cautious, as if she was patrolling the boundaries that existed between them. He didn't give a rat's arse about boundaries. The longer things went on, the less he saw her as his solicitor. He could see the two of them walking out of the place. He could see a key turning, a door opening into a darkened apartment. He could see her face turning up towards his. He could see her in a bed of soft pillows and clean sheets.

As she told him about how the recession was really hitting the Pauls' practice big-time, he reminded himself that he hadn't been with a woman since Stephanie. That was an age ago when he lived in a different world.

'So Henry, well, yes, he isn't having it easy, but at the same time, he's, I don't know, how could I best sum him up?'

'A prick?'

She pointed a finger at him. 'You have a way with words.'

Soon after that, she twirled her glass once more with feeling and the genie appeared in the nick of time. She raised the glass and her eyebrows to order another and asked Molloy how he was fixed. His glass was half full and he shook his head.

She got to her feet. 'I'm just nipping off to powder my nose,' she said. She began giggling. 'Oops, not the best way of putting it in this day and age, is it?'

He admired the way she shimmied out from behind the table and took off with grace, considering all she had on board.

He gave her twenty seconds, then got up himself and tried to find his way back outside. Up at ground level, dusk had settled on the evening. He put fire to a Marlboro and watched the slow procession of traffic down the quays. Two suits approached, en route to the pub. They were lost in conversation as they passed him.

After a while, he noticed that the tip of the cigarette had lengthened into a glowing cone. He had been pulling hard on it, drawing in the tobacco to fill something.

He still didn't know where the evening was heading. In another lifetime, he would have gone with the flow. Now there was no flow, just dry land.

She had returned when he arrived back at the table. She smiled up at him, as he pulled out the stool and sat down. She had a fresh Bailey's in front of her. His Coke looked flat.

'Do you mind if I ask you something?' she said.

'Bang away.'

'Do you know a man by the name of Junior Corbett?' She was looking intently at him now, pleading almost that he not think badly of her for straddling a boundary.

He picked up the Coke, took a sip. Yeah, it was flat. 'Is he a client of yours?'

'No, it's just his name came up today when they were firing me.'

Molloy raised his glass again. 'I know him. I've known him a long time.'

'Really?' She leaned forward, her eyes widened.

'What did the Pauls want to know about him?'

'It wasn't what they wanted to know. Henry said he might have had some dealings with my husband.'

Now it was his turn to say, 'Really?'

'What do you know about him?'

'What do you want to know? He's not the kind of person you'd find drinking in a place like this.'

'He's a criminal, isn't he?'

'He's Big Chief Sitting Bull out west. If I was your husband, I'd unmix myself from him pronto.'

'I didn't say my husband was mixed up with him. The Pauls said it.'

'OK.'

Her face had changed. There was something approaching concern drifting over it. He didn't want to go down this road.

'What more can you tell me about him?' she said.

'Junior gave me my big break. I was at a loose end, out of school with no prospects – at least, that's the way it looked to me. He showed me how to make some money, and then some big money.'

'Until you got caught.'

'Until I got caught. I was working for him when I was nabbed in England.'

'My God.'

'That surprise you?'

'Just the connections. You never came across my husband?'

He laughed. 'No. At the level I was operating, I'd never have met him. Unless I was fixing him up with a few grams of coke.'

'Can I ask you something else?'

'Don't stop now.'

'I looked up your court case. When they caught you that time, the panel in the car was ripped open. It was nearly as if you wanted to be caught.'

His foot was tapping now. He felt fidgety. This wasn't where he had wanted the conversation to drift. 'What do you think?'

'Do you mean what would I like to think?'

'You're on a roll now.'

She took a sip of her Bailey's. He could see that she was nearly halfway gone.

214

'I'd like to think that you'd had enough. That everything was getting to you. The life, your drink problem, the stress of a baby on the way. And you wanted out. You didn't want to live like that any more, but you didn't know how to stop. So, you got caught.'

'Jesus.'

'How does that sound?'

'Are you a solicitor or a shrink?'

She smiled weakly, accepting he wasn't going to go any further with this.

'And Junior Corbett, what do you think of him now?'

'Much the same you think about your ex-boss.'

'Henry Paul wouldn't shoot people to get what he wants.'

'He doesn't have to, does he? Why use a gun when you're able to use the law? They're out of different worlds, my Junior and your Mr Paul, but they're from the same side of the street.'

The apartment was just as Slate had imagined. There was soft lighting and soft furnishings, two beanbags and a bottle-green throw covering the couch. There was also a thin contraption, which Karen Small had told him was actually an African coffee- table. It was supported on one leg, about a foot high, and carved in the figure of the wise man who hears no evil. The table was on the guy's head, and it was only maybe a foot or so in diameter, as if he was balancing a tray with no hands.

They obviously weren't into big coffee mornings in Africa, he said. Karen Small just smiled, didn't appear to get the joke. He had noticed a bong on the window sill, before she drew the curtains. He hoped she wasn't one of those potheads who could identify humour only when halfway out of their skulls.

He complimented the place, said it looked cool, and was

really handy being just off Henry Street and a literal stone's throw from the Luas. He knew what her reaction would be. He all but mouthed it as she said it.

'Negative equity, but I suppose it's a home.'

She wore a green print maxi dress and sandals. He had on a striped Italian shirt and khaki trousers. He had been advised to wear striped shirts in deference to his ballooning potter. The stripes acted to camouflage the midriff expansion, he had been assured, although he had his doubts. He still hadn't signed up for membership of a gym.

The plan had been to go out for dinner. That was before he'd got a call from his new best friend, Inspector Phil Wright. There was a lead on the Luas-line murder. Two brothers were involved, rising stars in Junior Corbett's operation. There was nothing yet to pull them in on, but he would keep Slate posted.

Slate made a few follow-on calls, rang the Garda Press Office just to see what the official word was. As usual, it was no comment and that was off the record.

Work wasn't going to make the date easy for Karen Small either. She had been called at short notice to do a phone interview with the Ting Tings.

'Who?' Slate had never heard of them.

'The Ting Tings,' Karen Small said. She was at the sink, running the tap over a mountain of bowls and cups, which he reckoned must predate her breakfast.

'They're going to be huge,' she said.

'The Thing Things?'

'No. The Ting Tings. T-I-N-G. They're an indie outfit. From England.'

'I'll keep an eye out for them.'

Between their respective busy lives, neither of them got around to booking dinner anywhere. It was Slate who suggested Marks & Spencer. They were doing a dinner deal at the moment, big pizza, salad and a bottle of wine for little more than fifteen euro. As soon as he told her, he thought he might have sounded cheap, bringing her on a supermarket take-out date. So he immediately said that of course he'd get a few extras on top.

She didn't object, which he took as the nod. She even seemed relieved that they could forgo the effort required to venture out into public. And here they were now, lights down low, a candle burning on the table between them, James Morrison crooning in the background. Their plates were wiped clean and the plonk was rapidly disappearing from tall-stemmed glasses.

'It must be so exciting,' she said.

'What I do?'

'Yeah, I mean the criminals and the police and the crime scenes, like something out of those TV shows.'

'You mean *CSI*?'

'Yeah, and those detectives who always dress so badly but emit that animal magnetism.'

'A lot of that stuff rubs off on me,' he said.

She got up and went over to change the CD. He rose and poured the dregs of the bottle into the two glasses, giving himself a little extra, as he reckoned she had been throwing the stuff back at a ferocious rate. She was bent down into the music centre, her ass in the air. It was a good ass, just slightly on the heavy side of perfect, but it wasn't as if he was Charles Atlas.

She turned and smiled. And then Barry White came on. Barry White. She did a little wiggle in response to the opening bars of 'My First, My Last, My Everything'.

When she picked up her wine glass from the African coffee-table, she said, 'Was crime always your thing?' She sat down next to him, her fingers delicately holding the stem.

'When I was in college doing journalism, I never thought

things would end up this way. I wanted to be a foreign correspondent.'

'Me too.'

'You did?'

She giggled. 'Well, for about a week. But entertainment was always my thing.'

Alan Slate looked into the distance. 'It was what got me interested in journalism in the first place. I wanted to go to far-off places, wars and that, and report for the people back home what was actually happening out in the wide world.'

'Wow.' She looked at him, saw that he was heading into deeper territory. 'Anywhere in particular take your fancy?'

'I wanted to tell the story of the Kurds. I know it's not professional, strictly speaking, but I wanted to help them.'

'The Kurds?'

'Yeah.'

'Are they a band?'

'You never heard of the Kurds?'

'Sorry.'

'They're a people without a home, over there in Kurdistan, between Turkey and Iraq. Nobody wants them and they've been pushed around all their lives, serious human-rights abuses. They were in the news a lot when I was in college.'

'Wow.'

'That's how I started out in journalism. With big dreams of putting the world to rights. These days, I find myself doing stories like how serious crims splash around their cash on hookers in the sun.'

'Deadly.'

'Yep, that's the long and the short of it.'

'Where did it all go wrong?'

'How did I become a highly paid, award-winning crime reporter?'

'No, just, like, when did you abandon the Kurds?'

'Life gets in the way of your dreams. You just have to go with the flow.'

'Wow.'

He leaned over and kissed her. Her mouth felt wet and warm, and she wrapped her arms around his neck. He couldn't handle the thought of another wow.

Later, when they lay in the dark, she broke the silence. 'What happened to them?'

'Who?'

'The Kurds.'

'I don't know. I think they got sorted. I kind of moved on and I haven't heard much about them since.'

'These friends of mine, they're starting out. You wouldn't mind if I suggested the name for their band?'

'Be my guest.' He felt good. He wondered whether there might be a book in this gangster Molloy and all the shit he had stirred up. He was due a book. And now, with things on a roll, maybe it was time to ride the wind.

Caroline left work early. These days, it was no big deal. Up until the crash, there was no way you'd get out of the office before eight at the earliest. Back then, leaving work had been a wrench. There was just so much money to be made. She used to fantasise about inventing a way to go without sleep. All that time wasted when you could be making money and partying.

The PR game was no longer operating off that charged battery: one of the first things to go when costs were tightened. The company was feeling the pinch now, and Caroline wondered just how long they would hold on to business, to her.

She dropped into the new Fresh store to pick up dinner

for herself and Noelle. Beef Stroganoff, side portion of garlic potatoes and a good bottle of sauv blanc.

Then she drove out to Killiney. She had told her sister that she would pop in occasionally to pick up the post. Understandably, Noelle didn't want to have to go back there and wrestle with ghosts and memories. There was no question but she wouldn't be returning to Skellig. The way things were looking now, the place would be on the market within weeks, a nice little bargain for anybody who still had a few euro and was reckless enough to believe the market wasn't going to collapse further.

Once out there, she could see why Noelle didn't want to return. There was an eerie pall over the place. It gave her the creeps. She remembered the parties she had attended out here, and the nostalgia eased her into a temporary warm refuge.

She scooped up the post and left.

Back at the apartment, a shower beckoned. She put the meal in the oven. When she emerged from the bathroom in her dressing-gown, a towel on her damp hair, she heard the scratching in the door's lock. For a second, she froze. It had to be Noelle. But what was the problem? What if it was somebody else? How could they have got into the building? The scratching stopped. She heard voices, muffled behind the door. Curiosity and caution pulled her in opposite directions. She walked over and placed her face next to the door. No sound. She slipped the chain into place, slowly pulled open the door.

Noelle – well, it was Noelle, she could tell her sister from behind – appeared to be eating the face off a man. A man who wasn't her husband, the missing solicitor. The man was looking at Caroline while her sister lashed into him. He didn't look to be in control of the situation. Suddenly Noelle pulled back, ran her hands down her body in an attempt to straighten up. She raised her right hand, which still had a key in it and turned. Caroline was still looking out from behind the chained door.

'Caroline?'

'Hi.'

'Could you open the door, please?' She was gone all right, just about able to string the words together. The man had surprise written on his face.

'Hello,' he said. Good-looking guy. Caroline wondered where she'd picked him up.

The Luas-line murders are directly linked to the gangland war that kicked off last week with the attempted murder of Junior Corbett, Inside Out *can exclusively reveal.*

According to a garda source, the main suspects for the murders, which were carried out in front of hundreds of Luas-line passengers, are two brothers closely associated with Junior Corbett. 'All hell has broken loose,' the garda source told Inside Out. *'These lads may have been acting off their own bat looking for Brownie points with Junior, but he is lashing out in every direction after the attempt on his life. Gangland is about to get a lot uglier.'*

One of the suspects has a vicious reputation as a killer in gangland. He is wanted in connection with four murders over the last two years. His brother is believed not to be as vicious although, according to sources, he would have to have psychopathic tendencies to be as bad as his brother.

The man at the centre of the latest war is keeping a low profile until he can locate the would-be assassin who tried to snuff him out last week. One name that keeps coming up in garda contacts is that of the man known as the Dancer, who was recently released from prison in England.

'It looks like he came home with the intention of removing Corbett and setting up himself,' one impeccable source told Inside Out. *'But he didn't get his way and who knows where the bloodshed could lead from here?'*

Inside Out *can also reveal that our leading reporter,*

Alan Slate, is currently in negotiations with a number of publishers to write a book about modern gangland in Dublin, with particular focus on the current war. As always, though, it is the readers of this magazine who will be the first to know the real truth every time there are any developments in gangland.

Alan Slate, crime reporter of the year 2000, 2002, 2004

15

The waiter was a wiry guy with the kind of leathery face that comes from the sun and cigarettes. Donal Diggins asked for coffee with milk. The waiter turned on his heels and left. Diggins was sitting at a table outside the Café Central on the Plaza de la Constitución in central Málaga. The tables were protected by umbrellas and penned inside a little barrier at the entrance to the café.

The Plaza de la Constitución was busy at this time of day. Shoppers and tourists and the odd flock of birds milled around on the tiles, which looked clean and shiny. As his eyes swept the plaza, they returned to the tables beside his own at the entrance to the Café Central. Sitting four tables away, Ponce was busy looking busy behind a newspaper.

Diggins still couldn't get over his name. When they met, he asked him a few times to pronounce it, but didn't bother explaining what it meant back home. This Ponce was no ponce, and if he turned out to be one, you wouldn't bother informing him as he stood at six three and must have weighed nigh on eighteen stone. He was an ugly man, pointy ears, flat nose and a cap of thin, sandy hair fitted to his oversized head. He charged three hundred euro a day, which wasn't cheap but didn't come near the cost of whores.

Two nights previously, Diggins had succumbed again. He had been out for dinner with an ex-pat Scot with whom he was hoping to do a little business further down the coast. The Scot claimed to have a cold and disappeared back to his hotel at the conclusion of the meal.

Diggins sat at the bar alone, a stranger in a strange land, exiled and pining for a home that was no longer there. On his third glass of San Miguel, his defences were lowered and all resolve began to dissipate. He pulled out his mobile and thumbed down his contacts until he had the number.

At seven the following morning she left, and within minutes he flushed the dregs of the gram down the toilet, even though there was enough for a few more toots. The rest of the day had been lost to snatches of sleep and a burden of guilt. When he couldn't find the peace to sleep, he got up and strolled the length of Marqués de Larios. He distracted himself by imagining the lives of the casual shoppers with generous curves who went home to their husbands in the suburbs, living mundane lives inside a warm bubble.

At this stage of the game, Donal Diggins was all in favour of a bit of mundane. When everything was sorted, he would be heading that way himself. Not in this town, though. Not here where whores tracked his every move, waving bags of coke. No. Portugal sounded good, somewhere down the Algarve. The right climate, the right kind of people, the right environment to get back into the game. They could really forge something down there, Noelle keeping home, himself back to normal, but he would rein in his more extravagant impulses. The madness that had a grip on him for years was now gone.

'Afternoon, Señor.' Diggins looked up and the man was

removing his shades. He felt cold. He looked at Ponce, who was now busy gazing out on the square. The man pulled out a chair and sat into it. He didn't offer his hand in greeting. He was wearing a silk Hawaian shirt that was full of lanky orange palm trees against a backdrop of black. His arms were pale and glistened with sun block.

The waiter appeared with a little tray. He placed a circular napkin in front of Diggins, then the coffee and stainless-steel jug of milk. He stood there, awaiting further orders. Diggins looked at Johnny Cash.

'A glass of milk,' Cash said.

'Milk?'

'Yeah. I think I'm getting an ulcer.'

The waiter left, with a bemused look on his face.

Cash took off his shades. Diggins looked over at his protector again, just for reassurance that he hadn't fled.

'How does this lovely day find you in Paradise?' Cash said.

'It's not all it's cracked up to be.'

'Come home to the rain for a few weeks and you'll see what you're missing. Things work out, I could see myself moving here permanently.'

Diggins gave him the once-over. He never would have believed that a day would come when he had to deal with this pond life. He wondered whether Johnny Cash had ever killed anybody with his hands. 'You wouldn't like the food,' Diggins said.

'Not a problem in Torremolinos. Had the full works for breakfast this morning. Sausages could do with a bit of sprucing up, but apart from that you could be popping into a caff in Talbot Street.'

The waiter arrived with the glass of milk on a tray. He placed it on the table and stood back to wait for payment, but nothing was forthcoming from Johnny Cash. Diggins fished in his pocket for a note, placed it on the tray and waved away the waiter. 'How are things back home?' he said.

'We're getting there.'

'I've been reading the newspapers.'

'And I'm sure your missus has been keeping you informed of what's going on.'

'Leave my wife out of this.'

Johnny Cash leaned in closer. Diggins caught a whiff of aftershave that cheapened the air.

'Junior doesn't have the same respect for your wife that you might. As far as he's concerned, your missus is all he's got right now, and he's keeping her in his sights.'

'Does he know that we're meeting?'

'Are you fucking serious?'

Diggins pulled a handkerchief from his pocket and wiped his brow. Out of the corner of his eye, he could see Ponce looking out on the plaza to where a flock of birds had just scattered and taken to the air. 'This has nothing to do with me, but as I understood it, you said that Junior wouldn't be around for much longer.'

'Nothing to do with you? Mr Diggins, I know you wouldn't be the type of man to get your hands dirty, but this has everything to do with you. Before you came to me with your proposal, why, me and Junior were as tight as a nun's knickers. You came between our friendship with all that filthy money you've stacked away.'

Diggins moved his arms on to the table, nearly toppling his coffee. He caught the cup in time, pushed it aside. 'You're not pulling me into this thing. What we agreed was that you would arrange for Junior to accept a debt write-down. Let's just be clear on that.'

Johnny Cash tasted his milk. He turned his head at the sound of a trumpet from the plaza. 'Not the way I remember it, Mr Diggins. From what I can recall, you were ordering a hit.'

Diggins looked around, as if somebody might have heard

what was said. He leaned in to Johnny Cash. 'No way. No way. Whatever you people do to each other, whatever games you play with your lives, that's your business. It has nothing to do with me. Order a hit? You're talking about having somebody killed. Do not try to drag me into that pit.'

'How's the weather up there on your high horse?'

'I'm telling you. It has nothing to do with me.'

'Listen to me, you fuck-head. You're not telling me anything. You're lucky that you're still breathing after all you've tried to pull on Junior and me. You watch your mouth.'

Diggins's eyes drifted over to Ponce. This time he was earning his crust, looking good and hard at his employer's table. Johnny Cash met his stare. 'Who's the gorilla?'

'A friend.'

'Yeah, and I'm giving Madonna one. Who the fuck is it?'

'He's here to ensure no harm comes to me.'

'I hope you're paying him top dollar,' Johnny Cash said. ''Cause he's going to earn it.'

It had been a mistake. Easy to say that now, but the situation had been unfolding. Diggins thought at the time he could ride it out. How was he know that things would ever lead this far?

The day after he fled the country, Junior Corbett rang. Diggins was in London. He took the call. Mistake number one. But at the time his confidence was still topped up.

Junior wanted to meet . Diggins told him he was just out of the country for a few days.

'Where are you? I'm having second thoughts about my investment,' Junior said.

'You're kidding.'

'I don't kid about money. Something else has come up. This

Cape Isis thing is beginning to look like a dung pile. I need my cash back.'

'It doesn't work like that, Junior.' There was silence on the line. Since first encountering Junior Corbett more than six months previously, Diggins had done a bit of homework. He knew the man was unsavoury, to put it mildly, a staple of the tabloid crime pages. But, as he knew only too well himself, getting a reputation for major achievement through judicious publicity wasn't exactly rocket science. In his own line, the publicity served to enhance his reputation as a property mogul with the Midas touch. He could see why somebody like Corbett would like to acquire a name for being a hell of a lot nastier than he actually was.

Having met the guy, he didn't believe Corbett could be responsible for all the things they said he was. And now that a little misunderstanding had arisen in their relationship, he wasn't about to curl up on the floor and wail. Maybe this guy was accustomed to using silence as a weapon of intimidation. Maybe he didn't appreciate that Donal Diggins was a tough guy himself – had to be or he wouldn't have got to where he was.

'It doesn't work like that, Junior. The money is committed.'

Another pause followed.

'Well, then, you better start reworking it.'

It went on like that for a few minutes, Diggins trying to explain the ways of the world to a thug who usually solved everything through brute force and threats. They agreed to meet up, but Diggins knew he would never keep the appointment.

And he didn't. Two days later, when he was supposed to meet Junior Corbett in a Mayfair hotel, he was sitting in his underwear at the laptop in the apartment in Chiswick, scouring the property markets of Europe for an opening.

The next time Junior phoned, he ignored it. The voice message was hopping with anger. An incoherent flood was let loose, including something about extracting fingernails with pliers and his balls with a carving knife. Diggins let it pass, but the second voice message got his attention.

They had located Noelle, put her under surveillance. Gave him twelve hours to call back – or else, according to a calmer Corbett, his wife would be abducted and used to play Pass the Ride among his mates.

He rang back within an hour.

'The money?'

'Can we talk about this in a reasonable manner?'

'We tried that. You didn't show.'

'Please, Junior. This is not straightforward. I know your situation is different from that of my other investors. Let's just discuss it.'

'OK, you're down one chance. This is your second. Except this time I'm sending my representative.'

'Junior, there's no need to get solicitors involved in this.'

'Don't worry. My man hasn't crawled out of the same hole as you.'

'OK, OK. I'll meet him. What's his name?'

'Johnny Cash.'

They met at a pub on the Thames, up the road from Chiswick. The place was dark and perfumed with a log fire. Diggins arrived early, ordered a cup of coffee, and found a seat near the back. He watched three men walk in on their own over the following ten minutes. The third patron to walk through the door was well dressed, dark suit, black shirt, striped black and white tie. The threads might have been expensive, but the guy's face was hard, and the handlebar moustache was less than presentable in polite circles. When his eyes scoped the place, Diggins stiffened. This was his guy all right. He got up and approached him as he was leaning against the bar.

'Mr Cash, I presume,' he said.

The man looked him up and down, said nothing.

'I'm Donal Diggins.' He extended his hand, but Cash just examined it as if it might contain a gun or a knife. Slowly, he reciprocated. His handshake was limp, the flesh rough and coarse.

Diggins ordered him a drink and they repaired to a seat at the back. They circled each other with a few niceties about the neighbourhood, and the differences between Irish and British pubs. Then it was down to business.

'This is a straightforward matter for Junior,' Johnny Cash said. 'I might as well tell you, he must like you because he's cutting you a huge amount of slack.' He drained his pint. The barman was keeping a professional eye on them, and Cash raised his glass.

Diggins placed his cup on the table. He was feeling warm. He regretted sitting so close to the fire now. He slipped his arms out of his sports jacket, folded it and laid it carefully on the bench next to him. The barman came down with Cash's pint of bitter. He accepted it and looked at Diggins, who reached for his wallet.

When the barman left, Diggins leaned forward. 'There's no panic,' he said. 'Everything is as on course as it always was. I'm just over here as a precaution, but as far as Junior's investment is concerned, the whole thing is hunky-dory. He can begin to expect cheques on the far side of the summer.'

'No can do.'

'What are you saying?'

'The credit crunch. It's making Junior antsy.'

'The credit crunch.' Diggins was trying to sound incredulous.

'The fucking credit crunch. It's crunching down on Junior's operation too. He needs cash to invest. That's where I come in. I'm Johnny Cash. I persuade debtors to hand the cash over to Junior.'

Diggins tried explaining to Johnny Cash in detail why he no longer had control over the money. The cash had already been invested in the Cape. Cash sat there, nodding, as if the words were just washing over him.

'Could we cut a deal?'

'A deal?'

'Say I was able to come up with half the money.'

'Junior would regard that as an insult.'

'What about you?'

'It's not my cash.'

'Not yet.'

'Mr Diggins, what the fuck are you getting at?'

'In my line of work, debt-collection agencies often buy the debt that's owed and then make a settlement.'

Cash was keeping eyes front, towards the bar. Two middle-aged women had entered and were standing before the barman, enquiring about the menu. 'Mr Diggins, I don't do riddles or shit like that. What are you proposing?'

'Well, one option from your point of view is to take over the debt.'

Johnny Cash was reaching for his pint. He stopped and looked at Diggins. 'You want me to take Junior's action?'

'I'm just asking whether the possibility has ever occurred to you. In business, as I'm sure you're aware, an executive leaving an operation to set up on his own often takes clients with him.'

'You think I should go into business for myself?'

'It's an opportunity.'

'An opportunity?'

'Not many around at the moment.'

'You know what you're saying?'

'I'm just facilitating your thought process, Mr Cash.'

'And if your facilitation were to continue to a further point, and remembering all of this is just between you and me and the wall there, and none of it is ever going to happen, how much?'

'Half.'

'Half of one point eight million is …'

'Nine hundred grand.'

'Make it an even million.'

Diggins paused to give a two-second effect. 'That's fair enough.'

'And you're definitely good for that amount?'

'Look, if Junior was willing to take a hit on his investment, if he would accept fifty cents in the euro, we wouldn't be having this conversation.'

Cash leaned in close. Diggins was assaulted by the whiff of aftershave. There ought to be a law against whatever it was being worn in public.

'You're suggesting, in that roundabout, head-stuck-up-your-ass kind of way, that I take Junior out.'

'I think you've the wrong end of the stick there, Mr Cash.'

'The fuck I have.'

'I'm just offering you a deal. How you go about your end of it is your business.'

Cash was looking at him now as if he was a different person from the one he'd met twenty minutes earlier. 'Let's be clear on one thing. This meeting never happened. We never met. I came over here and you didn't show up again. Understood?'

'Perfectly.' Diggins extended his hand to shake on it. He had never felt as scared shaking on anything in his life.

After the woman ended her share, there was a long silence. There were three other women, two within Molloy's line of sight. Both had tears in their eyes. He saw that the big guy, Brick Shithouse who guarded the tea, now wore a face on the edge of crumbling. Molloy didn't feel too secure in his own composure.

The woman had given her name as Shauna. Her body was

a rake, but if you looked at her face long enough, you could see that she might well have been beautiful once upon a time. She told them about her daughter, and how they had been reunited six years after the daughter had been taken into care. The daughter had left for London three years after that when she was eighteen, and now she was back and had agreed to the meet-up.

Shauna was sober nearly a year now, and was on Step Nine, making amends. The meeting had gone well. Her daughter had been cautious, leaving all the big questions hanging in the air between them. But the main thing was no anger had been directed at her. They hadn't hugged or anything when they'd parted, but they had resolved to meet again.

Shauna couldn't have asked for more. It had been a good day. The good days, she said, were mounting up. She wasn't getting ahead of herself or anything but, damn it all, there were times when celebration was in order.

The meeting moved on. Next up was a man who began his every contribution with the declaration that he'd been in and out of the rooms for more years than he cared to remember. Every time he talked about the state of the country and the politicians who got on his wick. His sharing was generally greeted with a silent communal groan. You could nearly feel it. People were there to get well, not to fix the country. He spoke very little about himself, except to point out now and again that, like the country, he too was on the slide.

After a few minutes, the secretary reminded him of a group conscience decision that all sharing be kept to four minutes to allow everybody a chance to get in. The man finished up saying he was full of resentment, and the group fucking conscience fed into his resentments. When he stopped, silence took hold for a long four seconds.

Then Molloy heard himself talking. 'I'm Josh. I'm an alcoholic.'

They murmured the standard greeting: 'Hi, Josh.'

He could see some of them looking intently at him. He'd been coming here for a fortnight now with stitched lips, and suddenly he was finding his voice. 'I just want to say I'm glad to be here. It was good listening to Shauna.' He caught her staring at him from her hooded eyes.

'I have a son of my own I've never seen. Maybe I didn't deserve to see him until I started getting sober, but that's the way it goes. His mother is in a bad place. We used to party together but I've stopped and for her the party goes on.

'There's a lot of problems with the situation now, and I'm full of resentment. I'm pissed off at her, and at the system, and at life for dragging me down the road I took. There's other stuff too that's getting in the way of it all happening with my son, and dealing with that isn't easy.

'But I know there's nothing I can do about a lot of that now and I just got to deal with it. I know I'm ready for whatever happens. I'm not hiding from myself any more. I'm not drinking, looking for a way out. Today I have a chance.

'Coming to these rooms, listening to people like Shauna, it made me realise that anything is possible. I don't know if I'm making any sense, but I'll finish on this. I'm out of prison a few weeks, but I was on early release once I began going to the rooms inside. I'm free now. No matter what happens, the bastards can't touch me no more. Thanks.'

The man in the chair looked him in the eye. 'Thanks for your share. Keep coming back,' he said.

Another man piped in: 'Hi, I'm Daniel and I'm having a really shit day …'

Molloy tuned out. He felt lightened, but he didn't want to make a big deal of it. Ten minutes later, the meeting ended, and he got up and made his customary bolt for the door. One day at a time. He had shared, but he wasn't yet ready to hang about afterwards.

At the top of the steps the Praetorian Guard was still in place. They were on their feet, stretching their legs. The older of the pair looked to be in particularly bad shape, signs of blood ringing his eyes. He nodded at Molloy. The other kept his eyes on the cap at the end of his right arm.

Molloy pulled a two-euro coin from his pocket, dropped it into the cap.

''Twas a good meeting so,' the younger guy said. The older guy grinned, life fleeting across his eyes.

Molloy was thinking of a reply when his mobile beeped. He fished it out and pressed the read button for a text received: 'Want to see your son?'

Noelle had draped a sheet over Michael O'Leary before falling into bed; she'd stuck it to the wall with masking tape. For that, she was now grateful. When she awoke, there was nobody looking in on her pain. She remained still, as if any movement might place her in peril. She lay like that for a while, before exploring whether or not she was all present and accounted for.

Her feet were there. Check. She wriggled her hands. Check. Then the biggie: her head. She raised it from the pillow. There was an almighty movement within, as if somebody had decided to rearrange the furniture of her brain as a bad joke.

She tried to speak but no words would come. Her mouth felt as if it had been the location for a day-long demonstration on the attributes of a steel Brillo pad. She lay down and gave it another twenty minutes.

Sleep was no longer her friend. Instead images came to her, conveyed with a note of spite. Snogging Joshua Molloy on the doorstep. Her sister's face as she entered the apartment with a man in tow, two parts horror, one fascination. Breaking down and melting into Caroline's arms. None of it was pretty. None of it was welcome right now.

When she thought the time was right, she raised herself from the bed. Caroline must have helped her into pyjamas, because there was no way she would have managed herself. The room appeared to be going through a number ten on the Richter scale. She moved with caution, groping for the door handle, her eyes narrowed to slits in an effort to stave off the bastard who was beating the daylights out of a gong in her head.

Caroline, the dear, had left the curtains drawn in the living room. Noelle felt a powerful strain of love for her sister.

In the kitchen, the cold-water tap was as pure as day. She rinsed a tall glass and then drank long from it, introducing the beginnings of acceptable consciousness to her body. She refilled it and padded across to the couch. It took her a few minutes to find her bag, on the floor at the far end of the couch. She said a little prayer as she lifted it and her prayer was answered. Two Solpadeine tablets lay within.

Readapting to Planet Earth took another half-hour in the decompression chamber of a darkened apartment. There was a successful attempt at a slice of toast, some melted butter and a film of marmalade. It was so good, she had another. She tried the TV. A programme on baking. Another involving insufferable chat among heavy, ugly people. There was a western that looked like it dated from the seventies. She turned it off.

Daytime radio held no attractions for her at the moment. And the pop stations were more than her head could deal with. She fingered her way through Caroline's CDs, lined up across a shelf on the hi-fi unit. There was a CD with the name Cavatina, a guitar on its cover, mention of the movie The Deer Hunter. She slipped it into the player and returned to the foetal position on the couch. The music was like a balm.

She dozed for a while, trying hard to stay in the moment, while ignoring the tide of pain that was thankfully receding.

After some time, she got up, intending to go for a walk to clear her head. But just then a shower assaulted the wall-window, spitting with fury on the glass. She could put on her rain gear, head out to Killiney beach. But that would require bags of energy, which she did not have right now.

The kitchen was in a bit of a mess. She tidied the counter tops, emptied the bin and washed a saucepan that Caroline must have used for a sauce the previous evening before she'd arrived on the scene.

There was a stack of mail on the table. She remembered Caroline saying something last night about having been out to Skellig. She took up a sheaf of letters, leafed through them. There was one for her from a charity for deaf people in the developing world to which she had subscribed. Another was a circular from her mobile-phone company, advertising new deals. The rest was Donal's.

She peered at the envelopes. One had a British stamp. It looked as if it had originated in a bank. What was she going to do? Forward it? To where? Why not open it and tell Donal if it conveyed anything significant? She tore open the envelope at the top. It was an itemised credit-card bill. Most of the outgoings were small, one or two hitting more than two hundred euro. But a number were for a thousand. Curiosity brought her eyes to these items. She read one. She read it again. She felt weak. Maybe it was the hangover leaving her body, or maybe something else was taking flight.

Caroline had a laptop hooked up nearby. She picked it up and placed it on the table. Outside, the shower had passed, and the sun was back to take charge.

The computer booted up within ten seconds. She hit 'favourites' and scrolled down to Google. She typed in the name. A wide range of results came up. She tapped into a few and found comment boards. She read the comments and read again. Through it all she was feeling a sense of shock.

She pushed the laptop further on to the table, and buried her head in her hands, elbows digging into the cherrywood. She could feel the tears on her wrists.

Johnny Cash popped outside to ring Esther. Told her he was tied up with this bit of business. Of course she blew a gasket. What was the point of going on holidays if she was left on her own to stroll the boardwalk of Torremolinos or haunt the bars like a hungry cougar?

'You have two choices,' he told her. 'You can hang out there, get a drink for yourself, read a book or whatever it is that you do on holidays, or you can fuck off home.'

She slammed down the phone. He couldn't believe it. He goes to all this trouble, takes leave from work at a time of high stress, to bring her on a break. And this is the thanks he gets?

He rejoined the others at the bar. Ponce was still nursing a soda water. Diggins had his hand wrapped around a glass of beer. Cash nodded, said the women in his life were like the ulcers, always hanging about bugging the shit out of him. He picked up his vodka and Coke, raised a glass. The other pair didn't bother to respond.

The three of them were standing at a bar in a little place off the Plaza de la Constitución. It was a long, low affair, with spot lighting on ceiling and wall. The bar was complemented by a little restaurant just feet away on a raised platform and cordoned off by a carved railing. The walls were ringed with large prints of Picasso's work, showing off the local boy who had made good.

Everybody was chilled. Any potential for misunderstandings had been eliminated. Johnny Cash no longer felt the compulsion to kick seven shades of shite out of the local muscle. Mr Diggins had shown his goodwill this time around. He had presented him with an envelope of cash, which, when he counted it in the toilet, yielded just short of eight thousand euro.

'A small deposit,' Diggins had said. 'Our agreement still stands.'

After another drink, and more bullshit talk, Cash brought up the small matter of the elephant that stood in the way of the agreement between them. 'I'm just curious,' he said, leaning into Diggins's orbit. 'What do you think Junior would do if he found out about this little arrangement of ours?'

Diggins affected a pose that suggested he was considering the question deeply. 'You'd know him better than I do. What do you think?'

'What he would want to do is have our balls for breakfast. Now, in your case, he might well achieve that, but I'd be hopeful I'd make a better job of surviving.'

Diggins nodded, determined not to betray his fear.

Cash said, 'Just for the record. I think we need to be clear. Our agreement still stands.'

'I'm a man of my word.'

'You're what?'

'A man of my word.'

'And I'm Tony Soprano. And much as you mightn't like talking about these things, you do know that this means Junior has to check out, leave this world, meet his maker.'

'I understand,' Diggins said.

'Once we're clear.'

'All I know, Johnny, is that we have a deal. The rest of it is your business.' Diggins raised his glass. One for the road. If he could get this little issue out of the way, his new life would open up before him.

16

Molloy boarded the Luas in Abbey Street, travelled the length of the quays and disembarked at Heuston station. As he set off from the stop, he noticed a chill in the day, as if it was reluctant to let go of the departing winter. He walked back across the Liffey, which was offering up its low-tide smells, mined from the foulest corner of the earth's core.

He was at the entrance to the Phoenix Park within minutes. Stephanie had said to head straight up the main drag, Chesterfield Avenue. At the zoo, a gaggle of schoolchildren were being corralled together by two adults. He had been there just once as a child. He could remember an ice-cream, and his mother unwrapping sandwiches from tinfoil. Another retrievable memory was of throwing the remains of the food on to water, ducks waddling towards it, his wonder at the basics of nature. Little else from the day had stayed with him. The animals obviously hadn't made much of an impression.

He had other history with the park. After his mother died, when things went off the rails, he slept under the stars up here for a few nights, full of drink and longing. At fourteen, he was old enough to take it all on board. But he felt as if he'd been cast adrift, and wanted to find a way home.

The booze took him to a place where he felt he could make contact with his ma, just to get some reassurance that all was well with her. An epiphany told him to get to the park, where contact could be made in peace. So he slept out here, waiting, talking to her through a chain of cans of Bavaria. Eventually, he went home to an earful from Ivan who'd been worried sick.

Now, as he moved along the main drag, he looked to his left, over at the grove of trees where he had spent those few nights. All it held now for him was memories of pain, and the gun that was at the centre of his current woes.

At the big roundabout with the monument, he saw the sign for the visitor centre. The road snaked around, cutting a swathe through fields of knee-height grass.

He could see what must have been the playground in the distance. The sound of children floated to him on the air, dozens of them playing, running, climbing up a red contraption that was the centrepiece of the playground. There were a number of slides and swings. But what stood out was the noise, the incessant sound of voices lifted to a higher plane by excitement, wonder and now and again, fear. It was worse than prison.

He was standing there, gaping at all before him, when she appeared through the crowd. She had on a light pea-green dress over a pair of jeans and a beige sweatshirt, wearing the clothes in an effort to fill herself out, he reckoned. It wasn't working. Her face was different, though. She wore a smile where there had been scorn the previous day.

'How're you?' he said.

'I come in peace.'

'That makes a change. You look good.'

'And you're still full of shit.'

'Where's your lord and master?' Once it was out he knew he shouldn't have said it.

'If you want to be a prick, we can end this now. He don't know about any of this. I don't want him knowing. Just leave it, OK?'

A little boy ran up beside her and began tugging at her dress. She looked at him and bent down to his level. 'Mammy, Mammy,' he said. 'You push me on the swing.'

Molloy felt something welling inside him. The boy had chestnut hair, worn long over his shoulders. It matched the colour of his eyes. He was dressed in a pair of faded jeans and a navy sweatshirt emblazoned with the words 'I'm a little monster'.

His mother was talking to him, telling him this was somebody she wanted him to meet. He looked up at Molloy, then drew back into his mother's leg.

She picked him up. She looked to be suffering under the strain of his weight.

'Alex, this is your daddy.' His head was buried in her breast. He looked round. Molloy held out his hand. The boy stared at it, as if examining it for emotional contamination, then took it. His little hand felt warm and soft.

For a second Molloy was thrown back into that dank cell. Nights he had stared at the ceiling, impotent to the passage of time in the world where his son was feeling his way. Nights where he had tried to grapple with his fate, with the clock. Nights when he had seen a bundle being fed a bottle, the first cries, words, a step and then another, a smile. Nights haunted with worry and guilt that he wasn't there to guide his son.

Molloy pulled out a packet of chocolate buttons from his pocket. 'Is it OK?' he said. He didn't know whether he should be giving a child chocolate.

Stephanie laughed. 'I think he's seen a lot worse than buttons,' she said.

Molloy passed the sweets over. The boy took them with a smile. 'Could your daddy push you on the swing?' Stephanie said.

Alex nodded.

They walked through the playground. Stephanie introduced Molloy to a friend of hers, Gina, who was standing by a slide, watching a little girl. Gina looked to have the same dietary requirements as Stephanie, the junk all but oozing out of her pores.

Molloy put his son on the swing and began pushing him. Alex turned his head. 'I'm three,' he said.

'You're a big boy,' his father said. He reckoned he was too. Tall kid, looked like he had good balance, centre back maybe, or if he had a bit of pace, he could do a job out on the right wing.

Stephanie stood at the side of the swing, her arms folded, watching, perhaps wondering what it would have been like if things had worked out. The sun was shining now.

After a while, Alex said, 'I have enough.' Molloy lifted him from the swing. He was heavier than Molloy had thought he would be. Once on the ground, he ran over to where Stephanie's friend and her little girl were, at the slide. The boy tugged at the little girl, and pointed towards Molloy. He couldn't make out what was being said, but he imagined the kid was pointing out his father.

Stephanie gestured towards a picnic bench outside the playground, said she needed a smoke. 'What do you think?' she said.

'He's amazing,' Molloy said.

'Not at three in the morning, he's not.'

'Give the kid the break.'

'He's great. He's doing fine, with all he has to put up with.' She dropped her head when she said it, shame urging her to keep her eyes from his.

'And what about you?'

'I'm alive, amn't I? You look good, and that's not a bullshit line. How are you doing?'

'With what, your pals?'

'Back off, Josh. They're not my pals. I mean with you. Sober. Clean. How are you managing it?' She sat into the bench.

He went around and sat in opposite her. 'I'm not drinking but sobriety is a different ball game.'

'You on a programme?'

'Not really, just meetings.'

'Been that soldier.'

'You went to AA?'

'NA. AA, NA, most of the time it's not worth sweet FA.'

He laughed, and she smiled at him, reaching back for a moment to a shared past from a different world.

'There are days when I crave a hit. Just one drink. But there isn't one drink, never was.'

'Tell me about it.' She was still smiling, touching the chemistry that was once between them.

'Did you have to call him Alexander?'

The smile vanished. 'I was in a bad place at the time. You know. Alexander the Great. Maybe I was just hoping that whatever he was born into, he'd make a good go at it.'

'You must have been doing some heavy shit then.'

'I was. Anyway, he's Alex. Nobody calls him anything else.'

'So, do I need the solicitor, or is this some peace offering?'

She was looking away now, into the distance, the approach to the playground, where parents and kids were walking towards and away from them. 'Johnny knows nothing of this. If he found out he would rearrange my face.'

Molloy said, 'The Steph I knew would have told him to go fuck himself a long time ago.'

'The Steph you knew didn't have a habit strangling her.'

'And how's Alex with that?'

Stephanie blew some more smoke, ran her fingers along the table. 'He manages. I manage. It's not easy on your own.'

'Well, maybe I can take some of the load.'

'Do you want to see more of him?'

'Course I do.'

She pulled her legs out from under the picnic bench, stood over him.

'I mean, do you want see a lot more of him?'

'How much more?'

'Gettin' scared now?'

'Steph, what are you saying? Spit it out.'

She reached over, picked up the packet of cigarettes, began playing with it. 'I'm gonna try to get well once and for all. I'm going to go into a programme, end it all. It's going to be hell for a few months. I don't want Alex around.'

Now it was Molloy's turn to pull himself out of the bench. He stood up and lifted the cigarettes from her fingers, as if he had a right to take liberties after what she had just laid on him. Slowly he placed one between his lips. 'Fucking hell,' he said.

'That's nice, that is,' she said. She extended a lighter, put fire to his smoke and then her own. 'You go to the bother of getting a solicitor to get you access to your son. Then when you're told you're needed to take care of him you're like a fella who's been sentenced to run a crèche.'

Molloy walked away from her, towards the playground. Through the wire mesh he could see his son climbing a ladder to the top of a slide.

Stephanie said, 'It could be worse. He's out of nappies.'

'Nappies?'

'Yeah, Josh. Nappies. Little boys piss and shit in them. He's toilet-trained since after Christmas. It's one less thing you gotta worry about.'

'Right,' he said.

'Look, I don't want him going into care. Once he's in that

system it's a job to get him back, and they fuck up kids in there. Anything's better than that. You look like you're getting your shit together. This is a chance to get to know your son. I'm going to make a go of things. I'm going to kick this. I have to. But he can't be around. It's going to be hell on earth for a few months.'

'Jesus.'

'I'll come and visit.'

'Thanks.'

'So, what do you think?'

'Yeah, I want to do it. Once I get over the shock. I'm going to have to sort some things out, though. I've got a few things on, but I'll manage.'

'What about your brother?'

He looked at her but she had diverted her attention back to the playground.

'Great minds,' he said.

There were a few house rules. No coke, or at least not until such time as progress had been made. No violence, or at least not until such time as it was obvious that absolutely no progress was being made. Fionn Higgins was to be allowed what he requested in terms of food, but no drink.

He was permitted to rest on the bed, which was in his room, but that was to be monitored to ensure the fucker didn't just stay in bed all day, or even all night for that matter. He was allowed a supervised call to his bird twice a day.

No music. No music to listen to, and particularly no music to make. Fionn had requested an acoustic guitar, as if that was something that might be hanging around a broom cupboard in the kitchen.

Rocco told him to forget about it. He quietly explained to

Fionn that Kyle was not a great music fan, and if any sounds were heard escaping under the bedroom door, Kyle might get notions that Fionn was not taking his task seriously. When Fionn did grab forty winks here and there, Kyle usually popped into one of his dreams, standing there with the big scar across his face, violence in his eyes.

All Fionn Higgins wanted was to get back to his gaff so he could practise for next week's gig. He could also have done with a quick toot just to keep the show on the road or, at the very least, a few fingers of JD. But he knew deep down that that was negotiable, once he had fed Rocco some bullshit about how much progress he was making. If the truth be told, he wasn't even sure what he was looking for.

Fionn Higgins was in a child's bedroom, somewhere out west, as far as he could make out. In the back of Rocco's SUV, he had noticed signs for Cavan and Navan, but he wasn't up on this side of the city. What was there to be up about?

He was seated in the centre of the bedroom, on a chair that must have been commandeered from the kitchen. The table before him, on which lay the laptop, was long, narrow and made of cardboard, and looked like it was used for wallpapering or decorating of some sort.

He felt like an alien who had landed in this child's room with his incongruous table, chair and computer. There was a pair of Bob the Builder slippers, which he had lifted in a vacant moment and begun playing with on his fingers.

There was a miniature hurley and a sliotar. There was a shelf full of Lego. And the bed was covered with images of Spiderman.

Earlier, he had lain on the bed, although rest didn't come easy as he had to crowd out thoughts of Kyle coming through the door looking for blood.

He tried to concentrate on the screen. He had been through most of the available files, but there was little of interest there. He had been told that he was looking for something that indicated where this Diggins bastard might have stashed money. Yeah, right, guys, and check out the needle lying somewhere inside that giant haystack.

Downstairs Junior Corbett was sitting at the kitchen table. Kyle was standing at the work counter, fingering a K100 semi-automatic. Right now, Junior didn't like the idea of Kyle with a gun in his hand. If things went according to plan, Kyle wasn't long for this world, another day, two at the most. Innate caution drove Junior to conclude it was better that a condemned man be nowhere near a weapon in the last days of his life, lest he possess any information about the fate lined up for him.

'Put the gun away, Kyle, will you?' he said.

Kyle pointed the weapon towards the back door, lowered it and stuck into the back of his waistband. 'When are you going to let me at the prick upstairs?' he said.

'When he's no more use. There has to be something in that computer about what I'm looking for. There just has to be. Once this guy finds it, he's all yours.'

Kyle grinned. Junior nodded at him. It was his own fault. Taking out those two useless fuckers over nothing. You can't carry on like that, as if Dublin was some lawless outpost of Afghanistan. There was too much at stake to put up with that craziness.

'How long are we going to give him?' Kyle said.

Longer than you're getting. 'A few days, Kyle. This thing is coming to a head. Your brother is going to have a little chat with Diggins's wife today and we'll see what comes of that. Right now, I'm just about pissed off with all the faffing about. I want my money back.'

Donal rang four times over the course of the morning. Her phone first went off as she was stepping into her car outside the apartment. She looked at the caller display and saw his name there, buzzing like a plea. She let it ring, sat in and started the engine.

The day was fine, a rinsed sky full of blue promise, the sun burning last night's showers from the street. Even the Liffey looked good, high tide and a surface of crystal. This morning was going to be all about me-time. The case for the defence could wait till later.

She needed the sea. At times like this, she always headed for the coast. There was comfort in trawling through her thoughts at the edge of the ocean. At home, whenever doubts surfaced, whenever she and Donal had rowed, it was a quick nip down to Killiney strand. This time she didn't want the interference of recent memories. She turned the car north.

Traffic out of town was light. She tuned into Lyric FM, looking for something to take her away for a few hours. Out on the Clontarf Road she turned right for Dollymount, and drove towards the wooden bridge, which could only accommodate traffic one way. The light was green. She proceeded across the bridge. The North Bull pier came into view ahead, presided over by the statue of Mary, Queen of the Sea, green and ancient. Noelle left the road and followed the sandy path leading to the beach. She felt something scrape at the car's undercarriage, prompting her to apply greater caution to her driving. The path opened out into Dollymount strand, stretching off to the left, like a sandy necklace, as far as the Hill of Howth.

A couple of cars and a camper van were parked in front of large boulders that formed a car park of sorts on the beach. She pulled up, got out and opened the boot, from where she took her walking boots. She was standing on one foot, swapping footwear, when she heard her phone ring again from inside the vehicle. It rang out.

The boots were one size too big, but that was no big deal. She walked up and down beside the car, getting used to them.

Caroline's purple windbreaker fell loosely on her shoulders. She smiled to herself. Little girl lost, that's me.

She closed the boot and took the mobile from the dashboard. Two missed calls. Donal's second attempt.

A fair wind whipped in off the bay. It felt fresh on her face. There were large mounds of sand that looked wet and gave off the smell of a sewer, piled up at intervals along the beach. The tide was low, out beyond damp flats of sand, the wash from passing ships rippling across the water to shore. A couple, barely on the cusp of adulthood, were at the controls of a kite, the boy adopting the pose of teacher, guiding the girl's hands from behind.

She knew what was coming. Whenever she found herself in this mood, her thoughts always dragged her back to the point she considered to be the fork in her road.

It was a few weeks before the Leaving Cert that she told her mother her secret ambition to be a dancer, to make a career out of that which had been her passion since she was a child. There was no reply. Her mother looked at her as if she was listening to somebody unload grief, which demanded no response, only a sympathetic ear. Her mother eventually pulled her into a hug, maternal concern etched on her face. It was out of the question, of course. She didn't have to follow her father into law if she felt that strongly about it. But dancing, well, that was something you did at weddings and parties. It wasn't a career.

After the heart attack took her father, the practice was sold. By then Noelle had been working there for less than a year. There was no way she was going to stay on in the business. She bought a round-the-world ticket and struck out for Australia. She probably never had been as happy as she was during that year. Back home, the drifting went on, delivering her to Paul & Paul, delivering her to Donal's front door, the nagging doubt never leaving her. She was living somebody else's life.

The phone was hopping in the pocket of the windbreaker as she turned on the beach, placing the wind at her back. She didn't need to check who it was. She wondered whether he was doing coke. A few years back, at the height of the madness, she had found a vial one morning after a hectic night before.

She was amazed she hadn't copped what he was at. Drugs scared her, but as Donal had pointed out, she wasn't shy of the sauce and that was as much a drug as anything. There had been times after that when she suspected he might be on something, but he had always denied it in that reassuring way of his.

By the time she got close to the car park, she broke off towards the rear of the strand, where stumps of beach grass were bent against the wind. There was a wooden picnic table there, frayed and chipped, beaten senseless by the elements. When she sat into it, she could see right across to the southern reaches of the bay. Over there was Killiney, where once she had made her home with her husband.

She pulled the wedding band from her finger. It was a white-gold ring with the Celtic Trinity knot embossed in it. Donal had been nonplussed with her choice. He would have preferred something more extravagant, something to reflect both his love and where they were heading. The poor bastard.

She took the ring and lodged it between two of the frayed panels that made up the table. It might make somebody's day.

She felt lighter walking back to the car, as if she had shed a skin. From here on, she would beat her own path.

At the car, she untied her boots and returned them whence they'd come. Her mouth was filled with the taste of hot chocolate. Maybe there was somewhere on the way back into town where she could stop. She sat in behind the wheel, her whole body feeling refreshed. As she pulled the door closed, a man walked into the field of her vision, traipsing across the sand. Her first instinct was that it was the reporter. An impulse prompted her to start the car, turn it around and mow him down. But within seconds, it dawned on her that this was no reporter.

He wore a navy hoodie, the tails of a football jersey escaping beneath the bottom flaps. His face was full of purpose. He kept his eyes on her. There was something wrong. This guy wasn't looking for directions or the time of day. Noelle reached over and grabbed the windbreaker, ran her hands around it, looking for the pocket.

She could feel the keys through the fabric, but couldn't locate the pocket. The man was now less than ten yards away. Out on the beach, a couple were halfway down the strand, too far away to respond promptly to any cry for help. Her two hands were now feeling around the windbreaker. She felt the cold metal of the keys and pulled them out.

The man was now arriving at her door. He had a cap of hair that looked like it had been cut with a bowl. His face still didn't offer a smile. Everything about him confirmed her first instincts.

The engine came to life. The man knocked on the window. Lyric FM filled the cab with the sound of Vienna. Strauss was giving it welly. She didn't look up, her left hand pulling the gearstick into reverse. The couple on the beach had broken away from their path and were moving towards the car park now, but still too far away to be of any help.

She heard her name. She looked up at him. He was mouthing it again, as if to offer reassurance that he wasn't some crank. She eased her foot off the clutch and the car began to move. He stood there, still stooped, watching her reverse away. She swung the wheel around and pointed the car towards the road the hell out of here. By now, the man had broken into a jog, although he wasn't running towards her. She figured he was heading for his own car. Jesus Christ, he was going to follow her.

She heard a scraping noise underneath, and slowed down, her right foot touching lightly on the brake. The rear-view mirror gave up the image of a Toyota Avensis behind her. The car eased out on to the road again, heading for the wooden bridge. She stole another look at the mirror. It was him all right behind the wheel. What did he want? It had to be something to do with Donal. Why now, just after she had made her pledge, released herself from the marital coupling? It was as if she wasn't going to be left alone. He was sending somebody after her.

The traffic light at the bridge was red. She brought the car to a stop. He was still behind her. There was nothing approaching on the bridge. He got out of the car. He began walking towards her. The light was still red. There were fates worse than breaking a red light. She took off, caught him on her wing mirror, throwing his arms in the air. His anger was almost palpable, even at this distance.

As she approached the turn on to the main road, the light was green. She swung left and slipped out of the bus lane, heading towards the city. Against her better judgement, she looked for solace to the rear-view mirror again. He was still on her tail.

At the first set of lights, he was right behind her. She told herself not to panic. She was out here in the open. What was he going to do? Run up and try to drag her from the car? Shoot her? Of course not. Don't be crazy. Why would he do that?

The lights changed. She let down the handbrake and took off again. She noticed that her hands were trembling on the wheel. She felt a well of emotion rise up through her, like a tide. Keep things even. What in the name of God was Donal involved in? Who were these people?

She passed Fairview Park on the left, heading straight towards town. Once she arrived in the city centre, the traffic would thicken, presenting him with the opportunity to race up and snatch her or shoot her. She had to do something. She couldn't lead him all the way back to where she lived. Or did he know that already?

Then she saw it. Up ahead on the left, a squad car was pulled over on the bus lane, right up the arse of another car, having collared the driver for some indiscretion.

She indicated, the sound of the beeping thumping through her brain like a homing call to a sanctuary. She pulled up behind the squad car. A uniform was leaning in the window of the vehicle in front of it. He looked up when he saw her.

She caught a glimpse of her pursuer, staring across at her as he passed. She refused to meet his eyes. She sat back and closed hers. The phone began ringing. Donal. Fourth time. The garda was walking towards her.

'Wally?'

'Yo.'

'All wrapped up for the evening.'

'Is that the dumbest Irishman I know?'

'How are you?'

'Good, my friend. Another day down. Those two imposters fear and pride been hangin' about my cell earlier on but I sent them on their way. No room for resentment here, not when I'm on my ownio.'

'You're the only fucker I know could start a fight in a cell on your own.'

'Not today, brother. Today I know what I can and can't change.'

'Met my son.'

'Hey, that's cool, man. All went OK?'

'It's some feeling.'

'He as ugly as you?'

'Listen, it's good, you know. Going through all this stuff being able to feel it like it's real. It's hard, but it's good.'

'Check out the dude walking into the light. And his mother?'

'It's going to be OK. She's getting sorted and I'm going to take care of Alex for a while.'

'You serious?'

'I'm going to be a dad. And I'm shitting bricks.'

'As you would. Take it from me, it's no picnic.'

'What the fuck would you know? You said you weren't around much when your kids were growing up.'

'Even not being around was no picnic. And the other business. That monkey on your back waving a semi-A.'

'I'm taking your advice. Getting out of Dodge. Going down to my brother's place, check out how he would be about looking after Alex until I get fixed up. Hold on, there's somebody at my door. Listen, give you a shout when I'm out in the country, free and easy.'

'Till then, brother.'

'Hi. God, I've been trying to get you all day.'

'I know.'

'Why didn't you pick up?'

'I didn't really want to talk to you.'

'Noelle, what's going on?'

'Are you alone now?

'What?'

'Are you alone or have you got one of your prostitutes there?'

'Noelle, what are you saying?'

'The credit-card bills.'

'Go on.'

'Do you really want me to spell it out?'

'Noelle, it's not what you think.'

'I don't want to think about it at all, Donal. I've gone beyond it. But thank you for enlightening me on the state of my marriage. I knew there was something terribly wrong but I just couldn't put my finger on it. Thanks for straightening that out for me.'

'Noelle, please, you have to listen to me. It's not what you think. You have to stay focused. We have a job to do. We have to secure our futures. You have to get the money and bring it over here. Then we can move on from all this.'

'I have moved on, Donal. All that's left is to complete the formalities. You know, it's strange how when your world is turned upside down you can see the wood for the trees for the first time. I knew things weren't right, but not for a minute did I think you had to get comfort from prostitutes.'

'Noelle, calm down. Just listen for a minute, OK? I've got a problem, OK? There, I said it. I have a problem with cocaine.'

'Excuse me?'

'The coke. It's been getting out of hand.'

'Oh, I see.'

'Yeah. It's just … the way things were going for the last few years, you fall into a trap and—'

'The last few years? How long?'

'I don't know – since things began to take off with the business. You get offered stuff and get into a routine.'

'A routine? Donal, you need some help.'

'I know, I know, I'm going to. Look, once we get the money—'

'You don't understand. I'd like to see you sort yourself out, I really would, but it's not on my watch any more. We're finished. This is goodbye. I'll get a solicitor to give you a bell about the divorce.'

'Wait, wait. Noelle, you're not going to let a couple of hookers come between us? What about the money?'

'You're something else, Donal. You don't get it, do you? Your hookers, as you call them, are not the disease, although I shudder to think what they might be carrying. They are the symptom. It's over, Donal. I'm just glad I saw the light before I got further into this mess with you.'

'Noelle, wait. We can talk about this. If you go down and get the money and fly out here, we'll sort things out. Everything will be like it used to be before all this stuff blew up.'

'That's what I would be afraid of.'

'Noelle, the money—'

'I'm hanging up now, Donal, before I start smashing this phone on the floor. Goodbye.'

17

Johnny Cash looked in the mirror and liked what he saw. He had on a Gino Valentino jet black suit. The shirt was black silk, the tie a striped dark forest-green number. His feet were shod in Prada. He looked good. Sure, the years were there on his face and on his swept-back rug. But he looked good. Nobody could question that.

He was standing in front of the wardrobe with the full-length mirror in his bedroom. Well, it wasn't his bedroom in the technical sense. The house was Esther's, but he had bought it for her from the council. Since he had moved in four years ago, he had made a home of the place with Esther and her daughter Stella. That way the CAB couldn't show up and claim he'd bought the house with dirty money.

His phone was groaning in his pocket. He pulled it out. 'Everything OK?'

'Couldn't be better.'

'Rocco?'

'The Dubs are playing tonight. He wouldn't miss it for the world.'

'And our other friend?'

'Twinkle Toes?'

'Yeah.'

'His dancing days are behind him.'

'OK. I'll see you later at the garage.'

He hadn't been in favour of the mirrored wardrobes when Esther had first suggested them. What was it about women and mirrors? He was partial to mirrors himself, but women needed to have one within reach at all times, like a junkie needs her gear.

It wasn't the money. It was just that in matters like this he didn't have full control over his own home and that irritated him. Control was what life was about. Once it began to slip, chaos was around the corner, and Johnny Cash was acutely aware of the random nature of chaos.

Today the mirror was being called into action to ensure that he looked the business. Whenever a big day like this came around, he had a need to demonstrate his self-respect. The downside was that this was the last time he would wear these threads. Everything would have to go up in smoke once the business was done. But so what? What was any of it worth if he couldn't show this measure of respect for the job?

He checked the canvas holdall on the bed. Sock, jocks, Fruit of the Loom jogging pants, a black hoodie and a pair of runners. There was also a can of Sure deodorant, the .357 magnum revolver and two plastic bags with zippers. He patted his right-hand suit pocket where the Sig Sauer felt just a little too bulky. He pulled it out and stuck it into the waistband at the small of his back.

He zipped up the bag and moved to the door. On the threshold he turned back for one more check. Yeah, he looked the business. The next time he entered this bedroom he would be a different man. His destiny would be fulfilled. The leap from number two to number one was the biggest you could make. He should know: he had climbed the greasy pole over the last twenty-odd years, inch by inch.

Not for the first time he tried to remove from his mind the fuck-up that had brought him to this point. What had he been thinking? OK, the notion of putting Harms Sullivan in there had made sense, but he had never for a second thought the fella would make such a balls-up of the job. Afterwards, he had even got a kick out of doing him on the doorstep in his mother's arms. Fellas like him didn't deserve to live when they played around with the lives of others in such a cavalier manner. And now everything was coming full circle. He was cleaning up the final stains of the mess from the first day, and finishing the job himself.

The phone groaned again. Kyle. 'Johnny, you were looking for me?'

'Yeah, something's come up. I got to meet you in town.'

'Sure, except Rocco's gone to the Dubs game. Is it urgent or you want to leave it till after the game?'

'We can manage without big brother for one night, can't we?'

Silence filled the line for a few seconds.

'No prob, Johnny. You know me. Anything Rocco can do, I can do better.'

'We got to meet somebody about his last waltz.'

'The what?'

'The last ... our friend, the Dancer. He's hanging up his shoes.'

'Hey, now you're talking, Johnny. Say where and when. This is my night.'

They arranged to meet in Parnell Square in twenty minutes.

Downstairs, Esther was curled up on the couch, all eyes and ears on one of those talent shows where nobody had any talent. He could see Stella inside at the kitchen table, opened books spread around her and a cup at her elbow. Saturday night and she was in doing her homework.

Stella was a big girl. Whenever Johnny Cash looked at her he couldn't help thinking about wrestling. He often wondered whether she'd ever thought of getting into it. It was so big in the States it was only a matter of time before it took off here. He was always on the look-out for legit opportunities, and it had often occurred to him that women's wrestling was a game that had massive potential. Teenagers like Stella, nice faces, plenty of meat on the bone, could be a big attraction.

Esther had notions of sending the kid to college, but Johnny Cash doubted that they'd let her in on account of her being about two steps away from retarded.

He'd been standing there for at least twenty seconds before Esther pulled her eyes away from the box. She smiled at him, returned to the show and then did a double-take. She took in the threads, the canvas bag, and her face dropped. He'd known that would be her reaction and he still got a kick out of it.

'Hot date,' she said, unable to keep what he recognised as rising panic from her voice. He leaned down and kissed her. She wrapped her arms around his neck, pulled him into her, but he resisted, making sure to extricate himself gently.

'Don't worry, it's work.'

'Will you be late?'

'Don't wait up.'

'Why not? Maybe it'll be worth my while if I do.'

He walked into the kitchen. 'Night, Stella,' he said. She didn't look up, but raised her middle finger, then turned her face, which bore a smile of mischief.

The pair of them were standing there. Johnny Cash looked like a man who was on his way to get married. Kyle had on a fleece, but the red trimming of the Liverpool away strip was visible at the collar and the tail of the jacket.

'Let's go,' Cash said.

'Where?'

'Your missus wants to see you. She thinks it's time you got involved in raising the kid.'

Molloy went cold. He looked at Cash, who was staring intently at him. Kyle was moping around, as if checking out the place for something he could lift. 'No prob,' he said. He bent down to tie the lace of his runner. 'Just have to take a leak before we go.' When he looked up, Kyle had turned his head.

'Where's the pisser?'

'Why? Do you want to join me?'

Kyle smiled. Another stab of fear hit Molloy. The thick fucker wouldn't be reacting like that unless he had revenge close at hand. One thing was sure. Stephanie wasn't expecting them. She would have called. Most likely, they weren't going anywhere near her. Molloy arched his back, like a man stretching after an uncomfortable sleep. He saw a dark road. He saw himself kneeling at the margin, wet grass seeping into his trousers. He saw Kyle smirking. 'Down on the landing,' he said.

Cash moved towards the door. 'I gotta take a squirt first.' He went out the door.

Kyle was sweeping his eyes around the room. 'It can't be easy, staying in a shithole like this.'

Molloy wasn't going to play ball right now. He had to think. If he made a move, he could take Kyle, but Cash would be through the door like a shot. The window was still a long way up. He probably wouldn't survive the leap. One way or the other, he had to make a move. This thing looked completely fucked. 'Big brother let you out on your own tonight?' he said.

A flash of anger crossed Kyle's face. Molloy could see it was killing him to hang everything together, like a kid in a sweet shop who's been promised a treat if he keeps his hands in his pockets until he gets home. 'Escort duty doesn't need two of us,' he said.

'Rocco at the Dubs match?'

'What the fuck is it to you?'

Cash came back through the door. If he'd taken a piss, it was the shortest in history. 'OK, go on,' he said.

Molloy made for the door. He could feel eyes on his back as he descended the stairs. If he made a run for it now, he'd never get outside. He saw himself thrown against the door, reaching for the lock, the smell of cordite filling his nostrils, bullets slamming into his back.

The bathroom was its own prison. As Cash had just discovered, there was no way out. The smoked-glass window could only be opened at the top. A midget on a crash diet might make it, but otherwise it was only good for air. It was open now. He could hear the patter of soft rain on a roof outside.

He turned on the cold tap, splashed water on his face. He looked up. Deep breaths. Water was dripping down his cheeks. He had to stay alert. Think of nothing else. Block everything from his mind, particularly his son. He had to trust now. Trust his instinct.

Once they got him into a car, it was most likely all over. The best he could hope for was that they'd shoot him there if he lashed out. He'd leave the world with the grim satisfaction that his killers would have a job cleaning up afterwards. He saw a car abandoned on the side of the road, a pedestrian passing it and peeking in. He saw himself on the back seat, life ebbing from his body.

When he came out of the bathroom, Johnny Cash was standing on the landing, trying to look casual. He had Molloy's jacket on his arm, like a husband hurrying along his wife. Kyle was up at the door to the flat.

Molloy said he had to lock the door. Cash handed him the

jacket and stood aside. Once the door was locked, all three descended the stairs.

The evening was damp. Molloy felt the rain on his head. He could smell cooking escaping an open window. Music drifted from somewhere. It sounded like Abba.

The street was one way, traffic flowing top to bottom. Parking was busy, the spaces all taken up. He saw Johnny Cash's BMW just ahead of them. It was now or never. A Hiace van turned on to the street. Molloy heard the change of gears.

Two cars before the BMW he made a run for it. He ran straight in front of the Hiace. He heard the screech of brakes. He could see the driver, his face a study in anger. Beside him a woman had a hand to her mouth. He heard his name being shouted. He heard a bang rend the air. On the far side of the road, he ducked and ran, ducked and ran between the parked vehicles. Another bang rang out. He turned and thought he saw Kyle with a weapon extended into the night. There was no sign of Cash. He could hear his heart thumping, like a bell tolling.

The sound of voices came into his orbit, but it was too late when he looked up. A woman screamed as he crashed into her, another flung to the inside of the street. He saw a metallic skirt and platform heels. He felt himself hit the wet pavement, his left shoulder exploding in pain. The woman was slumped against a parked car. She looked at him, all confusion. Another was lying on her stomach beside Molloy. He couldn't see her face, but she was moaning. He slipped as he got to his feet. He saw Kyle running towards him. He got up and slid between two cars out on to the street. Another car was coming, deep red, the colour of blood. He ran out in front of this one, threw himself on the bonnet and sailed to the other side, landing with another crash. Brakes screeched. He got up and ran between cars again to the other side of the pavement. A car door opened, introducing an angry voice. He heard another bang.

At the top of the street, he straightened and kept running. The ground beneath his feet felt wet, slippery here and there. He tried to regulate his breathing. He had been in some sticky set-ups before, but this was the first time he had had literally to run for his life.

When Johnny Cash saw the two men ahead he slowed to a walk. He was sure Molloy had turned down this street, which was really a lane. On one side there was the high brick wall that must have enclosed a school. On the other, he walked past the shuttered front of a shop. The two lads were standing outside some form of a hall. They didn't look like upstanding members of the community. One had a can of Bavaria in his hand, a dirty woollen hat covering his crown; the other was pulling hard on a cigarette. Two more cans of Bavaria were at their feet. They were all eyes on him, as if he was a ghost, or somebody who was about to change their lives for ever.

When he arrived next to them he saw that they were standing beside a railing with an entrance to steps descending to a basement. 'Fella come running down here?' he asked.

The two looked at each other. The one wearing the woolly hat addressed him: 'Lots of fellas come running down here,' he said.

'How many came running down here in the last thirty fucking seconds?'

It was the other's turn to pipe up. 'Was he an alcoholic?'

Cash took the revolver from his pocket and pointed it at the head of Woolly Hat. 'Let's count to three,' he said. 'One …'

'Down there,' Woolly Hat said, his left hand covering his eyes, his right index finger pointing to the stone steps leading to a basement. 'Down there with all those other fuck-ups.'

Cash lowered the weapon. He looked down the steps. He

dug into his trouser pocket, pulled out a red ten-euro note and handed it to the bareheaded one. 'Sorry 'bout the hard arm, fellas, but this guy has fucked me over big-time. What's going on?'

'Alcoholics. They meet down there and, if the truth be told, they wouldn't give the steam of their piss to the crows.'

'Is there any other way out of there?' Cash said.

The two lads looked at each other, before the bareheaded one said, 'How would we know? Never had any cause to go down there.'

As he descended the steps, Cash could see through a window what looked like a gathering in progress. There was no sign of Molloy. He pushed open the door. A few heads in the room turned towards him. There were signs up around the place about thinking and letting go, and other stuff that was for the birds. The room was full of mostly men. At the top, two were facing everybody else. He thought he recognised the one who was talking, but he made a point of not meeting the fella's eyes.

He spotted a free chair a few feet away and slipped into it. The man in the chair next to him, who wore a beard and eyes that drooped with sadness, thrust out a hand. Johnny Cash looked at it as if it might carry a disease.

He scanned the room until he spotted his prey. Molloy was at the far end, beside an entrance to some form of a kitchen, sitting next to a fella who was built like a brick shithouse. What to do now? He had one target in his sights here, but he had to keep tabs on the other out there on the streets, wandering around like Moses in the desert.

Right now, all he could do was sit tight and wait for Molloy to make his move.

'Each and every one of us has our own journey and tonight I see that an old friend of mine has taken a big step on his.' Johnny Cash looked up at the top table. The prick was staring down at him. He could place him now. Foley: hung around the fringes a few years back before heading into the Joy on something stupid. Never heard any more from him after that. What the fuck was he playing at? Over at the far end of the room, Molloy was bent into the ear of Brick Shithouse.

'I don't want to embarrass him but it says something to me that he has made it here to the rooms tonight. I could tell some stories about the scrapes we've been in.'

Johnny Cash's hand moved around to the side of his waistband, felt the handle of the revolver through his jacket. The prospect of taking it out and starting a massacre occurred to him. He could certainly pop this Foley prick, and would be hard pressed to miss Molloy. Of course, even if he himself made it out through the door, he might as well turn the weapon on himself. Twenty or so witnesses, all sober. And, from the look of them, more than a few were capable of taking care of themselves.

'We don't usually do this but, Johnny, I would just like to welcome you here tonight. Is there anything you'd like to say?'

The eyes of the room turned on Johnny Cash. Every one of them, taking in all of his features, his threads, the gelled hair, the colour of his eyes, all of the killer punches if he ever found himself in a line-up. He could feel his face burning. He stared at Foley, trying to bore through the prick's skull, transmitting the sentiment that if Cash ever again in this life got the chance to do him some serious harm he would grab it with both hands. The room was very quiet, apart from a chair scraping near Molloy. Johnny Cash shook his head.

'Sorry about that, Johnny. In your own time,. We all know what the first time is like. Hope I didn't embarrass you. Just remember. Keep coming back. Don't pick up that first drink and keep coming back.'

Johnny Cash didn't move a muscle. The prick resumed his spiel, something about a higher power. Mother of Jesus, Cash had been at some tense meetings where territories were carved up, and sentences handed out to good men. He had never felt as tense as he did now.

When he looked over, Brick Shithouse was giving him the eye. The seat next to him was vacant. Cash's gaze shifted to the entrance to the kitchenette. He got up and walked over. Brick Shithouse got to his feet too and moved in front of the entrance.

He stood there, his arms folded, quiet defiance in his eyes. Beyond his shoulder, Cash could see a fire door that had been left ajar. He moved to go past the big man but there was nothing doing. The room had gone quiet. 'Move it,' he said. Brick Shithouse stiffened. He wasn't going anywhere.

When he got to the top of the stone steps, the two lads were still there. The one with the woolly hat pointed in the general direction of Dorset Street. He had a look on him as if he expected another tip. Johnny Cash walked on by. There were two chances now of finding Molloy. He pulled out his mobile.

Kyle was like a woman on the phone. He was at the top of the street where Molloy's place was. The law was all over the place. The whole area was alive now, heads sticking out of windows, the flashing blue lights and gentle rain lending the street an eerie texture. From where Kyle was, he could make out a knot of uniforms and ordinary heads around where one of the women had fallen.

Cash felt his left fist ball. Why, oh, why was he always condemned to be around such amateurs? He comforted himself with the idea that tonight was the last time he would have to put up with this muppet. The main thing now was to rescue the situation. He had to regain control before it all began to slip away.

He told Kyle to forget about the BMW. There was no point in taking the chance of getting nabbed if he went back down for it. Chances were they wouldn't cop it, and even if they did, it wouldn't amount to much. Kyle was to get a taxi back to his own place and pick up some wheels. He'd meet him at the junkie's paradise.

Out on Dorset Street, he slipped into a pub, The Big Tree. He ordered a large Powers. The place was sparsely populated. At one end a crowd was gathered in front of a big screen, watching a match. The commentary was boring through his head. He didn't need this right now. He sat down at a small round table, his back to the wall. The whiskey felt good, warming him, steadying the ship. All was not lost. He would have to return to Molloy, but that fella wasn't going anywhere. He would get the woman in the morning, beat the head off her if he had to, but he was going to do that fucker once and for all. He had been nothing but trouble since he returned.

The noise level from the vicinity of the screen was rising. The commentator began to sound like a man badly in need of a Valium or two. Of course, it was the Dubs. He detected that the match was on the bend for home, with what, Jesus, less than ten minutes left. Once that was over, Rocco was back in the game. He could walk through the door any minute.

Cash threw back the dregs of the whiskey. He pushed away the table and got to his feet. There had been enough fuck-ups for one night without Kyle's big brother walking in and spoiling everything.

He alighted from the taxi about ten minutes from the place. Rain was still falling in a fine curtain as he walked. You wouldn't put a dog out on a night like this. He began to feel the dampness through his clothes. The overcoat was in the back seat of the abandoned BMW. He found it hard to let go of the anger.

By the time he arrived at the lane, he was soaked through. Kyle was sitting in the Avensis outside the place. All he needed now was for a junkie to be cowering out of the rain. There should be nobody there, but on a night like tonight all available dry space would be coveted.

He rapped on the car window, and Kyle jumped. He threw his hand in the air and walked into the place. At the threshold, he heard a car door slam behind him. Inside, there was just darkness. He moved delicately, ensuring that nothing was going to trip him at this stage.

In the middle of the front room, where he had brought together Molloy and his whore, Johnny Cash stood and turned. He moved his right foot around, clearing a space for himself, as if he was going to do a little dance.

Kyle came through the door. He flicked on a lighter, sparked a smoke.

'I have an idea,' he said.

'Yeah. Tell me your idea.' Johnny Cash brought the revolver out, held it by his side in the darkness.

'We get the two women, the solicitor and Stephanie, bring them out here and get Molloy on the phone. He can listen as we go to work on them. Explain to him exactly what's going to happen if he don't get his ass out here. What do you think?'

'Would you like that, Kyle?'

'Fuck it, wouldn't you? If you like, you could leave it to me and Rocco.'

'You been on to Rocco since the match?'

'Naw, he's on the razz. Be tomorrow morning before he surfaces.'

'Good. Come here. Look what I did manage to get off Molloy tonight.'

Kyle walked towards him, slowly, his feet feeling the way

across the floor. He pulled from the cigarette, its orange glow lighting his nose but barely making it as far as his eyes.

The noise was deafening, startling even Johnny Cash. Kyle reeled back, spun, and fell on his face, crashing on to a milk crate, before falling to the floor. Johnny Cash walked over. He heard moaning from the body. He bent down, flicked on his lighter next to Kyle's face. He wanted Kyle to see him. He began patting down Kyle's jacket, moving his hand across the blood until he found a pocket. He pulled the keys out. He could feel the dampness now, getting into his bones. He bent down close to Kyle's ear. 'One too many fuck-ups,' he said. He placed the revolver three inches from Kyle's head and pulled the trigger again.

He was still buzzing by the time he got back to the garage. Over the years, he had noticed that killing had that effect, irrespective of who was getting it. For a few hours afterwards, you never felt so alive.

The shutter on the small door was down but not locked. There was a faint hint of light inside. He lifted the shutter, wincing as it squealed along the runners. Once inside he pulled it down after him. He felt the handle of his Sig Sauer in his waistband. The revolver was now lying at the bottom of the Royal Canal.

'Junior?' There was no reply. A hint of light came from the office. The rest of the garage was shrouded in darkness. He could make out a shape, raised on the hydraulic jack. The back, where Junior did his weights, was just a black hole that might have gone on for ever.

He walked over to the office. He pushed open the door, heard it creak on its hinges – he'd never noticed that before. He half expected Junior to pop up from behind the desk. He lifted the gun from his waistband. The first thing he heard was Junior's voice from behind.

'Don't turn around. Put it on the floor.'

He knew if he turned that that was it. He felt alive. He dropped the piece to the floor, heard the dull crack on the concrete. He was looking ahead now, straight at the reindeer dressed as Santa Claus.

'Kick it.'

'What's the problem, Junior? I know I'm dolled up, but don't tell me you don't recognise me.'

'Kick it and then we talk.'

'Talk about what?'

'Kick it or we don't talk.'

Johnny Cash kicked the Sig Sauer. It hit off the metal leg of the desk. He turned and faced down the barrel of a sawn-off shotgun. Junior was togged out in running gear, black, working clothes. He didn't look like a man who was dressed up for any life-changing event.

'Where's Kyle?'

'He's moved on.'

'And Molloy?'

'Still out there. It's was Kyle's last fuck-up.'

There was only business on Junior's face. But then again, Cash could now see, it was all business. Whatever was going to happen, there would be no emotional connection. They had met through business, they would depart the same way. All that mattered now was which of them would be continuing in business. Johnny Cash wasn't a betting man, but he could see the odds were stacked against him. All he had left was his mouth, which had never been his greatest asset.

'What was the plan?'

'You know the plan, Junior. It didn't come off, but that's not the end of things. Kyle is in the bag and I'll get my hands on Molloy. There's no problem.'

'What was the plan for me?'

'Junior, what the fuck is up with you?' Control was what it was about now. He had to stay in control of himself, his bladder. It wasn't over until it was over. There was no point in appealing to the fella's better nature, just as he knew it would have been futile for Junior to do so if their roles were reversed. He saw Esther opening the door to two pigs, a look on her face that said she didn't need to hear the news, she knew it already.

He wouldn't be going back to the house himself.

'When did you get greedy, Johnny?'

'Come on, what's all this about? How long have we been together, Junior?' There was no change in his face. Blank. Focused. Unyielding.

'Now that the end is near.'

'So why are you doing this?'

'The time for bullshit is past, Johnny.'

'You've got the wrong end of the stick.'

'I had somebody keep tabs on you over in Spain. I knew something was up but, by Christ, when I heard you were hooked up with Diggins, that threw me. You and that fuck-wit coming together to do me. How much?'

'Junior, I just heard that the guy was down there. I arranged to meet him, see if we could get some of your money back. I was going to fill you in when this stuff with Kyle and Molloy was out of the way.'

'Keep talking, Johnny. I love the sound of a dying man pleading for his life. I'll let you know when it starts boring me.'

'Junior, you're making a big mistake. We can sort this out.'

'The thing I haven't figured out was when you hooked up with this cunt. Obviously it was before that toe-rag Sullivan tried to do me. I knew he couldn't have been behind that on his own. It's only since getting the lowdown from Spain that I've nailed that it was you and Diggins. But when did you hook up with him? Was it that time I sent you to London?'

Johnny Cash could feel pain rising in his stomach. The night was closing in. There was but a crack of light left. He had seen others in this situation, how they had abandoned all dignity on the precipice, blubbering, shitting themselves, surrendering any claim that they were real men. Not him. He was still in control.

There was nothing to lose now. The darkness might give cover. He could still smell the prize, just out there a small way beyond his reach. The Sig Sauer was at the foot of the table behind him. He framed his words as if they were the last confession Junior was looking for. 'That time in London. We met up. He wanted— Jesus, I told him he was crazy, that you and me went back so far—'

Johnny Cash turned and dived for the floor. He saw the Sig Sauer as he came down. His fingers reached out, touched the chequered rosewood of the grip. Then his world exploded. The shotgun blast pushed him under the table, to the far side. He couldn't breathe, fading, going, lying there, looking up. The reindeer stood above him. It was Christmas all year round here, all year round. And then no more.

18

The Woodstock Café was crawling with cops. There were four uniforms at a window table. Two more were seated to the rear, wearing tall boots as if they had just been wading around in water. Another group included three in plainclothes although, like all their ilk, they weren't in plainclothes as much as clothes carrying a large sign saying, 'We are members of An Garda Síochána.'

The café hummed with conversation; a radio played wallpaper pop in the background. Lionel Richie. 'Easy'.

The place was in the heart of Phibsboro, just across the road from the local shopping centre. There was a scattering of wooden tables and chairs and copies of the daily newspapers left out for perusal. The long display case where Molloy queued had the pick of dinners, meat and two veg, a curry, even a pie.

As Molloy picked up a tray, two more of them came through the door. This pair were brandishing helmets and wraparound shades, and bursting out of leather outfits. No wonder the country was fucked, all these pigs in here with their snouts in the trough while the crims were at play outside. Right now, he saw them not as a threat to his liberty but as a protective shield around his life. Nobody this side of a kamikaze pilot was going to walk in here waving a gun around the place.

He felt calm, despite the Glock weighing on his pocket and on his mind.

Ever since he'd gone up to the Phoenix Park the previous evening and dug it up, the gun had been on his person.

He ordered a white coffee from a girl who transacted in a foreign accent and with a shy smile. Where to sit was the next problem. He had a quick scour, and noticed that one of the plainclothes boys was looking at him. Just as he knew who they were, they knew where he was coming from, even if they couldn't put a name to the face.

He found a two-seater table tucked away in the corner. He sat with his back to the wall. Lionel Richie gave way to Men At Work, 'Down Under'.

Seven minutes later, Noelle Diggins walked through the door. Just like the cops she was in plainclothes, except she looked the business. She wore jeans, a white cotton shirt and a black leather jacket. Her white runners had pink trimmings. She wasn't wearing her glasses.

She scoured the room and he raised his hand, but not high enough that everybody else would notice. Her eyes were narrowed in a squint. She saw him, nodded, and a smile raced across her face. He got up and shifted on his feet, not knowing whether to reach out and hold the chair for her, but then he thought better of it.

'Thanks for coming,' he said. He was half hoping she might be embarrassed about the other night. It would give him an advantage in what he was about to deliver.

He asked what she would like and she said a cappuccino.

There were only two people queuing at the till. He gave

the order and stood looking back at her as the coffee machine spluttered and squealed.

She had slipped out of her jacket when he returned with the frothy mug.

'About the other night,' she said.

'What night?'

'Thank you.' She took a sip of her coffee and winced.

'I got sorted with my son,' he said.

She looked up, an even expression on her face. 'Really?'

'Steph agreed to meet me, brought Alex along. He's a great kid.'

'I'm sure he is. Does he take after you?'

'Give him a chance. He's only three years of age.'

She laughed. 'I mean in looks.'

'Yeah, she thinks so anyway. Can't see it myself, but who am I to argue?'

She was looking at him now, like she was seeing something for the first time. He wondered what her reaction would be if he told her about the Glock. 'I need your help with one more thing.'

'Ask away.'

'I'm taking my son down to my brother's place.'

Noelle looked around and lowered her head. 'You're what?'

'Don't worry, I'm not kidnapping him. I have to go down and check with the brother first, but Steph asked me to do it. She wants to make a go at kicking her habit, a proper go. She can't have Alex around. I agreed to take him and bring him down to the brother's place. He's got kids of his own.'

Noelle straightened up. 'Every time we meet, you pull out another surprise.'

It was on the tip of his tongue to say he hadn't even got started yet, but he let it pass. 'I need to know if there's any problem legally. I want to do this properly.'

She took a sip of her coffee. 'It's highly irregular,' she said.

'Everything is highly irregular right now.'

The fingers of Noelle's right hand tapped the mug. Her left hand was flat on the table. Molloy noticed that her wedding finger was now bare.

'We need to get you signed up as a guardian, but that won't be a problem if the child's mother has no objection, which seems to be what you're telling me.'

'OK, thanks. There's one more thing. You asked me the other night about Junior Corbett.'

She smiled but didn't meet his eyes. 'I remember, believe it or not. You said something about him giving you your big break.'

'There's other stuff I didn't tell you about.'

'Before you start, has it anything to do with you?'

'Lots.'

'Yes, well, maybe you're better off not telling me. If you reveal any crime you've committed, I can't represent you unless you're going to plead guilty.'

'I'm not looking for a solicitor. I just want to level with you.'

Her face tightened into a question. 'Off you go.'

He told her everything. He told her about how when he'd got out he'd thought he was facing into a brand new day, with just a few matters of the night to clean up. He gave her the specifics of the hit on Corbett.

He told her about Harms Sullivan, and how he had pleaded for his life, pleaded to the wrong man. He told her how he had felt when he had heard about Sullivan in the waiting room of Paul & Paul, the news mocking him even as he was crawling back up the sides of the hole he'd fallen into.

She nodded through most of it. Here and there her eyes widened, lines appeared on her forehead. He got the impression she was trying hard not to give her true reaction, which might be to dial somebody like her sister and say, 'Get me the hell out of here.'

As he went on, he kept looking her directly in the eye, but

she wasn't really up for it, her gaze lowering to the table every so often. When he told her about being tied up in the kid's room awaiting his sentence, concern crept over her face.

Then he came to the tricky bit, where she was as likely to walk out the door as to reach over and slap him across the head. She was looking around her at this stage. He thought she might be worried about being overheard, but there was no danger of that. 'What's the matter?' he said.

'Water. Where can I get a drink of water?' She sounded like she was gasping.

He got up and poured a glass from a counter where two jugs of water stood next to stacks of plastic cups and napkins. When he handed it to her she produced the Solps, tore them open and dropped them in, like depth charges, to blow away a headache.

'This stuff about me is giving you a pain in the head,' he said.

'No, no, I just get headaches.'

'Maybe you'd want to see a doctor.'

'I have.'

'And what did he say?'

'He told me I need to stop taking Solpadeine.'

'But what about the headaches?'

'He said if I stopped taking the Solpadeine, the headaches would go away.'

'Some of those doctors aren't worth a hoot.'

'Just go back over that bit about you being tied up in the room. What did they tie you up with?'

'Plastic ties.'

'I see. OK, so this Corbett man walks in.'

He took a little more care with this bit of the story. 'And then they told me the terms of my reprieve,' he said. 'I was to keep an eye on you. See where things led. Suss out about your husband and where he might be.'

'Hold on, hold on.' Now her face was all business again. She was no longer concerned or confused. She was scared.

'All they told me was that your husband owed Junior a lot of money. Junior said he'd made an investment with your husband and that your husband had done a runner with the money. Except he didn't put it like that. He was more colourful about it, especially when he described your husband.'

He tried to read her face but it was no good. When she spoke, she was using her solicitor's voice again. 'You were to spy on me?'

'That's how they saw it.'

'And how did you see it?'

'I saw it as choices. I could have told him to do his own spying and then asked that I might be given a proper burial.'

'So you went along with it.'

'I told them what they wanted to hear. After that I told them nothing. I had nothing to tell. I still don't know the first thing about your husband, apart from the fact that he's pissed off Junior big-time. The only reason I'm here is to warn you. These people don't fuck around. Take it from me, as somebody who had some debt issues. The money gets paid back or somebody doesn't come home.'

'I don't know what to believe any more.'

'You can believe this. I've never told you a lie. And I'm not now.'

Molloy felt the presence of somebody beside him. He looked up, his right hand moving to his pocket. There was a uniform standing there. Molloy let his hand fall from the jacket. The uniform was stapled on to a clean-cut guy, about his own age, looked like he might have a future on some crime-stopping TV programme.

'Mrs Diggins?'

She looked up at him but the face meant nothing to her.

'Dick Dillon. I met you at the Bridewell court last year. With Johnny Foley. You were defending him.'

'Oh, yes,' she said, hoping the brevity of the reply might prompt him to clear off.

'How's Johnny getting on?'

'He couldn't be better. Off the drink last time I saw him.'

The uniform looked down at Molloy. He didn't bother extending his introduction. Nobody else bothered either. The awkward silence lasted all of five seconds before he said he'd be off.

Noelle wrapped her hands around the empty mug. 'Is there more?'

'Things have moved on. Last night they came to kill me. I'm no longer any use to them. That means they've probably found what they're looking for. Or else they've decided to go directly to you. You've got a problem. If I was you, I'd give a call to that nice inspector who drove you out to your house the other day.'

She leaned back in her chair, her shoulders sagging, as if she was feeling a great weight. 'Please tell me there's nothing else.'

'I thought that would be enough to be going on with. Look, if you want to tell me to—'

'Go and take a flying fuck at a rolled doughnut?'

'Yeah, something like that, you'd be right to do it. OK. I don't blame you. But I just want you to know, I never ratted on you, never told them a thing.'

'You'd nothing to tell.'

'That's right. But even if I did … Anyway, you know the score now.'

She looked up towards the counter, as if debating whether or not to chance another coffee. He copped and asked her, but she shook her head. Johnny Cash was singing U2's 'One' in the background. She turned back towards him but then looked again at the counter. Her eyes widened. She got up and walked to the counter, picked up a newspaper and looked at the front page. Her mouth was open now.

She held up the paper to Molloy. It was the *Evening Herald*, and the headline screamed: 'KILLER DIES'. Beside it there was a large photograph of Kyle Sansom.

Now it was Molloy's turn to experience a sharp intake of breath. He read the first paragraph: 'Gangland figure Kyle Sansom who was killed in an execution-style hit on Tuesday night was a suspect in at least four murders.'

Noelle sat back down, leaned over towards Molloy. She stabbed her index finger into the photograph on the paper. 'This man followed me the other day. He scared the living daylights out of me.'

'It mightn't have been him.'

'I'm telling you, it was. I couldn't forget that face.'

'He's a twin. It could have been his brother, Rocco.'

'There's two of them?'

'And counting. I'll tell you one thing. He was one of the guys who came to my flat to take me away the night before last. Jesus, that's the second time I've met somebody who gets killed a few hours later.'

'So what happened to him?'

'All I know is I need to get the hell out of here. Too many people are winding up dead.'

Noelle looked down at the newspaper again. She lifted her hand to her forehead. 'I don't know if I can take any more surprises,' she said. 'My head is hurting from it all.'

'These people are serious. If I was you, I'd go to the law.'

'And what about you?'

'I'm gone. Tomorrow I go down to my brother's place, as far out of town as you can go on this island. If everything is OK with him, I'll bring my son down there.'

'Where?'

'Kerry, the very bottom of it, place called Kells Bay.'

She nodded slowly, gathering thoughts, formulating some kind of a plan.

'You said the only reason you rang me to meet up was to warn me?'

'That wasn't entirely true.'

'OK.'

'You're not wearing your wedding band.'

'Very observant of you. How're you travelling?'

'Bus. Why?'

'I have some business myself in Kerry, not too far, I think, from where you're going. Do you want a lift?'

Fionn Higgins came tearing down the stairs. He had the answer, what they were looking for, his ticket to ride. The two men were in the kitchen, Junior seated at a table, a mug of tea at his elbow. Rocco was standing by the sink, leafing through a stack of mass cards, which his ma had asked him to sort out. Both men were dressed in black suits, white shirts and black ties. There were a stack of floral wreaths near Rocco's feet. Most of them were fashioned into rings, two were arranged to spell out Kyle's name. One, a small number in red carnations, was shaped like a handgun.

Fionn Higgins stopped abruptly at the door, remembering where he was, what was about to go down. He hadn't been invited to the funeral, which was to take place in two hours' time, and, under the circumstances, he didn't feel it right to ask permission to attend. It wasn't as if he missed Kyle.

When he heard the news, a chill came over him. He knew these people didn't fuck around. He had often wondered what would have befallen him if any misunderstandings had developed between him and the twins over finance or merchandise. He had envisaged pain, possibly broken bones, and an overwhelming sense of fear. Like everybody else, gangland was brought to him in cartoon images across the pages of tabloid newspapers, and through TV images of blue and white crime-scene tape. Now he could say that he actually knew somebody who had been shot.

Rocco had come up to the room yesterday to tell him. By then, regulations had been relaxed. When the twins had left, their replacement was a goon with a heart. Eventually, he had taken pity on Fionn Higgins and brought up to him a naggin of JD. Fionn got nicely toasted, kicked back and allowed himself some downtime, although he took care to keep the laptop open on a page, just in case anybody came barging in.

He must have dropped off because the next thing he knew Rocco was walking through the door. The man was wearing a face of grief and, for a panicked second, Fionn thought Rocco was arriving to deliver the news that he was to be shot.

Rocco sat on the edge of the bed. He looked at Fionn as if they were brothers.

'He's gone,' he said.

'Who?'

'Kyle.'

'Gone where?' Maybe he had found the loot and taken off with it himself, betrayed his brother and the gang.

Rocco looked to be on the edge of tears, and it finally dawned on Fionn Higgins what had gone down. 'Oh, man, I'm so sorry.' He tried to locate a sympathetic image of Kyle, but none would come to him. All he saw was that scar, and a face that always appeared to be on the cusp of exploding into violence. Still, Kyle was gone now and Rocco needed support. He looked around for the naggin, saw it on the floor at the foot of the table. All the whiskey was gone. He reached over and patted Rocco's right arm. Rocco lifted his other hand and patted Fionn Higgins's hand.

'What happened?'

'Johnny Cash.'

'That motherfucker. I knew he was bad news. 'Ring of Fire', my ass.'

'Yeah, well, he got what was coming to him.'

Now Fionn was wide awake. 'You shot him?'

'No. Junior did. Copped what was going on, and he did him. He's been fed to the rats up the Dublin mountains.'

'Jesus.' It began to occur to Fionn that he might be better off knowing none of this. They sat there for a few seconds, captured and captor joined in grief.

After a while, Rocco got up and moved towards the door. 'How you doing?' he said.

'Me? Good, man, good. This is slow, but I'm getting there. Any luck and I'll have some answers for you by tomorrow at the latest.'

Rocco nodded. 'We're burying Kyle tomorrow. I feel like a part of me is going to be put in the ground. We arrived in this world together, and now he's leaving without me.'

Fionn Higgins nodded. He didn't know what else there was to say. He did know that this was the kind of occasion that should be filed away and resourced the next time he was sitting down to write a song. He thought of Bob Dylan's 'Joey', the ballad about some thug who bought it out on the street. Maybe this was the chance for him to locate his inner Dylan.

Images and words began to whirr in his mind. When he looked up, Rocco was gone. Why wait? He got up and sat down at the laptop. He opened a new document, began typing words. He picked up the empty bottle from the floor, raised it to his lips and sucked hungrily for any stray drops. All he needed to set him on the path was a big fat line of Colombia's finest.

Now he had the answers. The two men looked up as he came to a halt in the doorframe. 'I have it,' he said.

Junior Corbett's eyebrows went north. Rocco gazed at him as if he had bellowed down into the shaft of grief. Fionn didn't look too hot, even by his standards. His eyes had taken off for outer space. His jeans were after a low-rise fashion, but not on purpose, no belt, and his belly was pushing out the stringy vest. He didn't so much need a shower as a hose.

'It's in Kerry, right down the arse end of the country. Place called Coomastow. When I saw it first I thought it was a code, not a place.'

'Coomastow?'

'Yeah, side of a mountain, really in the middle of nowhere.'

'What the fuck's it doing down there?'

'Our friend, looks like he had a development going on. He called it Buckingham Gate. Can you believe that?'

'Like the palace.'

'Like the fucking palace.' Fionn Higgins was full of drama now, loving his moment in the sun. He threw a printed sheet on to the table. Rocco walked over, getting into it despite himself. The sheet was a computer mock-up of the estate as envisaged, taken from a paved road, with houses, which, to Rocco's mind, would pass for mansions, running up each side. The houses were wrapped in cedar shingles, with white window frames. Money shone out from each pore of the buildings. There must have been ten of them. It wasn't like any other estate Rocco had ever seen.

Fionn Higgins said, 'There you have it, man, Buckingham Gate.' He began reading from another sheet, another printout. '"A salubrious retreat for the people who have it all but want more. Buckingham Gate offers an oasis of nature and quiet, located in a secluded corner just off the Ring of Kerry. We will keep your dreams warm for you in this corner of Paradise."'

Junior looked up. 'He was a great man for dreams all right.'

'Yep, well, this place does sound good. It's got the works, outdoor Jacuzzis and, get this, he started out flogging them for one point five million euro a pop.'

'How many fools bought into that?'

'Not a single one. It's a ghost estate right now. Got this piece from the local paper, says some of the locals are complaining it's an eyesore, like some kind of deserted village from the Famine, except they didn't have Jacuzzis and that shit in the Famine.'

'How do you know it's what I'm looking for?'

'He had a file, had to unlock it, took me the longest time, man. Inside there was a list of people with figures beside their names. You were there, Mr Corbett. You had the biggest number, one point eight million euro.'

'Never mind me, what else was there?' Junior looked over at Rocco, who was staring at him. Fionn Higgins sensed he had just introduced some information to which poor Rocco hadn't been privy before now.

'Anyway, there's all sorts of names there. The total comes to just under three million.'

At this Junior got up, his voice rising with him: 'And where, where the fuck is it?'

'Coomastow. He has it written here.' Fionn Higgins brought another sheet of paper over to Junior. 'Here, deposited Coomastow the twenty-first of September 2008. That's where it is, that's where all that fucking money is.' The second he said it, Fionn Higgins knew it was a mistake, as if he had trodden hard on toes and was now about to get a reaction, delivered in a bullet. He didn't know why he felt that. It must have been something in the air, something only somebody like him, with the heightened sensibility of a poet, could spot. 'I mean, you know, I just presumed it was money. Nothing to do with me.'

The two of them were exchanging glances, Junior holding the printed sheets in his left hand. 'What do you think?' he said, addressing Rocco.

'He doesn't know anything.'

'He knows enough.'

'I know absolutely nothing, man, zilch.'

'Shut the fuck up.'

Junior said, 'I wouldn't like to take any chances.'

'I'm with you on that, Junior, but what's the fella going to do? What has he got?'

Junior stood up, straightened himself. 'He could put me in this place for one. Say they want to play around with false imprisonment. I don't need that shit at this stage of my life.'

Rocco nodded, turned to Fionn. 'Were you kept here against your will?'

'No way, you know that. I could have walked at any time. I was just helping you out because neither of you knew anything about computers. There was nothing illegal here that I saw. I couldn't even get a decent bit of blow since I set foot in this place. I know nothing, man. I saw nothing. All I want to do is play my music.'

'OK, Fionn, take it easy. Junior, he's harmless.'

'Is he fuck. Why take a chance?'

'Because there is no chance. And because I'm burying my brother today. Just out of respect for Kyle. He was kinda fond of Fionn. Kyle wouldn't have wanted to see him be put away for no good reason.'

'Are you sure about that? From what I could see Kyle couldn't wait to blow his brains out.'

Rocco looked to be on the point of tears. 'Look, I'm having

nothing to do with it. You want to, you can do it yourself. I don't see the point.'

'OK. We'll leave it. Out of respect for Kyle. You, you can fuck off out of here now. But remember, if you ever ...'

'Hey, man, I wouldn't ...' The sobs came slowly at first and then they racked right through Fionn Higgins. He brought his hands up to his face.

Rocco went over to him, took him by the shoulders. 'Put a sock in it. You're going home. You're going back to your girlfriend and your guitar. It's OK. Nothing's going to happen to you.'

Fionn Higgins looked out through the tears. 'Thanks, man.'

'Listen, Fionn, I know it might be a bit short notice, but do you want to come to the funeral? I'd appreciate it if you could.'

Fionn Higgins raised his head again. He couldn't cope with this. If he didn't get something for his nerves in the next few minutes he was liable to collapse on the spot.

Alan Slate replaced the receiver. It was pushing five o'clock, but there was still plenty to do. He had just received another golden nugget from his new best friend, Inspector Phil Wright. The killing of Kyle Sansom could have been more than just your average gangland hit. Johnny Cash was missing. The word was that Cash had been planning to upend his boss, Junior Corbett, and young Kyle had got word of it. Cash had plugged him, but Junior, the survivor that he was, had got in first. Johnny Cash was out of the game, most likely food for the worms up in the Dublin mountains. One more scoop coming right up.

Slate looked up and saw Fastneck's wife, Julie, the new advertising manager, walk into the room. She had lent an air of propriety to the place since her arrival earlier in the week. Julie Fastneck was nearly as tall as her husband, and any time Slate saw her she had a silk scarf of various bright colours tied tightly around her neck. She wore the trousers, no question about that.

She looked into her husband's vacant office. 'Where's Frank?' she asked nobody in particular. There were four reporters in total sitting at terminals. Three heads popped up in response. One set of shoulders shrugged.

'He mentioned something about a meeting,' Slate said. She looked at him as if he was something the cat had dragged in. She turned on her heels and exited the room. Two of the reporters looked at Slate, all smiles. He twisted his face in mock anger and snapped the fingers of his right hand down on his thumb, yada, yada, yada. That got a laugh out of them.

Right now, Fastneck's wife wasn't the only one looking for Frank. Slate wanted to get the nod to head down to Kerry on the tail of his main focus, Dancer Molloy. Slate's new best friend was so full of info he had also passed on details about Molloy's family. Turns out the Dancer has a brother, guy who managed to steer on the straight and narrow. Might be worth a visit.

Experience told Slate that guys like that generally fell into two categories. There were the types who ran a mile from any coverage, often with a threat of violence. But sometimes the relative was only too happy to unburden the fraternal load they had been forced to carry all their adult lives. When that happened, it was often gold, plenty of human-interest stuff, with a splash of victim thrown in.

He scrolled down his contact list to the Fuhrer, and texted a question. 'Where are you?' The reply came in seconds: 'The Oarsman'.

The pub was dozing when Slate entered. The Oarsman was a great survivor in the massacre of the innocents that had gone on through the boom years, when most traditional businesses had been sacrificed on the altar of apartment fodder. It retained the authentic smell of stale beer, and gave no concession to natural light. The only food available was toasted sandwiches: ham, cheese, ham and cheese, or ham, cheese and tomato. The pride of the house was the Toasted Special, which had everything topped off with onions. The Special had acquired legendary status in the offices of *Inside Out*.

There were two men at the bar who looked like they were well into a day dedicated to quenching thirst. A besuited guy, three or four stone and twenty years past his prime, sat at a table with a young woman. Deeper into the cave, Slate spotted Fastneck at a table on his own, a half-drained pint of stout before him. Slate waved and imitated drinking to enquire from afar whether Fastneck was up to another. He raised an index finger to indicate he wouldn't say no.

'Thanks for coming,' Fastneck said, when the fresh pint was put before him.

'No problem,' Slate said. 'The missus was looking for you just now. I told her you had a meeting.'

Fastneck nodded, and Slate thought he detected a flash of fear run across his face.

'Just a couple of things I wanted to talk about in terms of the magazine and where I see us going.'

Alarm bells sounded in Slate's head. Whenever Fastneck raised anything that sounded mildly strategic, it was time to head for the hills.

'How you getting on with the Ciara Savage stuff?'

He'd known this was coming. 'OK. Hard to get a handle on it. Could be libel problems if we bring that cop into it.'

Fastneck took a long draw on his pint and licked the froth from his upper lip. 'His name is Inspector Phil Wright. He's a serious guy. It would make a good yarn, the fact that he was even in the same room as that criminal, and both of them buying property from Diggins. Have you contacted this Wright man?'

'Can't get hold of him, Frank. I think he's giving me the run-around. Tried him a few times.'

'Maybe we just need to move on it. Run the story and see what falls out.'

'Frank, a libel action from the likes of him could close the place down.'

Fastneck ran a finger across condensation on the pint glass. The furrows on his brow had deepened since their last sit-down, but you had to hand it to the guy: no matter what pressure he was under, his tie remained knotted tightly to his neck, the starch in his shirt as white as a ghost.

'On the subject of the place being closed down, you don't know any investors, do you?'

'Any what?'

Fastneck looked up and lowered his voice: 'As I've mentioned to you before, things are tight.'

'Sure, I know that, Frank. There's less to go around for everybody.'

'Yeah, well, they've just got a lot tighter. Julie's getting herself familiar with the workings of the advertising department, and she's come to the conclusion that things are not what they seem. Do you know any investors?'

It was beginning to sound like a mantra, as though he thought that if he kept repeating it Slate would eventually give in and admit that he had a clutch of investors hiding up his sleeve. 'You mean people who want to put money into this place?'

'Alan, when you say it like that you make *Inside Out* sound like a zoo.'

Slate caught himself before throwing back the obvious response. 'The credit crunch, Frank. There isn't much cash about.'

'Yeah, well, I know one man got plenty of that.'

'You were roped in too, weren't you?'

'What are you talking about?'

'Diggins. Cape Isis. You invested. Just like the cop, and your friend Ciara Savage.'

Fastneck took another draw from his pint. He finished it in one. He stood up, glanced down at Slate's pint and saw that it was barely touched. He walked to the bar and ordered another. When he returned, he sat down, and said, 'Julie was all against it.' Slate nodded. 'It was that phrase that hooked me.'

'"Releasing the equity"?'

'Yeah, makes you think you're holding something captive instead of sending it out to work for you. Anyway, I bought six. I'm in for over half a million. Should have seen him coming. A friend introduced us at an international in Lansdowne Road. Seemed like a get-ahead type of fella. He knew how to turn on the charm. Knew how to sell. Fifteen years, Alan, fifteen years as a pro footballer, and I haven't a bean. Julie, well, she's standing by me for now, but I don't know for how long. The magazine needs investment and all the savings I had are tied up in some island off the west coast of Africa. I've never even been to the place. If I got a hold of him now, I'd strangle him. I'd fucking—' Fastneck balled his fists. His face tightened in rage.

Slate was grateful that he wasn't the focus of the man's ire, but it was still scary enough. 'If I hear anything, I'll let you know, Frank. I'll do a bit of digging tomorrow, but after that I've got to go down to Kerry, follow up on this Dancer guy. He's got a brother down there.'

Fastneck nodded. 'Sure, and hopefully we'll still be open for business when you get back.'

Slate got up, shook hands with his boss. His evening had just got a whole lot busier. He had to get on the phone, pull out all the old contacts and try to find himself a real job.

19

She picked up Molloy at the top of O'Connell Street, pulling in between two buses that were swallowing queues of passengers. Inside the Honda Civic, he caught a hint of flowers from her perfume. Her smile was different today, from somewhere outside the solicitor/client relationship.

Traffic was fair to middling all the way through town. Within fifteen minutes, they were on the Naas road, dodging between the trucks and the grey fumes. It felt good to be leaving the city behind.

A car came up past them on the inside lane. The driver looked across, his mouth twisted in anger. Molloy felt a momentary stab of fear. They weren't free of the city yet.

'What's his problem?' Noelle said.

'Asshole. He thinks everybody in this lane should be going like the hammers of Hell.'

'Asshole,' Noelle said.

A few miles further on, she indicated and pulled in at a service station. She got out, lifted the fuel pump and filled it up. Afterwards she opened the driver's door and asked him did he want anything in the shop. He said he was fine. His eyes followed her as she walked across the forecourt, grace in her stride. He looked around for any stray eyes on him. He reached to his bag on the back seat, unzipped it, and rooted around until he felt the steel. He took the gun and placed it under his seat. If things got rough at any stage, if one of Junior's goons showed up with a gun waving out of the window of a passing car, he would be ready.

Back on the road, the traffic began to thin out as the motorway reached further from the city. Molloy relaxed, the tension seeping from his body with each passing mile. Van Morrison came on the radio, singing 'Moondance'.

'So what are you going to do?' Noelle said.

'About what?'

She thrust her head forward. 'About your ... life, making a career, earning a living.'

'Haven't thought much about it since I came back,' he said.

'Isn't that the time to really get thinking about it?' She stopped herself. Christ, there she was now, just like her sister, ending her sentences with a question mark?

He had given it some thought, a lot of thought, since he'd begun going to the meetings inside. He could try his hand at house painting. When he was fourteen his mother had sent him to work with his uncle, who was a house painter, running errands, holding ladders, getting bored out of his skull. He could see now that she'd wanted to get some sort of a work ethic going with him while he was groping around to find something that might interest him. Something to have if the football didn't work out. He didn't think much of the work, and at the end of the summer he had made a pact with himself never to go back.

'I did a bit of house painting when I was a kid,' he said.

Noelle nodded, dropped a gear and overtook a truck. 'Sorry.'

'What?'

'Not now. Anything construction-related is a no-no. Is it a trade you're after?'

'I don't know what I'm after. A bit of peace. Beyond that, I just don't know.'

'Was there ever anything that grabbed your interest?'

'Apart from the football? No, not really. That was my dream since I was a kid. But then things didn't work out and dreams just turned to regrets. Fuck-all I can do about it now.'

'Were you that good?'

'I don't know, but you just got to live with that stuff, park it, move on.'

'There must be something else you could have a go at?'

'Brain surgeon?'

'Sure, why not?'

'I could kick off with a DIY job on my own brain and take it from there.'

'I know a few people who could do with a lobotomy.'

'Yeah, and I know a few heads I'd like to brain.'

'What about counselling? With all you've been through, who knows?'

'Are you serious?'

'I've often read about people with addiction problems getting into that field. They've a lot to bring to it.'

'The blind leading the blind sort of thing.'

'Exactly.' They both laughed. The sound of an angry car horn came from behind them.

Noelle looked to the rear-view mirror, where lights were flashing. Molloy leaned forward in his seat, his hands dropping down towards the floor, inches from the Glock.

'Oops,' Noelle said. 'I've been cruising in the overtaking lane.' She indicated and pulled across. A powder blue Toyota Camry flew by, the driver wearing a sour face above his shirt and tie, his fisted right hand jerking up and down in the air in a wanking motion.

Molloy leaned over and gave him the finger. 'Asshole,' he said.

'Asshole,' Noelle said.

Michael Bublé began to croon from the radio.

'What about you?' he said.

'Me?'

'You're out of a job now. What you going to turn your hand to?'

'Might put on a bit of weight, try a spot of Japanese mud wrestling.'

He liked the way she kept a straight face when she threw it out there. 'There's one thing I don't understand about you and that job you had. What made you travel all the way from Killiney into town and up to the northside every day? It must have been like crossing between worlds.'

She was fully focused on overtaking a truck. Once back in the cruising lane she glanced at him. 'I used to wonder about that myself. So did my husband. He reckoned I was uncomfortable with money. I think I was just uncomfortable with where I had ended up. Anyway, I try not to think too much about it. That's all over for me. It was never really my thing. I just did it because ... it was there.'

'I know the way.'

'I had my own dreams,' she said. 'I wanted to be a dancer.'

'Yeah? That's what they used to call me, the Dancer, on account of the way I played.'

She laughed. 'So we were both dancers in our imagination, and look where we are now. A couple of bums on the road to Palookaville.'

'Is it too late now, for you?'

'The body doesn't wait around for careers like that. You get one shot at it and if you don't take it ... yeah, it's too late.'

Silence settled between them for a few minutes, before Molloy said, 'I could set myself up in business.'

'Would you be good at that?'

'Sure I would. I saw somewhere that recession is a good time to set up. I could open up dealing drugs to the high end of the market. There's still plenty of money up there.'

Noelle gave him a look. 'That's not funny. Since all this blew up, I've found out my husband, my ex-husband, had a serious drug problem. At the high end of the market, as you call it.'

'Sorry,' he said. He felt tired. He hadn't had a proper night's sleep for the guts of a week. Adrenalin was all that had kept him going over the last couple of days in particular.

His head fell forward into his chest. Nobody was going to have a pop at them out on the motorway. He felt safe here in the car. He could be back in the cell, lockdown for the night, knowing all grief for the day was beyond his door. Creedence Clearwater Revival faded in his ears as sleep crept over him.

At the end of the five-hour journey, Rocco couldn't make up his mind whether he wanted to shoot Junior. The car ride had been OK. They clipped along at a fair pace, careful not to fuck around with the speed limit. Junior did the driving. Rocco rode shotgun. That was what Junior called it, riding shotgun, as if they were a pair of cowboys heading out into Injun country. All he had to do was keep an eye on the navigation, which was a piece of piss. It was a straight road to Limerick. Not much navigation in that.

Junior was OK to travel with. He didn't talk too much, and when he did he said nothing that might crank up tension, the way so many fellas in the game just had to do.

But something was tugging at Rocco like an impatient child. What did Junior have to do with the death of his brother?

Junior's version just didn't add up. Johnny had been planning a takeover. He wanted Kyle and Rocco out of the picture as well, and had decided to move against Kyle and Junior while Rocco was at the Dubs match. Junior copped what was going on when Johnny showed up at the garage, but it had been too late for Kyle.

And then there was Molloy. He had been in cahoots with Johnny all along. That was how Junior told it, anyway. Junior promised him that Molloy would be taken and kept alive until Rocco did what he wanted with him.

The story was full of holes. But it wasn't something you could sit down and discuss with Junior. You just had to make up your own mind what you believed and act on that.

And now they were on the road to Kerry. Rocco had been there once, a family holiday, when he and Kyle weren't long out of short pants. That was the only family holiday he could remember. Not long after it, their father fucked off, gone without a word. In Rocco's memory, it was always the family holiday that did it for his old man. He couldn't take the scene any more.

It had taken an age to get there: a long train ride to Killarney and from there a bus to a seaside town with big cliffs and plenty of dodgem cars. The four of them had stayed in a cramped mobile home set among sand dunes, a stone's throw from the beach. Each morning, while their parents still slept, he and Kyle would put raincoats on over their swimming togs and head down to the seashore to muck around. The beach would be deserted except for the pair of them. Rocco really got a kick out of the tides. The sea kept coming and breaking in gentle folds a few feet from the shore, even when nobody was there to see it. He tried explaining this to Kyle, but Kyle didn't seem to get it. There was a lot Kyle didn't get when he was alive, and he sure as hell wouldn't get it now that he was dead, leaving Rocco behind, half dead himself, like a man whose limbs had been hacked from his body.

Just after five p.m., they stopped at Adare, a little tourist village on the far side of Limerick. Junior ordered a sirloin steak, Rocco tried the house burger, and then, after he was done, he told Junior he had to stretch his legs.

'You're not doing a runner, are you?' Junior said.

'Where am I going to run?'

He walked the length of the main street twice, past the tourist shops and restaurants, trying to shake the stiffness from his legs. He knew he was trying to shake something else as well.

On the second leg of the journey, Rocco brought out a map and relayed to Junior the names of the towns they were encountering. Newcastlewest, Abbeyfeale, Castleisland, Farranfore. When they drove past Kerry Airport at Farranfore, both of them hit on the same idea. 'Why the fuck didn't we fly down here and hire wheels?' They looked at each other, neither smiling, as each tried to lay blame for the cock-up on the other.

Cahirciveen was the nearest town to where they reckoned Buckingham Gate to be. They arrived just shy of eight o'clock, both of them cranky and stiff. The conversation had dried up. The car radio at that hour of the evening provided little more than sport, which was fine by Rocco, but Junior had no interest.

At the hotel, a woman in Reception was wearing a twenty-four-hour smile. She told them they could have a double room or two singles. Junior said they'd take the double. Mean bastard just didn't want to fork out. Or maybe he was keeping an eye on Rocco. Junior hadn't survived as long as he had without carrying suspicion around like a spare shirt.

After showering, they repaired to the bar and sat on high stools. The barman was a dapper little man in a stripy waistcoat and a cap of fitted sandy hair. Two drinks into the evening, Junior began to pump him about Coomastow. The barman didn't know the place. He disappeared and returned with another guy, who wore the same waistcoat but plenty more hair and poundage.

This guy pronounced the place differently: 'Coo-mash-thou,' he said.

Junior tried it. 'Coomastoo.'

The guy shook his head. He said it again, slowly this time: 'Coo-mash-thou.'

Junior tried again, managed to make it most of the way. 'Ever hear of Buckingham Gate?' he asked, in his best innocent-tourist voice.

The man's face broke out in a knowing smile. 'The banshee,' he said.

'The what?'

'The banshee. It's not just any ghost estate, it's a top-of-the-range one, and you need a top-of-the-range ghost for that. The banshee.'

Junior was trying to get his money back and this guy was making a big joke of it. 'Anybody living out there?'

'Nobody this side of the grave. You think you had it bad in Dublin? Some bright spark got the idea that that place would be the ultimate get-away-from-it-all stop-off point for people coming down here from the cities and across from England. Coo-mash-thou's in the back-of-beyond, the middle of nowhere. He was some boy all right that he thought he could pull that one off.'

Rocco piped up, 'You met him?'

'Sure, used to stay here when he was down. He's the guy who's been on the news a bit lately, solicitor done a runner. Man by the name of Diggins.'

'What did you make of him?' Junior said.

'Smooth character, no doubt about that. Good man to have the bit of crack with. You could see how he's capable of charming the birds off the trees, but after a while all the stuff wears thin. I used to have a chat with him here in the bar, and it doesn't take too long to cop that he's flying by the seat of his pants.' The guy looked around him, as if to ensure other parties wouldn't overhear what he was about to deliver. Then he leaned into the orbit of the two men at the counter. 'To tell you the truth, and I wouldn't say this out loud here, you'd want to be soft in the head to have bought anything from Mr Donal Diggins. I mean, when you look up close, the fella had "conman" written across his forehead.'

Junior was looking at the guy now, a fat fool bursting out through his uniform. He saw a baseball bat smashing into the guy's fat belly. He saw him doubled over in pain. He saw the baseball bat cracking down on his head. Laugh now, you fucker.

Rocco touched his arm, raising a drained pint glass. 'Another one?'

Ivan's directions were on the button. They knew they were nearing their destination when the road turned out on to the side of a mountain, nothing below but the sea, an old railway line just above them, tracking the road. And off in the distance another land bank, which had to be the Dingle peninsula.

A few miles on, they could see the bay down on the right, a curve of sand, a little pier advancing out into the sea, a few little white blobs of anchored pleasure craft.

Molloy read out the instructions. Leave the main road when you come to the restaurant-cum-shop, head down a lane that twists like a hairpin; take a right and keep going for a half-mile, before turning left; the cottage is the third house on the right.

They were upon it in minutes. The cottage was set down from the road, whitewashed walls, sea blue trimmings. There was a neat little garden split into quadrants in front of the house, brightened with petals of purple and yellow. Molloy rapped on the door.

Ivan's hair had grown since they last met. It was swept back in a ponytail that fell between his shoulder-blades. He wore a grey knitted waistcoat over a white linen shirt and khaki trousers. It took him a few seconds to smile, but then his face opened wide. He thrust out his hand. Molloy felt a tight grip.

'Welcome to Kerry,' he said. Kathy was at his shoulder now. His sister-in-law was as Molloy had remembered her, a petite woman with an open face and green eyes that could be used as a weapon or a wand by one less innocent than she.

The occasional meetings the three had had when she and Ivan were in the shallows of their relationship had been less than successful, Kathy more often than not attempting to act as mediator. She had always been prepared to give him the benefit of the doubt.

Two boys were now looking out between Ivan's legs. Molloy introduced Noelle, and hands were extended to shake and pat the heads of Aaron and Sam, who quickly exited out the front and went around the side of the house. The living room was spacious but dark, dating the cottage to a time when windows were small and compact to keep out the cold rather than let in the light.

The new arrivals were seated at a table, while Kathy arranged for teas and coffees. She produced a tray with freshly baked muffins and placed it on the table.

Kathy conducted most of the small-talk, Ivan interjecting here and there to provide support. Molloy asked about the area, the kids, schools, and that kind of stuff.

Through a window it was possible to see the sea, and in the foreground a children's swing and plastic slide, on which Aaron and Sam were amusing themselves.

When they had finished their drinks, Kathy broached the subject that had hung unspoken between them since their arrival. 'So you're thinking of moving down this way,' she said, caution in her voice.

Noelle wasn't sure whether she meant them as a couple. 'I'm just visiting,' she said, and laughed drily to let the other woman know things might not be as they seemed.

'It's to do with Alex, really,' Molloy said.

Kathy looked at her husband. 'The city's no place to raise children, these days. What do you think, Ivan?'

He turned to his brother. 'You said something about taking him in.'

Molloy brought them through the scenario. Of course his brother and sister-in-law knew all about Steph. Once upon a long time ago, one of the periodic attempts at bonding had involved a night out for the four of them. It had ended with Steph storming out of the place in a huff, although they all knew that her frustration on the night in question was wrapped up in the need for a lift, which she wasn't getting from the vodka and Coke.

They knew, too, about her descent since Molloy went away. Ivan had tried to keep tabs on her for the child's sake, but he had been told to take a running jump, and had lost contact. Molloy explained that she was trying to kick her habit. Kathy received the news with a sympathetic nod but Ivan's face betrayed scepticism.

'I was wondering, you know, if Alex could maybe stay here until things are sorted out.'

Kathy's hand was flat on the table, as if she could barely contain herself in reaching across to Molloy. 'We've discussed it and that's not a problem. Alex may have some difficulty in readapting to life here, but if it's for the better . . .'

Ivan said, 'How long do you reckon?'

Molloy shrugged his shoulders. 'Hopefully no more than a month.'

'And what about you?'

Now he exchanged glances with Noelle. 'I've a few things to clear up from … my past. Once that's out of the way, and I get sorted out with some place to start, I'll take him back up. What do you think?'

His brother nodded. 'It's not a problem,' he said. 'The young lad is family.'

The morning was damp when they came down to breakfast. Both of them went for the heart attack on a plate, full Irish with lashings of butter.

'What now?' Rocco asked, mopping up the last of his egg with a slice of toast.

Junior was sitting back, like a man who had some thinking to do. He was dressed in a salmon pink shirt, the second button open, matted grey hair moving in on a gold medallion. 'We keep the rooms here,' he said. 'Don't know how long this is going to take. We could get done today, but maybe not. All we have is an address.'

'Coo-mash-thou,' Rocco said slowly.

'Coo-mash-thou,' Junior said.

At a time like this, in the morning, when the day rolled out in front of him, like an ache, Rocco wondered how long he and Junior could last while the business of Kyle still stood between them. Then again, as far as he could see, Junior thought Kyle was yesterday's business.

Back in the car, both men assumed their positions. Junior slipped behind the wheel, Rocco unfolded a map before him, this one a local Ordnance Survey. They drove out of the town, heading along the Ring of Kerry. The sea was visible off to the right, pushing in against headlands and small islands. To the left, mountains reached up to low-lying banks of fluffy white clouds.

About four miles outside the town, there was a signpost for Coomastow, pointing towards a side-road. They followed it. Now, behind them, the sea was disappearing beneath a headland that moved out like an ancient whale. On the left, a mist was coming down from the mountain. Bogland and rough fields of scrub and stubble grass opened up on the right. Junior switched on the wipers. Rocco kept looking at the map, as if it might yield up some secrets.

They met a tractor. The road was not wide enough for the two vehicles to pass. The man on the tractor looked out at them from under a flat cap. He wore what looked like a suit jacket, as if he was heading to work in an office. He just sat there, waiting, as if the right of way yielded to whoever had the greater patience.

'What the fuck do I do?' Junior said. This shit was out of his comfort zone.

'We could shoot him,' Rocco said.

Junior looked at him. 'Are you serious?'

Rocco smiled. 'Even if we did, the tractor would still be in the middle of the road. Reverse. We just passed a house, you can pull into the driveway.'

Junior reversed the car and pulled in. The man on the tractor gave them a big wave, and a smile of victory.

They pushed on. Ahead there was more mist, like a movable white wall standing guard over further advance.

For at least a mile there had been a sliver of grass in the middle of the road, which was growing as they advanced further. They could hear the undercarriage of the car rub against it. They passed a fleeting canyon of trees where the branches squealed against the car's windows. Fewer houses appeared on the side of the road now than had been the case closer to civilisation.

They kept going, into the heart of the mist.

'Are you sure about this?' Junior said.

Rocco looked at the map again. 'By my calculations, we're entering Coo-mash-thou now.'

'Coo-mash-thou.'

Then they saw it up ahead, rising like a sore on the side of the mountain. Buckingham Gate stretched down from the foothills to the road ahead. The white mist had settled just a few feet from the house at the top, as if even the mist was cautious about taking on a ghost estate.

They were upon it within seconds. A stone pier, about four foot square, stood at the entrance, the words 'Buckingham Gate' carved out in script. The estate itself was corralled inside a wall standing at just above knee height, unfinished and bearing all the signs of sudden abandon.

Just after the pier, sticking out of the earth on the side of the road, a placard was mounted on a five-foot-high stick. The words 'Private Property' were handwritten on it.

Junior dropped a gear and turned into the estate. The road splitting the two rows of houses was paved about a third of the way up. After that, it looked to be all rough stone. Junior's foot touched lightly on the accelerator as he drove up the road. Rocco looked out at the houses, as if they were advancing through some post-apocalypse village.

These were serious fuck-off houses, no question about that. All were wrapped in cedar shingles the colour of slate. Each had four large windows on the ground floor, five on the floor above, flanked by decorative shutters. The first two houses on each side of the road were fronted by a lawn, and a driveway led to a garage which was separated from the main building and also done in cedar shingles.

Further up the road, things went downhill. The two men felt a bump as the car left the tarmac and landed on the unfinished surface. From there on, the houses were just about built, but the landscaping left a lot to be desired. There had been no time to lay lawns before the crash had kicked in. Some of the garages had no doors. The windows on the main houses had white tape across them.

Junior reversed the car down the road towards the entrance. He switched off the engine and they got out. The first thing Rocco noticed was the silence. 'Fuck me,' he said.

'Yeah. You can see where he was coming from, though.'

'Who?'

'Diggins. The dream-maker. This place is really hidden away from everything. If you were a millionaire footballer or an actor, you wouldn't have to mingle with the riff-raff here. It would have been a perfect getaway.'

'There's no pub, no shop, none of that shit.'

'Listen, these people, they can manage fine without that. All you need is a hot tub out the back, just like they have here.'

Rocco counted ten completed, and two that were little more than skeletal timber frames. He began to feel the cold and shivered in his fleece jacket. If he shot Junior now, nobody would know the difference. The sound might echo through the valley out here, but there would be no problem getting rid of the body. He could head back to town, pay the hotel bill to avoid any hassle and drive back to the real world.

Junior moved around the half-built wall. He stepped over it into what was the inside of the estate. There would be no point in shooting him before they found the money.

Junior laughed, but there was more bitterness than mirth in it. He raised a hand in the general direction of the houses. 'Here we are,' he said. 'Like those boys who all rushed west to find gold. The gold is in there somewhere.'

'Are you sure?'

'As sure as I can be. It's brilliant. Diggins must have a big bag of cash, and what does he do with it? He puts it in a house in the arse end of nowhere.'

'The back of beyond.'

'Coo-mash-fucking-thou. He's no fool, you have to give him that.'

'Junior, how are we going to find it?'

Junior looked back at him, and Rocco saw something in his face that he hadn't seen before. Desperation, maybe, or a wild madness that had just surfaced. 'Fuck knows,' he said. 'Fuck knows.'

Somewhere in the distance a cow mooed, as if answering a call from another.

'Inspector Wright.'

'Yeah.'

'You know who this is.'

'Keep talking, and it'll come to me.'

'We met last Christmas, Mountjoy station. You were a complete prick but we came to an arrangement.'

'With an attitude like that, sonny boy, I'm already reaching for the red button on my phone.'

'We had a minor disagreement on account of the two bags of amyl nitrate you found on my person.'

'Ah, yes, now I have you. Victor, isn't it?'

'No fucking names, man.'

'To what do I owe the pleasure?'

'I have something for you.'

'And any minute now you're going to spit it out.'

'I hear you're looking for that solicitor who made fools of half the country with his goings-on in the property lark ... Hello, Inspector?'

'I'm here.'

'You know who I'm talking about?'

'Yeah, yeah. Out with it.'

'What's it worth?'

'Listen to me. Do you want me to go out there and find you, and drag you in here and kick seven shades of shite out of you? Tell me what you know and I'll fix up with you.'

'OK, OK. Jesus, don't get personal. He's on his way home. Well, not home, but he's flying into Cork. Has an itchy nose so he got in touch with a friend of mine.'

'When?'

'Later on today. My friend is driving down to meet him in the Radisson Hotel near the airport.'

'Anything else?'

'That's the lot, Inspector. Glad to be of assistance. This could be the start of a beautiful relationship. What do you think?'

20

Donal Diggins fingered the stuff on to his gums, pressing it in. He had one last sniffle, hoovering up what was left. He flushed the toilet. There were a few bodies in the common area of the Gents in Málaga Airport. None of them looked like they had arrived hotfoot from a Dublin gang. None of them looked like cops, but you never knew, these days.

One guy, who had the pale skin of an Irish sky and was dressed in a linen suit, could have been from the CAB or the Revenue, but he knew that was the paranoia nudging him. Still, just because you were wired, it didn't mean they weren't out to get you.

He walked out into the shopping area. He found a seat, sandwiched between the female half of an elderly couple, and two kids of about nine or ten years of age competing for a single seat.

He was feeling better about the whole shebang now. Since he had made the decision, he had been haunted by an image of arriving at Cork Airport to be met by detectives, tipped off to pounce on the celebrated fugitive. He saw himself being marched across a concourse, press cameras flashing, his arms pinned behind his back, the coked-out personification of a boom gone wrong.

He wasn't going to give them the satisfaction. It wouldn't be easy, but he would fly home with nothing on him, like a compulsive gambler walking into a bookie's with empty pockets.

Noelle had shown her true colours. The brief conversation they had shared had enlightened him on two fronts. She knew about the whores. She was blowing the whole thing out of proportion. He knew that at the heart of her ire was a simple fact. She had got cold feet. Instead of seizing the opportunity to escape, she had frozen. And in her cowardice, he saw their love turn sour.

He had explained it all to last night's whore, a gentle and petite brunette from Siberia. She had understood where he was coming from. All he had wanted to do was talk to her and keep his nose powdered. In terms of a counselling session, he could have bought a full day with a top shrink for what those few hours had cost him.

But the main thing now was that he had a suss once he got to the other side. Two hours earlier, he had rung an old source in Dublin, delighted to find that, in these straitened times, it was a buyer's market. The guy would arrange for somebody to meet him in Cork. He felt relief flood his body like a speedball. At least now he would be fit for anything that might be thrown up.

In any event, it was a straightforward operation. Hire a car, drive down to south Kerry, pick up the money and head for the hills. If you stood back and applied some common sense, you'd have to come to the conclusion that there was no risk involved at all. It was child's play.

What was bugging him now was that he hadn't done this at

the outset. Why had he thought it would be such a big deal? How had he worked himself into a frenzy of worry over what was in effect a simple job that just couldn't involve any hassle?

If he had taken the initiative himself, Noelle would be at his side now. He could have whisked her out of the country along with the money and they would be en route to their new life together. Now, instead, he had to face it alone. But he was up for it. The men were about to be separated from the boys, and he knew where he stood.

After breakfast, Noelle and Molloy brought the children for a walk. There was no problem. Noelle was cautious asking Ivan and Kathy. They had just met the previous night. Ivan and Molloy hadn't had much contact in God knew how long. How would Ivan and Kathy feel about allowing their sons to go off with this strange couple?

But Kathy acquiesced immediately, as if instinctively she knew her brood would be safe in these childless hands. Well, technically childless, in Molloy's case. Kathy said to just stay down from the main road and don't let the kids near the water.

It was tough going, keeping a rein on the boys. They followed the road as it snaked down towards the beach. Aaron and Sam pointed out the cows and Molloy wondered about his own son, who had seen more hypodermic spikes than cows in his short life. As the road dipped, trees closed in overhead, creating a tunnel. Noelle and Molloy stole glances at each other in reaction to the wonder spilling from the kids.

He had left the Glock under the seat in the Honda Civic. If Ivan discovered it anywhere in the house, it would have been all over.

Last night had been good. They had been billeted together in the kids' room, like kids themselves. Kathy showed them to it, just off the kitchen. She didn't ask whether the arrangement suited, but neither did she presume they would be sharing a bed.

The door had hardly closed when he moved to her and she grabbed him in a needy embrace. They pulled at each other's clothes and fumbled in their rush to be naked before any questions could come between them. She was against the wall, next to the door, her eyes closed to her longing. He reached across and killed the light, then eased her down on to a rug that lay between the two beds. It was all over quicker than they would have liked, but they lay there for a long time, the sound of the TV and a crack of light coming under the door. Molloy tried to remember the last time he had sex when both parties had been in full control of their moods. He was still rooting through his memory when Noelle said, 'Who would have thought?'

Later, in one of the beds, they tried again, but the groaning of timber beneath them grew towards a wail. He felt Noelle's breath hot in his ear. 'It's a child's bed,' she said. With that, he tumbled to the rug and she fell on him.

When it was over, they lay there again. By then there was no light from beyond the door; the TV had long since been silenced. The only sound was their heavy breathing, until their bodies cooled and she shivered, then pulled a duvet down on top of them. Molloy felt free there in the dead of night. He hadn't felt so good since he didn't know when. If it wasn't for the threat casting a dark shadow over his life, he would be walking on air.

The beach was deserted. There was a little slip leading down to the sand, and off to the left a pier advanced into the bay. A few pleasure craft were out there, moored to anchors, awaiting fairer weather. And, beyond, there was more mist, shrouding the mountains on the far side of the bay.

Kathy had packed buckets and spades. There was a retaining

wall separating the beach from the car park above, and it had a ledge on which Molloy and Noelle sat as the kids dug their way to hunger.

When they got back to the house, Kathy had lunch laid out. Sausages and fried potatoes for the kids, a salad with mozzarella for the adults, with soda bread on the side.

Afterwards, Ivan said he had to go into town for a few bits and bobs.

'Why don't you go with your brother?' Noelle said.

The thought hadn't occurred to Molloy, but why not? A little brotherly bonding wouldn't go astray.

Slate had to drive back and forth for a while around Kells Bay before pinpointing the place. The journey down had been long, hitting on for five hours, with one stop for an overpriced sandwich outside Limerick. Then, as he drew closer, he began to take his time. He stopped at a petrol station-cum-restaurant for a coffee, and pumped the waitress for information. She consulted with a middle-aged customer and came back with specific directions to the place he was looking for.

Fifteen minutes later, he pulled into the side of what was little more than a laneway and killed the engine. He could hear birds, and the distant rumble of a truck up on the main road. He put his notebook into his inside breast pocket, got out and locked the car. Meeting guys like this, you just never knew. This Ivan didn't have any form, but violence was never far from the surface where he had grown up.

He rapped twice and left it at that. There was movement. A woman opened the door, her face brightening into an instinctive smile. 'Hello,' she said.

'Hi, is Ivan home?' She still had her hand on the door handle. A little boy appeared at her side and grabbed her leg.

'He's down in Cahirciveen. We send him out for provisions now and again to make sure we don't starve.'

Slate felt the tension ease from his body. This woman had the air of somebody who was naturally open and welcoming. 'Will he be long? I'm down from Dublin to see him.'

Her expression hardened into curiosity, as if the mention of Dublin could bring only trouble. 'He didn't tell me he was expecting anybody.'

Slate raised his hands. 'It's nothing to worry about. We just have a mutual friend who said he might be able to help me. I'll only take a few minutes of his time.'

It didn't do the trick, her face was tightening into questions. She looked down at her watch. 'He might be another hour or so. I'd invite you in but I have visitors already and we're pretty busy.' She moved sideways as if to allow him see how busy the house was.

Slate looked beyond her shoulder. There was a boy at a table with a woman, and not just any woman. It was one of those moments in his career that Slate cherished, that he recognised as delivering him something that could be as good as it got. The solicitor, Noelle Diggins, was sitting making a jigsaw with the boy. He reached for composure. 'That's OK,' he said. 'I think I might know your guest.'

The woman stood aside, to give him a better view. 'Really? Noelle, this man, sorry I didn't get your name, he says he knows you.'

Noelle Diggins turned around with a smile lingering from something the kid had said. The smile died on the spot.

The hardware shop was on the main street. There were wheelbarrows and shovels and pairs of wellington boots on the footpath, advertising its wares. Inside, a middle-aged woman stood behind the counter, reading from a trade magazine. She looked up when the two men entered, smiled, and returned to her reading.

Junior patrolled the shop's aisles, picking up stuff as he went, handing it to Rocco, who was soon weighed down by it all. First there were the windcheaters. The rain had been a constant since their arrival. Junior picked up a plastic packet in which a navy windcheater was wrapped. He looked at Rocco, decided he was a medium and took a green one from the shelf.

He selected a shovel and a pick. Rocco brought them over and stood them next to the counter. Then there was a torch, large, advertised as 'multi-use'. Junior turned to Rocco. 'What use could you have for a torch other than shining a light? What the fuck is multi-use?'

Rocco shrugged. He was wondering whether there was any situation in which Junior would admit to having had anything to do with Kyle.

Junior handed Rocco a set of chisels. He picked up a hammer, swung it through the air, as if he was laying into Diggins, then handed it to Rocco. Next he came to a stop beside a long box that depicted an electric saw. He opened it, and took out the contraption. He moved it back and forward in his hands, in a jerk.

There were all sorts of rumours about Junior and how he had come up. Rocco didn't believe too many of them, but the way he held the saw suggested he had used one before, and not for cutting wood.

Junior put the saw back into its box.

'What exactly are we going to do?' Rocco said.

'Go through the houses, one by one, until we find what we're looking for.'

'They're big houses. It could be a needle in a haystack. You don't even know the money is there.'

'Trust me. It'll be worth it.'

Rocco saw them stumbling across a suitcase, a black

suitcase, with straps and zips. He saw Junior opening it and looking down at cash, stacks of cash stuffing the case out. He saw himself pulling out the Beretta and giving Junior one in the base of his skull. Except, before doing anything, he'd like to know about Kyle. What he did know was that he couldn't keep the situation under wraps. Once Junior detected anything, he was likely to move first. Coming down here was a distraction for everybody. Getting their hands on some serious cash would be a big bonus. But this shit couldn't go on for ever.

The only other purchase was a packet of thick, stumpy candles. 'No electricity out there,' Junior said. 'We're going back to the Stone Age.'

The woman behind the counter didn't remark on the purchases, as if it was quite normal that somebody would come in looking for this amount of gear of a damp Tuesday. She commented on the weather and that was it. Rocco wasn't sure exactly what she said. He found it hard to understand what anybody round here was saying. They all spoke too fast.

Ivan's car was an old Toyota Corolla, one of those models that were popular around the same time Moses had come down from the mountain. The silencer on the engine had had its day. There was no CD player, and the radio was kaput. A yellow tree-shaped air-freshener hung from the rear-view mirror, as if to ward off malfunctions as much as smells.

'Not the job for long journeys, is it?' Molloy said.

'I suppose you'd be used to something a little plusher. And a little stolen.'

He'd had to get the dig in, even a small one, but Molloy wasn't going to dwell on it. 'At least you don't have to worry about anybody stealing this.'

Ivan laughed, and Molloy smiled, both reaching out across the big divide.

'You've got a good set-up down here,' Molloy said.

'Yeah, Kathy likes it. Not much money but we can get by. Good place to raise kids. The winters are long.'

'Place is like a sanctuary, different world from Westwood. That beach, man, you could pitch a tent there.'

'Fuckin' tourists in the summer.'

'No noise, no hassle.'

'Don't have much in the way of exotic food.'

'You've got it made.'

'You know, it rains more down here, a lot more.'

'Are you taking the piss?'

'I know what I got. I'm grateful for it every day.'

They passed a man wearing a flat cap. He stood in against the ditch at the side of the road to let the car pass. The sleeves of his white shirt were rolled up to the elbow. Ivan waved to him. The man's face lit up with recognition and he waved back, his arm describing a big circle. Ivan said, 'Have you been to the grave?'

'The day after I got back. Seems like a long time ago now. There were some fresh flowers there, carnations and a wreath.'

'We were up about six weeks ago. Went out there with the kids while Kathy was visiting her parents. The place is kept well.'

'Yeah.' Molloy knew what was coming next. They might have been back there again, the empty house that was already losing the warmth of a home, Ma not a month in the grave and Ivan laying out her dying concerns.

Ivan said, 'How do you think she would have felt?'

'About me?'

'About everything. She never got to see her grandkids. I often wondered what it would have been like – she could have come down here, stayed for a while, away from everything up there. She would have been glad to see you getting your act together.'

'Yeah?'

'You are getting your act together, aren't you?'

Molloy could see the town in the distance now, a collection of bright colours set low between a brown mountain and the blue sea. 'I'm getting something together.'

'And Noelle?'

'Don't go there. I haven't a clue what's going on.'

'But you are out of the game. You are finished with that?'

'There's one matter needs to be cleared up before I can put it behind me.'

Ivan looked across at him. 'Whatever it is, do whatever you have to do, don't drag it down here. Go back up and get your son, bring him down. But I don't want any trouble. I've too much to lose.'

They arrived at the town within minutes. Ivan drove down a long street. A huge church loomed on the right, out of proportion with everything else. He pulled off the main street, and swung around into a car park, which opened up like a bay. Molloy noticed that his brother didn't bother locking the doors. They began walking up through the parked vehicles. Ivan said something about a great fruit-and-veg shop at the top of the car park, but by then Molloy wasn't listening.

He was watching two men getting into another car. He stopped in his tracks. Ivan didn't notice, just kept on walking. Molloy called after his brother, said he'd forgotten something in the car. He turned to walk back. He had to get out of sight. Jesus Christ, they had followed him all the way down here.

'That didn't take long.' The waitress was standing over him, brandishing a menu. She had a nice smile that was just on the wrong side of curious.

Slate said he'd have coffee and waited for her to go in behind the service counter. He pulled out his phone. It answered on the second ring.

'How're you, Inspector?'

'OK, and you?' He could hear the sound of a car engine in the background.

'I'm down in the deep south.'

'Oh, yeah, the brother. Have you got anywhere with him?'

'He wasn't home, but there was a surprise guest in the house.'

'Go on.'

'Your friend's wife.' There was a silence on the line.

'Where are you, Alan?'

'Place called Kells, right on the lip of the Ring of Kerry. There's something going on. I just haven't figured it out yet.'

'OK. I've an idea that we might be hooking up in the next few hours. This can't be a coincidence. I'm on my way to Cork Airport. My friend, as you call him, is flying in. And I'm beginning to see what's happening.'

Slate killed the phone. He was buzzing now, in a way that he recognised from an old day. It was as if he had downed half a dozen espressos, unable to stay still. When he had started out in the business, he used to feel like this all the time. The newness had grabbed him and sent him into a frenzy of excitement. Now he was back there again, the sense of wonder recaptured.

His phone rang him out of his happy cloud. Fastneck. The editor was getting his knickers in a twist over something. Trust Frank Fastneck to ruin his buzz, reminding him that he still hadn't found a proper home for his skills. He had a good mind to let it go, but native curiosity wouldn't leave him alone.

'Alan?'

'Hi, Frank.'

'Where are you?'

He didn't want to play his full hand with this guy. He certainly didn't want him charging down here. 'On my way to Kerry. Remember, I told you about the Dancer, his brother. I'm going down to meet him.'

'Alan, if I was you, I'd turn the car around. The bank is pulling the plug. This week's edition is going to be our last.'

Molloy opened the passenger door of the Corolla and pretended to rummage around on the floor. He heard a car pass behind him. He stole a glance in its wake. The man behind the wheel had Junior's bald head. That was most likely it, all right. Still, he held on to his caution as he rejoined Ivan.

'Find what you were looking for?'

He pulled out a key and nodded. They spent the best part of half an hour in town. First the fruit-and-veg shop, then a walk up through the main street to a supermarket. Molloy said little. Ivan pointed out various things about the town, mentioned the size of the church as they passed it. He just nodded, and tried to suppress the anger that was rising within him, like a wave. There would be no end to it. If they had already traced him down here, how far would they be behind him wherever he went? And what could he tell his brother? Right now, the main thing was he had to move. He had to get out of here and take his trouble with him before they showed up at Ivan's door.

When they got back to the cottage it was obvious that things had changed there too. Noelle and Kathy were seated at the kitchen table, an air of anxiety hanging between them. Noelle got to her feet as the brothers walked through the door. 'Guess who called here a few minutes ago?'

Molloy tensed himself. His first instinct was to go out to the car and get the gun.

Noelle spoke again: 'The reporter, Slate. That man who

has been hassling me for the last fortnight. He came here and knocked on the door. How did he know we were here?'

Molloy put a hand on her shoulder. 'We need to talk,' he said. He turned to Ivan. 'Excuse us a minute.' Ivan shrugged his assent. The two of them walked out the door, and back around to the front. The two boys were at the swing, Sam pushing Aaron. They were wearing coats against the chilly air. Sam waved across at the adults.

'We have a problem,' Molloy said. 'Our friends are here. I saw them in the town. We can't stay. I'm not dragging Ivan into this.'

He noticed the hint of bags around her eyes now, as if the weight of the last few weeks was settling on her face.

'How is this going to end?' she said.

'I don't know. I'll do whatever has to be done, but I don't want to deal with it on their terms.'

'Would money help?'

'What are you talking about?'

She turned away from him, towards the bay. The mist had lifted now. She could see all the way across to the other peninsula. 'When you said you were coming down here, I had another motive. Apparently there is a suitcase of money in an estate Donal developed down here. Somewhere on the far side of the town.' She turned back towards him.

It was his turn to look confused. 'Could you run that by me again, in English this time?'

She went through it all. Donal, London, the plan. He listened, his head bent towards the ground. The kids swapped around on the swing. Sam began singing 'Old MacDonald' as Aaron pushed him. 'It's called Buckingham Gate.' She pulled a folded A4 piece of paper from the pocket of her jeans. 'I just got this from my bag after the reporter left here. I knew we wouldn't be sticking around.' She read down through it. 'Coomastow. That's the name of the place.'

'How come this is the first I've heard of all this?'

'I've known you for all of ten days. Do you want me to hand over everything to do with my life?'

'No, but—'

'And you were spying on me, remember?'

'I wouldn't call it spying.'

'How could I tell you anything until … Well, I don't know. I don't know that I should be telling you now, but I am. I decided that I wanted the money. I'm as entitled to it as anybody, certainly as much as Donal.'

'Hold on, whose money is it?'

'All different people Donal dealt with. He took their cash and kept it for a rainy day. He was running rings around everybody, clients, the banks, the lot.'

'Is Junior's money there?'

'How should I know? But if he can be paid out of it, this might go away.'

'I can see it all now. That's why they wanted me to keep tabs on you. They knew there was money stashed away somewhere and they figured you might lead them to it.'

She turned away again. 'Donal must have known about all of this. And he didn't say one word to me. He just sent me off to get his money without ever mentioning that some gang of criminals were after it too.' When she turned back towards him her face was all thunder, as if he was in some way responsible for how her husband had treated her. She said, 'Do you think they know where it is?'

'Not unless your husband told them.'

'No way, absolutely no way..'

'OK, let's take a punt. We leave here now, find out where this place is and get the money. We can decide after what to do with it.'

'We?' She had a look on her face, no longer anger. He couldn't make out whether it was suspicion or a question for which she wanted the right answer.

'It's your money. Let's just get going.'

Ivan appeared at the back door, and shouted to the kids to come inside. 'Hey,' he said to the adults, 'Kathy has just got those biscuits out of the oven. A cuppa?'

'Sure,' his brother said. They began walking towards the house. 'Ivan, you ever hear of a place called ...'

He turned to Noelle, who said. 'Coomastow.'

'Doesn't ring a bell, but if it's somewhere round here, we'll find it.'

Cork Airport was dozing through a midday lull when Donal Diggins passed through into the arrivals hall. There were about half a dozen faces waiting to meet and greet. He scanned them all through hooded eyes and satisfied himself that none were there to arrest or kill him.

How would he look to any casual observer at that time of day? He wore a brown suit, white shirt, no tie, and was carrying only hand luggage. He was the same as any number of businessmen, flying back and forth to the country. He kept telling himself this as he paced across the concourse towards the Avis desk.

The woman behind the counter didn't betray any recognition. She didn't even smile, which he found a bit off-putting. He filled out the forms for a mid-range Nissan Almera. She gave him instructions on where to locate the vehicle outside, but he had to ask her twice. Fatigue was attacking his body like a virus. He badly needed to get back up where he belonged.

Once through the outer doors he stopped momentarily, and noticed the sharp breeze that told him he was home. He hadn't packed a coat. On the threshold of the terminal he made an effort to savour this moment for posterity. The next time he arrived in the country would most likely be years down the line. He would be in a much better place, his life rebuilt, a new fortune made. If Noelle couldn't see what she was going to miss, that was her problem.

En route to the car park, he phoned his man. The response was positive. He was already *in situ* at the bar of the Radisson. The news gave Diggins a little perk-up. It took him all of six minutes to locate the car, minutes that appeared to drag out into infinity.

The Radisson was just down the road. Inside, the lobby was thickening with afternoon traffic. He walked through the door into the bar and stopped with a jolt. Standing at the counter in front of him two men were bent low towards each other in animated conversation. Diggins immediately turned on his heels and headed for the front door. One of the men, a large guy with a small brain and a short fuse, had been involved with him on a development in the Midlands, completed less than six months ago. It had been an exciting project, in which an estate of high-end holiday homes was built more or less on the lip of a bog. It had seemed like a good idea at the time but, as it turned out, proper provision hadn't been made for the bog. The place was now more or less abandoned, and Diggins was sure that the guy at the bar blamed him for the vagaries of business. It was the same with so many of them. They thought that they were investing in a sure thing, not understanding that business simply didn't work that way. And when the whole shebang went belly-up, it was to him they turned to unleash their fury.

Back at the car, he phoned his man again. Ninety seconds later, the man opened the passenger door. He had a grin on his face, the stupid grin of power.

'Long time no see,' he said. He wore a light navy hoodie, and a low-necked T-shirt that was in the wrong season but complemented the gold chain around his neck.

Diggins detected an immediate whiff of BO. 'Hasn't been that long,' he said.

'Where have you been?'

'Spain. Have you got it?'

'Hold your horses now for a minute. Tell me how you've been getting on. This credit crunch is a right bastard, isn't it?'

Approximately sixty yards across the car park from where Donal Diggins was being put through the final agonies before relief, Inspector Phil Wright sat behind the wheel of his own vehicle.

21

From the get-go, Rocco knew the whole affair was crazy. They arrived back with the tools. Junior parked up inside the wall, just on the off-chance that somebody might stumble across them out here and begin wondering about the motor. The two of them stood on the track between the first two houses. Junior had a grip on the shovel, Rocco held the pick.

'What way do we do this? Working the houses together or separately?' Rocco said.

'Together. Look at the odds. If we hit on the right house, we should find what we're looking for quicker. But if we take one each, even if it is the right house, it's going to take us a longer time.'

Rocco couldn't follow the logic. 'What if we pick the wrong house first?'

'Then we'll get to the next one quicker. Trust me.'

Rocco was long past that. The two of them stood there for a few minutes, thinking. Overhead, a bunch of indigo clouds was drifting in from the sea. Rocco had enough of the rain. 'So what about number one?'

'I was thinking about that. See, if you were Diggins, I don't think you'd put it in number one.'

'Too obvious.'

'Too obvious, and it would be the showhouse. I mean, if you have a big bag of cash, you don't want loads of heads trooping through the gaff where they could stumble across it and then, bam, there goes your future..'

'I don't think they had to worry about that. Who in their right mind would ever have bought a place out here?'

The two men turned their heads to the house on the other side of the track.

'Number two,' Rocco said. Junior walked over, across the uneven stones where a driveway had been planned. He looked through a window, his face pressed up against the glass. He went around to the side, his shoes kicking up the topsoil as he moved down between the house and garage. A few seconds later Rocco heard the sound of smashing glass.

When he got around to the back the hardwood decking was littered with shards. There was more glass just inside where the sliding doors had been. Junior was reaching inside to unlock the door, his grip high on the shovel.

They walked into a huge room that had no furniture. The floor was of maple, but nobody had got round to putting in the skirting boards. Junior went through a door at the far end. Rocco heard him moving between rooms before reappearing. 'Let's bring the stuff in here and see where we go,' he said, his voice echoing across the room.

Rocco brought in the tools and the box with the electric saw. He stood the pick and shovel next to the broken glass door, took the saw from the box, and unfurled the electric lead. His eyes scoped the walls. He spotted four sets of loose wires protruding from where there should have been sockets. 'Shit. What use is this saw? There's no electricity here.'

Junior looked at him for a second, the reality of their

situation dawning on his face. He shrugged. 'We have other tools.' He walked over and lifted the pick.

Rocco threw the saw on to the floor. 'Junior, this is crazy. The money, it could be anywhere. How do we know where to look? I mean, you could spend a month out here taking these houses apart one by one and get nowhere.'

'What the fuck are you saying? That we give up? There's no option. Do you understand that? I need my money back.'

Rocco noted the desperation in his voice, the sound of power leaving him. 'Why don't we try and get the plans for this place and work off them?' Rocco said. 'If we were to start pulling the place apart it would attract attention at some time. Those fucking cows out there? Somebody has to be looking after them. If we're up here for days battering the shit out of these houses, somebody is going to find it very strange. Why don't we head back into town and see if we can get our hands on the plans or even on some better tools?'

Junior Corbett had to admit it: the kid made sense. Dark vistas had been forming in his head of stacks of broken shingles piled high, walls knocked down and no result. He threw the pick on to the floor. 'Let's go,' he said.

There was a car up ahead, blocking the road to Coomastow. Molloy turned his head to check whether there was somewhere they could reverse and pull in. There was nothing within sight.

He refocused on the car ahead. 'Come on, move it back, will you?' he said to nobody in particular.

Noelle's fingers were tapping on the steering wheel. 'What's the matter with them?'

A man got out of the car from the driver's side. He was wearing a green windcheater. Another man got out from the other side. His windcheater was navy and his head was bald. He pulled a blue woollen hat over his head. The engine was still idling.

'Jesus.'

'What?'

'It's them.'

The two men began walking towards the car. Molloy recognised Junior Corbett at the same moment that a gun materialised in Junior Corbett's right hand.

Molloy reached under the seat, felt the cold metal of the Glock.

Noelle was staring at him as he brought the gun up. 'What is that?'

'I'll explain later. Get down and stay down until I'm clear of the car. I'll draw them after me. Then reverse and drive like a blue-arsed fly.'

Noelle's head was already down at the handbrake. He reached out and touched her hair. 'You're going to be OK. This time please phone the cops.'

'What about you?'

'It's time to piss or get off the pot,' he said. He pulled at the door handle.

She looked over, saw him crouched behind the open door. His arms were extended, holding the weapon with both hands.

'Drop the gun, Junior,' she heard him say. 'Now.' A momentary silence followed.

A shot rang out. Noelle put her hands to her ears. The handbrake felt cold against her cheek.

Molloy looked at her. 'I'll draw them after me. Just drive.' He ran from the car.

'Wait,' she said. She could see him hopping over a fence. Another shot. She could nearly smell her own fear. Molloy was her guide through this world into which she had been thrust, and now she was abandoned, as surely as if he had left her alone in a dank sewer.

She heard shouts rending the air with curses. The smell of burning hung around her. Another shot. A voice shouting instructions. She could feel herself trembling. Another voice, this one further away. She counted to twenty. What mattered most now was to keep it together.

She sat up. The engine was still idling, rocking gently. It had never sounded so loud before. The wipers were still lazily making curves on the windscreen. There was nothing out there but the other car. She looked to the field on her left, rising into the foothills of a mountain. At the far end, at least a hundred yards away, a figure, the one wearing the navy windcheater, appeared to be running through the soft rain. There was nobody else in sight. She leaned over, crawled across the passenger seat and reached out to pull the door closed. As she did so, she caught a glimpse of a cow with a black and white hide staring at her over a low ditch.

Her mobile phone was in her handbag on the back seat. She dipped her hand in and came out with it. She punched in 999. A beep told her there was no signal available to connect her to the network. She pushed the gearstick into reverse. The engine whined as she drove, her eyes alternating between the rear-view and wing mirrors. There was nowhere to turn. She kept going.

At last there was an entrance to a field behind her, the side of the road dipping down towards a gate of galvanised black pipes. She swung the car around into the dip. She threw the gearstick into first. The car roared, the rear wheels spun. She tried again, the engine squealed in protest. In the rear-view mirror, there was a man climbing over the gate. She slammed her foot to the floor, the car roared back, as if in pain, but there was no shifting it.

The door beside her flew open. He was standing there, one

hand out towards her, the other on the gun. He was the same man who had pursued her that day on the beach.

When Molloy leaped the ditch into the field, he landed in water. It was some sort of a shallow dike, and he was soaked to his ankles. He pulled himself from it and made for a grove of trees off to the right. He jogged across the field, stumbling now and again on the hoof prints with which the field was pockmarked. He pulled his woolly black hat from the pocket of his jacket.

Looking over his shoulder, he could see that he had a head start. No sign of the two lads yet. Then a shot rang out and he threw himself on the ground. He was still intact but damp now. Once in the grove, he ducked behind a stout trunk and peered around it to see Junior Corbett in his navy windcheater, emerging from the dike, looking at his right foot, as if it might have been attacked by some alien being in the water.

Corbett scanned the field and began plodding towards the far end. Molloy caught his breath. He leaned against the tree trunk, felt the bark on his cheek. This had to end here today. He wasn't carrying it around any more.

He gave it a few minutes, then moved back up through another field, and another after that. There was a lean-to of corrugated iron at the entrance to the next field. He stepped under it, and took in the smell of dry cowshit.

He stayed put for some time; how long he wasn't sure. Every moment he expected to hear the wail of a siren. The soft rain stopped falling and the night began gathering in around the hills.

He drew long breaths. From somewhere, a sheep bleated. There was a peace about the mountain, as if nothing had changed, as if the bad things that are done had no place here.

He waited for the sirens, but they didn't come. He pulled the cigarettes from his pocket, the box of Marlboro damp to the touch. He lit one and dragged hard on the filter. Time passed slowly. He felt a calm come over him. He remembered the nights in the Phoenix Park all those years ago, when there was just him and the darkness. He had been looking for different things then. Right now, what he wanted was real. Right now, there was a lot more at stake. He was through with being hunted, by men, by his own demons.

Presently he felt it was time to move back down. He retraced the route he had taken up the hill, but the evening was closing in and he sensed that he had strayed from the path. He moved cautiously across the uneven ground as the light faded. At one point, he nearly slipped on a saucer of fresh dung, just about keeping his balance. Briars tore at his sleeves as he leaped one ditch into another field. He stopped again a little while later in a copse of undergrowth, around which gorse stood like a yellow-tinged moat. Down in the lowlands, a few lights were coming on in the loose scattering of homes.

Maybe he was losing track of time, but Noelle had to have got back to the town by now and located the law. At the very least, she must have rung. Unease washed over him. He had invested his hope in the law showing up and bringing an end to this. Out here in the wilds he could get rid of the gun and walk down into the commotion an innocent man. But that scenario was quickly receding. Where the fuck were they?

By now, night had fallen like a blanket. The going underfoot was soft and sticky, and his toes felt like blocks of ice. At last, he spotted dry land. He climbed over a rusting gate on to the road. Now the night was his friend as he could spot anybody approaching from either end. He got his bearings and decided that the main road and civilisation were to the right. He turned left.

The squelching in his shoes moved to the beat of a march as

he made his way along the dark road. He passed a house, set back, two-storey and fronted by a yard on which were littered bits of farm machinery. A tractor stood just inside the gate, hooked to a trailer. There were two plastic five-gallon drums on the trailer. Lights burned from two of the windows on the ground floor. He could walk up to the front door, explain that there was a serious problem and he needed to use the landline to call the law.

He stood on the road in front of the house for a few moments. The silence was as if from the tomb.

He couldn't do it. If Noelle had rung them, that was OK. But he couldn't bring himself to do it. For one thing, he'd have too much explaining to do.

He walked over to the trailer. The plastic drums smelt of fuel, petrol or maybe diesel. One was full to the brim. He tried to lift it, but it took both his hands. He wouldn't be going too far with that. The second was half full. It was manageable. He lifted it clear of the trailer and got back on the road, his right hand gripping the handle.

Within a few minutes he came upon the Honda Civic, nosing from the entrance to a field. The interior felt cold. He checked for the keys, but they were gone. The cab light threw a dirty yellow glow on to the front seats. There was no sign of blood.

From what he remembered her saying, the housing estate couldn't be too far away. Christ knows, much further and it was in danger of being swallowed by the mountain.

He returned to the road. Between the moon and the rinsed aftertaste of the rain, the night was clear and fresh.

After the thug took her from the car, they walked back along the road, his hand tight on her arm. Twice she asked him to lay off but he told her to shut the fuck up both times.

When they arrived at the other car, the one out of which this man and his companion had emerged, he opened the door and shoved her into the passenger seat. He started the engine, and put the car into gear. She saw her chance, pulled at the door handle and lunged through. She felt his hand tearing at her jacket, but she broke free and began running, back out towards the way they had come in here, back down a passage out of this nightmare. She felt the rain on her face, thought she had the better of him. But he was no slouch. She hadn't gone twenty yards before an arm grabbed her around the neck, hauling her back and on to the road. She landed on her side. A pain shot out from her arm. He kicked her legs and she cried out.

'Try that again and I'll put a fucking bullet in you,' he said.

He dragged her to her feet and held her by the arm as they walked back to the car. This time she didn't try anything. He threw the car into reverse, kept his eyes on the road behind. She saw the gun between his legs. She willed it to go off and shoot his balls halfway into next week. She was afraid now. All control of her fate had been taken from her. It was a feeling she recognised from whenever she took a flight. She had no influence over what was going to befall her. Except this was a lot worse than any aeroplane.

She saw the sign carved into stone at the entrance to the houses. Buckingham Gate. The first time Donal had mentioned it to her, she had thought he was having her on. But he had worked his persuasive charm, explaining that it was merely taking to its logical conclusion the trend in naming new estates after English shires and villages.

'They'll love it,' he had said. 'It evokes exactly the correct image for the end of the market we're servicing here. It won't be a home, it will be an experience.'

The thug pulled up in front of a house, got out and came around to her side. No words had passed between them during the short drive. She was brought around the back, up on to decking and through double glass doors, one of which had been broken. Inside there was a large kitchen space, as big as her own back in Skellig, but bare to the world.

He dragged her to a corner of the room and pulled from his pocket a plastic tie. He twisted her hands behind her back. She felt the tie on her wrists. He threaded the flex of an electric saw between her wrists and tied a knot with it. Then he got a pick, tied a string around the shaft and handle and attached that to the flex. If she had any notions of going anywhere, she'd be dragging a racket behind her.

The man walked through an inner door. She could hear his footsteps as he marched about, sounding as if he was just pacing rather than going anywhere specific.

Eventually he came back into the room. 'You've caused some trouble,' he said. 'Where's the money?'

She kept her eyes on the floor. She noticed the maple, similar to the floor back in Skellig. There were all sorts of things you could do with a maple floor. She could feel him standing above her.

'The money,' he said. He lowered himself to his haunches, and when he spoke, his voice had dropped an octave towards civility. 'You can tell me, or you can wait for Junior. If I was you, I'd tell me because I won't hurt you. Just say where I need to go and that's it. I'll set you free and you can find your own way out of here.'

Noelle refused to meet his eyes. She tried to concentrate on the floor. It could do with a coat of Ronseal, but the big problem was the little lumps that would form if it wasn't applied with great care. A four-inch brush should do the job.

The man raised himself up to his feet again. She heard his footsteps walk towards the back door. The rain had stopped, but a chill breeze was blowing through the broken glass. The man walked around the kitchen, through the rooms and back again, as if impatience wouldn't leave him alone.

When she looked up again, another man was walking in through the back door. The sound of his shoes on the wooden floor echoed out across the empty room. He looked to be in some pain. 'This fucking place,' he said. His shoes squelched. The sleeve of his jacket was ripped, leaving flesh exposed, blotched in a dark shade of red.

'Where is he?' the younger guy said.

'He won't be far away.'

'You didn't get him?'

'I said he won't be far away. Not now that this little lady is here to help us with our enquiries.' He walked over to her, took her face in his right hand. She reared against him, fear taking over her whole body.

'Mrs Diggins, to hook up with one loser was a bad move on your part. To hook up with two makes you a loser yourself. Now, where is the money?'

He was squeezing her cheeks between his thumb and finger. She couldn't have spoken even if she'd wanted to, which she didn't. She looked at him, trying to convert her fear into defiance.

'No talky? We'll see if that can be rearranged. Rocco here might be interested in getting intimate with your good self.' He pushed her face back, and looked to examine his injured arm. 'Nobody who has given me as much grief as this fucker Molloy has ever lived so long. But when he goes it will be slow, and it will be painful. I presume he's poking you at this stage.'

Noelle's cheeks still hurt. She had never known fear like this, the idea that she was at the complete mercy of these men. She tried not to think about what they might do to her, and whether afterwards they would let her live. She thought of Molloy. With any luck, he would have overcome his reservations and phoned the guards. There was no coverage here, but there were houses a way back. She tried to picture him at the door of one of those bungalows, explaining that it was an emergency, that a couple of hardened criminals had kidnapped a woman down the road, and were now deciding whether or not to rape her.

They wouldn't go that far. They must know that it would involve cutting off nose to spite face. The younger one, he didn't look to be as vicious as the other. He had scared the living daylights out of her that day on the beach, but he seemed different now, not as crazy, not as focused on what he was doing.

Noelle hadn't believed in God since she was a child. She had never put much thought into it, but the nuns had sent her scurrying in the opposite direction from whatever they believed in. She closed her eyes and opened a conversation with the mystery of her childhood. If you are really out there, God, I could use you right now.

The traffic in the town was heavy. Here they were, in the arse end of nowhere, and the cars were backed up as if it was the M50. Detective Inspector Phil Wright could see Diggins's silver Nissan Almera four vehicles ahead of his own. There was a Mace convenience-store truck between them but it was possible to make him out.

He tapped in Slate's number, and got an immediate response.

'I'm outside the bank, halfway down the town, past the church,' Slate said.

Wright looked up, saw a huge church coming up on the right. 'He's in a Silver Almera. Keep your head down.' He rang off.

A few minutes of crawling traffic later, Wright saw him idling beside an ATM. Slate spotted him and walked across, his eyes darting about the place as if he was starring in some crime drama.

Once in the car he extended his hand. Wright took it limply.

'Strange times.'

Wright didn't reply. He kept his eyes on the traffic.

'Any idea where we're headed?' Slate said.

'I've been looking into this bastard in minute detail over the last few weeks. He developed a place just a few miles from here. Sold it as the ultimate getaway for high-net-worth individuals, the kind of people he used to hang out with.'

'Not too many of them left now.'

'That's the only place I can think of.'

'What do you reckon with the wife?'

'Could be that she and Molloy are in cahoots with him.'

'This gets better and better. And when we get there?'

Wright lifted himself off the seat as if trying to get comfortable. 'We'll have to see. See what's there. See how he reacts to our presence. Alan, you're coming along for the ride, but whatever goes down, you run it by me before it sees print. Nothing comes out without my say-so. Are we clear on that?'

'Sure, Phil, no problem.'

'You're in the big league now, playing senior inter-county hurling, if you know what I mean. We don't fuck around up here.'

'You can depend on me, Phil.'

'You know it's all bollocks?'

'What?'

'Cape Isis.'

'I don't get you.'

'There is no Cape Isis. He made the whole thing up. I began checking it out after the first time you and I discussed it. I don't know why it took me that long, but I went at it thoroughly. I've been on to four different countries in west Africa. Nobody's ever heard of it. Estate agents. Tour operators. I've been on to the Gambia, to Mauritania. A guy in the chief of police's office in Sierra Leone reckons the place must have disappeared into the sea.'

'But the presentation, the slides, the brochures.'

'How many African villages do you have to pick from? Nobody there would know whether that place was in eastern Kenya or Bongo Bongo Land. How the fuck would anybody know? All they wanted was what I wanted, a piece of the action.'

'Jesus.'

'And the man behind it all is just ahead of us there. If he doesn't lead me to my money, I'm going to have to kill him.'

'Steady on, Phil.'

'I am steady. I've never been as steady in my life.'

It had begun to rain again by the time Molloy came upon Buckingham Gate. The houses were silhouetted against the moon and fine sheets of soft rain. He moved slowly once he passed the stone pier. A dull pain was now where his toes used to be. His right arm was aching with the weight of the drum. He dropped it on the ground at the stone pier and moved ahead slowly.

The sight of the SUV heightened his caution. He tried the door, which was open – there was nothing of use to him in the cab – and eased it closed again.

He could go up there and begin shooting. There were two of them, but compared to the odds stacked against him so far, that wasn't too bad.

Noelle was the only problem. She had to be in there somewhere with them. He knew he could go up and bargain with them, take-me-and-let-the-girl-go sort of thing. And he knew they would agree to it, shoot him, then turn on her. There had to be some other way.

He picked up the drum and made his way along the outside of the half-built perimeter wall. Voices drifted out from the first house. He dropped to his knees and moved along, dragging the drum. His hands slid on muck and wet grass. He raised his head above the wall. There were figures in there, moving around in shadows set against flickering candles. He lowered his head back down and kept going.

His wet knees scraped on stones. Rain and sweat congealed on his forehead and slid in salty drops down his nose and into his mouth. When he gauged himself to be far enough up from the first house, he raised his head above the wall again. Four dwellings separated him from the one with the voices.

He leaped over the wall and reached over to pull the drum after him. The ground beneath him was spongy. He stepped on to decking. A hole had been cut from it into which a plastic tub had been placed. It was almost full of rainwater. Out at the front of the house, all was silent. He couldn't see or hear anything from down the road. He crossed to the next identical house on the far side of the track through puddles and soft earth. The rain shifted down a gear. He shivered inside his wet clothes.

At the side of the house, he uncapped the drum. The fumes caught him unawares, but he breathed in hard, as if the smell might warm him. He trailed it all the way around the side of the house, and on to the decking at the back. When the last drop fell from the drum, he placed it on the decking and moved back around towards the front. There was still no sign of anybody from down the road.

Once he was squatting on his haunches the fumes were in his nostrils again. He flicked the lighter and the flame came. He moved it to the shingle and it caught fire. The blue flame began moving back along the wall, flickering here and there against the rain and wet timber, but quickly it spread.

Molloy looked out again. He ran back across the road and positioned himself at the gable end of the house directly opposite.

Across the road, a wall was already burning brightly. Now he just had to wait and watch them come running. He still needed some luck, but the odds were shortening.

22

Strange how some things stay with you. Diggins remembered the road, even with night closing in. The sea on the right, its blue deepened by the fading light. Out there, somewhere beyond the headlands and inner islands, stood the Skellig Rock. He'd been fascinated by that place since he'd read about it in school. He'd clung to the idea that monks used to live out there a thousand years ago, persevering against the worst of the elements, and had taken the rock's name for the marital home, a place where he and Noelle would endure against all the elements, and all the hard knocks lapping up against their sanctuary. Now it was gone. Just as wild storms and foreign invaders had sent the monks scurrying for the mainland, he and Noelle had abandoned their Skellig, after coming under attack from whores as battle-hardened as any Vikings.

Right now, he was fading. The blow had been less than satisfactory. If he was totally honest, it had been garbage.

But that was the kind of risk he had to take under the circumstances.

Soon after leaving the main road, en route now to Coomastow or, as they called it round these parts, Coo-mash-thou, he pulled in. He switched on the light in the cab and took out his stash. Two quick lines disappeared up his hooter, but he knew he was chasing diminishing returns.

He had been down here at least half a dozen times, dealing with the plans and then the construction. This time, though, he wouldn't be sticking around. Apart from anything else, there were a clutch of subcontractors in the general area who would gladly have his balls for breakfast.

The most pressing thing at the moment was the headlights that appeared to be following in his wake. Since leaving the main road, the lights had been with him. He hadn't noticed anybody on his tail on the drive from Cork Airport. He stopped just once on the way down, at a petrol station in a one-horse town somewhere near the county boundary. After filling up, he nipped across the road to what looked like a small hardware shop. Inside, he bought a mallet and chisel, the only tools he would need to root out his money.

Now, though, these lights appeared to be following him all the way into the mountain. He was perfectly willing to believe in a coincidence. There were houses in along here; civilisation didn't end completely. But now, a good two miles since they left the Ring of Kerry, the lights were clinging stubbornly to his rear-view mirror.

Maybe he should pull in and let it pass. On the other hand, if it was somebody on his tail, a confrontation would ensue, and that he could not handle.

He passed a farmhouse with yellow light burning behind curtains. Then a few bungalows. On the only occasion he had been out here at night before he had noticed how darkness tightened around the place. He reached for the car radio and a wail of static replied. The headlights fingered along the road. A rabbit appeared, ran along beside the ditch and was swallowed by the night.

The lights were still in his wake. His attention was now equally divided between road and rear-view mirror, between the future waiting for him at Buckingham Gate, and the past chasing him like a debt collector.

Then a stray thought hit him. He had no light to take him through the house once he arrived at Buckingham Gate. He was coming out here into the back of beyonds without even a torch to show him the way. He could stop at one of the bungalows before he got too far into the mountain. Then again, why take the risk? Why walk into a house only for somebody to recognise him, effect a citizen's arrest and get some big bogtrotter to sit on him until the law arrived?

The car was still in his wake, following him all the way into the mountain. He had to stay calm. It had to be a coincidence. Nobody knew that he was back in the country.

He concentrated on how to manage without any light. The layout of the houses was such that maybe he could drive the car up to the front window and shine the headlights in. It was worth a try.

The road snaked on. The distances between houses grew longer. He sought out the moon, but it was little more than a shadow behind a bunch of black clouds. If there were any ghosts out there with a notion of haunting him, they wouldn't get a better chance than this.

The headlights were still pursuing him. He passed what appeared to be an abandoned car, a Honda Civic, as far as he could make out. That was the same make as Noelle's, although he couldn't make out the reg. Not that it could be hers anyway. Every track he wandered down in his imagination led back to her. By now his sense of loss had been displaced by anger. How could she have abandoned him just when he was about to put his life, their lives, back together?

There was no point in trying to outrun them, no escape. All he could do was keep going. Once he got there, he could just make straight for number seven. He could have the bag out from its hiding place in jig time and be off. If necessary he would take to the fields. OK, none of this was ideal, but he would do whatever was required to secure his future. Some fucking wife – abandoning him at this time of his greatest need! It told him all he needed to know about her.

The candles were lit around the room, as if the place was getting ready for a seance. They came and went, moving through the shadows. She knew their names now: the older guy was Junior, the other Rocco. There was nothing else in the room, apart from a shovel, the pick and the electric saw, which had been fashioned into her ball and chain.

They had had a row about the saw and not having any electricity. The older guy had said he couldn't be thinking of everything, and Rocco had retorted that Junior's thinking had got them where they were. For a second, Noelle thought violence might flare between them. She felt her own fear grow at the prospect, but it receded, both men appearing to back off at the last minute.

If she told them what they were looking for, what then? She would be of no further use to them. They would kill her, out here in this ghost estate where nobody might find her for days, weeks, months.

The pair of them were now at the far end of the room, their heads bent down in a huddle. She sensed something was about to happen and braced herself. They turned and walked across the floorboards towards her. The older guy began to unbuckle his belt. She strained against the ties that bound her hands. He dropped his trousers, moved in and grabbed her arms. 'Last chance.'

A rising tide of panic washed over her. Her head began to spin. 'All I know is that he said something about number seven.'

'Where? There's a whole lot of house in any of these places. Where in the house?'

She was sobbing. 'I don't know. I just don't know.'

The younger one spoke up: 'She's lying.'

'I'm not. I just want … Could you leave me alone.'

The older one pulled up his trousers and refastened the belt. He leaned down, moved his face up against hers. She could see in his eyes that he was capable of anything. He smelt like an animal.

'You were on your way out here. For what? You know exactly where the money is and you were going to take off with your new lover boy. I'll give you one more chance. And that's it. After that, it doesn't matter what you say, I'm going to ride you every which way before handing you over to Rocco here.'

He grabbed her face in his hand again, then pushed her head back. Pain shot through her cheeks. She couldn't take any more of this. 'There's a utility room, next to the kitchen.' She paused to catch her breath. 'Donal said there was a raised platform at the back of the cupboard, like a step. He got a carpenter to put it in there. That's where the money is. In a leather bag.'

She closed her eyes to await her fate. There was so much she hadn't been able to do. She'd lived a lie for so long and had been looking forward to seeking out her own life. And now they were going to take it away from her.

She felt one of them behind her, pulling the tie free.

'OK, let's go. Rocco, get the pick. And if there's nothing under those boards, this little lady is going to have one horrible end.'

They walked out of the back door on to the half-finished deck. Junior was pulling her along by the arm. The moon had escaped the cloud cover. It sat in the dome of black inside a fuzzy blanket of yellow, high above the falling rain. She stumbled as they stepped from the deck on to the soil.

As soon as they rounded the house, they saw the flames. Something up there was on fire. It had to be one of the houses. And it was around where number seven ought to have been.

Molloy's back was against the gable end of the house across the road from the pile that was catching fire. He saw the flames lick around the shingles first, spreading from the back. Twisted columns of smoke, rising into the night sky, were now bleeding together into a solid wall. They had to be on the way. He lifted his feet one by one, shook them in the air, trying to get life back into his toes. He kept his anger in check. The priority was to get Noelle the hell out of here. After that, he could play the hand he had been dealt. It was going to end here one way or the other.

The crackle of burning timber came from across the road, flames rising against the rain. They had to have seen it by now.

Voices drifted to him from down the road. He moved along the gable to the front wall. Three bodies were coming up the road. He could make out Junior Corbett leading the way, his bald head bare against the night. Behind him, Rocco was dragging Noelle, her feet catching on the unfinished surface.

He beat back an impulse to step out and put a bullet into Rocco.

Junior Corbett turned to Noelle. He was shouting in a voice on the edge of panic, a finger pointing behind him to the blaze. 'Is it in there? Is my fucking money in there?' He walked up to Noelle. Rocco held her by the arm. Corbett's hand rose in an arc and came down swiftly on Noelle's face. She fell to the ground in a heap. Molloy grabbed a shingle on the corner of the wall. If he went out now, gun blazing, she would be dead. He needed an edge. He moved back around the house, ran across the decking, stumbled when he kicked a plastic bucket. He slowed at the far side of the house, moving with stealth up the side. He could see them from behind now. The two men were staring at the flames. Noelle was on the ground. He looked to detect some movement in her body, but there was none.

He checked the clip on the Glock. He planted his feet, ready to take aim. He held the gun out, training it on the back of Junior's head. It was then he heard a shout from down the road: 'Get the fuck off my property!'

Before he knew it, his destination was upon him. The stone with Buckingham Gate written on it. The shadows rising against the moonlight. This was the last of Donal Diggins's great developments, and he was prepared to admit that it had been a dream too far. He stopped outside the entrance as he couldn't remember how far the road had been built before the subbies had walked off the job.

The rear-view mirror was now black. The lights on his tail had been taken by the night. He killed the engine and got out of the car. The rain felt fresh and pure and ancient. He walked towards the entrance, careful with his footing, and then he saw it: an SUV, as black as the night, standing at the entrance. He moved towards the vehicle. Images plucked from horror movies came crashing through his head. He expected to see a body in the car. But when he arrived there was none.

He looked up towards the houses and that was when he saw the flames. Something was badly wrong. He went back to the hired car, opened the passenger door and took out the mallet and chisel. He tapped his shirt pocket for reassurance that the coke was there but, much as he needed a quick toot, he had to sort this thing out first. It was going to be quick. In, out and away. He walked up the tarmac road and, from a distance of about thirty yards, he saw two figures silhouetted against the flames. There was a bag or something at the feet of one. They had to be local kids, vandals who had decided to burn the place to the ground.

Donal Diggins quickened his pace. His right hand tightened on the mallet. He wasn't a violent man but, if need be, he would see these people off.

It dawned on him that the house on fire must be … It couldn't be. He broke into a jog.

Ahead, where the two figures stood, he could see that the heap on the ground was a human. The fear within him intensified, but there was no turning back now. This was his future he was fighting for. He steeled himself for confrontation. 'Get the fuck off my property!'

The two men turned towards him. He moved closer, clinging tightly to his courage. 'What the hell do you think you're doing? If you don't make yourselves scarce, I'm calling the guards.'

He was upon them now, confused that his warnings were having no effect. The closer he got, the more he began to feel that this scene was much worse than he had first read it. These guys weren't local kids. One wasn't a kid at all. He walked right up to them and that was when he noticed the gun in the hand of the younger one. He could see now that the heap on the ground was a woman, although her face was turned away from him.

'Well, well, well,' the older guy said. Raindrops were bouncing on his head. The voice was familiar – and all at once Donal Diggins began to see his life flashing before his eyes. 'Look who we got here, Rocco.'

Rocco had raised his gun. Donal Diggins let the mallet fall from his hand. He could feel the heat from the fire on his face. The sound of crackling timber was growing in his ears.

'Where's my money?'

Donal Diggins felt the fight drain from his body. He should have known there would be complications, but nothing had prepared him for this. The money no longer mattered. Without his life, nothing would be happening. He nodded beyond the two men towards the flames. 'In there,' he said. 'That's number seven. That's where I left the money.'

'Well, you'd better go and get it now because either I have it or you are dead. The choice is yours. Move.'

Diggins looked at him. The guy had to be joking. Junior expected him to walk into a burning building? The younger guy was waving the gun.

'I said, move. Get. The. Fucking. Money.'

Diggins looked up at the house. The flames were now dancing twenty feet high into the air. Even when it was over, there was no way anything in there would be intact.

Junior Corbett moved towards him. Diggins cowered, crossing his hands in front of his face. There was something about the body on the ground. It … it couldn't be.

'Noelle,' he said. The body stirred. Junior grasped Diggins by the collar and dragged him towards the house. The heat of the fire was more intense the closer they got to the building. As it began to tower above them, Junior grabbed his jacket in a bunched hand and threw him to the ground, where a landscaped garden was meant to have been. Junior pulled a gun from his pocket. 'Last chance,' he said. 'You go in there, or you're toast.'

Donal Diggins raised his hand to shield himself from a bullet or whatever the man was going to do. His composure broke into sobs. He didn't deserve this. He had been a facilitator, a processor of dreams. He hadn't hurt anybody. All he had ever wanted was to take care of his family, his wife, and if it hadn't been for the coke getting out of control, he would merely be broke now, rather than lying here, his dignity being shoved into the soft earth by this thug.

Inspector Phil Wright had been uncomfortable for a while. It was the lights. Diggins had to know that he was being followed. They were driving into the back of beyonds and he would have wanted to be as thick as two planks not to cop it at some stage. He killed the lights.

'What are you doing?' Slate said.

'We need to take it easy. Diggins is going to cop us sooner or later. And the fella might be coked to his eyeballs, paranoid and the whole thing. I don't want him to panic. He can't be going too much further into this mountain.'

Progress was slow thereafter. Twice the car veered dangerously towards a ditch. Wright managed to keep the headlights of the car ahead in view most of the time. And then the lights went dead.

'He's arrived wherever he's going,' Wright said.

'Where are we?'

Wright ignored him, killed the engine, opened his door and put one foot on the road. He stuck his head back into the cab. 'OK, let's go.'

'We're walking?'

'And this car is staying on the road. Nobody is coming out of here until I say so.'

Slate pulled the collar of his jacket up around his neck. He tucked his notebook into the inside left breast pocket, checked the two pens in his trousers.

They were walking for less than a minute when Wright spotted the houses framed against the night sky. 'Jesus, it's an estate of some sort. Out here.'

Within five minutes they were upon the stone pier. Wright bent down and looked into Diggins's rented car. He moved on and did the same with the SUV parked a few feet away. Slate followed in the inspector's footprints, wielding his pen and notebook, scribbling details. He could barely keep his excitement in check.

When they turned into the road through the estate, they saw the flames. Wright reached under his jacket and pulled out his revolver. Slate scribbled that detail.

Wright grabbed the reporter and dragged him behind the gable end of the first house.

'There's somebody up there. You stay here and wait,' he said.

'Phil, you're not going to do anything crazy, are you?'

Wright was peering out from the gable end, up the road. He turned around.

'What do you think?'

'I think you'd want to be careful. No matter what happened, it isn't worth killing anybody over it.'

'You think I'm a killer?'

'No, no, I don't, but people put in strange situations, they can ... lose it.'

Wright moved past him towards the back of the house. His right foot stepped into a hole that was filling with water. He cursed and turned back to the reporter.

'I'll give you the exclusive when I'm convicted.' Slate

couldn't tell if he was taking the piss, but he hoped so. On the other hand, a detective inspector losing it and going out to kill: a story doesn't get much better than that. It didn't matter anyway: he had given his tuppence-worth and that was on the record. From here on, his duty was to observe and inform the public. He wasn't a player.

Wright disappeared around the back of the house. Slate moved to the front of the gable end and looked up the road. He could make out two bodies, one appeared to be holding the other, and beyond them two more, one walking towards the flames, the other in his wake. He looked at his watch and scribbled down the exact time: eight fourteen p.m.

Diggins got to his feet. 'It wasn't me, Junior,' he said. 'It was Johnny's idea.'

Junior moved the muzzle of the gun four inches from Diggins's face. 'Johnny, is it, your good pal, Johnny?'

'I wanted to pay you back the money, you have to believe me.' His body was jerking now to the beat of sobs. 'Please, Junior.'

'I'm going to count to three. If you aren't on your way, you get it between the eyes. What the fuck did you take me for? Did you really think I'd let you away with stealing my money? One … two …'

Diggins turned and began walking towards the flames. He raised his hands against the heat burning his face. He was a few feet from the door. Above him the flames were a wall that might collapse on top of him at any minute. He turned for one last plea, one last chance to make it out of here so he could repair what had been done, to get his life back on the right track. Beyond Junior Corbett's shoulder he could see the woman getting to her feet. It was Noelle, it was her. She had a dazed look on her face, as if she was walking through a crazy dream. She looked towards him. He took a step forward, called her name. She was going to rescue him. She had come through in the end, just like he'd thought she would.

Junior Corbett shot him in the forehead, an inch below his hairline. Diggins fell back in the direction of the house. Junior walked up to him, but he was dead already. He kicked the lifeless body and turned to walk back to Rocco and the woman. He had to get away from the house. It was liable to collapse in a heap any second now. He wasn't going to get his money but, by Christ, he would have some fun with the woman before finishing her off.

Rocco was standing with her, holding her arm.

'You shot a man,' she said. She looked as if she had just seen a ghost.

He grabbed her face. 'Didn't you recognise him? Don't you even know your thieving bastard of a husband?' He pushed her away, and she stumbled and fell down, her head hitting the soft earth again. He turned to Rocco. 'Come on, let's go, and bring her.' He began walking down the road.

'What are we doing?' Rocco said, as Junior took off.

'Just come on,' Junior said, without turning back.

Rocco raised his voice. 'Junior, look at me.'

Junior turned and Rocco aimed low to be sure at this distance, and shot him in the chest. Junior looked down at his wound, then up at Rocco. A second shot rang out. Junior fell back on to the earth, a perplexed look on his face. The rain was falling on him, no longer gently, but in a torrent, beating him down into the earth, pushing him away from life, and towards the darkness, pushing him, until it was all over and there was just black.

Something crashed inside in the burning house and the flames reacted, getting a new kick of life. Rocco turned to the woman, who was pulling herself to her feet. Her head was buried in her hands. He had nothing against her, but he couldn't let her live.

He grabbed her arm. 'Let's go,' he said. And then he heard the barked instruction.

'Garda. Drop the weapon.'

Detective Inspector Phil Wright recognised Donal Diggins from his vantage-point at the gable end of the house on the other side of the road from the burning building. He saw Junior Corbett walk Diggins towards the fire. He had to consider his options. If he was to make himself known now, to come out with guns blazing, the woman would most likely end up dead, not to mind Diggins.

There were two of them, both armed and each focused on a hostage. There was no way he could take control of both situations at once. He would have to await an opportunity. He would have to see what fate befell Diggins. As far as he could make out, Diggins was being directed to walk into the burning building. The money must be in there, going up in smoke.

Wright knew Junior Corbett going way back. Smarter than your average crim, he hadn't seen the inside of a courtroom, not to mind prison, since he was a teenager. Wright had suffered some discomfort on the day he had seen himself and Corbett buying into the Diggins dream, but he had put aside any concerns. Property was the great democratic leveller and if he didn't like others in the room he was free to leave.

Now, though, Junior was all but toast. There he was with a gun in his hand, threatening a civilian. When this was over, Junior would be heading for the Joy and Detective Inspector Phil Wright would have acquired a major scalp.

Diggins was on the ground now, Junior standing over him. Wright looked towards the other one with the woman. Maybe he'd have a better sight on taking the two of them if he moved to the far end of the house.

The gunshot threw him. He looked back up at the burning building. Junior was kicking a lifeless body. Jesus Christ, he'd killed the man in cold blood. Wright watched him turn and walk away from the burning house and the body beneath it.

Wright turned and ran towards the back of the house. Puddles were now forming on the decking. He slipped, but regained his balance. He was just coming to the gable end when he heard another shot. He could see Junior Corbett now, on the ground, writhing, then heard the next shot.

He looked out and saw the other one, with the Diggins woman. She was mixed up in the middle of the whole thing. He had waited long enough. He stepped out to the front of the house.

'Garda. Drop your weapon.'

The man grabbed the Diggins woman and ducked behind her. She had a glazed look on her face, as if she wasn't there at all. The gunman scanned to see where the instruction had come from.

'I said drop the weapon.'

Wright began advancing out on to the road. They faced each other, the woman between them. 'It's over,' Wright said.

'Fuckin' right it is,' the man said. 'It's over for her if you don't throw that gun over here. Now.'

Wright weighed it up. There was no way he could try a shot on him. The woman was dead if he did. He knew this guy. He was one of the twins, the Sansoms. Junior's up-and-coming muscle. The other one, Kyle, had copped it three days ago. A scenario began to form in Wright's head. There was a reason why this one had done in Junior Corbett. What was his name? Roy or Richie or …

'Don't make things worse, Rocco. I know why you shot Corbett. He did your brother, didn't he?'

'Shut the fuck up. The gun. Over here. Now.'

Wright placed two fingers on the butt of his weapon and threw it out a few feet in front of himself. 'Let the woman go, Rocco. She has nothing to do with this. Just get in your car and get out of here.'

Another wall collapsed in the fire, falling outwards on to what would have been the front garden. The flames crept towards the body of Donal Diggins. At that moment, Rocco saw something on the road below. He aimed and fired and a cry rent the air. Alan Slate's notebook fluttered into the sky as he fell to the ground. 'That's one dumb partner you got there,' Rocco said.

'He's a reporter, Rocco, just along for the ride. There was no need to kill him. Is that what you want? To kill everybody? Is that going to solve it all?'

Rocco took his arm from around Noelle Diggins's neck. He shoved her hard in the back propelling her in the direction of the cop. Wright grabbed her before she fell again. She lodged her face in his chest.

'On your knees, both of you,' Rocco said. He was pointing the gun at Wright's chest. 'On your fucking knees.'

Wright looked at him and shook his head. He was cradling the woman in the crook of his arm. He wasn't going to end his life on his knees before this kid. He pulled the woman around behind him, turned and wrapped her inside his arms. He was about to close his eyes when he saw a figure in a woolly hat at the far end of the house from where he himself had emerged, pointing a gun directly at Rocco.

Molloy saw Junior go down, and felt nothing for the man who had brought him into the game, who had ordered him dead. He saw Rocco shoot Junior a second time.

He had to make his move. Anything could happen from here on. Rocco was as likely to shoot Noelle as he was to walk away. Molloy straightened his grip on the gun and swung around, the weapon held in his outstretched right hand, steadied by his left. Then he heard the shout from the far end of the house where he stood.

'Garda. Drop the weapon.'

He leaned back into the wall once more. The man walked out, his weapon trained on Rocco. Molloy could make him out now. The lawman who had called to his house that morning, the same one who had brought Noelle to her burgled home. What the fuck was going on?

Rocco was telling the cop to drop his weapon. Molloy could see through the rain that Noelle had come to and her eyes were wide now with fright. Rocco turned and fired a shot down the road. Molloy heard a cry. Then he heard Rocco saying, 'On your knees, both of you.'

Molloy took the position once more. He had Rocco in his sights now.

'Rocco.'

The twin turned, his eyes narrowed in confusion. He saw Molloy at the side of the house. Both men now had guns pointing at each other.

'Well, well, well,' Rocco said. 'If it ain't the Dancer. This is some party we have going now. And look who turns up to be the hero.'

Molloy shot him in the chest. Rocco's gun went off as he was falling back, firing towards the clouds. He rolled over on the ground, his head turning into a puddle of rainwater. Detective Inspector Phil Wright moved across to him, prised the gun from his fingers. He pulled Rocco on to his back. His eyes were open now, looking up at the sky. The rain had stopped and a bunch of indigo clouds was scudding across the sky, lit by the moon. The garda held his right hand. Rocco looked into the other man's eyes and held on tightly. He tried to lift his head from the ground, his lips moving. Wright lowered an ear. 'Coo-mash-thou,' the dying man said, and held tightly to Wright's hand, until death loosened his grip.

Wright got to his feet. Noelle was looking at him, and at the dead man, shock written across her face.

Beyond her, at the side of the house opposite, Molloy stood where he had shot, legs apart, the gun in his right hand, pointing now at the ground beneath his feet. Wright shouted, 'The gun, Molloy. Put the gun down now.'

In the distance, the sound of a siren echoed through the mountain. Another crash came from the fire, another wall collapsing to the ground.

23

Thank you, thank you very much. Thank you. No, please, take your seats. Hey, it feels good to be up here again collecting this award. I have to tell you, this is the sweetest one. The other three all meant something to me but to be voted Crime Reporter of the Year this time around is on a different plane.

Excuse me while I just lean against the lectern here, my leg is still not the best. When they tried to get the bullet out they said it might take a few months to get back to normal. As you know, that was six months ago. And look at me now. But that's the price we pay for doing the job we do. There we go. That's better.

As I was saying, this award is the biggie. That's mainly because I won it out there in the field, literally, where the bullets were flying.

Let me just say a few things about the fateful night that formed the centrepiece of my winning entry.

I didn't know it at the time, but I was no longer chasing a story. I was the story. I was a player. Not that I ever set out to be one, but circumstances, and my own reckless character, blew me towards the action. I was chasing the story, but the story ended up chasing me.

Let me tell you something, fellow hacks. Just hope that none of you is ever exposed to what I went through that night. Sure, you might think it would be great to be in the centre of the story. Isn't that where we all want to be? But it sure ain't pretty. In fact, it's hell out there.

And it's just by the grace of God and the help of a brave member of An Garda Síochána that I made it through.

There's a few people I would like to thank for helping me get to where I am today. First off, my former editor Frank Fastneck. Come on, let it out, you can give the guy a round of applause. Ah, come on.

Well, I wouldn't be up here today if it wasn't for Frank Fastneck. Some of you may think that I'm up here entirely due to my own talent and perseverance, and maybe you're not wrong, but Frank did help me along the way. He was the one who gave me the OK to chase this story all the way down to Kerry and back. While he grappled with the finances at Inside Out, he was still keeping his eye on the ball, putting the story before everything else. Frank showed confidence in me. He brought me back to the frontline, and when it was time for me to go over the top, he was right there behind me.

It's a pity that his magazine was not destined to survive, but when I visited him last week, he was delighted that the cover story for the final edition was being honoured with your award. I want to wish Frank well. The mind can be an awful thing when it begins playing tricks on you but, hopefully, Frank will be let out of hospital soon to further his career. Soccer punditry just hasn't been the same since he went off the air.

Somebody else who I must thank is the man formerly known

as Detective Inspector Phil Wright. If anybody put me up here today, it's Phil. As you all know, Phil resigned from the force after receiving the highest commendation for the performance of his duty in rescuing not just me but a civilian as well.

Let me tell you, as somebody who was there that night, it's impossible to speak highly enough of Phil Wright. He had to face down the worst that humanity can throw up and he did it with huge grace under pressure. I want to wish Phil well in his new political career. At trying times like these for our country, it's a man like Phil we need leading from the front. He has dealt with the scum from one side of the street. I'm confident that he can bring the white-collar criminals to justice when he makes it into the Dáil, as I expect him to at the first available opportunity. I, for one, will be out there pounding the streets to get a people's person elected to show us the way forward from here.

Finally, I want to thank you for, well, putting me back up where I feel I belong. My recovery hasn't been easy, and it was good that I had the distraction of writing the book – which, by the way, goes on sale next Monday. But I'm back in the market now, ready to serve, ready to put my life on the line once more.

Thank you.

The Woodstock was quiet for the time of day. Coldplay were coming over the radio, on the station that said it played songs to pick you up and make you feel good in the world's greatest city. Two women were seated at the window with a buggy. A couple were hunched over their full Irishes at a table halfway in. Apart from that, Molloy spotted only one table seating the law.

He got his coffee and parked himself down the back. The warmth in the September day permeated the restaurant. He took off his jacket and hung it on the back of the chair. He wouldn't be here long. He detected in himself that feeling he used to experience whenever he returned to Westwood, the fear of encountering ghosts. Now he seemed to feel it whenever he came back to the city. Keep the head down and let the ghosts go about their business. He would be in and out in two shakes of a lamb's tail, and back to the present.

He didn't recognise her immediately when she walked through the door. She was wearing a red summer dress and a denim jacket. Her hair was longer now, falling below her shoulders. But other than that, he wouldn't have recognised her anyway with the shades on. After all that had gone down, he couldn't blame her, but she had to know that she wasn't in Camden Town now: wearing shades indoors in Phibsboro was a plea to be noticed.

He got to his feet and waved as she scanned the restaurant. She had to do a double-take. He waved again and saw the two cops give him the eye. She spotted him and began walking over. He willed her to take off the glasses, but she didn't.

She extended her hand, then leaned in and kissed him on the cheek. He squeezed her arm. He didn't want to overdo the delicacy, but you couldn't be too careful with somebody bearing her scars. At last, she lifted the shades and folded them. There was a glaze on her eyes, but she still looked good.

'Hi,' she said, 'you're looking well.' Her voice had thickened.

'You look great yourself.'

'I look like shit. I'm dying with a cold right now.'

She sat down. He remembered that it was a cappuccino. She was coughing into a hankie when he returned.

'Bit of a dose you have there,' he said.

She waved away his concern. 'Withdrawal,' she said.

'From what?' His voice was incredulous. Surely she hadn't turned to the gear in her despair.

'The Solpadeine. I stopped last week. Jesus, I hadn't realised how dependent I'd become. Before I knew it I was all bunged up. It's the codeine. Has to work its way out of my system having been in there for the last few years. That's it now, though. No more Solps. I'm clean, as you might say yourself.'

He laughed. 'And how's London treating you?'

She kept her eyes on the table for a few seconds, formulating an answer.

'It's different. Easy to lose yourself in it, which I suppose is why I moved there. Takes a bit of getting used to. The course is interesting. Never thought that interior design would be my thing, but I'm getting into it.'

He nodded slowly. 'You're managing OK?'

'Being a widow? Yes, I think so. The counselling helps. I think I'm beginning to see life open up in front of me again. Except this time it's for real.'

He looked at her and saw vulnerability breaking out all over her body. He saw her looking out at the bay in Kells. He saw them walking hand in hand across the beach, his brother's kids running ahead of them with buckets and spades. He saw them in bed in the home he was now making with his son. The longing wouldn't leave him alone.

'I heard about Stephanie,' she said.

He nodded. It was strange to hear her mention Steph like that, as if the two of them had known each other. It had been all over the papers. Another junkie dies, but guess who this one is connected to? 'Let me put it this way,' he said. 'It hasn't been a picnic.'

After he was arrested, they brought him back to the station in Cahirciveen. All they would tell him was that Noelle was

OK. She'd been transported to the hospital in Tralee and was under observation, but she was suffering from little more than shock.

They brought him to the station in Tralee the following day. Wright was there to meet him. They shook hands, and it became obvious to all the other guys there that this was not going to be your run-of-the-mill arrest and interrogation.

Two lads were dispatched down from Dublin. They went gently with him. The second night during lock-up, the sergeant in charge had a chat with him. He wasn't giving much away, but he did say it had been noted that Molloy had saved a member's life. Things like that counted for something.

He told them nothing about the fuck-up attempt on Junior. Whatever had gone down, whoever was no longer around, old habits didn't die with them. It was pointed out to him that the gun he had used to kill Rocco Sansom matched the weapon that had been used on the attempted murder of Junior Corbett.

When they pressed it, he said that Junior Corbett was dead, that the man they believed to have been involved in the hit, Harms Sullivan, was dead. That the man who had ordered the hit, Johnny Cash, was dead, as far as he could make out. What was the point? They asked him what he knew about Cash, and he told them nothing. They were interested in where his body might be found. But they didn't push anything, as they stepped gently through the motions.

Later, they wanted to know how he knew Donal Diggins. He told them he had never met the man in his life. The first time he ever saw him was when he stood against the burning house, Junior Corbett's gun in his face.

They wanted to know what had brought him down there. He went through his child-custody issues and told how at the time in question he was in Kerry trying to sort out his son's future. He knew nothing about Buckingham Gate until Noelle

Diggins told him about it the very day they went out there. He knew nothing about any money.

Noelle did tell them about the money. They didn't know whether to believe her. All they had was her word on what her dead husband had said, although it was a reason why Corbett and his sidekick found themselves at the scene.

The remains of a leather bag were retrieved from the house, but if there had been any money, it had been converted to ash.

On the third day, Wright appeared, taking a break from the TV appearances he had been clocking up. He told Molloy he had made extensive enquiries about what he had been up to since his return to Dublin. A file was to be prepared and passed on to the DPP. He couldn't see it going anywhere. There would be no prosecutions. He was free to go.

They shook hands again. Then Molloy asked him, 'What brought you down there anyway?'

Wright gave him a look that said he should get out while the going was good. 'A hunch,' he said. 'Nothing more than a hunch. I heard that Diggins might be flying back into the country. I wanted to see where he would go.'

It was when he got out that things took a turn for the worse. He collected Alex from Stephanie and brought him down to Ivan's place. There was an unspoken tension between the brothers at first, but after Ivan got his hands on a copy of the magazine article laying out the whole thing, he relaxed.

Molloy was there for over a fortnight when word came through about Steph. She had left the treatment centre to score in one of her old haunts. She made no provision for the collapse of her tolerance for the stuff during the weeks she had been clean. They found her in an apartment squat just off Gardiner Street, her body already cold.

Molloy's main concern after that was Alex. It took three months to get a house under the Rural Resettlement Scheme, but eventually he was offered a little bungalow in north Kerry, about sixty miles from his brother's place, near enough for family, far enough away for the two brothers.

Father and son had set about making a new life there. None of it was easy, particularly on Alex, but the wounds were being bound up and given time to heal. Molloy was back in education, studying for his Leaving Cert. He wasn't looking any further down the road than that.

'Every morning that I wake up, I'm grateful,' he said. 'Does that sound fucked up?'

Noelle sniffled again, pulled a hankie from her pocket and blew her nose. 'No,' she said. 'It sounds like living.'

The café was filling up now, a queue forming at the counter. Molloy got up to get a second cup for both of them. When he returned to the table, he could see she had wound up to get something off her chest.

'It's still painful to rake over it, but there's one thing I'd like to know about that night,' she said.

'Shoot.'

'Did you know?'

'Know what?'

'Which house you were setting alight. Did you know that the money was in there?'

He leaned back on his chair. 'What do you think?'

'I don't think you could have known. I didn't tell you what number it was. There was no other way you could have found out. Unless you went in there and discovered the money and decided to set it alight afterwards.'

'You think I could have gone in there, taken the money and then started a fire?'

She smiled. "I'd like to think you had more pressing issues on your mind at the time.'

Molloy looked around and leaned across the table. 'Was there any money in there?'

She leaned in to meet him, and whispered, 'Who knows? And at this stage, who cares?'

They finished their coffee, and she mentioned something about meeting her sister in town. She had a good three hours before her flight, and she had a few things to do.

They walked from the café and stood outside, neither sure how exactly to bring things to a close.

'The place me and Alex have, you know, it's plenty big for three of us,' he said. 'Maybe you might like to visit some time.'

She hooked her bag on to her shoulder, tossed her hair out from inside the collar of her jacket. 'That would be nice,' she said. 'Let's stay in touch and see if I get a chance to come across.'

She came to him and they kissed and embraced. He felt her grip tighten around him, and then she pulled back. She gave him a little wave and turned to go. He watched her move out on to the road to hail a taxi. She turned and waved again as she got into the back seat, the smile back on her face.

He walked around the corner and waited at the bus stop. Once he got into town, it was down to Heuston Station and off out of there, back to his life.

He was standing at the stop when his phone began rattling in his pocket. It was a blocked number.

'Yo.'

'Who that?'

'Your guardian angel.'

'I always thought you were a fairy.'

'How goes it now, brother?'

'Pretty good. Just leaving the city, heading back down to my son. How's things with you?'

'Getting better, brother. Just got word that I'm back on the streets next week.'

'Good result for you, bad for humanity maybe.'

'You'd better believe it. I can't wait. Once I walk through these gates, there's a pub just around the corner. Can't wait.'

'You're kidding?'

'What do you think? First thing I do when I get out is look for my first meeting as a free man. And once I get in there I'm going to bore the bollocks out of the place with all my war stories from inside.'

'You might get over this side of the pond?'

'I was going to talk to you about that. You living down the country and all with your boy.'

'The welcome sign is always up. Listen, by the way, all bullshit aside, thanks. Thanks for … being an asshole when I needed one.'

'That's just one of the things I can't change, brother. See you soon.'

Molloy pressed the call-end button. The double-decker bus pulled into the stop. He boarded, paid the fare and found a seat upstairs. He was going home.